THE STATE OF IRELAND

THE STATE OF
IRELAND

A Novella & Seventeen Stories by

BENEDICT KIELY

with an Introduction by

THOMAS FLANAGAN

DAVID R. GODINE · PUBLISHER
BOSTON

First published in 1980 by
David R. Godine, Publisher, Inc.
306 Dartmouth Street, Boston, Massachusetts 02116

Library of Congress Cataloging in Publication Data
Kiely, Benedict, 1919 –
  The state of Ireland.
  1. Ireland – Fiction. I. Title.
PZ3.K547St   1980 [PR6021.I24]   823'.914 79-92210

ISBN 0-87923-320-6

*The following stories have been previously published in
somewhat different form:*
In *The New Yorker:* The White Wild Bronco, The Heroes in the Dark
House, The Little Wrens and Robins, A Great God's Angel Standing,
Homes on the Mountain, A Journey to the Seven Streams, The Dogs in
the Great Glen, There Are Meadows in Lanark, Maiden's Leap, A Room
in Linden, The Night We Rode With Sarsfield, Bluebell Meadow
In *Kenyon Review:* A Ball of Malt and Madame Butterfly
In *TriQuarterly:* Proxopera, Make Straight for the Shore

MANUFACTURED IN THE UNITED STATES OF AMERICA
SECOND PRINTING DECEMBER 1980

for
John Kiely, Valerie,
Adrienne and Tomas

Contents

THE STATE OF IRELAND

INTRODUCTION

by Thomas Flanagan

BENEDICT KIELY, a writer in whom are joined magnificent lyrical and comic gifts, is one of the most admired of literary figures in his native Ireland. Although a number of his novels have been published here and his short stories have appeared in *The New Yorker* and elsewhere, he has not had the kind of American reputation enjoyed by Frank O'Connor and Sean O'Faolain. This selection of his short fiction, which concludes with 'Proxopera,' a recent and extraordinary novella, should redress the balance. It exhibits not only the remarkable continuity of his themes, attitudes, and abiding concerns, but also the ways in which, over several decades, these have deepened and enriched themselves.

Kiely's art begins with a profound sense of place, of both physical and human geography, and of the integuments by which people and landscape are bound together. It would be entirely wrong, however, to 'place' him as a regional writer, for the strong center of his craft, in his novels no less than his short stories, is the shaping voice of the narrator. This voice may seem at first to be that of the *seanachie*, the traditional Irish storyteller, but in fact it is a far more complex and sophisticated instrument. Kiely moves very close indeed to the people of whom he writes – farmers, tradesmen, mechanics, journalists, doctors, priests, publicans – but the voice can complicate itself suddenly, distancing the speaker and reminding us that Kiely is a man of wide literary culture, with a deep, unyielding tolerance for almost every range and variety of human experience. It is this shaping voice within the stories that, I suspect, has fallen strangely upon the ears of a generation schooled to expect from art only a stern, ironical impersonality. But fashions have changed once more, and allow

3

us now to see in his work a sensibility and an intelligence engaged in an exchange both with his readers and with his created world.

Benedict Kiely was born, in 1919, in County Tyrone in what now is Northern Ireland, and grew up in Omagh, its county town, built where the Drumragh and the Camowen rivers join to form the Strule. James Joyce once boasted that if Dublin were ever destroyed, it could be replaced brick by brick, with *Ulysses* as a blueprint. It is one of the few claims made for that great novel that exceeds the mark, for in fact only sections of the city are represented, and the characters are drawn from a narrow banding of the petty bourgeoisie. But Omagh, its banks and courthouse, cinema, barracks, back lanes, public houses, churches, and the roads, fields, hills, villages, and streams that stretch away from it, could be reconstructed from Kiely's stories and novels with extraordinary completeness, a slow and massy accretion of details remembered with an affectionate precision. And indeed, as his dark recent stories suggest, the destruction being wrought upon Northern Ireland by the present troubles may one day make necessary such a blueprint.

It would be a temporal as well as a spatial reconstruction. Level with the eye of imagination would be the remembered Omagh of his childhood and youth, a warm, enveloping community whose inhabitants are raised by his voice to mythic significance. It is not an isolated world – there is a barracks of British soldiers to bring a drum roll of distant empire, and letters from emigrants bind it to Dublin, to England, to America – but it is self-contained. And it is a world of two communities, one Catholic and one Protestant, shaped apart from one another by conflicting traditions, schooling, mythologies, and yet held together by a sense of shared society. With a delicacy that seldom strays toward the sentimentally pastoral, Kiely contrives to suggest that even deep and bitter sectarian divisions are so wedded to landscapes and weathers that they have become part of the natural order of things, emotional and communal signposts, ambiguously reassuring.

Beneath that Omagh of the twenties and thirties, remembered or revisited, is the limestone and the rich, loamy soil of a history that has shaped its people. That history is visible in landmarks, the humpbacked bridge across which King James rode in his retreat from Derry, the Augustan austerity of the eighteenth-century courthouse. But it is more richly present to the ear, in song, anecdote, tradition, conversation, scraps of local verse. The people of Kiely's Omagh – which on occasion is anonymous or given a different name, but which is always Omagh – are aware that they live not only in space but in time, and that time stretches toward them from the distant past. And the narrator, too, lives in time. Omagh changes, decade by decade, as we move through the stories, but so, too, does the man who returns to it in fact or in memory, stays for a visit, and then returns to what conventional wisdom calls a larger world.

Kiely himself left Omagh for that world at the age of eighteen, when he entered the Jesuit novitiate at Emo Park in the Ireland that was the setting of his 1955 novel, *There Was an Ancient House.* A year later, however, a serious back illness sent him to the hospital for a prolonged course of treatment and convalescence, and there, with the help of several of the nurses, he discovered that his vocation was not a priestly one. Instead, he attended the National University, married and began a family, and then established for himself in Dublin a double career in literature and in journalism. Literary Ireland and the city of Dublin were to give to both his life and his art a second center, which in the fiction is subtly joined to that of rural Ireland.

Thus far, he has published eleven novels, three volumes of short stories, and four books of social and literary history. Had he limited himself to journalism, however, he would have earned for himself something that approached his present position in Irish life. Kiely's is not a fractured sensibility, and he is one of those fortunate few writers who can turn to fiction or to journalism with equal craft and pleasure but remain faithful to the discipline of each. He endows the journalist in 'The Weavers at the Mill' with one of his own habits: she carries two notebooks. 'One of the notebooks was paper-backed, spined with spiral wire, and with tear-out leaves. It was for ephemera and temporalities – in other words, her work. The other book was stiff-backed, with stable, ruled leaves for the recording of the experiences she would use when the day would come and she'd sit down really to write.'

When I first met Kiely and became friends with him, some

twenty years ago, he was literary editor of the *Irish Press*, for which
he also wrote an idiosyncratic column of travels around the
country. I used often to accompany him, and like other friends
found it an exhilarating but disconcerting experience. A trip that
by ordinary clock time should have taken four or five hours at
most would mysteriously stretch itself into days or even a week. At
every twist in the road there would be a stream to watch or a
crooked bridge to lean upon, and in every other village there
would be someone to visit. And, later, one or the other of the
notebooks would come out, either the paper-backed one or the
stiff-backed one. This became for me in time an emblem of his art.
His stories seem to move as easily as a mountain stream, but his art
is that of the mosaic, whose design is grasped only when one
stands back from it.

Kiely began his literary career in the Ireland of the 1940s. His
first novel, *Land Without Stars* (1946), takes its title from the
eighteenth-century Munster poet, Egan O'Rahilly, who wrote of
'a land without dry weather, without a stream, without a star.' ✗
O'Rahilly's reference was to the defeat of Gaelic Ireland, and
Kiely's is to Ulster during World War II. Many, however, would
find the phrase applicable to what was then the condition of the
culture itself. The isolation created by Irish neutrality during the
war, a harsh and puritanical clericalism, a stupid and hysterical
policy of censorship, had lowered every horizon. Three of Kiely's
own novels were banned, or as he puts it, 'received the national
literary award for being in general tendency indecent or
obscene.' It was that Ireland that Frank O'Connor opposed in the
bitterness of a temporary exile, and it is the subject of a fine, fierce
essay by Kiely, 'The Whores on the Half-Doors.'

But it is impossible to imagine Kiely in Joycean exile. He has
always lived deeply within his society, savoring its essences, its
smells, its textures and colors, its contradictions. Like his characters, he is bound to the world that has shaped him, but unlike
them, he is, as an artist, distanced from it. He is a man in whom
great personal warmth, wit, and generosity of spirit are curiously
joined to a deep inner reserve, a privateness, and this is reflected
in his fiction. Of all my friends, he has, I think, the most copious
and variously equipped memory – stored with Balzac, Chekhov,
Shelley, Carl Jung, Hilaire Belloc, Plato, the verses of obscure or

✗ Tír gan uisce gan 6uinne gan peżżean

anonymous local bards. All, great or small, are given a democratic welcome, as though his memory were a public house into which they have strolled for a drink or a chat.

And works of literary art, great or rustic, appear in his stories with extraordinary frequency, not merely as sources of apposite quotation but as central, organizing symbols, or as an atmosphere, a weather, within which the stories assume their final meanings. In 'The Night We Rode With Sarsfield,' it is a nineteenth-century patriotic ballad. In 'Down Then by Derry,' it is an emigrant's song celebrating and lamenting Omagh's river, 'the serpentine Strule.' In 'A Great God's Angel Standing,' a title that has both a religious and a discreetly priapic significance, it is a poem by William Morris that exhibits, in the words of Pascal Stakelum, the rural rake, 'odd stuff about a great God's angel standing at the foot of the bed, his wings dyed with colours not known on earth, and asking the guy or girl in the bed, the angel has two cloths, you see, one blue, one red, asking them, or him or her, to guess which cloth is heaven and which is hell. The blue one turns out to be hell. That puzzles me.' 'A Ball of Malt and Madame Butterfly' has to do with the denizens of a half-pub/half-brothel on the Dublin quays – whores, publicans, a fireman, sailors, cattle farmers up from Longford for a bit of fun – but the story is shadowed by Yeats's love for Maud Gonne, and lines from his love poetry move almost unnoticed through the prose, the spiritual and the profane in complex counterpoint. It is by voice, by the shifting contours of the narrator's words, that the harmonies of art and the random varieties of human intercourse are held in balance.

In *The Captain with the Whiskers*, the finest of Kiely's novels, the captain is 'a certifiable monster,' a vicious, sardonic bully who maims the spirits of his children and those who serve him. But the final verdict upon him is spoken across the bars of a song sung in a distant Dublin pub, by men remembering Omagh. 'And when in Quebec, we're safely landed, kind friends will greet us upon the shore. But the hills that stand above Magheracolton and the Gap of Gortin we will see no more.' As voices fall silent in the smoky room, Owen Rogers, the narrator, remembers the works of his dead father. 'He was a re-organizer, that's a destroyer. He changed the name of Magheracolton to Bingen. There was a good song once about the hills that stand above Magheracolton. Would that be a sufficient reason for hating a man like the captain?

For Kiely, it would indeed be a sufficient reason. He is a deeply conservative man, not in the political but in the Virgilian or Wordsworthian sense. Names are wedded to fields and hills: to put them asunder is an act of violence. Story after story, whether grave or comic, celebrates a conjunction of setting and feeling. The narrator of 'A Journey to the Seven Streams' remembers a father who knew all of the real or legendary history of the lands beyond his town. 'Townlands like Corraheskin, Drumlish, Cornavara, Dooish, the Minnieburns and Claramore, and small towns like Drumquin and Dromore were all within a ten-mile radius of our town and something of moment or something amusing had happened in every one of them. The reiterated music of the names worked upon him like a charm.' And upon Kiely and the reader. The story chronicles a family expedition in the twenties to visit 'in one round trip those most adjacent places of his memories and dreams.' They come at last, to the entwined music of his father's voice and the splutterings of Hookey Baxter's decrepit motorcar, to the seven streams. 'Then the seven made into one, went away from us with a shout and a song towards Shaneragh, Blacksessiagh, Drumragh and Crevenagh, under the humpy crooked King's Bridge where James Stuart had passed on his way from Derry to the fatal brackish Boyne, and on through the town we came from.' The father says, 'All the things we could see, if this spavined brute of a so-called automobile could only be persuaded to climb the high hills. The deep lakes of Claramore. The far view of Mount Errigal, the Cock of the North, by the Donegal sea. If you were up on the top of Errigal you could damn' near see, on a clear day, the skyscrapers of New York.' In his imagination, the towers of Atlantis rise glimmering from the deep. 'What matter,' the mother says. 'The peace of heaven is here.'

But the story has been told in retrospect, and the final paragraphs return us to the present. The father, we learn there, is dead. And every house on the funeral road along the Erne shore to the home places now has a television aerial. There are no longer crossroads dances. The Drumlish schoolhouse is gone, 'and in its place a white building, ten times as large, with drying rooms for wet coats, fine warm lunches for children, and even a gymnasium. But the belt of trees that he and Paddy Hamish planted to break the wind and shelter the children is still there.' Tone and detail modulate what might otherwise be a sentimental pastoralism. Past and present are linked by a natural, communal kindliness. And the engine of Hookey Baxter's car has survived, turning a farmer's circular saw near Clanabogen. 'As the Irish proverb says: It's a little thing doesn't last longer than a man.'

In the most significant of his recent work, however, Kiely's created world has grown more somber. Omagh, like all of Northern Ireland, has become implicated in an evil to which he has responded with the passion of a personal outrage. Indeed, it is only when one has become familiar with the world of his earlier fiction and with the depth of his psychic involvement in it that this outrage can be properly weighed.

A premonitory note is struck in 'Down Then by Derry' when, near midnight in a hotel bar, the talk turns to a local murder, the second that year. It is not a 'patriotic' murder, but only a filling-station attendant killed for his money, and it is a detail in a story whose emotional center lies elsewhere. But as the commercial travelers in the bar reflect upon it in philosophic jest – 'This town is getting to be as bad as Chicago' – the clock strikes midnight. With its chimes, the weather of Kiely's Omagh begins to turn.

Two stories, 'The Night We Rode With Sarsfield' and 'Bluebell Meadow,' mark, in their contrasting attitudes and tonalities, Kiely's deepening concern with the present tragedy of Northern Ireland. The first asks us to assume that for a time, in his infancy and outside the town of Omagh, the Kielys lived under one roof with a Presbyterian couple, Willy and Jinny Norris. To be precise, there had been two small houses, joined by a thatched roof. The friendship between the families had continued into later years, and the core of the story concerns a visit to the Norrises by Kiely, then a boy of nine, and his two older sisters. The differences between the two communities, the Catholic and the Protestant, are sketched in swift, delicate lines. The Kielys come from a world of priests and nuns, of stern nationalist politics, of vague and half-acknowledged links to the outlawed Irish Republican Army.

But at the scrupulously neat Protestant house of the Norrises, Orange lilies are in bloom on the lawn, the Bible and copies of *The Christian Herald* are in view; and on a tailor's dummy, in anticipation of the Twelfth of July march, are Willy's bowler hat and his Orangeman's sash of true blue. The precocious Kiely is invited to sing a song for the company, and to the embarrassment of his sisters, obliges with the most notorious and bellicose of I.R.A. songs – 'Our bayonets flash like lightning / To the rattle of the Thompson gun.' The teakettle, a loyal Orange kettle, sputters and spits, but 'Willy was weeping with laughter and wiping the back of his left hand sideways across his eyes and his red moustache.'

But all that, the narrator reminds us, was long ago. Willy and Jinny have been dead for years. 'My father walked at their funeral and entered their church and knelt with the congregation: a thing that Roman Catholics were . . . by no means then supposed to do. Not knelt exactly but rested the hips on the seat and inclined the head: Ulster Presbyterians don't kneel, not even to God above.' The Norrises had died when the house burned down – by accident. 'Nowadays when you say that a house or a shop or a pub or a factory burned down, it seems necessary to add – by accident.'

Both the deep divisions and the social and personal closeness of the two communities are implied by the two small houses, divided by stone and plaster yet joined by the roof of inflammable thatch. And of course the fire, although an accident, is also a foreshadowing. There is a darker and more sinister foreshadowing in the second story.

Bluebell Meadow, which gives the story its title, is a public park that is almost an island, between a river coming out of deep waters and a rough mountain stream. The bluebells grow in the woods on the far side of a millrace. Here a Catholic girl and a young Protestant named Lofty meet and fall hesitantly in love. For a joke one day, Lofty gives her six bullets as a present. 'She spread the bullets on the table and moved them about, making designs and shapes and patterns with them, joining them by imaginary lines, playing with them as if they were draughts or dominoes or precious stones. It just wasn't possible that such harmless mute pieces of metal could be used to kill people.' Then one day, as she sits on a bench in the park, she is warned off Lofty by a man named Samuel McClintock, who is a butcher by trade but also a member of the black preceptory, a special branch of the Orange Order. It will not do, he tells her, a romance between a Catholic girl and an Orangeman: the Order would not stand for it, and neither would Mother Teresa, at her school. The butcher is firm but kindly. He is reminding her of implacable tribal truths, which none of them can change. And he explains the bullets: Lofty is a B Special, a member of an armed and exclusively Protestant militia, hated and feared by the Catholic minority. 'He stood up and patted her on the shoulder. He was really just a big rough friendly man.'

Now, in the present, and remembering her, the narrator revisits Bluebell Meadow, rank grass a foot high and 'a wide track of sand and gravel where the river in fierce flood had taken everything before it.' In the town, 'the soldiers go about in bands, guns at the ready, in trucks and armoured cars. There are burned-out buildings in the streets – although the great barracks is unscathed – and barricades and checkpoints at the ends of the town. As a woman said to me: Nowadays we have gates to the town. Still, other towns are worse: Strabane which was on the border and easy to bomb is a burned-out wreck. And Newry, where the people badly needed shops and factories, and not ruins. And Derry is like Dresden on the day after.'

When one comes to a story such as 'Bluebell Meadow' after a rereading of Kiely's earlier work – in which the deep moral and psychic significances of his town and its countryside have been established in slow, loving accumulation – the full weight for him of the present devastation becomes palpable for the reader and almost intolerable. Kiely is not a political man and therefore is not a political writer: he has too rich and too humane a delight in fallen human nature. Ideally, one suspects, he may have wished to see the two Northern communities joined in the business of daily life yet nurtured by separate traditions, as in those two houses of his childhood, divided by plaster, sheltered by a common thatch. Yet he also knows that the I.R.A. song sung in the polished parlor, the Orange lily, and the Orange sash are the ultimate sources of that violence by which men are killed and houses set afire. Move the bullets about into what designs you will, they are not harmless mute pieces of metal. It is this dual vision, lenses disclosing irreconcilable perspectives, that brings his recent stories into an uneasy and troubled focus.

There are resemblances between Kiely's Omagh and Faulkner's Yoknapatawpha. Within each of the two created worlds an imagination that is at once conservative and radically wayward is brought to bear upon a society shaped by history and wedded to traditional modes of feeling and action. Nowhere, however, is the resemblance more clear than in the presence, within each world, of a grave and deep evil, which rises at last to challenge both the society and the artist. The rich soil of Yoknapatawpha sustains black and white alike, and the two races respond to each other by complex silences and ambiguous pacts that, in day-to-day matters, involve a mutual respect. But slavery, and those tribal loyalties to race and caste that are its historical legacy, is a destructive evil buried beneath the soil, cancerous and dehumanizing. So too, in Kiely's Omagh, the seeming innocence, indeed the childishness, of sectarian badges and slogans issue at last into the moral and physical corrosion of the society. And these are truths that the two writers, the Southern American and the Northern Irishman, confront with reluctance, for they challenge and mock those versions of the pastoral to which each has been committed. For this reason, the response of each has been impassioned and unmodulated.

'Proxopera' is Kiely's *Intruder in the Dust*, an indictment of those people, passions, and malignant principles by which the culture that claims his deepest loyalties has been savaged. A retired schoolmaster named Binchey is taken prisoner, together with his son, his daughter-in-law, and his two grandchildren by a gang of three masked men. As it happens, they are members of the Provisional I.R.A., but could as easily have been their Protestant-extremist counterparts. Binchey is to drive into town with a creamery can loaded with explosives, and his family will be held hostage to make certain that he does so. He begins the journey, but discovers that he is morally and emotionally incapable of bringing destruction to the town, and in consequence ends in a hospital bed, with his son wounded and his house burned to the ground.

That is the narrative plot of 'Proxopera,' but the meanings of the story reside less in its narrative than in its accumulation of symbolic detail, and in Binchey's consciousness and his memories. The unnamed town (which is Omagh), the roads, streams, houses, and lake that lie beyond it, his own long, white house with its avenue of beeches, have become for Binchey a geography of the spirit. It has always been, from one perspective, a troubled geography. On the hills around the lakeshore the thatched cottages have always been divided between Orange and Green, Protestant and Catholic. The division is perpetual, for 'the two main paths in the graveyard are cruciform, Protestants to the left as you enter, Catholics to the right, the cross that had divided them in life divided them also in death.' But Binchey's wife, who lived and died a Protestant, lies buried on the Catholic side, beside his father and mother. As a child, the Orange processions had delighted him – noise, music, color and song – but at twelve or so he had begun to understand the words: 'Slewter, slaughter, holy water, harry the Papishes every one, drive them under and cut them asunder the Protestant boys will carry the drum.' And the other side had its tribal pieties, Caithlin Ni Houlihan and Patrick Pearse and the sainted dead who died for Ireland. 'What it was all about was hate which, as always, bred hate.'

Binchey's own pieties, which are also Kiely's, deeper and more ancient than deforming tribalisms, are directed to the abiding forms of nature itself, and to nature's humanizing faculties. Like Wordsworth, he has discovered in nature's primitive gifts of 'sun and sky, the elements and seasons as they change,' a source of 'simplicity, and beauty, and inevitable grace.' But the savage hatreds within his society have sullied nature itself. The body of a man murdered by Protestant gunmen has been dredged up from his lake, and – the phrase echoes through the story – 'the lake will never be the same again.' The I.R.A. gunmen who invade his house are masked, a sock for one of them, black felt and a soldier's cap for the second, a gasmask for the third, and in their blank-visaged anonymity they resemble Faulkner's Popeye, whose face seems to have been stamped out of tin, depthless and metallic, bespeaking a spirit cut off from nature. Binchey guesses the identities of two, Bertie and Mad Minahan, stunted products of local hatreds. The third, their leader, is an implacable stranger with a Cork accent ('Corkman' in the tale) and, in his devotion to an abstract principle, more deadly than the others. Binchey's choice, to shield his town with all its imperfections of Orange and Green, is prompted in part by his pitying contempt for the gunmen. 'Hissing into a sock or something Corkman couldn't know what a town is.'

But still more is it prompted by Binchey's act of loyalty to his own local deities of place, to his memories, to the life he has lived. His wife, remembered in her graveyard, offers him an image of the town, 'the sleeping beauty inaccessible in a sleeping wood, and thorns and thorns around her and the cries of night.' On the opening page of the story Binchey, thinking of the murdered Catholic in the lake, says for the first time, 'The lake will never be the same again.' 'The water never knew what was happening,' his son says. 'I doubt that,' Binchey says. 'Water may know more than we think. And grass. And old rocks.'

The catastrophe that 'Proxopera' addresses is still unfolding, and Kiely's angry grief is so immediate that it cannot be wholly contained by his fable. 'And if every blade of grass were an eye watching me,' Binchey thinks, 'to hell with them, let the grass wither in the deepest Stygian pits of gloom, and blast and blind the bastards and Bertie Bigboots and Mad Minahan and that creepy half-literate Corkman.' In fact, the Corkman is condemned not by Binchey's uncontrollable outburst but by his own language. Pointing proudly to his bomb – ammonium nitrate, fuel oil, and three pounds of gelignite – he says, 'Technologically we've made big advances .' It is the voice of an ignorant and dehumanized modernity, and is reproved by those other and sweeter voices that have shaped Binchey's imagination – old songs, old proverbs, the voices of dead friends.

It is, finally, Kiely's sense of the humane that emerges from his stories as their strongest presence. The community by which he was himself shaped has possessed, more fully perhaps than it has realized, strong, traditional powers to humanize, and these the stories have celebrated. But the process has been reciprocal. Kiely's imagination, realizing itself in art through form, attitude, and, especially, through voice, is kindled by the rich variety of traditional society. His stories create a world faithful to the actualities of a given place and time, but faithful also to his own hard-won perceptions of human value. And, like all true art, they strengthen and enrich our own respect for life.

PART ONE

The White Wild Bronco

T THE AGE of five, when asked what he wanted to be when he grew up, Isaac said he wanted to be a German. He was then blond and chubby and not at all pugnacious. Because he stuttered, he pronounced the word, German, with three, sometimes with six, initial consonants. He had heard it by his father's bedside where, propped most of the day on high pillows, the old fusilier remembered Givenchy and Messines Ridge in the hearing of his friends: Doherty the undertaker; Mickey Fish, who sold fish on Fridays from a flat dray and from door to door, and who stopped young women – even under the courthouse clock – to ask them the time of evening; Pat Moses Gavigan who fished pike and cut the world's best blackthorns; and the Cowboy Carson, the only man in our town who lived completely in the imagination. Occasionally the old fusilier read aloud out of one or other of the learned anthropological tomes dealing with the adventures of Tarzan the ape man, but mostly the talk was about Germans. Isaac, quiet on his creepie stool, liked the sound of the word.

Bella, the loving wife of the old fusilier, had received her husband home from the war, we were told, in a glass case, the loser by a stomach shot away when – all his superior officers dead – he, the corporal, gallantly led an action to success, carried the kopje or whatever it was they carried in Flanders, and stopped just short of advancing, like the gallant Dublins, into the fire of his own artillery. Back home, stomachless in his glass case, he cheated the War Office on the delicate question of expectation of life, collected a fine pension and lived at ease until the world was good and ready for another war. No crippled veteran, left to beg at the town's end, was the old fusilier. Secure in his bed, in his lattice-windowed room in his white cottage that was snug in the middle of a terrace of seven white cottages, he talked, read about Tarzan, told how fields were won and, on big British Legion days, condescended to receive homage from visiting celebrities, including, once, Lady Haig herself. On the creepie stool, chubby Isaac absorbed the wonder of half-comprehended words, pondered the girth of the undertaker, the lean, loveless face of the fish merchant who thought that only beauty could tell him the time on a June evening, watched the hands of Moses as they cut a thorn or measured the monstrousness of an escaped pike, studied the cowboy's eyes that squinted, by way of twopenny paper-covered books, back to the Texas Panhandle and the Old Chisholm Trail.

The undertaker, or the pike fisherman, or the fish merchant, or the Cowboy would say: Isaac, what do you want to be when you grow up?

Isaac would say: I want to be a German.

Then the four visitors would laugh. His father, pale on his pillows, would laugh – forgetting Germans once seen in the sulphurous haze as he charged roaring through shot and shell to become a hero. His father would read the next instalment:

When Tarzan of the Apes realised that he was in the grip of the great jaws of a crocodile he did not, as an ordinary man might have done, give up all hope and resign himself to his fate...

His body trailed out beside the slimy carcass of his captor, and into the tough armour the apeman attempted to plunge his stone knife as he was borne to the creature's horrid den...

Staggering to his feet the apeman groped about the reeking, oozy den...

In the moonlight the Cowboy walked home, pulling imaginary guns and talking in admonitory tones to Wyatt Earp: Stand there, Earp. You may be a big man, but I'll cut you down. Do I have to push you into slapping leather?

Alone in the moonlight on the hill that went down to the red-and-white creamery, the brook, the Cowboy's hut, the fields beyond, he pulled and whirled and fired three times. With satisfaction he listened to the echoes dying away at the town's last fringe of shabby, sleeping terraces, over the tarred iron roofs of Tansey the carter's stableyard, over the railway-engine shed and the turntable. On green-and-white moonland beyond the Dublin railway a mystic, white bronco galloped in circles as, noiselessly, the Cowboy slipped the smoking Colt back into the holster. He turned then and went on down the hill to Tansey the carter's, and supper. Every day he worked, carrying bags of meal to clumsy four-wheeled drays, in the warehouse of Dale, the grain-merchant, nicknamed Attention, who was an amateur astronomer and had a telescope installed in a beehive-shaped structure at the back of his store. Every night after the fusilier's reading the Cowboy ate his supper of yellow Indian porridge and buttermilk in the huge coppery kitchen where Tansey the carter was a smiling extrovert Buddha in the middle of six stout sisters who had never shown the least inclination towards matrimony.

—Every day, Cowboy, Attention's back is stiffer and stiffer, Tansey said.

—He sat on a poker, said the third sister.

The sisters were all red-faced and brown-haired. The fourth one cooked the porridge.

—I hear he got drunk on wine gums in Devlin's sweetie shop in Bridge Lane, Tansey joked. The sergeant had to wheel his bicycle home for him.

Seriously resenting the imputation, the Cowboy, thumbs in the armholes of his patched and darned grey vest, drawled: The Big Boss is a fast man on the draw. He never touches hard likker.

—We heard he can stare the sun in the face up in that spinning beehive of his, said the second sister.

The carter said: It takes a good man to stare the sun in the face.

On a hook behind the broad oak door the first sister considerately hung the Stetson that a rope juggler in a travelling circus had once given to the Cowboy.

—What goes on between the sun and himself is his own business, said the Cowboy reverently. There was a cattleman in Wyoming had as big a spyglass. Could spot an Injun or a stray ten miles off.

—You and Wyoming, gently said the sixth sister.

—The Big Boss reaches me my wad. At the door of the bunkhouse. Your pay, Michael, he says. Count it. I counted one pound, nineteen and eleven pence. A penny short, boss, says I. One penny deducted, Michael, for a box of matches purchased on credit last Tuesday at eleven ah em. He misses nothing.

—Your porridge, said Tansey the carter, and give us another bit of the story.

—The place I was in at that time, said the Cowboy. Down Deep South. There was a river. Alligators. As plentiful as trout in the brook. This day I went for a swim. Just the way you'd go for a swim above the salmon leap by the hospital on the Camowen River.

—Showing off and strutting before the nurses, said the third sister. For shame, Cowboy.

—And what should happen when I was out in deep water but an alligator. Silent-like he grabs me by the arm. I could show you the marks still. But cute enough, he doesn't take the arm off. He needed it, you see, to drag me down.

—In this life you'll always get somebody to drag you down, said the second sister.

—Down to where? asked the carter.

—Not down the town to a pub or the pictures, anyway. Down to his cave. They live in caves in that river.

—No homes to go to, said the third sister.

—Was he big? asked the carter. Would he be the size now of the last pike Pat Moses Gavigan caught at Blacksessiagh?

—Size! Ten times the size. A mouth that wide. And the growls of him. Well, there was I. My body beside the slimy carcass of my captor. But I had a knife. A stone knife. Never swam without it. Wouldn't be safe in those parts. And as I was borne to the creature's horrid den I attempted to plunge my knife into the tough armour of the reptile.

—Cowboy, said the carter, you're the lucky man to be alive and eating porridge there this blessed night.

—Lucky! Quickness: that's what does it. An ordinary man might have given up all hope and resigned himself to his fate.

From the stables came a wild volley of hooves on cabbining wood, then a second volley, then a slow thud – thud – thud and one mad, high, equine scream.

—That savage you bought, said the fifth sister. He'll never cart.

—He'll cart, said Tansey. More India-buck porridge, Cowboy?

That was the time when Isaac desired – as every child, male or female, sometimes desires – a pony. It was, of course, long before he found his vocation and in a green lane above the engine shed – the town's unroofed gymnasium — learned to become the best fighter our town ever had. Poise and stance, dynamite right and cunning left, footwork, speed, quick eye, cool head and iron muscles, the fusilier's son was a natural champion. And, graduating from the green lane, he brought belts, cups, medals, honour and glory home with him from every part of the country. We were proud of him.

But in the days of his desire for the pony there were no blows struck but one. Where would a boy go who wanted a pony or a stable to house him but to Tansey's yard where the great carthorses stamped with the assured gravity of savants, where the Taggarts, the horse dealers, displayed the shaggy, sullen-eyed animals they brought in droves from the mountains away to the south-west, even from tinker camps in the province of Connacht. Roosted high on the shaft of an idle dray, Isaac was there the day Tansey bought the wild, white horse. In among the brown, shaggy brutes he was white-limbed Tarzan among the ape people of Akut and, until he felt on his quivering flanks the confining shafts, he concealed horror in docility. Then he reared to the perpendicular, assaulted the heavens, came down again and lashed out backwards, did the rounds of the yard like a Derby winner while old and young, Isaac among them, ran for shelter. With great Tansey swinging from the reins the horse went round and round and round until the cart was in firewood and broken shafts trailed the ground.

—Powerful God, said Tansey to the Taggarts, where did you get this one?

—In Ballinasloe in the County Galway, they said.

As if that explained everything.

—Take him back to Ballinasloe, said Tansey.

—But no, linger now, he said. There's life in him. He'll cart. I'll coax him.

Dreaming at a safe distance, Isaac saw himself coaxing the savage with gently proffered lumps of sugar, and all through the white one's novitiate under Tansey, Isaac was in constant, reverent attendance. But no coaxing, no lump sugar, no whispers or magic hands, could reconcile the untamed tinker-spirit of Ballinasloe to the base servility of the shafts of a dray.

—He has good blood in him, Tansey said. I'll try him in a trap.

Some of the fragments of the trap, they say, were found fifty yards away on the railway line, and the great white creature stood shivering as if, if it were human, it would burst into hysterical sobs. For a whole fortnight, with Isaac perched on high walls or drays or snug on the hay in the hayshed, the wooing went on, and it was one evening in the stable that Isaac said: Give him to me, Mr. Tansey. I'll tame him for you.

For one half second while the carter, distracted, turned and laughed, the horse lunged and snapped, the razor teeth grazing the back of Tansey's skull and gashing the lobe of his left ear. The blood came out like a spout and Tansey dyed his hand in it. Then, disregarding it, he looked sadly at the animal. With no sign of temper he went to the back of the stable, picked up a crowbar from a heap of rusting metal and, with the deliberation of God, struck the animal between the eyes and stunned it. When it woke up an hour later it went, almost of its own accord, to the shafts. Isaac's sugar lumps were never needed.

By the fusilier's bedside that evening the Cowboy was sitting straddle on a stool, knees in, feet out, hands wide, showing how he had held the reins and stayed in the saddle when lesser men had bitten the dust of the rodeo ring. Isaac chewed toffee.

He said: Tansey the carter broke a bronc today. I saw him.
He told his story.

—Tansey's a brute, said Doherty the undertaker. He'd slay
his six sisters before he'd lose two pounds sterling.

—You'd benefit, said Pat Moses Gavigan. Six coffins.

—They're six fine big girls, said Mickey Fish.

—Not a watch between them, said the fusilier. Time doesn't
count in Tansey's.

The fusilier read: Screaming with terror the Maoris were
dragged from their lofty perches. The beasts, uncontrolled by
Tarzan, who had gone in search of Jane, loosed the full fury of
their savage natures upon the unhappy wretches who fell into
their clutches...Sheeta, in the meanwhile, had felt his great
fangs sink into but a single jugular....

Afterwards when the guests had gone Isaac said: The Cowboy Carson had a ranch once on the Rio Grande. He told me
he had seventy pinto ponies.

—Son, said the fusilier, I hate to rob you of your fancy. But
better for your father to do it than for the hard world and the
black stranger. The Cowboy Carson was never out of this town
except perhaps to carry Pat Moses Gavigan's bag as far as the
pike-water at Blacksessiagh. It all comes out of the wee books
you see in the paper-shop window: Deadwood Dick and Buffalo Bill, and Hit the Tuttle Trail with Hashknife and Sleepy.

—But he was a gun-slinger, Da, in Texas.

—Guns, he never saw guns, said the fusilier – musing for
a minute and remembering Flanders and the roar of the
iron monsters.

In the dusk the Cowboy walked home, spurs jingling, stiff
and stilted on high heels, bowlegged from the saddle, left to
right and right to left practising the cross-draw and remembering with affection his deceased friend, Buck Duane, the
Lone Star Ranger. He was light and elated. There was no
pressure of crushing bags of grain on his old, bony shoulders.
Melodious with beeves, a freight train from the West truckled
on towards Belfast. The Cowboy made his customary crooked
way to the kitchen of Tansey the carter.

—You broke the bronc today, I'm told, he said to Tansey.

—I broke the bronc, Cowboy, the only way my father taught me. If I buy a horse to cart he has to cart. Or a woman to cook.

—He never bought a woman, said the third sister, and the six sisters laughed.

—Your porridge, Cowboy.

—Did I ever tell you about the time I was in New Zealand?

—You never did, said Tansey the carter.

When the Americans came to our town on their way to meet Hitler somebody told them about the Cowboy and one of them, meeting him, said: Haven't we encountered you before?

—Was it in Tucson? said another.

—More whisky, said a third, it was in Tombstone.

—Not there, said the Cowboy. I guess and calculate it might have been in Deadwood.

—Deadwood it was, said the three of them. Well, we'll be doggone darned.

—Tell us about Deadwood, Cowboy, said the man behind the bar.

—I was riding shotgun at that time, said the Cowboy. Stiff knee, you see. Couldn't mount a bronc.

For corroborative purposes he displayed his stiff knee. They listened with a little laughter. They weren't cruel. They were, in fact, kind, because the worst thing you could have done was to tell him he was never there.

By that time the old fusilier was dead, and buried by Doherty the undertaker; Attention Dale had been succeeded by a nephew who couldn't face the sun and sold the telescope; Mickey Fish was confined to a mental home for chasing young girls to ask them the time of evening; and arthritis prevented Pat Moses Gavigan from fishing pike or cutting blackthorns. And Isaac, the fusilier's son, had realised that he would never be a German. He came like a bird as a paratrooper into Narvik, came out again alive, and possibly helped the three Americans who had listened to the Cowboy to storm the French shore. Until he was killed at the Rhine crossing he remained the best fighter our town ever had.

The Heroes in the Dark House

THEY WERE GONE in the morning, the old man said. His name was Arthur Broderick, and the young folk-tale scholar sat quietly, listening for the story that had been promised him.

—Lock, stock and barrel, said the old man. The whole U.S. garrison, off for the far fields of France. Jeeps, guns, and gun-carriers. In the dump behind the big camp at Knock-nashee Castle the handful of caretakers they left behind slung radio sets and bicycles and ran a gun-carrier with caterpillar wheels over the lot, and as good as made mash of them. Very wasteful. War's all waste. Those bicycles would have kept every young boy in the county spinning for the next five years.

Like the plain girl that nobody wanted Mr. Broderick's nine-times rejected manuscript-folk-tales set down with such love and care in high-spined script lay between them on an antique drawing-room table. The table's top, solid oak and two inches thick, was shaped like a huge teardrop pearl with the tip abruptly nipped off.

—Oak, Mr. Broderick said through the smoke. Solid oak and two centuries old. In 1798, in the year of the Rising, it was the top of a bellows in a smithy. Look here where the British yeomanry sawed the tip off it so that the rebels could no longer use it for the forging of the pikes. When I was the age of yourself I converted it into a table. Sixty years ago last July.

Around them in the ancient, musty, tapestried room the wreathing smoke might have come from the fires of 1798. Birdsong outside, sunshine, wind in the creepers were as far away as Florida. The greedy, nesting jackdaws held the flues as firmly as ever at Thermopylae or the Alamo or Athlone, or a score of other places all around the battered globe, unforgotten heroes had held passes, bridgeheads or gun-burned walls. And unforgotten heroes had marched through the smoke in this room: Strong Shawn, the son of the fisherman of Kinsale, triumphant, with the aid of white magic, crossed the seven-mile strand of steel spikes, the seven-mile-high mountain of flames, the seven miles of treacherous sea, and came gloriously to win his love in a castle courtyard crowded with champions and heroes from the four sides of the world; the valiant son of the King of Antua fought with Macan Mor, son of the King of Soracha, in the way that they made rocks of water and water of rocks, and if the birds came from the lower to the upper world to see wonders it was to see these two they came.

Mr. Broderick went on with his tale. All night long through the village below the old, dark, smoky house that had once been a rectory the lorries had throbbed and thundered on the narrow, twisted street and above, in the upper air, the waves of planes had swept east towards Europe.

—They were gone in the morning, he said. Lock, stock and barrel. There was never a departure like it since the world was made. For quick packing, I heard afterwards, they drove the jeeps up the steep steps of the courthouse below. It reminded me of the poem about the three jolly gentlemen in coats of red who rode their horses up to bed.

—They were gone, he said, like snow off a ditch.

It was as much as the young scholar could do to see him for smoke. But with an effort that would have done credit to Macan Mor or Shawn of Kinsale he managed to control his coughing.

In the old dizzy chimney the jackdaws were so solidly entrenched that at times Mr. Broderick had found it hard to see the paper he transcribed the folk-tales on. The smoke no longer made him cough, but at eighty-five his eyes were not as keen as they had been when he was in his prime and from the saddle of a galloping hunter could spot, in passing, a bird's nest in a leafy hedgerow. Lovingly he transcribed the tales in the high, spidery handwriting that – like himself, like his work for Sir Horace Plunkett in the co-operative creameries, his friendship with Thomas Andrews who had built the Titanic and gone bravely with it to Wordsworth's incommunicable sleep – belonged to a past, forgotten time. For years of his life he had followed these tales, the people who told them, the heroes who lived in them, over miles of lonely heather-mountain, up boreens that in rain became rivulets, to crouch in mountain cabins by the red hearth-glow and listen to the meditative voices of people for whom there was only the past.

Peadar Haughey of Creggan Cross had sat on the long, oaken settle with his wife and three daughters and dictated to him the adventures of the son of the King of Antua, as well as the story of the giant of Reibhlean who had abducted from Ireland a married princess. Giants as a rule preferred unmarried princesses. Peadar told the story in Irish and English. His wife and daughters understood only English but together they rocked in unison on the settle and sang macaronic songs in a mixture of both languages. That simple world had its own confusions. At times in his smoky house he found it hard to separate the people in the tales from the people who told them.

Bed-ridden Owen Roe Ward, in a garret in a back-lane in the garrison town ten miles away, had told him the story of the King of Green Island and other stories that were all about journeys to the end of the earth in search of elixirs that could only be won by herculean labours. Hewing trees for hire in a tangled plantation whose wood had once paid for the travels and other activities of D'Orsay and Lady Blessington, Owen had brought down on his hapless spine a ton-weight of timber. Paralysed in his garret he travelled as he talked to find life-giving water in the well at the world's end.

A woman of eighty by the name of Maire John (she still sang with the sweet voice she had at twenty and displayed the fondness for embracing men that, according to tradition, had then characterised her) had told him of the three princesses who sat in the wishing chair. One wished to marry a husband more beautiful than the sun. The second wished to marry a husband more beautiful than the moon. The third stated her honest but eccentric preference for the White Hound of the Mountain. It was a local heather-flavoured version of the marriage of Cupid and Psyche, and Maire John herself was a randy old lady who would, in the days of silver Latin, have delighted Apuleius.

The stories had come like genii, living, wreathing from holes in the wall behind smoky hearths, or from the dusty tops of dressers, or from farmhouse lofts where ancient, yellow manuscripts were stored. By Bloody Bridge on the Camowen River (called so because of no battle, but because of the number of fine trout killed there) he had heard from Pat Moses Gavigan a completely new version of the story of Fionn MacCumhail and the enchanted Salmon of Wisdom.

Plain and mountain and river-valley, the places he knew were sombre with the sense of family, and folk-tales grew as naturally there as grass. Heroes, princesses, enchanters good and bad, he had marshalled them all, called them to order in his own smoky room, numbered them off right to left, made his roll-call, described them in that high-spined handwriting he had studied so laboriously in the old manuscripts. Properly thus caparisoned they would go out into the twentieth century. He made his own of them. He called them his children. He sent them out to the ends of the earth, to magazine editors and publishing houses. They came back rejected to him, as if being his children they could have no life when torn away from him. Then one day in the smoky room under the power of the squabbling enchanters of jackdaws he had the bitterness of discovering that his children had betrayed him. In a Dublin newspaper he read the review of the young scholar's book:

The scholar who has compiled, translated and edited these folk-tales has a wise head on young shoulders. Careful research and a wide knowledge of comparative folklore have gone into his work. He has gleaned carefully in the mountainous area ten miles north of the town where he was born. He presents his findings with an erudite introduction and in an impeccable style...

The smoke wreathed around him. The reviewer's weary sentences went on like the repetition of a death-knell:

His name is worthy to rank with that of such folklorists as

Jeremiah Curtin. Particularly notable is his handling of the remarkable quest tale of the King of Green Island...

Mr. Broderick couldn't blame the three princesses for leaving the wishing chair and making off with a younger man. That scholar, wise head on young shoulders, could be Cupid, more beautiful than the sun and the moon: he might even be that enigmatic character, the White Hound of the Mountain. But Shawn of Kinsale could have been kinder to old age, and so could all those battling heroes or venturesome boys who crossed perilous seas, burning mountains and spiked strands.

He wrote to the young scholar at the publisher's address: While I am loath to trade on your time, I have, it would seem, been working or wandering about in the same field and in the same part of the country. We may share the acquaintanceship of some of the living sources of these old tales. We certainly have friends in common in the realms of mythology. Perhaps my own humble gatherings might supplement your store. So far I have failed to find a publisher for them. If you are ever visiting your home town you may care to add a few miles to the journey to call on me. My congratulations on your achievement. It gratifies me to see a young man from this part of the country doing so well.

A week later he took up his stick one day and walked down the winding, grass-grown avenue. An ancestor was rector here long years ago, he thought, as in the case of William Yeats, the poet, who died in France on the eve of this war and who had an ancestor a rector long years ago in Drumcliffe by the faraway Sligo sea. Mr. Broderick's house had been the rectory. When the church authorities judged it a crumbling, decaying property they had given it to Mr. Broderick for a token sum – a small gesture of regard for all that in an active manhood he had done for the village. Crumbling and decaying it was, but peace, undisturbed, remained around the boles of the trees, the tall gables and old tottering chimneys, the shadowy bird-rustling walks. Now, as he walked, yews gone wild and reckless made a tangled pattern above his head.

Weeks before, from the garrison town in the valley, war had spilled its gathering troops over into this little village. Three deep, burdened with guns and accoutrements, they slouched past Mr. Broderick on the way down the hill to their court-house billet. Dust rose around them. They sang. They were three to six thousand miles from home, facing an uncertain future, and in reasonably good humour. A dozen or so who knew Mr. Broderick from the tottering house as the old guy who made souvenirs out of blackthorn and bog oak, waved casual, friendly hands. Beyond and behind them as they descended was the blue cone of Knocknashee Hill where the castle was commandeered and where a landlord had once stocked a lake with rainbow trout that like these troops had been carried across the wide Atlantic. The soldiers' dust settling around him in wreaths and rings, Mr. Broderick went down the road to collect his mail at the post-office. There had been no troops in this village since 1798 when the bellows had been mutilated and the soldiers then, according to the history books, had been anything but friendly.

The long red-tiled roofs and white walls of the co-operative creamery, the sheen of glasshouses from the slopes of the model farm were a reminder to Mr. Broderick of the enthusiasms of an active past. People had, in his boyhood, been evicted for poverty in that village. Now every year the co-operative grain store handled one hundred and fifty thousand tons of grain. An energetic young man could take forty tons of tomatoes out of an acre and quarter of glasshouses, and on a day of strong sunshine the gleam of the glasshouses would blind you. Crops burst over the hedges as nowhere else in that part of the country. It was good, high, dry land that took less harm than most places from wet seasons and flooding, and the cattle were as heavy and content as creamy oxen in French vineyards.

Over the hedge and railings by the parish church the statue of the old Canon, not of Mr. Broderick's persuasion, raised a strong Roman right arm. The pedestal described the Canon as a saintly priest and sterling patriot and to anybody, except Mr. Broderick, that raised right arm might have been minatory. To Arthur Broderick it was a kind memory of hero and co-worker, it was an eternal greeting in stone.

—Arthur, the statue said, yourself and myself built this

place. There was a time when you'd have clambered to the top of a telegraph pole if somebody'd told you there was a shilling there would help to make the village live. You did everything but say mass and I did that. You got little out of it yourself. But you saw they were happy and strong. Look around you. Be proud and glad. Enjoy your dreams of lost heroes in the mist. No young man can steal from you what you want to give away.

High above the dead stone Canon the Angelus bell rang. Before him, down the cobbled footwalk, so steep that at times it eased itself out with a sigh into flat, flagged steps, went a tall soldier and a small young woman. Mr. Broderick knew her. She was one of the eighteen Banty Mullans, nine male, nine female, all strawheaded and five feet high, the males all roughs, and the females, to put it politely, taking in washing for the Irish Fusiliers in the town below. She was ill-dressed, coarse-tongued and vicious. She carried in her left hand a shiny gallon buttermilk-can. Stooping low, the tall warrior eased the handle of the can from the stumpy, stubborn fingers and, surprised at a gentlemanly gesture that could never have come from a pre-war fusilier trained in the old Prussian school and compelled in public to walk like clockwork, she asked with awe: Aren't you feared the sergeant will see you?

—In this man's army, he said.

He could be a Texan. It was diverting to study their accents and guess at States.

—In this man's army, sister, we don't keep sergeants.

Suddenly happy, Arthur Broderick tripped along behind them, kicked at a stray pebble, sniffed at the good air until his way was blocked by the frail, discontented figure of Patrick who kept the public house beside the post-office and opposite the courthouse, and who sold the bog oak and blackthorn souvenirs to thirsty, sentimental soldiers.

—Lord God, Mr. Broderick, said Patrick. Do you see that for discipline? Carrying a tin can like an errand boy.

—But Patrick, child, it's idyllic. Deirdre in the hero tale couldn't have been more nobly treated by the three Ulster brothers, the sons of Uisneach. Hitler and Hirohito had to bring the dough-boys over here before one of the Banty Mullans was handled like a lady.

—Mr. Bee, said Patrick, we all know you have odd ideas on what's what. But Mr. Bee, there must be a line of demarcation. Would you look across the street at that for soldiering?

In sunshine that struggled hard, but failed, to brighten the old granite walls and Ionic columns of the courthouse the huge, coloured sentry had happily accepted the idea that for that day and in that village he did not have to deal with the Wehrmacht. Unlike the courthouse he looked as if he had been specially made by the sun. He sat relaxed on a chair, legs crossed, sharing a parcel of sandwiches with a trio of village children. Behind him on a stone ledge, his weapon of war was a votive offering at the feet of a bronze statue of a famous hanging judge who, irritated by the eczema of the droppings of lawless, irreverent birds, scowled like the Monster from Thirty Thousand Fathoms. Then clattering down the courthouse steps came fifty young men, very much at ease. Falling into loose formation they went jauntily down the hilly street to the cookhouse at the bottom of the village. To the rhythm of their feet they played tunes with trays and table utensils.

—Their morale is high, said Mr. Broderick.

Dark, hollow-cheeked, always complaining, persecuted by a corpulent wife, Patrick resented the young warriors with every bone in his small body. Some local wit had once said that he was a man constitutionally incapable of filling a glass to the brim.

—Those fellows, Mr. Bee, are better fed than yourself or myself.

—They're young and growing, Patrick. They need it more. Besides, doesn't the best authority tell us an army marches on its belly?

—They're pampered. Starve the Irish, Lord Kitchener said, and you'll have an army.

—Ah, but Patrick the times have changed. I had the pleasure of serving under Lord Kitchener. But he never impressed me as a dietician.

—Soft soles on their boots, said Patrick, and their teeth glued together with chewing gum and all the girls in the country running wild since they came.

—Life, said Mr. Broderick, we can't suppress. Every woman worth breathing loves a warrior who's facing death.

—Once upon a time, Patrick said, your old friend, the Canon, made a rake of a fellow kneel at the church gate with a horse collar round his neck to do public penance for his rascalities with the girls.

—Lothario in a leather frame, Patrick.

Mr. Broderick laughed until his eyes were moist, at the memory and at the unquenchable misery in the diminutive, unloved, unloving heart of hen-pecked Patrick.

—Today, Patrick, there wouldn't be enough horse collars to go round. The horse isn't as plentiful as it was. The Canon had his foibles. He objected also to tam o'shanters and women riding bicycles. That was so long ago, Patrick. We'll drink to his memory.

Everything, he thought as he left the public house and stepped on to the post-office, was so long ago. Patrick could hardly be described as part of the present. His lament was for days when heroes went hungry, when the fusiliers in the town below were forbidden by rule to stand chatting on the public street, were compelled to step rigidly, gloves like this, cane like that under the oxter – like a stick trussing a plucked chicken in a poulterer's shop. Patrick in his cave of a pub was a comic, melancholy, legendary dwarf. His one daring relaxation was to brighten the walls of his cave with coloured calendars of pretty girls caught with arms full of parcels and, by the snapping of some elastic or the betrayal of some hook or button, in mildly embarrassing situations. With startled but nevertheless smiling eyes they appealed to Patrick's customers.

—Your souvenirs sell well, Mr. Bee, Patrick said. The pipes especially. But the sloe-stone rosary beads too. Although it puzzles me to make out what these wild fellows want with rosary beads.

—They may have mothers at home, Patrick, who like keepsakes. They're far from home. They're even headed the other way.

At the post-office the girl behind the brass grille said: Two letters, Mr. Broderick.

He read the first one. The young scholar said that he had read with great interest of Mr. Broderick's interest in and his collection of folk-tales. He realised that folk-tales were often, curiously enough, not popular fare but he still considered that the publishers lacked vision and enterprise. He had only had his own book published because of the fortunate chance of his meeting a publisher who thought that he, the young scholar, might some day write a book that would be a moneymaker. The young scholar would also in the near future be visiting his native place. He thanked Mr. Broderick for his kind invitation and would take the liberty of calling on him.

The second letter came from an old colleague in the city of Belfast. It said: Arthur, old friend, yesterday I met a Major Michael F. X. Devany – it would seem he has Irish ancestry – who has something or other to do with cultural relations between the U.S. troops and ourselves. He's hunting for folk-tales, local lore, to publish in book-form for the army. I thought of you. I took the liberty of arranging an appointment and of loaning him a copy of some of the stories you once loaned me.

Mr. Broderick went to Belfast a few days later to keep the appointment. From the window of the major's office the vast, smoky bulk of the domed City Hall was visible. He turned from its impressive Victorian gloom to study the major, splendidly caparisoned as any hero who had ever lived in coloured tales told by country hearths.

—Mr. Broderick, said the major, this is real contemporary.

—Old tales, major, like old soldiers.

—This spiked strand and burning mountain. I was in the Pacific, Mr. Broderick. This seven miles of treacherous sea. A few pages of glossary, Mr. Broderick. A few explanatory footnotes. How long would that take you?

—A month, major. Say a month.

—We'll settle for a month. Then we'll clinch the deal. These tales are exactly what we want, Mr. Broderick. Tell the boys something about the traditions of the place.

He took the train home from the tense, overcrowded city to the garrison town in the valley. The market-day bus brought him up over the ridge to his own village. All that warm night the lorries on the steep street robbed him of his sparse, aged sleep as the troops moved; and they were gone in the morning, lock, stock and barrel, and on the far French coast the sons of the Kings of Antua and Soracha grappled until they made rocks of water and water of rocks, and the waves of the great metal birds of the air screamed over them.

High in the sky beyond Knocknashee one lone plane droned like a bee some cruel boy had imprisoned in a bottle to prevent it from joining the swarm. At his hushed doorway sad Patrick the publican looked aghast at the newspaper headlines and more aghast at the cold, empty courthouse that once had housed such thirsty young men.

—You'd swear to God, he said, they were never here at all.

Arthur Broderick left him to his confusion. He walked home under twisted yews, up the grass-grown avenue to his own smoky house. The heroes had gone, but the heroes would stay with him for ever. His children would stay with him for ever, but, in a way, it was a pity that he could never give his stories to all those fine young men.

—Come in, Mr. Broderick said to the young scholar, you're welcome. There's nothing I'm prouder of than to see a young man from these parts doing well. And we know the same people. We have many friends in common.

—Shawn of Kinsale, the young scholar said, and the son of the King of Antua.

—The three princesses, said Mr. Broderick, and the White Hound of the Mountain.

He reached out the hand of welcome to the young scholar.

—Publishing is slow, the young man stammered. They have little vision . . .

—Vision reminds me, Mr. Broderick said. Do you mind smoke?

He opened the drawing-room door. Smoke billowed out to the musty hallway.

—My poor stories, he said. My poor heroes. They went away to the well at the world's end but they always came back. Once they came very close to enlisting in the U.S. army. That's a story I must tell you sometime.

The manuscript of his tales lay between them on the table that had once been part of the rebels' bellows. Around them in the smoke were the grey shadows of heroic eighteenth-century men who, to fight tyranny, had forged steel pikes. And eastwards the heroes had swept that earth-shaking summer, over the treacherous mined sea, over the seven miles of spiked strand, over the seven and seventy miles of burning mountain.

The Little Wrens and Robins

COUSIN ELLEN WROTE poetry for the local papers and was the greatest nonstop talker you, or anybody else, ever listened to. The poetry was of three varieties: religious poetry, love poetry and nature poetry that went like this, the nature poetry, I mean:

> *Farewell to the dreary Winter,*
> *Welcome to the days of Spring*
> *When the trees put on their coats of green,*
> *And the birds with joy will sing.*
> *The daffodils put on their gowns,*
> *How proudly they stand up,*
> *To shake their dewy golden coats*
> *On the smiling buttercups.*

After reading the poem of which that was the opening stanza, I was ever afterwards somewhat in awe of Cousin Ellen: her daring in rhyming only one little up with all those buttercups, her vision of the daffodils as tall fashion models swaying and pirouetting in extravagant golden gowns, of the smirking of those sly little gnomes and peeping-toms, the buttercups, who were so delighted that the stately ladies should shake the dew of their coats to be caught in and savoured from the yellow cups. No one could deny that Cousin Ellen had a poetic mind and a special vision, except my father who loved quietude, and long calm silent days, and a garden growing, and who was driven out of all patience by Ellen's ceaseless clickety-clack when, once a month, she travelled twenty-five miles by train from Hazelhatch to visit us.

39

—And Uncle Tommy, did you hear that Peter McQuade of
Lettergesh sold that bay mare he had at an unimaginable high
price, I don't know what the exact sum was, but it was, I hear,
absolutely over the moon and out of sight, he ran her at the
Maze Races and won all before her and he brought her south
to the Curragh of Kildare, and some rich American saw her
and bought her on the spot and flew off with her to Hialeah in
Florida, that was a travelled mare, they say Florida's lovely,
America that's where the money is, not that money's everything if you haven't happiness, get out there to America, Ben
boy, before it's too late, as I left it too late and this, Aunt Sara,
is an American fashion magazine I brought for you to look
over, the styles will absolutely blind you, you should have been
at Hazelhatch last Sunday when the Reverend Dr. Derwent
preached the most divine sermon about the Sacred Heart, I
wrote a poem in my head on the way home from church and
sent him an autographed copy, you see he clips every one of
my poems out of the papers and pastes them into one big
book, he says that he'll be the first person ever to possess my
collected works, he's just divinely handsome, too handsome for
a priest as they say although personally I see no harm at all in
a priest being handsome, Our Divine Lord himself was the
handsomest person that ever lived and exactly six feet in
height, and very much the favourite man of the bishop at the
present moment, he's leading the diocesan pilgrimage to
Lourdes, Fatima, Rome and home by Lisieux this year, an
all-rounder, and I have every intention of going, I never saw
Lisieux and I have always adored Saint Thérèse, they may call
her a little flower but she was in her own quiet way a warrior,
as Dr. Derwent says, and she wrote the divinest book, solid as a
rock just like Mamma who's in the best of health, nothing
shakes her, all plans to make the business prosper, we're expecting such a passing rush of tourists this year on the way to
West Donegal, they all stop to stock up with food and drink at
Hazelhatch Inn, that old picturesque thatch and the diamond-
paned latticed windows, particularly those high cosy dormers,
catch the eye, you'd be amazed the number of people who stop
to take pictures and then come in and buy, beauty and business mixed...

Like Molly Bloom she was no great believer in punctuation which is really only a pausing for breath, and Cousin Ellen's breath always seemed as if it would last for hours. My father said that after half-an-hour or less of her monologue, in which she needed no assistance except seemingly attentive faces, he always felt that he was drowning in a warm slow stream, drifting slowly, sinking slowly, brain and body numb, faraway bells in his ears, comfortable, but teetotally helpless. That talk, he claimed, threatened the manhood in a man, which was why all men had escaped, while there was still time, from Cousin Ellen, except Dr. Derwent who was sworn celibate and thus safe, and except for one other wretch whom she talked into matrimony and who lasted for a year and then vanished mysteriously: dead by asphyxiation, my father said, and buried secretly under the apple trees at the back of the old house at Hazelhatch.

Those were lovely apple trees.

Drowning in what deep waters of constant talk was I, the Saturday I walked her through the marketing crowds in from the country, from brown mountains and green river valleys, to our town? We went along John Street and High Street and Market Street, by the Catholic church with the high limping spires that could be seen for miles, by the eighteenth-century courthouse with Doric columns that was once admired by no less a person than Tyrone Guthrie who said that if you tilted the long sweep of High Street and Market Street the other way, the courthouse steps would be the perfect stage on which to produce a Passion play. Church and courthouse were our architectural prides. Cousin Ellen, as far as I can remember from my drowning swoon, talked about love. Being all of eighteen I was still interested.

—Your sister, Dymphna, in Dublin, she said, is very happy, Edward and myself called to see her two months ago, not rich but happy and happiness is all, I said to her if only Edward and myself can be as happy as yourself and your husband, you know, Ben, Edward and myself are to be wedded shortly and I do hope everything turns out for the best, and I hope that suitcase isn't too heavy, but oh you're so young and strong and athletic, and they really shouldn't allow these fruit-stalls on the open street any more, not with modern traffic and all that, although you have to admit that they're most colourful and picturesque but they really belong to the Middle Ages, and see me safely now on to the bus for Dromore, the crowd here is just fearful, and oh this letter I forgot, do drop it in the post-office for me, it's for Edward, love is all, just a perfect understanding between people and when human love fails there is always the love of the Sacred Heart which I wrote in a poem that Dr. Derwent read out from the pulpit, there is nothing on earth we may cling to, all things are fleeting here, the pleasures we so oft have hunted, the friends we've loved so dear...

Then off she went not, as it happened, to Dromore where she had wanted to visit some other relatives, but to Drumquin, because in the confusion into which she had talked me, I deposited herself and her suitcase on the wrong bus. To the casual observer there isn't much difference between Drumquin and Dromore, but one is twenty miles from the other, and it's a bind to be in one when you want to be in the other. But Cousin Ellen found some obliging commercial traveller who drove her to Dromore, and God help him if he had to listen to her for the time it took to drive twenty miles. She wrote me a most amusing letter about it all. She was easier to read than to listen to. The accident about the buses had really tickled her, she said, for life was just like that: you headed off for somewhere and ended up somewhere else. She bore no grudge and we would be better friends than ever, wouldn't we? We were, too.

About that time I headed off for Dublin to go through the motions of a university education, and didn't see Cousin Ellen again, although we constantly exchanged letters, until the husband had come and gone, and she herself was in hospital close to Hazelhatch with some rare ailment that was to stop her talk forever, and her poetry.

The letter to Edward that that day she gave me to post I found two weeks later when, pike-fishing on the Drumragh River, I had a little leisure and used it to clear out my pockets. Since it then seemed too late to send it to where it should have gone I tore it up into tiny pieces and cast it on the running water. My mother always said that you should never burn letters from friends or, indeed, anything that had to do with friendship. Fire destroyed. Water did not. So she was constantly making confetti out of letters and flushing them down the john.

The deep pike-water of the Drumragh, still patterned with froth from the falls at Porter's Bridge, bore away northwards the words of love that Ellen had meant for Edward. Life, she might have said had she then known, was also like that. Our friendship, at any rate, remained unaltered. After all, she was the only other writer in the family.

> *Ah, yes! And the tiny little lambs,*
> *They, too, will play and skip*
> *In the fields just decorated*
> *With the daisy and cowslip.*
> *The blackbird and the thrushes*
> *They are glad to see you here,*
> *The little wrens and robins*
> *To all you bring good cheer.*

She was, as you may remember, addressing the Spring. Her favourite picture hung on a wall of the old oak-timbered country kitchen at Hazelhatch. It was called: Springtime on an Ayrshire hillside, or, the Muse of Poetry descends to Robert Burns while at the plough.

But those words were a paltry effort to describe that picture and, out of respect for the memories of Burns and Cousin Ellen and, of course, of the Muse, I will try to do better.

The poet in the picture wears the height of style: a blue tailed-coat, knee-breeches a little off-white, strong woollen stockings and stout buckled shoes. He has taken one hand, the right, from the plough and is using that hand to raise with a sweep a tall hat of a type that in nobler times may have been general issue for ploughmen, or poets. His profile is noble, his head held high to escape extinction in an ample cravat. He salutes a plump girl in a white revealing nightgown sort of costume of the period, perhaps, of the French Directorate, and who is standing on a cloud about two feet above the backs of two patient and unnoticing horses. The girl on the cloud carries a wreath and it is clearly her intention to put the wreath where the tall hat has been. In the bottom left-hand corner a fieldmouse is playing the part of a wee sleekit cowering timorous beastie yet is clearly, to judge from the glint in her eyes, an intent observer of the coronation ceremony and, in the words of another poet, is confidently aware that a mouse is miracle enough to stagger sextillions of infidels. In the background, for it is spring in Ayrshire and a little late for ploughing, the birds are plentiful on the branches and in a pale blue sky.

That picture, I feel, had its influence on Ellen:

> The man whose work is in the field
> From you his joy can't hide,
> As he treads along at break of day
> With two horses by his side.
> He whistles all along his way
> And merrily will sing.
> This is a birthday once again,
> Each morning of the Spring.

That picture, too, is always very much present to me. When the Empress of Hazelhatch, as my youngest sister called Ellen's mother, our grass-widowed aunt by marriage, died, and Hazelhatch passed into the hands of strangers, she left me the picture. Ellen and myself, she said, had liked it, and each other. Was the old lady remembering, too, one sad lulled day of sunshine when we sat in the kitchen at Hazelhatch and looked at the picture and she told me what I had already partly guessed that morning, that Ellen would die in hospital?

All around us in the old kitchen were cases of brown stout just freshly bottled in a careful and religious ritual at which I had been allowed to assist, along with a new girl who was there, from the County Mayo, to work in the bar and grocery and learn the trade. A long procession of girls had come and gone and benefited, perhaps, from the strict wisdom of the Empress, even if they had most certainly sighed and writhed and groaned under her discipline. She still decanted her own port,

a good Graham, black as your boot – and solid, but that de-
canting she did on her own, no assistants, no encouragement
even to spectators. Certain things were just too sacred.

That port was famous.

—It fixed her marriage, my father said, good and proper.
Your good mother's brother could think of nothing but port
and running horses. Never left the bar except to go to Punches-
town or the Maze or Strathroy Holm or Galway or Gowran
Park or Tramore or Bellewstown Hill or the Curragh itself, or
the horsefairs of Ballinasloe or Cahirmee. When he ran away
to the States and never came back he was both bow-legged and
purple in the face.

—He couldn't come back, said my mother.

She felt very sore about the whole story. He had been her
favourite brother. She explained: He went to Canada, not the
States, and then jumped the line at Buffalo and could never
again get his papers in order. He got in but couldn't get out.
There were hundreds like him.

—I often wondered why he ran away, said that youngest
sister with the thin face and the dark hair and the whiplash of
a tongue. Then I met the Empress of Hazelhatch with her long
black gown and her hair mounted high on a Spanish comb,
and dyed horse-chestnut as sure as God, and her pince-nez,
sitting behind the bar all night to speak to the better sort of
people, but never demeaning herself by serving a customer,
and I knew then why he would run to Alberta, or farther if he
could get without beginning to come home again round the
world.

Because that sister was herself an embryo empress she was
never happy at Hazelhatch. For myself, as easy-going as my
father or a wag-by-the-wall clock, I loved my visits to the place,
the picture of the poet, the strong drone of the old lady's voice,
the odour of good groceries and booze, the glow of old oak,
the high bedroom with slanted ceiling and dormer window
and an angled criss-crossed vision of the road west to Mount
Errigal and the Rosses and the ocean, the apples in the
orchard, the procession of young, discontented and frequently
sportive girls. Memories of those visits stay with me, stilled,

separated from all else, not frayed by time. That particular day
the Empress said to me: How did Ellen look when you saw her
this morning?

Nobody except her mother could have considered or
enquired how Ellen looked. She talked so much you didn't see.
So, to answer, I had to think back painstakingly. That was all
the more difficult to do because we had left the kitchen and
gone, rather sadly, out to the orchard where it seemed unkind
and even sinful to think how somebody looked who was going
to die, and who had loved that orchard.

> *Oft times I sit and think,*
> *And wonder if God sends*
> *This season, Spring, so beautiful*
> *To all his city friends.*
> *Ah no! there are no green fields*
> *There are no little lambs to play...*

For one thing, that morning Ellen had not been in the least
like the Muse of Poetry descending to salute Robert Burns
at the plough. She had always dressed modestly, mostly in
browns or mother-of-god blues with the breast-bone well
covered in white frills and lace and such; and there had never
been a pick on her bones. Never before had I noticed that she
was so freckled, scores of tiny dark-brown freckles around her
eyes and down the slopes of her nose. The paleness of her
ailing face, perhaps, made them more than ever noticeable.
Freckled people are always great talkers and even illness
could not stop her tongue: only death or the last gasping that
preceded it.

—It must be heavenly for you, she said, to feel that you are
really and truly walking the paths of learning, and in a city that
has been ennobled by the footsteps of so many great scholars
and poets, how I envy you, I always so wanted to get to the
university, but when I'm up and about again and out of this
bed I promise you a visit in Dublin and you must show me all
the sights and famous places, promise, you'll find my mother
very quiet and brooding these days, I can't think what's wrong
with her, but sometimes she gets like that, it may be that the
new girl and herself do not get on so well, a strange girl from

the County Mayo, a great singer, she came to see me several times, and sometimes I think she resembles me, she wants to sing just as I write poems, a lovely voice, too, but it's so sad, such clean regular features and an exquisite head of dark hair, but that purple discolouration on one side of her face, God help her, she would have to sing always with one side of her face away from the audience...

Because there was winter and the end of things in the room, even if it was high summer outside the window, I told her about the letter forgotten, then torn into fragments and sent sailing on the Drumragh. I told her about my mother and her opinions on fire and water. She said that, perhaps, it would have been better for both of them, meaning the vanished husband and herself, if it had ended the way the letter did: gone peacefully on the easy water. She said my mother had always been kind. She stepped out of bed and walked with me as far as the door of the room. She wore a heavy blue dressing-gown. She kissed me. We never met again.

> *Ah no! there are no green fields,*
> *There are no little lambs to play,*
> *But walk out in the country*
> *On any fine spring day...*

So I in the orchard, all alone and sad, am fixing a puncture in the back wheel of the lofty ancient bicycle on which the Empress of Hazelhatch is wont to cruise forth in deep-green drowsy summers, her skirts high above the dust, her head high above the hedges, surveying the labour of the fields, occasionally saluting the workers. To me, and softly singing to herself for she is proud of her voice and the old lady flatters her about it, comes the Mayo girl with the face, flawless and faultless in shape but discoloured on the left cheek. She stands beside me, at my left hand. Our hands touch as we run the bicycle tube through a basin of water so as to raise a bubble and locate the puncture. The birds in the orchard trees are silent because it is the sultry month of least song. But the girl for a while sings in a sort of sweet whisper about, of all things, moonlight in Mayo. Then she says: It isn't my day off, and I want to get to Strabane.

—Why?

—What do you think? A fella.

—Ask her for the evening off.

—She's hell on fellas. You ask her. She'd grant you anything.

—I'm a fella.

—You're the white-headed boy around here. Say you want to take me to the pictures.

—What picture?

—Any picture. No picture.

> But walk out in the country
> On any fine spring day.
> And there you'll find what art can't paint
> Nature's gifts so fair:
> The trees, the flowers, the streamlets
> And the many birds so rare.

The road is dusty and the hedges high. Had Ellen never written a poem about summer? The girl sings as she walks. It is four miles to the village of Lifford, old houses shaggy with flowering creepers, then across the great bridge where the Mourne River, containing the water of the Drumragh, from Tyrone, meets the Finn River from Donegal to form, between them, the spreading Foyle; then half a mile across level water-meadows to the town of Strabane. She sings about the bird in the gilded cage. But walking through Lifford, curious faces looking out over half-doors, she stops singing and says: Mrs. Lagan is dying, isn't she?

Ellen's married name takes me by surprise. She says: You needn't talk about it if you don't want to. It's just that I like her.

—So do I.

—She's very clever. She's a great poet.

—Not exactly great.

—She gets printed.

—In local papers.

—Nevertheless.

We lean on the bridge and watch the mingling of the Mourne and the Finn, and the wagtails darting and diving over a shining triangle of sand and gravel. She says: The old lady is kindly but very strict. Mrs. Lagan is generous but very sad. They say there never was a man, but one, who could listen to her or talk her down. She should have lived in a world where men talked more.

—Like where?

—New York or Dublin or London or Milan. Big singing cities. Her soul's mate was a flowery preaching priest. They should have been allowed to marry, the old lady says. They'd have made a perfect couple. She'd have made a perfect minister's wife. Did you ever look at a minister's wife? They're all like that. All poetry and bazaars.

—She could have preached better than anyone.

We follow the level road across the water-meadows. There is a raised footwalk designed to keep pedestrians dry-shod in time of flood. The clock has stopped forever on that still day in Strabane. She says: She likes me to sing when I go to see her.

She sings: Ah, sweet mystery of life at last I've found you.

When she has finished singing I declaim:

> *You may have your city pleasures*
> *And its praises you may sing,*
> *But there's naught on earth that can compare*
> *With the country's dales in spring.*

—What's that?

—The voice of Cousin Ellen.

—I could sing that.

She sings it to a slow sweet tune I never heard before or since. Under the apple trees had Ellen's poetic soul taken possession of the girl?

We sit on the quiet river bank to pass the time until my train departs for Dublin or until her fella arrives. She sits at my left hand. When I hold her chin and try to turn her lips towards me she stiffens her neck, then looks away towards the town. So, when I hear the train whistle, I leave her unkissed there by the Mourne River, waiting for the fella. Often afterwards in Dublin I wonder what song she sings for him, what side of her face does she turn towards him.

A Great God's Angel Standing

PASCAL STAKELUM, the notorious rural rake, and Father Paul, the ageing Catholic curate of Lislap, met the two soldiers from Devon by the bridge over the Camowen River and right beside the lunatic asylum. It was a day of splitting sunshine in the year of the Battle of Dunkirk. Pascal and the priest were going to visit the lunatic asylum, Father Paul to hear confessions, Pascal to bear him company and to sit at a sealed distance while the inmates cudgelled what wits they had and told their sins. The two soldiers, in battle-dress and with heavy packs on their backs, were on their way home from Dunkirk, not home to Devon exactly but to Six-milecross, to the house of two sisters they had married in a hurry before they set off for France. It was, as you may have guessed, six miles from our garrison town of Lislap to the crossroads village where the two sisters lived, and it was a very warm day. So every one of the four, two in thick khaki, two in dull black, was glad to stop and stand at ease and look at the smooth gliding of the cool Camowen.

The bridge they rested on was of a brownish grey stone, three full sweeping arches and, to the sides, two tiny niggardly arches. In a blue sky a few white clouds idled before a light wind, and beyond a wood at an upstream bend of the river a two-horse mowing-machine ripped and rattled in meadow grass. The stone of the bridge was cut from the same quarry as the stone in the high long wall that circled the lunatic asylum and went for a good half-mile parallel with the right bank of the river.

—In France it was hot, said the first soldier.

—He means the weather was hot, said the second soldier.

The four men, priest and rake and soldiers two, laughed at that: not, Pascal says, much of a laugh, not sincere, no heartiness in it.

—Hot as hell, said the second soldier. Even the rivers was hot.

—Boiling, said the first soldier. That canal at Lille was as hot as a hot bath.

—Ruddy mix-up, said the second soldier. The Guards, they fired at the Fusiliers, and the Fusiliers, they fired at the Guards. Nobody knew who was what. Ruddy mix-up.

They took the cigarettes Pascal offered.

—Boiling hot and thirsty, said the second soldier. Never knew such thirst.

Father Paul said: You could have done with some Devon cider.

—Zider, said the first soldier. There were zomething.

—Zomerzet you are, said the second soldier.

They all laughed again. This time it was a real laugh.

The Camowen water where it widened over gravel to go under the five stone arches was clear and cool as a mountain rockspring. Upstream, trout rings came as regularly as the ticks of a clock.

The two soldiers accepted two more cigarettes. They tucked them into the breast-pockets of their battledress. They hitched their packs, shook hands several times and knelt on the motorless roadway for Father Paul's blessing. They were not themselves Arcees, they said, but in camp in Aldershot in England they had been matey with an Arcee padre, and they knew the drill. Blessed after battle, they stood up, dusted their knees as carefully as if they'd never heard of mud or blood and, turning often to wave back, walked on towards the two sisters of Sixmilecross.

—Virginia, Father Paul said, was the best place I ever saw for cider.

Just to annoy him, Pascal said: Virginia, County Cavan, Ireland.

They were walking together on a narrow footwalk in the shadow of the asylum wall.

—Virginia, U.S.A., Paul said. The Old Dominion. Very well you know what Virginia I mean. They had great apple orchards there, and fine cider presses, around a little town called Fincastle under the shadow of the Blue Ridge Mountains. That was great country, and pleasant people and fine horses, when I was a young man on the American mission.

It was a period out of his lost youth that Paul frequently talked about.

In those days of his strange friendship with Pascal he was thin and long-faced and stoop-shouldered with the straining indignant stoop that is forced on tall people when the years challenge the power to hold the head so high. That day the sun had sucked a little moisture out of his pale cheeks. He had taken off his heavy black hat to give the light breeze a chance to ruffle and cool his thin grey hair, but the red line the hat rim had made was still to be seen and, above the red line, a sullen concentration of drops of sweat. He was though, as Pascal so often said, the remains of a mighty handsome man and with such dignity, too, and stern faith and such an eloquent way in the pulpit that it was a mystery to all of us what the bishop of the diocese had against him that he had never given him the honour, glory and profit of a parish of his own.

—In the mood those two boyos are in, Pascal said, it will take them no time at all walking to the sisters at Sixmilecross.

That was the way Pascal, in accordance with his animal nature, thought; and Sixmilecross was a village in which, as in every other village in our parts, Pascal had had some of the rural adventures that got him his dubious reputation, and that made us all marvel when we'd see a character like him walking in the company of a priest. In Burma, I once heard an old sweat say, adulterers kill a pig to atone for their crime, so it was only apt and proper, and even meet and just, that Pascal should be a pork butcher. When he went a-wooing in country places he'd never walk too far from his rattly old Morris Cowley without bringing with him a tyre lever or starting handle, for country girls were hell for having truculent brothers and if they didn't have brothers they had worse and far and away worse, male cousins, and neither brothers nor male cousins, least of all the male cousins, had any fancy for Pascal

rooting and snorting about on the fringes of the family. That's
Pascal, for you. But at the moment, Paul is speaking.

—A man hungers to get home, Paul said. The men from
Devon won't count the time or the number of paces. Time,
what's time? They've come a long walk from the dreadful gates
of eternity. Once I told you, Pascal boy, you were such a rake
and run-the-roads you'd have to live to be ninety, to expiate
here on this earth and so dodge the devil.

Complacently Pascal said: The good die young.

—Ninety's a long time, Father Paul said. But what's time?
Here in this part of my parish...

They were walking in at the wide gateway. He waved his
black wide-brimmed hat in a circle comprehending the whole
place, as big almost as the garrison town itself, for all the
crazy people of two counties, or those of them that had been
detected and diagnosed, were housed there.

—This part of my parish, he said. As much happiness or
unhappiness as in any other part of the parish. But one thing
that doesn't matter here is time. As far as most of them know,
time and eternity are the same thing.

They walked along a serpentine avenue, up sloping lawns to
the main door. The stone in the walls of the high building was
cut from the same quarry as the stone that bridged the river, as
the stone in the encircling wall. The stone floor in the long
cool corridor rang under their feet. They followed a porter
along that corridor to a wide bright hospital ward. Unshaven
men in grey shirts sat up in bed and looked at them with quick
bright questioning eyes. The shining nervous curiosity of the
ones who sat up disturbed Pascal. He preferred to look at the
others who lay quietly in bed and stared steadily at points on
the ceiling or on the opposite wall, stared steadily but seemed
to see neither the ceiling nor the opposite wall, and sometimes
mumbled to nobody words that had no meaning. A few men in
grey suits moved aimlessly about the floor or sat to talk with
some of the bright curious men in the beds. Beside the doorway a keeper in blue uniform dotted with brass buttons sat and
smoked and read a newspaper, raised his head and nodded to
the priest, then returned to his pipe and his newspaper.

Father Paul moved from bed to bed, his purple stole about

his neck. The murmur of his voice, particularly when he was at the Latin, was distinctly audible. His raised hand sawed the air in absolution and blessing. Once in a while he said something in English in a louder voice and then the man he was with would laugh, and the priest would laugh, and the man in the next bed, if he was a bright-eyed man, would laugh, and another bright-eyed man several beds away would start laughing and be unable to stop, and a ripple of laughter would run around the room touching everybody except the staring mumbling men and the keeper who sat by the door.

Pascal sat beside an empty bed and read a paperbacked book about a doctor in Germany who was, or said he thought he was, two men, and had murdered his wife, who had been a showgirl, by bathing her beautiful body in nitric acid. That sinful crazy waste of good material swamped Pascal in an absorbing melancholy so that he didn't for a few moments even notice the thin hand gripping his thigh. There, kneeling at his feet, was a man in grey clothes, misled into thinking Pascal was a priest because Pascal wore, as did the gay young men of that place and period, a black suit with, though, extremely wide and unclerical trousers. Pascal studied, with recognition, the inmate's grey jacket, the scarce grey hair, the spotted dirty scalp. The kneeling man said: Bless me, father, for I have sinned.

—Get up to hell Jock Sharkey, Pascal said. I'm no priest. You're crazy.

He was, he says, crimson in the face with embarrassment. The keeper was peeking over his newspaper, laughing, saying Jock sure was crazy and that, in fact, was why he was where he was. The keeper also blew smoke-rings from thick laughing lips, an irritating fellow. He said: Fire away, Pascal. It'll keep him quiet. I hear him two or three times a week.

—It wouldn't be right, Pascal said.

He had theological scruples, the only kind he could afford.

Only once in my life, he was to say afterwards, did a man ever ask me to listen to him confessing his sins and, fair enough, the place should be a lunatic asylum and the man, poor Jock Sharkey, that was put away for chasing women, not that he ever overtook them or did anybody any harm. They walked quick, he walked quick. They walked slow, he walked slow. He was just simply fascinated, the poor gormless bastard, by the sound of their feet, the hobbled trot, the high heels, you know, clickety-click, thigh brushing thigh. Poor Jock.

—What he'll tell you, said the keeper, is neither right nor wrong. Who'd anyway be better judge than yourself, Pascal? Even Father Paul doesn't know one half of what you know. You, now, would know about things Paul never heard tell of.

The man on his knees said: I suppose you'll put me out of the confession box, father. I'm a terrible sinner. I wasn't at mass or meeting since the last mission.

—Why was that? said Pascal the priest.

—The place I'm working in, they won't let me go to mass.

—Then it's not your fault, said Pascal. No sin. Grievous matter, perfect knowledge, full consent.

He did, he said afterwards, remember from his schooldays that impressive fragment of the penny catechism of Christian doctrine: the stud-book, the form-book, the rules for the big race from here to eternity.

—But when I go to confession, father, I've a bad memory for my sins. Will you curse me, father, if I forget some of them?

—By no means, Jock. Just recite what you remember.

The keeper, more offensive as his enjoyment increased, said that Pascal wouldn't know how to curse, that he didn't know the language. The head of the kneeling man nodded backwards and forwards while he mumbled the rhythmical words of some prayer or prayers of his childhood. Now and again the names of saints came clearly out of the confused unintelligible mumble, like bubbles rising from a marshy bottom to the surface of a slow stream. Then he repeated carefully, like a child reciting, these words from an old rebel song: I cursed three times since last Easter Day. At mass-time once I went to play.

Pascal was seldom given to visions except in one particular direction, yet he says that at that moment he did see, from his memory of school historical pageants, the rebel Irish boy, kneeling in all innocence or ignorance at the feet of the brutal red-coated captain whose red coat was, for the occasion, covered by the soutane of the murdered rebel priest.

The keeper said: You should sing that, Jock.

—I passed the churchyard one day in haste, Jock said, and forgot to pray for my mother's rest.

—You're sure of heaven, said the keeper, if that's the sum total of your sins. The Reverend Stakelum himself, or even Father Paul, won't get off so easy.

The penitent looked up at Pascal and Pascal looked down at stubbly chin, hollow jaws, sorrowful brown eyes. Poor Jock, Pascal thought, they put you away just for doing what I spend all my spare time, and more besides, at: to wit, chasing the girls. Only you never even seemed to want to catch up with them.

For poor Jock was never more than what we called a sort of a mystery man, terrifying the girls, or so they claimed, by his nightly wanderings along dark roads, his sudden sprints that ended as sharply and pointlessly as they began, his shouted meaningless words provoked perhaps by a whiff of perfume in his nostrils or by that provocative tap-tippity-tap of high hard heels on the metalled surface of the road. A child might awaken in the night and cry that there was a man's face at the window. A girl might run home breathless and say that Jock had followed her for half a mile, suiting his pace to hers, like a ghost or a madman. He couldn't be a ghost, although he was as thin and harmless as any ghost. So we put him away for a madman.

He stared long and hard at Pascal. His thin right hand tightly grasped Pascal's knee.

—David Stakelum's son, he said. I'd know you anywhere on your father. Thank God to see you in the black clothes. Your father was a decent man and you'll give me the blessing of a decent man's son.

He bowed his head and joined his hands. Behind the newspaper the keeper was gurgling. Pascal said afterwards that his father wouldn't be too pleased to think that his hell's own special hell-raker of a son bore him such a resemblance that even a crazy man could see it. But if his blessing would help to make Jock content then Jock was welcome to it. So he cut the sign of the cross over the old crazy dirty head. He touched with the tips of the fingers of both hands the bald patch on the dome. He held out those fingers to be kissed. The most fervent young priest fresh from the holy oil couldn't have done a better job, Pascal had so often studied the simple style of Father Paul. The keeper was so impressed that he folded the newspaper and sat serious and quiet.

Father Paul walked slowly towards them, along the narrow passage between the two rows of beds. Walking with him came a fat red-faced grey-headed inmate. The fat inmate talked solemnly, gestured stiffly with his right hand. The priest listened, or pretended to listen, turning his head sideways, stretching his neck, emphasising the stoop in his shoulders. He said: Mr. Simon, you haven't met my young friend, Pascal.

The fat man smiled benevolently at Pascal but went on talking to the priest: As you know, sir, I am not of the Roman Catholic persuasion, yet I have always been intrigued by the theory and practice of auricular confession. The soul of man, being walled around and shut in as it is, demands some outlet for the thoughts and desires that accumulate therein.

He had, Pascal says, a fruity pansy voice.

—The child, he said, runs to its mother with its little tale of sorrow. Friend seeks out friend. In silence and secrecy souls are interchanged.

It was exactly, Pascal was to say, as if the sentences had been written on the air in the loops and lines of copper-plate. You could not only hear but see the man's talk: A Wesleyan I was born, sir, and so remain. But always have I envied you Roman Catholics the benefits of the confessional, the ease that open confession brings to the soul. What is the Latin phrase sir?

Paul said: Ad quietam conscientiam.

—Ad quietam conscientiam, Simon repeated. There is peace in every single syllable. There is much wisdom in your creed, sir. Wesley knew that. You have observed the spiritual similarity between Wesley and Ignatius of Loyola.

The keeper said: Simon, Doctor Murdy's looking for you. Where in hell were you?

—He asks me where I have been, sir. Where in hell.

Father Paul said: He means no harm, Simon. Just his manner of speaking.

Simon was still smiling. From elbow to bent wrist and dangling hand, his right arm was up like a question mark. He said to Father Paul: Surveillance, sir, is a stupid thing. It can accomplish nothing, discover nothing. If I were to tell this fellow where I had been, how could he understand? On this earth I have been, and beyond this earth.

He shook hands with the priest but not with Pascal nor the keeper nor Jock Sharkey. He walked with dignity past the keeper and back down the ward.

—There goes a travelled man, Pascal said.

Father Paul was folding his purple stole. He said: There are times when religion can be a straitjacket.

—It's not Simon's time yet for the straitjacket, the keeper said. When the fit takes him he'll brain the nearest neighbour with the first handy weapon.

At the far end of the ward where Simon had paused for a moment, there was a sudden noise and a scuffling. The keeper said: Too much learning is the divil.

He thumped down the passage between the beds.

—Now for the ladies, Father Paul said. You'll be at home there, Pascal. They say all over the town that no man living has an easier way with the ladies.

Pascal was to report to myself and a few others that if Paul had wanted to preach him a sermon to make his blood run cold and to put him off the women for the rest of his life, he couldn't have gone about it in a better way.

Is it true that, as the poet said, you never knew a holy man but had a wicked man for his comrade and heart's darling? Was it part of Paul's plan to pick Pascal as his escort and so to make an honest boy out of him or, at least, to cut in on the time that he would otherwise spend rummaging and ruining the girls of town and country? The thing about Pascal was that, away from the companionship of Paul, he thought of nothing but women when, of course, he wasn't butchering pork, and perhaps he thought of women even then. Like many another who is that way afflicted he wasn't big, violent, handsome, red-faced or blustering. No, he went about his business in a quiet way. His hair was sparse, of a nondescript colour, flatly combed and showing specks of dandruff. He wore horn-rimmed spectacles. He was one of those white-faced fellows who would, softly and secretly and saying nothing about it to their best friends, take advantage of their own grandmothers. The women were mad about him. They must have been. He kept himself in fettle and trim for his chosen vocation. When the two soldiers and Paul were, in the sunshine on the Camowen Bridge, talking of Devon cider, Pascal was thinking, he says, of sherry and raw eggs, and oysters, porter and paprika pepper.

On the day of Paul's funeral he said to me: A decent man and I liked him. But, my God, he had a deplorable set against the women or anybody that fancied the women.

—Except myself, he said. For some reason or other he put up with me.

—That day at the female ward, he said, at the geriatrics you call 'em, I cheated him, right under his nose, God forgive me. And may Paul himself forgive me, since he knows it all now.

Pascal stood at the threshold of this female ward while Father Paul, purple stole again around his neck, moved, listening and forgiving with God's forgiveness, from bed to bed. Pascal wasn't much of a theologian, yet looking at the females in that female ward he reckoned that it was God, not the females, who needed forgiveness. They were all old females, very old females, and as such didn't interest Pascal. He had nothing, though, against old age as long as it left him alone. His father's mother was an attractive, chubby, silver-haired female, sweet as an apple forgotten and left behind on a rack in a pantry, wrinkled, going dry, yet still sweet beyond description. But these sad old females, a whole wardful of them, were also mad and misshapen, some babbling like raucous birds, some silently slavering.

He couldn't make up his mind whether to enter the ward and sit down or to walk up and down the cool echoing corridor. He always felt a fool when walking up and down like a sentry, but then he also felt a fool when standing or sitting still.

He was just a little afraid of those caricatures of women. This was the first time he had ever been afraid of women, and afraid to admit to himself that these creatures were made in exactly the same way as women he had known. He was afraid that if he went into the ward and sat down he would see them in even greater detail than he now did from the threshold. He was young. Outside the sun was shining, the Camowen sparkling under the sun, the meadow grass falling like green silk to make beds for country lovers. But here all flesh was grass and favour was deceitful and beauty was vain. It was bad enough looking at the men. To think what the mind could do to the body. But it was hell upon earth looking at the women. Jock Sharkey, like a million lovers and a thousand poets, had gone mad for beauty. This, in the ward before him, was what could happen to beauty.

He stepped, shuddering, back into the corridor and collided with a tall nurse. He apologised. He smelled freshly-ironed, starched linen and disinfectant, a provoking smell. A quick flurried glance showed him a strong handsome face, rather boyish, brick-red hair bursting out over the forehead where the nurse's veil had failed to restrain it. He apologised. He was still rattled by his vision in the ward. Contrary to his opportunist instinct he was even about to step out of the way. But the nurse didn't pass. She said: It is you, Pascal Stakelum, isn't it? Did they lock you up at last? A hundred thousand welcomes.

He had to do some rapid thinking before he remembered. There were so many faces in his memory and he was still confused, still a little frightened, by those faces in the ward. She didn't try to help. She stood, feet apart and solidly planted, and grinned at him, too boyish for a young woman but still fetching. She was, if anything, taller than he was. Her brother, then he remembered, had gone to school with us, a big fellow, as dark as she was red, very clever but capricious, making a mockery of things that he alone, perhaps, of all of us could understand and, in the end, throwing the whole thing up and running away and joining the Royal Air Force. So the first thing Pascal said, to show that he knew who she was, was to ask about the brother, and when would he be coming home. She said: He won't be coming home.

—Why for not?

She said he had been killed at Dunkirk.

Coming right after the prospect of the mad old women, that was a bit of a blow in the face, but at least, he told himself, clean death in battle was not madness, deformity, decay; and the moment gave Pascal the chance to sympathise, to get closer to her. He held her hands. He said he was sorry. He said he had always liked her brother. He had, too. They had indeed, been quite friendly.

She said: It's war. He would always do things his own way.

She seemed proud of her brother, or just proud of having a brother dead at Dunkirk.

—This is no place to talk, Pascal said. And I'm with Father Paul. Meet me this evening at the Crcvenagh Bridge.

That was the old humpy scventeenth-century bridge on the way to a leafy network of lovers' lanes and deep secret bushy ditches.

—Not this evening, she said. I'm on duty. But tomorrow.

—Eight o'clock on the dot, said Pascal.

That was his usual time during the summer months and the long warm evenings. And he was very punctual.

She walked away from him and towards Father Paul. He lookcd after her, no longer seeing the rest of the ward. She was a tall strong girl, stepping with decision and a great swing. Jock Sharkey would have followed her to the moon.

Father Paul, the shriving done, was again folding his stole. He joked with a group of old ladies. He told one of them that on his next visit he would bring her a skipping rope. He told another one he would bring her a powderpuff. He distributed handfuls of caramels to the whole crew. They cackled with merriment. They loved him. That was one bond between Pascal and himself. The women loved them both.

—But if he meant to preach to me that time, Pascal said to us, by bringing me to that chamber of horrors, I had the laugh on him.

In the sunshine on the lawn outside, the superintending doctor stood with his wife and his dogs, three Irish setters, one male, two female. The doctor and his wife stood, that is, and the setters ran round and round in erratic widening circles.

Those smart-stepping Devon men were by now approaching

Sixmilecross, and the two sisters, and rest after battle and port after stormy seas.

The doctor was a handsome cheery fellow, even if he was bald. He wore bright yellow, hand-made shoes, Harris tweed trousers and a high-necked Aran sweater. The wife was small and dainty and crisp as a nut, and a new wife; and the two of them, not to speak of the three setters, were as happy as children. They talked – the doctor, the woman, Paul and Pascal – about the war, and about the two soldiers from Devon and their two women in Sixmilecross. Then Father Paul wished the doctor and his wife many happy days, and he and Pascal stepped off towards the town. At the gateway they met a group of thirty or forty uniformed inmates returning, under supervision, from a country walk. One of them was gnawing a raw turnip with which, ceasing to gnaw, he took aim at Pascal and let fly. Pascal fielded the missile expertly – in his schooldays he had been a sound midfield man – and restored it to the inmate who was still chewing and looking quite amazed at his own deed. All this, to the great amusement of the whole party, inmates and three keepers. But oddly enough, Paul didn't join in the merriment. He stood, silent and abstracted, on the grass at the side of the driveway. He looked at the sky. His lips moved as though he were praying, or talking to himself.

Pascal gave away what cigarettes he had left to the hiking party and he and the priest walked on, Paul very silent, over the Camowen. When they were halfways to the town, Paul said: Some men can't live long without a woman.

Pascal said nothing. He remembered that there was a story that Paul had once beaten a loving couple out of the hedge with a blackthorn stick. He remembered that Paul came from a stern mountain part of the country where there had been a priest in every generation in every family for three hundred years. He thought of the red nurse and the hedge ahead of her. So he said nothing.

—That new wife of his, Paul said, was American. Did you notice?

—She dressed American, Pascal said. But she had no accent.

—She comes from a part of the States and from a class in

society where they don't much have an accent, Paul said. At least not what you in your ignorance would call an American accent.

Pascal said: The Old Dominion.

—You're learning fast, Paul said.

The town was before them.

—Three wives he had, Paul said. One dead. Irish. One divorced. English. And now a brand new one from Virginia. Some men can't go without.

Pascal made no comment. He contented himself with envying the bald doctor his international experience. He resolved to travel.

—Most men, said Paul, aren't happy unless they're tangled up with a woman. The impure touch. But the French are the worst. Their blood boiling with wine. From childhood. How could they keep pure?

Pascal hadn't the remotest idea. So he made no comment. He didn't know much about the French but he reckoned that just at that moment in history they had enough and to spare on their plates without also having to worry about purity.

—But pleasures are like poppies spread, Paul said.

He was a great man always to quote the more moralising portions of Robert Burns. Pascal heard him out: You seize the flower, its bloom is shed. Or like the snow falls in the river – a moment white, then melts forever. Or like the borealis race, that flit ere you can point their place. Or like the rainbow's lovely form, evanishing amid the storm.

—Burns, said Father Paul, well knew what he was talking about. Those, Pascal, are the words of wisdom gained through sad and sordid experience.

Pascal agreed. He was remembering the nurse's dead brother who had been a genius at poetry. He could write parodies on anything that any poet had ever written.

When Pascal met the nurse at the Crevenagh Bridge on the following evening she was, of course, in mourning. But the black cloth went very well with that brilliant red hair. Or like the rainbow's lovely form. There was something about it, too, that was odd and exciting, like being out, he said, with a young nun. Yet, apart from the colour of her clothes, she was no nun. Although, come to think of it, who except God knows what nuns are really like?

Pascal, as we know, was also in black but he had no reason to be in mourning. It had rained, just enough to wet the pitch. Otherwise the evening went according to Operation Pascal. When he had first attacked with the knee for the warming-up process he then withdrew the knee and substituted the hand, lowering it through the band of her skirt, allowing it to linger for a playful moment at the bunker of the belly button. Thereafter he seemed to be hours, like fishermen hauling a net, pulling a silky slip out of the way before the rummaging hand, now living a life of its own, could negotiate the passage into her warm drawers. Pascal didn't know why he hadn't made the easier and more orthodox approach by laying the girl low to begin with and then raising skirt and slip, except it was that they were standing up at the time, leaning against a sycamore tree. The rain had passed but the ground was wet, and to begin his wooing by spreading his trenchcoat (Many's the fine rump, he boasted, that trenchcoat had kept dry, even when the snow was on the ground.) on the grass, seemed much too formal. Pascal Stakelum's days, or evenings or nights, were complex with such problems.

Later came the formal ceremonious spreading of the trench-coat on a protective mattress of old newspapers, and the assuming by both parties, of the horizontal. By that time the big red girl was so lively that he swore she'd have shaken Gordon Richards, the King of them All, out of the saddle. She kept laughing and talking, too, so as to be audible, he reckoned, thirty yards away but fortunately he had chosen for the grand manoeuvre a secluded corner of the network of lanes and ditches. He had a veteran's knowledge of the terrain and he was nothing if not discreet.

He was not unmindful of the brother dead in faraway France. But then the brother had been such an odd fellow that even in Pascal's tusselling with his strong red sister he might have found matter for amusement and mockery. As Pascal bounced on top of her, gradually subduing her wildness to the rhythmic control of bridle and straddle and, in the end, to the britchen of his hands under her buttocks, he could hear her brother's voice beginning the schoolboy mockery of Shelley's soaring skylark: Hell to thee, blithe spirit.

Pascal and the splendid panting red girl moved together to the poet's metre.

That was one brother Pascal did not have to guard against with starting handle or tyre lever. Working like a galley slave under the dripping sycamore he was in no fear of ambush.

Paul got his parish in the end, the reward of a well-spent life, he said wryly. He died suddenly in it before he was there for six months. That parish was sixty miles away from Lislap, in sleepy grass-meadow country where the slow River Bann drifts northwards out of the great lake. Pascal missed Paul's constant companionship more than he or anybody else would have believed possible and began, particularly after Paul's sudden death, to drink more than he had ever done before, and went less with the girls, which puzzled him as much as it did us. It worried him, too: for in the house of parliament or public house that we specially favoured, he asked me one day was he growing old before his time because he was growing fonder of drink and could now pass a strange woman on the street without wondering who and what she was.

--You're better off, Pascal, I said. What were you ever doing anyway but breaking them in for other men? You never stayed long enough with any one woman to be able in the long run to tell her apart from any other woman.

He was more hurt than I had imagined he would be. But he sadly agreed with me, and said that some day he hoped to find one real true woman with whom he could settle down.

—Like with poor Paul that's gone, he said. Some one woman that a man could remember to the last moment of his life.

—No, I'm not crazy, he said. Two days before his death I was with Paul in his parish, as you know. We went walking this evening after rain, by the banks of a small river in that heavy-grass country. That was the last walk we had together. The boreen we were on went parallel with the river bank. We met an old man, an old bewhiskered codger, hobbling on a stick. So Paul introduced us and said to Methusaleh: What now do you think of my young friend from the big garrison town of Lislap?

—The old fellow, said Pascal, looked me up and looked me down. Real cunning country eyes. Daresay he could see through me as if I was a sheet of thin cellophane. But he lied. He said: Your reverence, he looks to me like a fine clean young man.

—That was an accurate description of me, Pascal Stakelum, known far and wide.

Pascal brooded. He said: A fine clean young man.

—Then that evening, he said, we sat for ages after dinner, before we knelt down to say the holy rosary with those two dry sticks of female cousins that did the housekeeping for him. One quick look at either of them would put you off women for time and eternity. There's an unnerving silence in the houses that priests live in: the little altar on the landing, you know, where they keep the sacrament for sick calls at night. Imagine, if you can, the likes of me on my bended knees before it, wondering would I ever remember the words when it came my turn to lead the prayers. But I staggered it. Closed my eyes, you might say, and took a run and jump at it, and landed on the other side word perfect. It would have been embarrassing for Paul if I hadn't been able to remember the words of the Paterandave in the presence of those two stern cousins. One evening one of them sat down opposite me in a low armchair and crossed her legs, poor thing, and before I could look elsewhere I had a view of a pair of long bloomers, passion-killers, that were a holy fright. You wouldn't see the equal of them in the chamber of horrors. Six feet long and coloured grey and elastic below the knee. But when the two cousins were off to bed, and good luck to them, we sat and talked until all hours, and out came the bottle of Jameson, and Paul's tongue loosened. It could be that he said more than he meant to say: oh, mostly about Virginia and the Blue Ridge Mountains and the lovely people who always asked the departing stranger to come back again. Cider presses near Fincastle. Apple orchards. Dogwood trees in blossom. He went on like that for a long time. Then he got up, rooted among his books, came back with this one book covered in a sort of soft brown velvet with gold lettering and designs on the cover and, inside, coloured pictures and the fanciest printing you ever saw, in red and in black. He said to me: Here's a book, Pascal, you might keep as a memory of me when I'm gone.

—So I laughed at him, making light of his gloomy face, trying to jolly him up, you know. I said: Where, now, would you be thinking of going?

—Where all men go sooner or later, he said.

—That was the end of my laughing. That's no way for a man to talk, even if he has a premonition.

—Keep the book as a token, Paul said to me. You were never much for the poetry, I know. But your wife when you find her might be, or, perhaps, some of your children. You've a long road ahead of you yet, Pascal, all the way to ninety, and poetry can lighten the burden. That book was given to me long ago by the dearest friend I ever had. Until I met yourself, he said. Long ago in a distant country and the wench is dead.

—Those were the last words I ever heard Paul speak, excepting the Latin of the mass next morning, for my bus passed the church gate before the mass was rightly over, and I had to run for it. But bloody odd words they were to come from Paul.

—Common enough words, I said. Anybody could have said them.

—But you didn't see the book, Pascal said. I'll show it to you.

He did, too, a week later. It was an exquisite little edition, lost on Pascal, I thought with some jealousy, both as to the perfection of the bookmaker's art and as to the text, which was William Morris telling us, there in a public house in Lislap, how Queen Guenevere had defended herself against the lies of Sir Gauwaine, and a charge of unchastity. Fondling the book, I was not above thinking how much more suitable than Pascal I would have been as a companion for old Paul. So that I felt more than a little ashamed when Pascal displayed to me with what care he had read the poem, underlining here and there in red ink to match the rubric of the capitals and the running titles on the tops of the pages. It was, almost certainly, the only poem to which he had ever paid any particular attention, with the possible exception of that bouncing parody on Shelly's skylark.

—It's like a miniature mass book, he said. Red and black. Only it was by no means intended for using at the mass. See here.

He read and pointed with his finger as he read: She threw her wet hair backward from her brow, her hand close to her mouth touching her cheek.

—Coming from the swimming-pool, Pascal said, when the dogwoods were in blossom. You never knew that Paul was a champion swimmer in his youth. Swimming's like tennis. Brings out the woman in a woman. Arms wide, flung-out, breasts up. Oh, there were a lot of aspects to Paul. And listen to this: Yet felt her cheek burned so, she must a little touch it. Like one lame she walked away from Gauwaine.

—Time and again, Pascal said, he had heard it said that lame women had the name for being hot. Once he had seen on the quays of Dublin a one-legged prostitute. The thought had ever afterwards filled him with curiosity, although at the time he wouldn't have risked touching her for all the diamonds in Kimberley.

—And her great eyes began again to fill, he read, though still she stood right up.

That red nurse, he remembered, had had great blue eyes, looking up at him like headlamps seen through mist.

—But the queen in this poem, he said, was a queen and no mistake. And in the summer it says that she grew white with flame, white like the dogwood blossoms and all for this Launcelot fellow, lucky Launcelot, and such a pansy name. One day she says, she was half-mad with beauty and went without her ladies all alone in a quiet garden walled round every way, just like the looney bin where I met that nurse. And both their mouths, it says, went wandering in one way and, aching sorely, met among the leaves. Warm, boy, warm. Then there's odd stuff here about a great God's angel standing at the foot of the bed, his wings dyed with colours not known on earth, and asking the guy or girl in the bed, the angel has two cloths, you see, one blue, one red, asking them, or him or her, to guess which cloth is heaven and which is hell. The blue one turns out to be hell. That puzzles me.

It puzzled both of us.

—But you must admit, said Pascal, that it was a rare book for a young one to be giving a young priest, and writing on it, look here, for Paul with a heart's love, by the Peaks of Otter in Virginia, on a day of sunshine never to be forgotten, from Elsie Cameron. Usually the women give breviaries to the priests, or chalices, or amices, or albs, or black pullovers. She must have been a rare one, Elsie Cameron. Would you say now that she might have had a slight limp? It's a Scottish name. Paul was forever talking about what he called the Scots Irish in Virginia and the fine people they were. All I know is that Scottish women are reputed to be very hot. They're all Protestants and don't have to go to confession.

Pascal had known a man who worked in Edinburgh who said that all you had to do to set a Scotswoman off was to show her the Forth Bridge, the wide open legs of it. That man had said that the Forth Bridge had never failed him.

When I said to Pascal that all this about Paul could have been as innocent as a rose, he said he was well aware of that: he wasn't claiming that Paul had done the dirty on the girl and left her to mourn out her life by the banks of the James River. But that it may all have been innocent for Paul and Elsie only made it the more mournful for Pascal. Fond memories and memories, and all about something that never happened.

—Any day henceforth, Pascal said, I'll go on a journey just to see for myself those Blue Ridge Mountains. Were they ever as blue as Paul thought they were? Cider's the same lousy drink the world over. What better could the orchards or women have been in Virginia than in Armagh? You see he was an imaginative man was old Paul, a touch of the poet, and soft as putty and sentimental away behind that granite mountainy face. Things hurt him, too. He told me once that one day walking he met that mad Maguire one from Cranny, the one with the seven children and no husband, and tried to talk reason to her, and she used language to him the like of which he had never heard, and he turned away with tears in his eyes. He said he saw all women degraded and the Mother of God sorrowful in Nancy Maguire who was as bad as she was mad. An odd thought. He should have taken the stick to her the way I once heard he did to a loving couple he found under the hedge.

But pleasures are like poppies spread, as Paul would say, walking the roads with Pascal ad quietam conscientiam, looking at mad Nancy and listening to her oaths, seeing Elsie Cameron under the apple trees under the Blue Mountains in faraway Virginia. Once I wrote a story about him and it was printed in a small little-known and now defunct magazine. That story was all about the nobility of him and the way he used to chant the words of Burns; and then about how he died.

He came home to his parochial house that morning after reading the mass and sat down, one of the cousins said, at the breakfast table, and sat there for long time silent, looking straight ahead. That wasn't like him. She asked him was he well. He didn't answer. She left the room to consult her sister who was fussing about in the kitchen. When she came back he had rested his head down on the table and was dead.

Looking straight ahead to Fincastle, Virginia, and seeing a woman white with flame when the dogwood blossomed, seeing the tall angel whose wings were the rainbow and who held heaven, a red cloth, in one hand, and hell, a blue cloth, in the other.

There was no place in that story of mine for Pascal Stakelum, the rural rake.

Homes on the Mountain

THE YEAR I WAS TWELVE my father, my mother, my brother and myself had our Christmas dinner in the house my godmother's husband had built high up on the side of Dooish Mountain, when he and she came home to Ireland from Philadelphia.

That was a great godmother. She had more half-crowns in her patch pockets than there were in the Bank of England and every time she encountered me which, strategically, I saw was pretty often, it rained half-crowns. Those silver showers made my friend Lanty and myself the most popular boy bravados in our town. A curious thing was, though, that while we stood bobby-dazzler caramels, hazelnut chocolate, ice cream, cigarettes and fish and chips by the ton to our sycophants, we ourselves bought nothing but song-books. Neither of us could sing a note.

We had a splendid, patriotic taste in song-books, principally because the nearest newsagent's shop, kept by an old spinster in Devlin Street, had a window occupied by a sleeping tomcat, two empty tin boxes, bundles of pamphlets yellowed by exposure to the light, and all members of a series called Irish Fireside Songs. The collective title appealed by its warm cosiness. The little books were classified into Sentimental, Patriot's Treasury, Humorous and Convivial, and Smiles and Tears. Erin, we knew from Tom Moore and from excruciating music lessons at school, went wandering around with a tear and a smile blended in her eye. Because even to ourselves our singing was painful, we read together, sitting in the sunshine on the steps that led up to my father's house, such gems of the Humorous and Convivial as: When I lived in Sweet Ballinacrazy, dear, the girls were all bright as a daisy, dear. Or turning to the emerald-covered Patriot's Treasure we intoned: We've men from the Nore, from the Suir and the Shannon, let the tyrant come forth, we'll bring force against force.

Perhaps, unknown to ourselves, we were affected with the nostalgia that had brought my godmother and her husband back from the comfort of Philadelphia to the bleak side of Dooish Mountain. It was a move that my mother, who was practical and who had never been far enough from Ireland to feel nostalgia, deplored.

—Returned Americans, she would say, are lost people. They live between two worlds. Their heads are in the clouds. Even the scrawny, black-headed sheep – not comparing the human being and the brute beast – know by now that Dooish is no place to live.

—And if you must go back to the land, she said, let it be the land, not the rocks, heather and grey fields no bigger than pocket handkerchiefs. There's Cantwell's fine place beside the town going up for auction. Seventy acres of land, a palace of a dwelling-house, outhouses would do credit to the royal family, every modern convenience and more besides.

For reasons that had nothing to do with prudence or sense Lanty and myself thought the Cantwell place an excellent idea. There were crab-apple trees of the most amazing fertility scattered all along the hedgerows on the farm; a clear gravel stream twisted through it; there were flat pastures made for football and, behind the house, an orchard that not even the most daring buccaneer of our generation had ever succeeded in robbing.

But there were other reasons – again nostalgic reasons – why my godmother's husband who was the living image of Will Rogers would build nowhere in Ireland except on the rough, wet side of Dooish, and there, on the site of the old home where he had spent his boyhood, the house went up. There wasn't a building job like it since the building of the Tower of Babel.

—Get a good sensible contractor from the town, said my

mother, not drunken Dan Redmond from the mountain who couldn't build a dry closet.

But my godmother's husband had gone to school with Dan Redmond. They had been barefooted boys together and that was that, and there was more spent, according to my mother, on malt whisky to entertain Dan, his tradesmen and labourers, than would have built half New York. To make matters worse it was a great season for returned Americans and every one of them seemed to have known my godmother and her husband in Philadelphia. They came in their legions to watch the building, to help pass the bottle and to proffer advice. The acknowledged queen of this gathering of souls fluttering between two worlds was my Aunt Brigid, my mother's eldest sister. She was tiny and neat, precise in her speech, silver haired, glittering with rimless spectacles and jet-black beads. In the States she had acquired a mania for euchre, a passion for slivers of chicken jelled in grey-green soup, a phonograph with records that included a set of the favourite songs of Jimmy Walker, and the largest collection of snapshots ever carried by pack mule or public transport out of Atlantic City.

Then there was a born American – a rarity in our parts in those days – a young man and a distant relative. Generous and jovial, he kissed every woman, young or old, calling them cousin or aunt; but it was suspected among wise observers that he never once in the course of his visit was able to see the Emerald Isle clearly. For the delegation, headed by my Aunt Brigid, that met him in Dublin set him straight away on the drink and when he arrived to view the building site – it was one of the few sunny days of that summer – he did so sitting on the dickey seat of a jaunting car and waving in each hand a bottle of whisky. The builder and his men and the haymakers in June meadows left their work to welcome him, and Ireland, as the song says, was Ireland through joy and through tears.

Altogether it was a wet season: the whisky flowed like water, the mist was low over the rocks and heather of Dooish and the moors of Loughfresha and Cornavara, the mountain runnels were roaring torrents. But miraculously the building was done; the returned Americans with the exception of Aunt Brigid, my godmother and her husband, went westwards again

in the fall; and against all my mother's advice on the point
of health, the couple from Philadelphia settled in for late
November. The house-warming was fixed for Christmas Day.
—Dreamers, my mother said. An American apartment on the
groundwalls of an old cabin. Living in the past. Up where only a
brave man would build a shooting lodge. For all they know or care
there could be wolves still on the mountain. Magazines and
gewgaws and chairs too low to sit on. With the rheumatism the
mountain'll give them, they'll never bend their joints to sit down
so low.

Since the damp air had not yet brought its rheumatism we
all sat down together in the house that was the answer to the
exile's dream. Lamplight shone on good silver and Belfast
linen. My godmother's man was proud to the point of tears.

—Sara Alice, he said to my mother.

Content, glass in hand, he was more than ever like Will Rogers.

—Sara Alice, he said. My mother, God rest her, would be
proud to see this day.

Practicality momentarily abandoned, my mother, moist-eyed
and sipping sherry, agreed.

—Tommy, he said to my father, listen to the sound of the
spring outside.

We could hear the wind, the voices of the runnels, the spring
pouring clear and cool from a rainspout driven into a
rock-face.

—As far as I recollect that was the first sound my ears ever
heard, and I heard it all my boyhood, and I could hear it still
in Girard Avenue, Philadelphia. But the voices of children
used to be part of the sound of the spring. Seven of us, and me
to be the youngest and the last alive. When my mother died
and my father took us all to the States we didn't know when we
were going away whether to leave the door open or closed. We
left it open in case a travelling man might pass, needing shelter. We knocked gaps in the hedges and stone walls so as to
give the neighbours' cattle the benefit of commonage and the
land the benefit of the cow dung. But we left the basic lines of
the walls so that nobody could forget our name or our claim to
this part of the mountain.

—In Gartan, in Donegal, said my father, there's a place called the Flagstone of Loneliness where Saint Colmcille slept the night before he left Ireland under sentence of banishment. The exiles in that part used to lie down there the day before they sailed and pray to the saint to be preserved from the pangs of homesickness.

My Aunt Brigid piped in a birdlike voice a bit of an exile song that was among her treasured recordings: A strange sort of sigh seems to come from us all as the waves hide the last glimpse of old Donegal.

—Our American wake was held in Aunt Sally O'Neill's across the glen, said my godmother's husband. Red Owen Gormley lilted for the dancers when the fiddlers were tired. He was the best man of his time at the mouth music.

—He was also, said my father, the first and last man I knew who could make a serviceable knife, blade and haft, out of a single piece of hardwood. I saw him do it, myself and wild Martin Murphy who was with me in the crowd of sappers who chained these mountains for the 1911 Ordnance Survey map. Like most of us, Martin drank every penny and on frosty days he would seal the cracks in his shoes with butter – a trick I never saw another man use. It worked too.

—Aunt Sally's two sons were there at our American wake, said my godmother's husband. Thady that was never quite right in the head and, you remember, Tommy, couldn't let a woman in the market or a salmon in the stream alone. John, the elder brother, was there with Bessy from Cornavara that he wooed for sixty years and never, I'd say, even kissed.

The old people were silently laughing. My brother, older than myself, was on the fringe of the joke. As my godmother came and went I sniffed fine cooking. I listened to the mountain wind and the noise of the spring and turned the bright pages of an American gardening magazine. Here were rare blooms would never grow on Dooish Mountain.

—All dead now I suppose, my father said to end the laughing.

—Bessy's dead now, said my Aunt Brigid. Two years ago. As single as the day she was born. Like many another Irishman

John wasn't overgiven to matrimony. But in the village of Crooked Bridge below, the postman told me that John and Thady are still alive in the old house on Loughfresha. Like pigs in a sty, he said. Pigs in a sty. And eight thousand pounds each, according to all accounts, in the Munster and Leinster Bank in the town.

—God help us, said my mother. I recall that house as it was when Aunt Sally was alive. It was beautiful.

My father was looking out of the window, down the lower grey slopes of Dooish and across the deep glen towards Loughfresha and Cornavara.

—It won't rain again before dark or dinner, he said. I haven't walked these hills since I carried a chain for His Majesty's Ordnance Survey. Who'd ever have thought the King of England would be interested in the extent of Cornavara or Dooish Mountain.

—Get up you two boys, he said, and we'll see if you can walk as well as your father before you.

The overflow of the spring came with us as we descended the boreen. Winter rain had already rutted the new gravel laid by drunken Dan Redmond and his merry men. Below the bare apple-orchard the spring's overflow met with another runnel and with yet another where another boreen, overgrown with hawthorn and bramble, struggled upwards to an abandoned house.

—Some people, said my father, didn't come back to face the mountain. Living in Philadelphia must give a man great courage.

He walked between us with the regular easy step of an old soldier who, in days of half-forgotten wars had footed it for ever across the African veldt.

—That was all we ever did, he would say. Walk and walk. And the only shot I ever fired that I remember was at a black snake and I never knew whether I hit or missed. That was the Boer War for you.

Conjoined, innumerable runnels swept under a bridge where the united boreens joined the road, plunged over rock in a ten-foot cataract, went elbowing madly between bare hazels down to the belly of the glen. White cabins, windows already lamp-lighted and candle-lighted for Christmas, showed below the shifting fringe of black grey mist.

—This house I knew well, he said, this was Aunt Sally's. The Aunt was a title of honour and had nothing to do with blood relationship. She was stately, a widow, a great manager and aunt to the whole country. She had only the two sons.

By the crossroads of the thirteen limekilns we swung right and descended the slope of the glen on what in a dry summer would have been a dust road. Now, wet sand shifted under our feet, loose stones rattled ahead of us, the growing stream growled below us in the bushes. To our left were the disused limekilns, lining the roadway like ancient monstrous idols with gaping toothless mouths, and as we descended the old man remembered the days when he and his comrades, veterans all, had walked and measured those hills; the limekilns in operation and the white dust on the grass and the roadside hedges; the queues of farm carts waiting for the loading. Fertilisers made in factories had ended all that. There was the place (he pointed across a field) where a tree, fallen on a mearing fence, had lain and rotted while the two farmers whose land the fence divided, swept away by the joy of legal conflict, had disputed in the court in the town the ownership of the timber. The case never reached settlement. Mountainy men loved law and had their hearts in twopence. And here was Loughfresha bridge. (The stream was a torrent now.) The gapped, stone parapet hadn't been mended since the days of the survey. And there was the wide pool where Thady O'Neill, always a slave to salmon, had waded in after a big fish imprisoned by low water, taken it with his bare hands after a mad struggle and, it was said, cured himself by shock treatment of premature arthritis.

Once across the bridge our ascent commenced. Black brooding roadside cattle looked at us with hostility. On a diagonal across a distant meadow a black hound dog ran silently, swiftly up towards the mist, running as if with definite purpose – but what, I wondered, could a dog be doing running upwards there alone on a Christmas Day. The thought absorbed me to the exclusion of all else until we came to the falling house of John and Thady O'Neill.

—Good God in heaven, said my father.

For a full five minutes he stood looking at it, not speaking, before he led his two sons, with difficulty, as far as the door.

Once it must have been a fine, long, two-storeyed, thatched farmhouse, standing at an angle of forty-five degrees to the roadway and built backwards into the slope of the hill. But the roof and the upper storey had sagged and, topped by the growth of years of rank decayed grass, the remnants of the thatched roof looked, in the Christmas dusk, like a rubbish heap a maniacal mass-murderer might pick as a burial mound for his victims.

—They won't be expecting us for our Christmas dinner, said my brother.

To reach the door we went ankle-deep, almost, through plashy ground and forded in the half-dark a sort of seasonal stream. One small uncurtained window showed faintly the yellow light of an oil-lamp.

Knock, knock, knock went my father on the sagging door.

No dogs barked. No calves or cocks made comforting farmhouse noises. The wind was raucous in the bare dripping hazels that overhung the wreck of a house from the slope behind. An evil wizard might live here.

Knock, knock, knock went my father.

—Is there anybody there said the traveller, said my brother, who had a turn for poetry.

—John O'Neill and Thady, called my father. I've walked over from the Yankee's new house at Dooish and brought my two sons with me to wish you a happy Christmas.

He shouted out his own name.

In a low voice he said to us: Advance friends, and be recognised.

My brother and myself giggled and stopped giggling as chains rattled and slowly, with a thousand creaks of aged iron and timber in bitter pain and in conflict with each other, the door opened. Now, years after that Christmas, I can rely only on a boyhood memory of a brief visit to a badly-lighted cavern. There was a hunched decrepit old man behind the opening door. Without extending his hand he shuffled backwards and away from us. His huge hobnailed boots were unlaced. They

flapped around him like the feet of some strange bird or
reptile. He was completely bald. His face was pear-shaped,
running towards the point at the forehead. His eyes had the
brightness and quickness of a rodent's eyes. When my father
said: Thady, you remember me, he agreed doubtfully, as if
agreement or disagreement were equally futile. He looked
sideways furtively at the kitchen table half-hidden in shadows
near one damp-streaked yellow wall. For a tablecloth that table
had a battered raincoat and when our knock had interrupted
him Thady had, it would seem, been heeling over onto the coat
a pot of boiled potatoes. He finished the task while we stood
uncertainly inside the doorway. Then as if tucking in a child
for sleep, he wrapped the tails of the coat around the pile of
steaming tubers. A thunderous hearty voice spoke to us from
the corner between the hearth and a huge four-poster bed. It
was a rubicund confident voice. It invited us to sit down, and
my father sat on a low chair close to the hearth-fire. My brother and myself stood uncomfortably behind him. There was, at
any rate, nothing for us to sit on. The smoky oil-lamp burned
low but the bracket that held it was on the wall above the owner
of the voice. So it haloed with a yellow glow the head of John
O'Neill, the dilatory lover of Bessie of Cornavara who had
gone unwed to the place where none embrace. It was a broad,
red-faced, white-haired head, too large and heavy, it seemed,
for the old wasted body.

—It's years since we saw you, Tommy, said John.

—It's years indeed.

—And all the wild men that had been in the army.

—All the wild men.

—Times are changed, Tommy.

—Times are changed indeed, said my father.

He backed his chair a little away from the fire. Something
unpleasantly odorous fried and sizzled in an unlidded pot-
oven. The flagged floor, like the roof, had sagged. It sloped
away from the hearth and into the shadows towards a pyramid
of bags of flour and meal and feeding stuffs for cattle.

—But times are good, said John. The land's good, and the
crops and cattle.

—And the money plentiful.

—The money's plentiful.

—I'm glad to hear you say it, said my father.

—The Yankee came back, Tommy.

—He came back.

—And built a house, I hear. I don't go abroad much beyond my own land.

—He built a fine house.

—They like to come back, the Yankees. But they never settle.

—It could be that the change proves too much for them, said my father.

Then after a silence, disturbed only by the restless scratching of Thady's nailed soles on the floor, my father said: You never married, John.

—No, Tommy. Bessy died. What with stock to look after and all, a man doesn't have much time for marrying.

—Thady was more of a man for the ladies than you ever were, said my father to John.

Behind us there was a shrill hysterical cackle and from John a roar of red laughter.

—He was that. God, Tommy, the memory you have.

—Memory, said my father.

Like a man in a trance he looked, not at John or Thady, but into the red heart of the turf fire.

—There was the day, Thady, he said, when Martin Murphy and myself looked over a whin hedge at yourself and Molly Quigley from Crooked Bridge making love in a field. Between you, you ruined a half-acre of turnips.

The red laughter and the cackle continued.

—Tommy, you have the memory, said John. Wasn't it great the way you remembered the road up Loughfresha?

—It was great, said my father. Trust an old soldier to remember a road.

The odour from the sizzling pot-oven was thickening.

—Well, we'll go now, said my father. We wouldn't have butted in on you the day it is only for old time's sake.

—You're always welcome, Tommy. Anytime you pass the road.

—I don't pass this road often, John.

—Well, when you do you're welcome. Those are your two
sons.

—My two sons.

—Two fine clean young men, said John.

He raised a hand to us. He didn't move out of the chair. The
door closed slowly behind us and the chains rattled. We forded
the seasonal stream, my brother going in over one ankle and
filling a shoe with water.

We didn't talk until we had crossed the loud stream at Loughfresha Bridge. In the darkness I kept listening for the haunted
howl of the black hound-dog.

—Isn't it an awful way, Da, I said, for two men to live,
particularly if it's true they have money in the bank.

—If you've money in the bank, said my brother, who suffered from a sense of irony, it's said you can do anything
you please.

With a philosophy too heavy for my years I said: It's a big
change from the house we're going to.

—John and Thady, said my brother, didn't have the benefit
of forty-five years in Philadelphia.

My father said nothing.

—What I wonder, I said, was cooking in the pot-oven?

—Whatever it was, said my brother, they'll eat it with relish
and roll into that four-poster bed and sleep like heroes.

The black brooding roadside cattle seemed as formidable as
wild bison.

—Sixty years, said my father to himself. Coming and going
every Sunday, spending the long afternoons and evenings in
her father's house, eating and drinking, and nothing in the
nature of love transpiring.

Like heroes I thought, and recalled from the song-books the
heroic words: Side by side for the cause have our forefathers
battled when our hills never echoed the tread of a slave; in
many a field where the leaden hail rattled, through the red
gap of glory they marched to their grave.

Slowly, towards a lost lighted fragment of Philadelphia and
our Christmas dinner, we ascended the wet boreen.

—Young love, soliloquised the old man. Something happens

to it on these hills. Sixty years and he never proposed nothing, good or bad.

—In Carlow town, said the song-books to me, there lived a maid more sweet than flowers at daybreak; their vows contending lovers paid, but none of marriage dared speak.

—Sunday after Sunday to her house for sixty years, said the old man. You wouldn't hear the like of it among the Kaffirs. It's the rain and the mist. And the lack of sunshine and wine. Poor Thady, too, was fond of salmon and women.

—For I haven't a genius for work, mocked the Humorous and Convivial, it was never a gift of the Bradies; but I'd make a most iligant Turk for I'm fond of tobacco and ladies.

To the easy amusement of my brother and, finally, to the wry laughter of my father I sang that quatrain. Night was over the mountain. The falling water of the spring had the tinny sound of shrill, brittle thunder.

After dinner my godmother's husband said: Such a fine house as Aunt Sally O'Neill kept. Tables scrubbed as white as bone. Dances to the melodeon. I always think of corncrakes and the crowds gathered for the mowing of the meadows when I recall that house. And the churning. She had the best butter in the country. Faintly golden. Little beads of moisture showing on it.

—We'll have a game of euchre, said my Aunt Brigid.

—Play the phonograph, said my godmother's husband.

He loathed euchure.

So on the gramophone, high up on Dooish, we heard that boys and girls were singing on the sidewalks of New York.

I wondered where the hound-dog could possibly have been running to. In a spooky story I had once read, the Black Hound of Kildare turned out to be the devil.

My godmother asked me to sing.

—But I can't sing, I said.

—Then what do Lanty and yourself do with all the song-books?

—We read them.

Laughter.

—Read us a song, said my brother.

So, because I had my back to the wall and also because once

when visiting a convent with my mother I had sung, by request, *Let Erin Remember*, and received a box of chocolates from the Reverend Mother, I sang: Just a little bit of Heaven fell from out the sky one day, and when the angels saw it sure they said we'll let it stay; and they called it Ireland.

That spring, following my heralding of the descent from Elysium of the Emerald Isle, there was a steady downpour of half-crowns.

A Journey to the Seven Streams

MY FATHER, the heavens be his bed, was a terrible man for telling you about the places he had been and for bringing you there if he could and displaying them to you with a mild and gentle air of proprietorship. He couldn't do the showmanship so well in the case of Spion Kop where he and the fortunate ones who hadn't been ordered up the hill in the ignorant night had spent a sad morning crouching on African earth and listening to the deadly Boer guns that, high above the plain, slaughtered their hapless comrades. Nor yet in the case of Halifax nor the Barbadoes where he had heard words of Gaelic from coloured girls who were, he claimed, descended from the Irish transported into slavery in the days of Cromwell. The great glen of Aherlow, too, which he had helped to chain for His Majesty's Ordnance Survey, was placed inconveniently far to the South in the mystic land of Tipperary, and Cratloe Wood, where the fourth Earl of Leitrim was assassinated, was sixty miles away on the winding Donegal fjord called Mulroy Bay. But townlands like Corraheskin, Drumlish, Cornavara, Dooish, The Minnieburns and Claramore, and small towns like Drumquin and Dromore were all within a ten-mile radius of our town and something of moment or something amusing had happened in every one of them.

The reiterated music of their names worked on him like a charm. They would, he said, take faery tunes out of the stone fiddle of Castle Caldwell; and indeed it was the night he told us the story of the stone fiddle and the drowned fiddler, and recited for us the inscription carved on a fiddle in memory of the fiddler, that he decided to hire a hackney car, a rare and daring thing to do in those days, and bring us out to see in one round trip those most adjacent places of his memories and dreams.

—In the year 1770 it happened, he said. The landlord at the time was Sir James Caldwell, Baronet. He was also called the Count of Milan, why, I never found anybody to tell me. The fiddler's name was Dennis McCabe and by tradition the McCabes were always musicians and jesters to the Caldwells. There was festivity at the Big House by Lough Erne Shore and gentry there from near and far, and out they went to drink and dance on a raft on the lake, and wasn't the poor fiddler so drunk he fiddled himself into the water and drowned.

--Couldn't somebody have pulled him out, Da?

—They were all as drunk as he was. The story was that he was still sawing away with the bow when he came up for the third time. The party cheered him until every island in Lough Erne echoed and it was only when they sobered up they realised they had lost the fiddler. So the baronet and Count of Milan had a stone fiddle taller than a man made to stand at the estate gate as a monument to Dennis McCabe and as a warning for ever to fiddlers either to stay sober or to stay on dry land.

—Ye fiddlers beware, ye fiddler's fate, my father recited. Don't attempt the deep lest ye repent too late. Keep to the land when wind and storm blow, but scorn the deep if it with whisky flow. On firm land only exercise your skill; there you may play and safely drink your fill.

Travelling by train from our town to the seaside you went for miles along the green and glistening Erne shore but the train didn't stop by the stone fiddle nor yet at the Boa island for the cross-roads' dances. Always when my father told us about those dances, his right foot rhythmically tapped and took music out of the polished steel fireside fender that had Home Sweet Home lettered out on an oval central panel. Only the magic motor, bound to no tracks, compelled to no fixed stopping places, could bring us to the fiddle or the crowded cross-roads.

—Next Sunday then, he said, as certain as the sun sets and

rises, we'll hire Hookey and Peter and the machine and head for Lough Erne.

—Will it hold us all, said my mother. Seven of us and Peter's big feet and the length of the driver's legs.

—That machine, he said, would hold the twelve apostles, the Connaught Rangers and the man who broke the bank at Monte Carlo. It's the size of a hearse.

—Which is just what it looks like, said the youngest of my three sisters who had a name for the tartness of her tongue.

She was a thin dark girl.

—Regardless of appearance, he said, it'll carry us to the stone fiddle and on the way we'll circumnavigate the globe: Clanabogan, and Cavanacaw, Pigeon Top Mountain and Corraduine, where the barefooted priest said Mass at the Rock in the penal days and Corraheskin where the Muldoons live...

—Them, said the third sister.

She had had little time for the Muldoons since the day their lack of savoir faire cost her a box of chocolates. A male member, flaxen-haired, pink-cheeked, aged sixteen, of those multitudinous Muldoons had come by horse and cart on a market day from his rural fastnesses to pay us a visit. Pitying his gaucherie, his shy animal-in-a-thicket appearance, his outback ways and gestures, she had grandly reached him a box of chocolates so as to sweeten his bitter lot with one honeyed morsel or two, or, at the outside three; but unaccustomed to towny ways and the mores of built-up areas the rural swain had appropriated the whole box.

—He thought, she said, I was a paleface offering gifts to a Comanche.

—But by their own hearth, said my father, they're simple hospitable people.

—And Cornavara, he said, and Dooish and Carrick Valley and your uncle Owen, and the two McCannys the pipers, and Claramore where there are so many Gormleys every family has to have its own nickname, and Drumquin where I met your mother, and Dromore where you (pointing to me) were born and where the mail train was held up by the I.R.A. and where the three poor lads were murdered by the Specials when you (again indicating me) were a year old, and the Minnieburns where the seven streams meet to make the head waters of the big river. Hookey and Peter and the machine will take us to all those places.

—Like a magic carpet, said my mother – with just a little dusting of the iron filings of doubt in her voice.

Those were the days, and not so long ago, when cars were rare and every car, not just every make of car, had a personality of its own. In our town with its population of five thousand, not counting the soldiers in the barracks, there were only three cars for hire and one of them was the love-child of the pioneer passion of Hookey Baxter for the machine. He was a long hangle of a young fellow, two-thirds of him made up of legs, and night and day he was whistling. He was as forward-looking as Lindbergh and he dressed like Lindbergh, for the air, in goggles, leather jacket and helmet; an appropriate costume, possibly, considering Hookey's own height and the alti-tude of the driver's seat in his machine. The one real love of his young heart was the love of the born tinkerer, the instinc-tive mechanic, for that hybrid car: the child of his frenzy, the fruit of days spent deep in grease giving new life and shape to a wreck he had bought at a sale in Belfast. The original manu-facturers, whoever they had been, would have been hard put to it to recognise their altered offspring.

—She's chuman, Peter Keown would say as he patted the sensitive quivering bonnet.

Peter meant human. In years to come his sole recorded comment on the antics of Adolf Hitler was that the man wasn't chuman.

—She's as nervous, he would say, as a thoroughbred.

The truth was that Peter, Hookey's stoker, grease-monkey and errand boy, was somewhat in awe of the tall rangy metal animal yet wherever the car went, with the tall goggled pilot at the wheel, there the pilot's diminutive mate was also sure to go. What living Peter earned he earned by digging holes in the street as a labouring man for the town council's official plumber so that, except on Sundays and when he motored with Hookey, nobody in the town ever saw much of him but the top of his cloth cap or his upturned face when he'd look up from the hole in the ground to ask a passer-by the time of day. Regularly once a year he spent a corrective month in Derry Jail, because his opportunities as a municipal employee and his weakness as a kleptomaniac meant that good boards, lengths of piping, coils of electric wire, monkey wrenches, spades, and other movable properties faded too frequently into thin air.

—A wonderful man, poor Peter, my father would say. That cloth cap with the turned up peak. And the thick-lensed, thin-rimmed spectacles – he's half-blind – and the old tweed jacket too tight for him, and the old Oxford-bag trousers too big for him, and his shrill voice and his waddle of a walk that makes him look always like a duck about to apologise for laying a hen-egg. How he survives is a miracle of God's grace. He can resist the appeal of nothing that's portable.

—He's a dream, said the third sister. And the feet are the biggest part of him.

—The last time he went to Derry, said my brother, all the old women from Brook Street and the lanes were at the top of the Courthouse Hill to cheer him as he passed.

—And why not, said my mother. They're fond of him and they say he's well-liked in the jail. His heart's as big as his feet. Everything he steals he gives away.

—Robin Hood, said the third sister. Robbing the town council to pay Brook Street.

—The Council wouldn't sack him, said my eldest sister, if he stole the town.

—At the ready, roared my father. Prepare to receive cavalry.

In the street below the house there was a clanking, puffing, grinding tumult.

—God bless us look at Peter, said my father. Aloft with Hookey like a crown prince beside a king. Are we all ready? Annie, Ita, May, George, yourself ma'am, and you the youngest of us all. Have we the sandwiches and the flasks of tea and the lemonade? Forward.

A lovelier Sunday morning never shone. With the hood down and the high body glistening after its Saturday wash and polish, the radiator gently steaming, the car stood at the foot of the seven steps that led down from our door. The stragglers coming home from early mass, and the devout setting off early for late mass had gathered in groups to witness our embarkation. Led by my father and in single file, we descended the steps and ascended nearly as high again to take our lofty places in the machine.

There was something of the Citroen in the quivering mongrel, in the yellow canvas hood now reclining in voluminous ballooning folds, in the broad back-seat that could hold five fair-sized people. But to judge by the radiator, the absence of gears, and the high fragile-spoked wheels, Citroen blood had been crossed with that of the Model T. After that, any efforts to spot family traits would have brought confusion on the thought of the greatest living authorities. The thick slanting glass windscreen could have been wrenched from a limousine designed to divert bullets from Balkan princelings. The general colour-scheme, considerably chipped and cracked, was canary yellow. And there was Hookey at the wheel, then my brother and father, and Peter on the outside left where he could leap in and out to perform the menial duties of assistant engineer; and in the wide and windy acres of the back seat, my mother, myself and my three sisters.

High above the town the church bell rang. It was the bell to warn the worshippers still on their way that in ten minutes the vested priest would be on the altar but, as it coincided with our setting out, it could have been a quayside bell ringing farewell to a ship nosing out across the water towards the rim of vision.

Peter leaped to the ground, removed the two stones that, blocked before the front wheels, acted as auxiliaries for the hand brake. Hookey released the brake. The car was gathering speed when Peter scrambled aboard, settled himself and slammed the yellow door behind him. Sparing fuel, we glided down the slope, backfired twice loudly enough to drown the sound of the church bell, swung left along John Street and cleared the town without incident. Hands waved from watching groups of people but because this was no trivial event there were no laughs, no wanton cheers. The sound of the bell died away behind us. My mother expressed the hope that the priest would remember us at the offertory. Peter assured her that we were all as safe as if we were at home in bed. God's good green Sunday countryside was softly all around us.

Squat to the earth and travelling at seventy you see nothing from cars nowadays, but to go with Hookey was to be above all but the highest walls and hedges, to be among the morning birds.

—Twenty-seven em pee haitch, said Hookey.

—Four miles covered already, said Peter

—The Gortin Mountains over there, said my father. And the two mountains to the north are Bessy Bell and Mary Grey, so named by the Hamiltons of Baronscourt, the Duke of Abercorn's people, after fancied resemblance to two hills in Stirlingshire, Scotland. The two hills in Stirlingshire are so called after two ladies of the Scottish court who fled the plague and built their hut in the wild wood and thatched it o'er with rushes. They are mentioned by Thomas Carlyle in his book on the French Revolution. The dark green on the hills by Gortin Gap is the new government forestry. And in Gortin village Paddy Ford the contractor hasn't gone to mass since, fifteen years ago, the parish priest gave another man the job of painting the inside of the sacristy.

—No paint no prayers, said the third sister.

—They're strange people in Gortin, my mother said.

—It's proverbial, said my father, that they're to be distinguished anywhere by the bigness of their backsides.

—Five miles, said Peter. They're spinning past.

—Running sweet as honey, said Hookey.

He adjusted his goggles and whistled back to the Sunday birds.

—Jamie Magee's of the Flush, said my father.

He pointed to a long white house on a hill slope and close to a waterfalling stream.

—Rich as Rockefeller and too damned mean to marry.

—Who in heaven would have him, said the third sister.

—Six miles, said Peter.

Then, with a blast of backfiring that rose my mother a foot in the air, the wobbling yellow conveyance came to a coughing miserable halt. The air was suddenly grey and poisoned with fumes.

—It's her big end Hookey, said Peter.

—She's from Gortin so, said the third sister.

The other two sisters, tall and long-haired and normally quiet girls, went off at the deep end into the giggles.

—Isn't it providential, said my mother, that the cowslips are a glory this year. We'll have something to do, Henry, while you're fixing it.

Hookey had been christened Henry, and my mother would never descend to nicknames. She felt that to make use of a nickname was to remind a deformed person of his deformity. Nor would she say even of the town's chief inebriate that he was ever drunk: he was either under the influence or he had a drop too many taken. She was, my mother, the last great Victorian euphemiser.

—We won't be a jiffy, ma'am, said Hookey. It's nothing so serious as a big end.

The three sisters were convulsed.

The fields and the roadside margins were bright yellow with blossom.

—Gather ye cowslips while you may, said my father.

He handed the ladies down from the dizzy heights. Peter had already disembarked. Submitting to an impulse that had gnawed at me since we set sail I dived forwards, my head under Hookey's left elbow, and butted with both fists the black rubber punch-ball horn; and out over the fields to startle birds and grazing cattle went the dying groan of a pained diseased ox.

—Mother of God, said my father, that's a noise and no mistake. Here boy, go off and pick flowers.

He lifted me down to the ground.

—Screw off the radiator cap, Peter, said Hookey.

—It's scalding hot, Hookey.

—Take these gauntlet gloves, manalive. And stand clear when you screw it off.

A geyser of steam and dirty hot water went heavenwards as Peter and my brother, who was always curious about engines, leaped to safety.

—Wonderful, said my father to my brother, the age we live in. They say that over in England they're queued up steaming by the roadsides, like Iceland or the Yellowstone Park.

—Just a bit overheated, said Hookey. We won't be a jiffy.

—Does it happen often? said my father.

Ignoring the question, descending and opening the bonnet to peer and poke and tinker, Hookey said: Do you know a funny thing about this car?

—She's chuman, said Peter.

—You know the cross-roads at Clanabogan churchyard gate, Hookey said. The story about it.

—It's haunted, said my father.

—Only at midnight, said Peter.

As was his right and custom, my father stepped into the role of raconteur: Do you know that no horse ever passed there at midnight that didn't stop – shivering with fear. The fact is well attested. Something comes down that side road out of the heart of the wood.

Hookey closed over the bonnet, screwed back the radiator cap and climbed again to the throne. He wiped his hands on a bunch of grass pulled for him and handed to him by Peter. Slowly he drew on again his gauntlet gloves. Bedecked with cowslips and dragging me along with them the ladies rejoined the gentlemen.

—Well, would you credit this now, Hookey said. Peter and myself were coming from Dromore one wet night last week.

—Pouring rain from the heavens, said Peter, and the hood was leaking.

—A temporary defect, said Hookey. I mended it. Jack up the back axle, Peter, and give her a swing. And would you credit it, exactly at twelve o'clock midnight she stopped dead at the gate of Clanabogan churchyard?

With an irony that was lost on Hookey, my mother said: I could well believe it.

—She's chuman, said Peter.

—One good push now and we're away, said Hookey. The slight gradient is in our favour.

—Maybe, he said to my father and brother, you'd lend Peter a hand.

Twenty yards ahead he waited for the dusty pushers to climb aboard, the engine chug-chugging, little puffs of steam escaping like baby genii from the right-hand side of the bonnet. My father was thoughtful. He could have been considering the responsibilities of the machine age particularly because when it came to team pushing Peter was more of a cheer leader, an exhorter, a counter of one two three, than an actual motive force.

—Contact, said Hookey.

—Dawn patrol away, said Peter. Squadron Leader Baxter at the joystick.

He mimicked what he supposed to be the noises of an aeroplane engine and, with every evidence of jubilation, we were once again under way; and a day it was, made by the good God for jubilation. The fields, all the colours of all the crops, danced towards us and away from us and around us; and the lambs on the green hills, my father sang, were gazing at me and many a strawberry grows by the salt sea, and many a ship sails the ocean. The roadside trees bowed down and then gracefully swung their arms up and made music over our heads and there were more birds and white cottages and fuchsia hedges in the world than you would readily imagine.

—The bride and bride's party, sang my father, to church they did go. The bride she goes foremost, she bears the best show...

—They're having sports today at Tattysallagh, said Hookey.

—But I followed after my heart full of woe, for to see my love wed to another.

We swept by a cross-roads where people and horses and traps were congregated after the last mass. In a field beside the road a few tall ash plants bore fluttering pennants in token of the sports to be.

—Proceed to Banteer, sang my father, to the athletic sporting and hand in your name to the club comm-i-tee.

—That was a favourite song of Pat O'Leary the Corkman, he said, who was killed at Spion Kop.

Small country boys in big boots, knickerbockers, stiff celluloid collars that could be cleaned for Sunday by a rub of a wet cloth, and close-cropped heads with fringes like scalping locks above the foreheads, scattered before us to the hedges and the grass margins, then closed again like water divided and rejoining, and pursued us, cheering, for a hundred yards. One of them, frantic with enthusiasm, sent sailing after us a half-grown turnip, which bounced along the road for a bit, then sought rest in a roadside drain. Looking backwards I pulled my best or worst faces at the rustic throng of runners.

—In Tattysallagh, said my father, they were always an uncivilised crowd of gulpins.

He had three terms of contempt: Gulpin, Yob and, when things became very bad he became Swiftian, and described all offenders as Yahoos.

—Cavanacaw, he said, and that lovely trout stream, the Creevan Burn. It joins the big river at Blacksessiagh. That there's the road up to Pigeon Top Mountain and the mass rock at Corraduine, but we'll come back that way when we've circumnavigated Dooish and Cornavara.

We came to Clanabogan.

—Clanabogan planting, he said.

The tall trees came around us and sunlight and shadow flickered so that you could feel them across eyes and hands and face.

—Martin Murphy the postman, he said, who was in the survey with me in Virginia, County Cavan, by Lough Ramor, and in the Glen of Aherlow, worked for a while at the building of Clanabogan Church. One day the vicar said to him: 'What height do you think the steeple should be?' 'The height of nonsense like your sermons,' said Martin, and got the sack for his wit. In frosty weather he used to seal the cracks in his boots with butter and although he was an abrupt man he seldom used an impolite word. Once when he was aggravated by the bad play of his wife who was partnering him at whist he said: 'Maria, dearly as I love you there are yet moments when you'd incline a man to kick his own posterior.'

—There's the church, my father said, and the churchyard and the haunted gate and the cross-roads.

We held our breath but, with honeyed summer all around us and bees in the tender limes, it was no day for ghosts, and in glory we sailed by.

—She didn't hesitate, said Peter.

—Wonderful, said the third sister.

It was more wonderful than she imagined for, as the Lord would have it, the haunted gate and the cross-roads of Clanabogan was one of the few places that day that Hookey's motor machine did not honour with at least some brief delay.

—I'd love to drive, said my brother. How did you learn to drive, Hookey?

—I never did. I just sat in and drove. I learned the basic principles on the county council steamroller in Watson's quarries. Forward and reverse.

—You have to have the natural knack, Peter explained.

--What's the cut potato for, Hookey? asked my brother.

—For the rainy day. Rub it on the windscreen and the water runs off the glass.

—It's oily you see, said Peter.

—Like a duck's back, said the third sister.

—Where, said my father – sniffing, do you keep the petrol?

—Reserve in the tins clipped on the running board. Current supply, six gallons. You're sitting on it. In a tank under the front seat.

—Twenty miles to the gallon, said Peter. We're good for more than a hundred miles.

—Godalmighty, said my father. Provided it isn't a hundred miles straight up. 'Twould be sad to survive a war that was the end of better men and to be blown up between Clanabogan and Cornavara. On a quiet Sunday morning.

—Never worry, said Hookey. It's outside the bounds of possibility.

—You reassure me, said my father. Twenty miles to the gallon in any direction. What care we? At least we'll all go up together. No survivors to mourn in misery.

—And turn right here, he said, for Cornavara. You'll soon see the hills and the high waterfalls.

We left the tarred road. White dust rose around us like smoke. We advanced half a mile on the flat, attempted the first steep hill and gently, wearily, without angry fumes or backfiring protests, the tremulous chuman car, lying down like a tired child, came to rest.

—We'll hold what we have, said Hookey. Peter . . . pronto. Get the stones behind the back wheels.

—Think of a new pastime, said the third sister. We have

enough cowslips to decorate the town for a procession. With the sweet face of girlish simplicity she asked, Do you buy the stones with the car?

—We'd be worse off without them, Hookey muttered.

Disguised as he was in helmet and goggles it was impossible to tell exactly if his creative soul was or was not wounded by her hint of mockery, but my mother must have considered that his voice betrayed pain for she looked reprovingly at the third sister and at the other two who were again impaled by giggles, and withdrew them out of sight down a boreen towards the sound of a small stream, to – as she put it – freshen up.

—Without these stones, Peter panted, we could be as badly off as John MacKenna and look what happened to him.

—They're necessary precautions, said Hookey. Poor John would never use stones. He said the brakes on his car would hold a Zeppelin.

The bonnet was open again and the radiator cap unscrewed but there was no steam and no geyser, only a cold sad silence, and Hookey bending and peering and probing with pincers.

—She's a bit exhausted, Peter said.

—It's simple, Hookey said. She'll be right as rain in a jiffy. Going at the hill with a full load overstrained her.

—We should walk the bad hills, Peter explained.

—Poor John MacKenna, Hookey said, was making four fortunes drawing crowds to the Passionist monastery at Enniskillen to see the monk that cures the people. But he would never use the stones, and the only parking place at the monastery is on a sharp slope. And one evening when they were all at devotions doesn't she run backways and ruin all the flowerbeds in the place and knock down a statue of Our Lord.

—One of the monks attacked him, said Peter, as a heathen that would knock the Lord down.

—Ruined the trade for all, said Hookey. The monks now won't let a car within a mile of the place.

—Can't say as I blame them, said my father.

—Poor John took it bad, said Hookey. The lecture he got and all. He was always a religious man. They say he raises his hat now every time he passes any statue: even the Boer War one in front of the courthouse.

—So well he might, said my father.

Suddenly, mysteriously responding to Hookey's probing pincers, the very soul of the machine was again chug-chugging. But with or without cargo she could not or, being weary and chuman, would not assault even the first bastion of Cornavara.

— She won't take off, said Hookey. That run to Belfast and back took the wind out of her.

—You never made Belfast, said my father, in this.

—We did Tommy, said Peter apologetically.

—Seventy miles there and seventy miles back, said my father incredulously.

—Bringing a greyhound bitch to running trials for Tommy Mullan the postman, said Hookey.

—The man who fishes for pearls in the Drumragh river, said Peter.

They were talking hard to cover their humiliation.

—If she won't go at the hills, my father said, go back to the main road and we'll go on and picnic at the seven streams at the Minnieburns. It's mostly on the flat.

So we reversed slowly the dusty half-mile to the main road.

—One night in John Street, Peter said, she started going backways and wouldn't go forwards.

—A simple defect, Hookey said. I remedied it.

—Did you turn the other way? asked the third sister.

Artlessly, Peter confessed: She stopped when she knocked down the schoolchildren-crossing sign at the bottom of Church Hill. Nipped it off an inch from the ground, as neat as you ever saw. We hid it up a laneway and it was gone in the morning.

My father looked doubtfully at Peter. He said: One of those nice shiny enamelled pictures of two children crossing the road would go well as an overmantel. And the wood of the post would always make firewood.

Peter agreed: You can trust nobody.

Hurriedly trying to cut in on Peter's eloquence, Hookey said: In fact the name of Tommy Mullan's bitch was Drumragh Pearl. Not that that did her any good at the trials.

—She came a bad last, burst out the irrepressible Peter.

—And to make it worse we lost her on the way back from Belfast.

—You what? said my father.

—Lost her in the dark where the road twists around Bally-macilroy Mountain.

My mother was awed: You lost the man's greyhound. You're a right pair of boys to send on an errand.

—'Twas the way we stepped out of the car to take the air, said Hookey.

By the husky note in his voice you could guess how his soul suffered at Peter's shameless confessions.

—And Peter looked at the animal, ma'am, and said maybe she'd like a turn in the air too. So we took her out and tied her lead to the left front wheel. And while we were standing there talking didn't the biggest brute of a hare you ever saw set out as cool as sixpence in the light of the car. Off like a shot with the bitch.

—If the lead hadn't snapped, Peter said, she'd have taken the wheel off the car or the car off the road.

—That would have been no great exertion, said my father. We should have brought a greyhound along with us to pull.

—We whistled and called for hours but all in vain, said Peter.

—The hare ate her, said the third sister.

—Left up the slope there, said my father, is the belt of trees I planted in my spare time to act as a wind-breaker for Drum-lish schoolhouse. Paddy Hamish, the labouring man, gave me a hand. He died last year in Canada.

—You'd have pitied the children on a winter's day, my moth-er said, standing in the playground at lunchtime taking the fresh air in a hilltop wind that would sift and clean corn. Eating soda bread and washing it down with buttermilk. On a rough day the wind from Lough Erne would break the panes of the windows.

—As a matter of curiosity, my father said, what did Tommy Mullan say?

—At two in the morning in Bridge Lane, said Peter, he was waiting for us. We weren't too happy about it. But when we told him she was last in the trials he said the bloody bitch could stay in Ballymacilroy.

—Hasn't he always the pearls in the river, my mother said.

So we came to have tea and sandwiches and lemonade in a meadow by the cross-roads in the exact centre of the wide saucer of land where seven streams from the surrounding hills came down to meet. The grass was polished with sunshine. The perfume of the meadowsweet is with me still. That plain seemed to me then as vast as the prairies, or Siberia. White cottages far away on the lower slopes of Dooish could have been in another country. The chief stream came for a long way through soft deep meadowland. It was slow, quiet, unobtrusive, perturbed only by the movements of water fowl or trout. Two streams met, wonder of wonders, under the arch of a bridge and you could go out under the bridge along a sandy promontory to paddle in clear water on a bottom as smooth as Bundoran strand. Three streams came together in a magic hazel wood where the tiny green unripe nuts were already clustered on the branches. Then the seven made into one, went away from us with a shout and a song towards Shaneragh, Blacksessiagh, Drumragh and Crevenagh, under the humpy crooked King's Bridge where James Stuart had passed on his way from Derry to the fatal brackish Boyne, and on through the town we came from.

—All the things we could see, said my father, if this spavined brute of a so-called automobile could only be persuaded to climb the high hills. The deep lakes of Claramore. The far view of Mount Errigal, the Cock of the North, by the Donegal sea. If you were up on the top of Errigal you could damn' near see, on a clear day, the skyscrapers of New York.

In his poetic imagination the towers of Atlantis rose glimmering from the deep.

—What matter, said my mother. The peace of heaven is here.

For that day that was the last peace we were to experience. The energy the machine didn't have or wouldn't use to climb hills or to keep in motion for more than two miles at a stretch, she expended in thunderous staccato bursts of backfiring. In slanting evening sunlight people at the doors of distant farmhouses shaded their eyes to look towards the travelling commotion, or ran up whinny hills for a better view, and horses and cattle raced madly around pastures, and my mother said the country would never be the same again, that the shock of the noise would turn the milk in the udders of the cows. When we came again to the crossroads of Tattysallagh the majority of the spectators, standing on the road to look over the hedge and thus save the admission fee, lost all interest in the sports, such as they were, and came around us. To oblige them the right rear tyre went flat.

—Peter, said Hookey, jack it up and change it on.

We mingled unobtrusively with the gulpins.

—A neat round hole, said Peter.

—Paste a patch on it.

The patch was deftly pasted on.

—Take the foot pump and blow her up, said Hookey.

There was a long silence while Peter, lines of worry on his little puckered face, inspected the tube. Then he said: I can't find the valve.

—Show it to me, said Hookey.

He ungoggled himself, descended and surveyed the ailing member.

—Peter, he said, you're a prize. The valve's gone and you put a patch on the hole it left behind it.

The crowd around us was increasing and highly appreciative.

—Borrow a bicycle Peter, said Hookey, cycle to the town and ask John MacKenna for the loan of a tube.

—To pass the time, said my mother, we'll look at the sports.

So we left Hookey to mind his car and, being practically gentry as compared with the rustic throng around us, we walked to the gateway that led into the sportsfield where my mother civilly enquired of two men, who stood behind a wooden table, the price of admission.

—Five shillings a skull missus, barring the cub, said the younger of the two. And half a crown for the cub.

—For the what? said my mother.

—For the little boy ma'am, said the elder of the two.

—It seems expensive, said my mother.

—I'd see them all in hell first – let alone in Tattysallagh, my father said. One pound, twelve shillings and sixpence to look at six sally rods stuck in a field and four yahoos running round in rings in their sock soles.

We took our places on the roadside with the few who, faithful to athletics and undistracted by the novelty of the machine, were still looking over the hedge. Four lean youths and one stout one in Sunday shirts and long trousers with the ends tucked into their socks were pushing high framed bicycles round and round the field. My father recalled the occasion in Virginia, County Cavan, when Martin Murphy was to run at sports and his wife Maria stiffened his shirt so much with starch it wouldn't go inside his trousers, and when he protested she said: Martin, leave it outside and you will be able to fly.

We saw two bicycle races and a tug-of-war.

—Hallions and clifts, he said.

Those were two words he seldom used.

—Yobs and sons of yobs, he said.

He led us back to the car. Peter soaked in perspiration had the new tube on and the wheel ready.

—Leave the jack in and swing her, Hookey said. She's cold by now.

There was a series of explosions that sent gulpins, yobs and yahoos reeling backwards in alarm. Peter screwed out the jack. We scrambled aboard, a few of the braver among the decent people rushing into the line of fire to lend a hand to the ladies. Exploding, we departed, and when we were a safe distance away the watchers raised a dubious cheer.

—In God's name, Henry, said my father, get close to the town before you blow us all up. I wouldn't want our neighbours to have to travel as far as Tattysallagh to pick up the bits. And the yobs and yahoos here don't know us well enough to be able to piece us together.

Three miles further on Peter blushingly confessed that in the frantic haste of embarkation he had left the jack on the road.

—I'll buy you a new one, Henry, my father said. Or perhaps Peter here could procure one on the side. By now at any rate, they're shoeing jackasses with it in Tattysallagh.

—A pity in a way, he said, we didn't make as far as the stone fiddle. We might have heard good music. It's a curious thing that in the townlands around that place the people have always been famed for music and singing. The Tunneys of Castle Caldwell now are noted. It could be that the magic of the stone fiddle has something to do with it.

—Some day, he said, we'll head for Donegal. When the cars, Henry, are a bit improved.

He told us about the long windings of Mulroy Bay. He explained exactly how and why and in what year the fourth Earl of Leitrim had been assassinated in Cratloe Wood. He spoke as rapidly and distinctly as he could in the lulls of the backfiring.

Then our town was below us in the hollow and the Gortin mountains, deep purple with evening, away behind it.

—Here we'll part company, Henry boy, said my father. 'Tisn't that I doubt the ability of Peter and yourself to navigate the iron horse down the hill. But I won't have the town blaming me and my family for having hand, act or part in the waking of the dead in Drumragh graveyard.

Sedately we walked down the slope into the town and talked with the neighbours we met and asked them had they heard Hookey and Peter passing and told them of the sports and of the heavenly day it had been out at the seven streams.

My father died in a seaside town in the County Donegal – forty miles from the town I was reared in. The road his funeral followed back to the home places led along the Erne shore by the stone fiddle and the glistening water, across the Boa Island where there are no longer cross-roads' dances. Every roadside house has a television aerial. It led by the meadowland saucer of the Minnieburns where the river still springs from seven magic sources. That brooding place is still much as it was but no longer did it seem to me to be as vast as Siberia. To the left was the low sullen outline of Cornavara and Pigeon Top, the hurdle that our Bucephalus refused to take. To the right was Drumlish. The old schoolhouse was gone and in its place a white building, ten times as large, with drying rooms for wet coats, fine warm lunches for children and even a gymnasium.

But the belt of trees that he and Paddy Hamish planted to break the wind and shelter the children is still there.

Somebody tells me, too, that the engine of Hookey Baxter's car is still with us, turning a circular saw for a farmer in the vicinity of Clanabogan.

As the Irish proverb says: It's a little thing doesn't last longer than a man.

PART TWO

The Dogs *in the* Great Glen

THE PROFESSOR had come over from America to search out his origins and I met him in Dublin on the way to Kerry where his grandfather had come from and where he had relations, including a grand-uncle, still living.

—But the trouble is, he said, that I've lost the address my mother gave me. She wrote to tell them I was coming to Europe. That's all they know. All I remember is a name out of my dead father's memories: the great Glen of Kanareen.

—You could write to your mother.

—That would take time. She'd be slow to answer. And I feel impelled right away to find the place my grandfather told my father about.

—You wouldn't understand, he said. Your origins are all around you.

—You can say that again, professor. My origins crop up like the bones of rock in thin sour soil. They come unwanted like the mushroom of Merulius Lacrimans on the walls of a decaying house.

—It's no laughing matter, he said.

—It isn't for me. This island's too small to afford a place in which to hide from one's origins. Or from anything else. During the war a young fellow in Dublin said to me: Mister, even if I ran away to sea I wouldn't get beyond the three-mile limit.

He said: But it's large enough to lose a valley in. I couldn't find the valley of Kanareen marked on any map or mentioned in any directory.

—I have a middling knowledge of the Kerry mountains, I said. I could join you in the search.

—It's not marked on the half-inch Ordnance Survey map.

—There are more things in Kerry than were ever dreamt of by the Ordnance Survey. The place could have another official name. At the back of my head I feel that once in the town of Kenmare in Kerry I heard a man mention the name of Kanareen.

We set off two days later in a battered, rattly Ford Prefect. Haste, he said, would be dangerous because Kanareen might not be there at all, but if we idled from place to place in the lackadaisical Irish summer we might, when the sentries were sleeping and the glen unguarded, slip secretly as thieves into the land whose legends were part of his rearing.

—Until I met you, the professor said, I was afraid the valley might have been a dream world my grandfather imagined to dull the edge of the first nights in a new land. I could see how he might have come to believe in it himself and told my father – and then, of course, my father told me.

One of his grandfather's relatives had been a Cistercian monk in Mount Melleray, and we went there hoping to see the evidence of a name in a book and to kneel, perhaps, under the high arched roof of the chapel close to where that monk had knelt. But, when we had traversed the corkscrew road over the purple Knockmealdowns and gone up to the mountain monastery through the forest the monks had made in the wilderness, it was late evening and the doors were closed. The birds sang vespers. The great silence affected us with something between awe and a painful, intolerable shyness. We hadn't the heart to ring a doorbell or to promise ourselves to return in the morning. Not speaking to each other we retreated, the rattle of the Ford Prefect as irreverent as dicing on the altar-steps. Half a mile down the road the mute, single-file procession of a group of women exercitants walking back to the female guest-house underlined the holy, unreal, unanswering stillness that had closed us out. It could easily have been that his grandfather never had a relative a monk in Mount Melleray.

A cousin of his mother's mother had, he had been told, been a cooper in Lady Gregory's Gort in the County Galway. But when we crossed the country westwards to Gort, it produced nothing except the information that apart from the big breweries, where they survived like birds or bison in a sanctuary, the coopers had gone, leaving behind them not a hoop or a stave. So we visited the woods of Coole, close to Gort, where Lady Gregory's house had once stood, and on the brimming lake-water among the stones, we saw by a happy poetic accident the number of swans the poet had seen.

Afterwards in Galway City there was, as there always is in Galway City, a night's hard drinking that was like a fit of jovial hysteria, and a giggling ninny of a woman in the bar who kept saying: You're the nicest American I ever met. You don't look like an American. You don't even carry a camera. You look like a Kerryman.

And in the end, we came to Kenmare in Kerry, and in another bar we met a talkative Kerryman who could tell us all about the prowess of the Kerry team, about the heroic feats of John Joe Sheehy or Paddy Bawn Brosnan. He knew so much, that man, yet he couldn't tell us where in the wilderness of mountains we might find the Glen of Kanareen. Nor could anybody else in the bar be of the least help to us, not even the postman who could only say that wherever it was, that is if it was at all, it wasn't in his district.

—It could of course, he said, be east over the mountain.

Murmuring sympathetically, the entire bar assented. The rest of the world was east over the mountain.

With the resigned air of men washing their hands of a helpless, hopeless case the postman and the football savant directed us to a roadside post-office twelve miles away where, in a high-hedged garden before an old grey-stone house with latticed windows and an incongruous, green, official post-office sign there was a child, quite naked, playing with a coloured, musical spinning-top as big as itself, and an old half-deaf man sunning himself and swaying in a rocking-chair, a straw hat tilted forwards to shade his eyes. Like Oisin remembering the Fenians, he told us he had known once of a young woman who married a man from a place called Kanareen, but there had been contention about the match and her people had kept up no correspondence with her. But the day she left home with her husband that was the way she went. He pointed. The way went inland and up and up. We followed it.

—That young woman could have been a relation of mine, the professor said.

On a rock-strewn slope, and silhouetted on a saw-toothed ridge where you'd think only a chamois could get by without broken legs, small black cows, accurate and active as goats, rasped good milk from the grass between the stones. His grandfather had told his father about those athletic, legendary cows and about the proverb that said: Kerry cows know Sunday. For in famine times, a century since, mountain people bled the cows once a week to mix the blood into yellow maize meal and provide a meat dish, a special Sunday dinner.

The road twisted on across moorland that on our left sloped dizzily to the sea, as if the solid ground might easily slip and slide into the depths. Mountain shadows melted like purple dust into a green bay. Across a ravine and quite alone on a long, slanting, brown knife blade of a mountain was a white house with a red door. The rattle of our pathetic little car affronted the vast stillness. We were free to moralise on the extent of all space in relation to the trivial area that limited our ordinary daily lives.

The two old druids of men resting from work on the leeward side of a turf-bank listened to our enquiry with the same attentive, half-conscious patience they gave to bird-cries or the sound of wind in the heather. Then they waved us ahead towards a narrow cleft in the distant wall of mountains as if they doubted the ability of ourselves and our conveyance to negotiate the gap and find the glen. They offered us strong tea and a drop out of a bottle. They watched us with kind irony as we drove away. Until the gap swallowed us and the hazardous, twisting track absorbed all our attention we could look back and still see them, motionless, waiting with indifference for the landslide that would end it all.

By a roadside pool where water-beetles lived their vicious secretive lives, we sat and rested, with the pass and the cliffs, overhung with heather, behind us and another ridge ahead. Brazenly the sheer rocks reflected the sun and semaphored at

us. Below us, in the dry summer, the bed of a stream held only
a trickle of water twisting painfully around piles of round
black stones. Touch a beetle with a stalk of dry grass and the
creature either dived like a shot or, angry at invasion, savagely
grappled with the stalk.

—That silly woman in Galway, the professor said.

He dropped a stone into the pool and the beetles submerged
to weather the storm.

—That day by the lake at Lady Gregory's Coole. The exact
number of swans Yeats saw when the poem came to him. Upon
the brimming water among the stones are nine and fifty swans.
Since I don't carry a camera nobody will ever believe me. But
you saw them. You counted them.

—Now that I am so far, he said, I'm half-afraid to finish the
journey. What will they be like? What will they think of me?
Will I go over that ridge there to find my grandfather's
brother living in a cave?

Poking at and tormenting the beetles on the black mirror of
the pool, I told him: Once I went from Dublin to near Shannon Pot, where the river rises, to help an American woman
find the house where her dead woman friend had been reared.
On her deathbed the friend had written it all out on a sheet
of notepaper: Cross the river at Battle Bridge. Go straight
through the village with the ruined castle on the right. Go on
a mile to the crossroads and the labourer's cottage with the
lovely snapdragons in the flower garden. Take the road to the
right there, and then the second boreen on the left beyond the
schoolhouse. Then stop at the third house on that boreen. You
can see the river from the flagstone at the door.

—Apart from the snapdragons it was exactly as she had
written it down. The dead woman had walked that boreen as a
barefooted schoolgirl. Not able to revisit it herself she en-
trusted the mission as her dying wish to her dearest friend. We
found the house. Her people were long gone from it but
the new tenants remembered them. They welcomed us with
melodeon and fiddle and all the neighbours came in and
collated the long memories of the townland. They feasted us
with cold ham and chicken, porter and whisky, until I had
cramps for a week.

—My only grip on identity, he said, is that a silly woman told me I looked like a Kerryman. My grandfather was a Kerryman. What do Kerrymen look like?

—Big, I said.

—And this is the heart of Kerry. And what my grandfather said about the black cows was true. With a camera I could have taken a picture of those climbing cows. And up that hill trail and over that ridge is Kanareen.

—We hope, I said.

The tired cooling engine coughed apologetically when we abandoned it and put city-shod feet to the last ascent.

—If that was the mountain my grandfather walked over in the naked dawn coming home from an all-night card-playing then, by God, he was a better man than me, said the professor.

He folded his arms and looked hard at the razor-cut edges of stone on the side of the mountain.

—Short of too much drink and the danger of mugging, he said, getting home at night in New York is a simpler operation than crawling over that hunk of miniature Mount Everest. Like walking up the side of a house.

He was as proud as Punch of the climbing prowess of his grandfather.

—My father told me, he said, that one night coming home from the card-playing my grandfather slipped down fifteen feet of rock and the only damage done was the ruin of one of two bottles of whisky he had in the tail-pockets of his greatcoat. The second bottle was unharmed.

The men who surfaced the track we were walking on had been catering for horses and narrow iron-hooped wheels. After five minutes of agonised slipping and sliding, wisdom came to us and we took to the cushioned grass and heather. As we ascended the professor told me what his grandfather had told his father about the market town he used to go to when he was a boy. It was a small town where even on market days the dogs would sit nowhere except exactly in the middle of the street. They were lazy town dogs, not active, loyal and intelligent like the dogs the grandfather had known in the great glen. The way the old man had described it, the town's five streets grasped the ground of Ireland as the hand of a strong swimmer might grasp a ledge of rock to hoist himself out of the water. On one side was the sea. On the other side a shoulder of mountain rose so steeply that the Gaelic name of it meant the gable of the house.

When the old man went as a boy to the town on a market day it was his custom to climb that mountain, up through furze and following goat tracks, leaving his shiny boots, that he only put on, anyway, when he entered the town, securely in hiding behind a furze bush. The way he remembered that mountain it would seem that twenty minutes active climbing brought him halfways to heaven. The little town was far below him, and the bay and the islands. The unkempt coastline tumbled and sprawled to left and right, and westwards the ocean went on for ever. The sounds of market day, voices, carts, dogs barking, musicians on the streets, came up to him as faint, silvery whispers. On the tip of one island two tall aerials marked the place where, he was told, messages went down into the sea to travel all the way to America by cable. That was a great marvel for a boy from the mountains to hear about: the ghostly shrill, undersea voices; the words of people in every tongue of Europe far down among the monstrous fish and shapeless sea-serpents that never saw the light of the sun. He closed his eyes one day and it seemed to him that the sounds of the little town were the voices of Europe setting out on their submarine travels. That was the time he knew that when he was old enough he would leave the Glen of Kanareen and go with the voices westwards to America.

—Or so he said. Or so he told my father, said the professor.

Another fifty yards and we would be on top of the ridge. We kept our eyes on the ground, fearful of the moment of vision and, for good or ill, revelation. Beyond the ridge there might be nothing but a void to prove that his grandfather had been a dreamer or a liar. Rapidly, nervously, he tried to talk down his fears.

—He would tell stories for ever, my father said, about ghosts and the good people. There was one case of an old woman whose people buried her – when she died, of course – against her will, across the water, which meant on the far side of the lake in the glen. Her dying wish was to be buried in another graveyard, nearer home. And there she was, sitting in her own chair in the chimney corner, waiting for them, when they came home from the funeral. To ease her spirit they replanted her.

To ease the nervous moment I said: There was a poltergeist once in a farmhouse in these mountains, and the police decided to investigate the queer happenings, and didn't an ass's collar come flying across the room to settle around the sergeant's neck. Due to subsequent ridicule the poor man had to be transferred to Dublin.

Laughing, we looked at the brown infant runnel that went parallel to the path. It flowed with us: we were over the watershed. So we raised our heads slowly and saw the great Glen of Kanareen. It was what Cortez saw, and all the rest of it. It was a discovery. It was a new world. It gathered the sunshine into a gigantic coloured bowl. We accepted it detail by detail.

—It was there all the time, he said. It was no dream. It was no lie.

The first thing we realised was the lake. The runnel leaped down to join the lake, and we looked down on it through ash trees regularly spaced on a steep, smooth, green slope. Grasping from tree to tree you could descend to the pebbled, lapping edge of the water.

—That was the way, the professor said, the boys in his time climbed down to fish or swim. Black, bull-headed mountain trout. Cannibal trout. There was one place where they could dive off sheer rock into seventy feet of water. Rolling like a gentle sea: that was how he described it. They gathered kindling, too, on the slopes under the ash trees.

Then, after the lake, we realised the guardian mountain; not rigidly chiselled into ridges of rock like the mountain behind us but soft and gently curving, protective and, above all, noble, a monarch of mountains, an antlered stag holding a proud horned head up to the highest point of the blue sky. Green fields swathed its base. Sharp lines of stone walls, dividing wide areas of moorland sheep-grazing, marked man's grip for a thousand feet or so above sea-level then gave up the struggle and left the mountain alone and untainted. Halfways up one snow-white cloud rested as if it had hooked itself on a snagged rock and there it stayed, motionless, as step by step we went down into the glen. Below the cloud a long cataract made a thin, white, forked-lightning line, and, in the heart of the glen, the river that the cataract became, sprawled on a brown and green and golden patchwork bed.

—It must be some one of those houses, he said, pointing ahead and down to the white houses of Kanareen.

—Take a blind pick, I said. I see at least fifty.

They were scattered over the glen in five or six clusters.

—From what I heard it should be over in that direction, he said.

Small rich fields were ripe in the sun. This was a glen of plenty, a gold-field in the middle of a desert, a happy laughing mockery of the arid surrounding moors and mountains. Five hundred yards away a dozen people were working at the hay. They didn't look up or give any sign that they had seen two strangers cross the high threshold of their kingdom but, as we went down, stepping like grenadier guards, the black-and-white sheepdogs detached themselves from the haymaking and moved silently across to intercept our path. Five of them I counted. My step faltered.

—This could be it, I suggested with hollow joviality. I feel a little like an early Christian.

The professor said nothing. We went on down, deserting the comfort of the grass and heather at the side of the track. It seemed to me that our feet on the loose pebbles made a tearing, crackling, grinding noise that shook echoes even out of the imperturbable mountain. The white cloud had not moved. The haymakers had not honoured us with a glance.

—We could, I said, make ourselves known to them in a civil fashion. We could ask the way to your grand-uncle's house. We could have a formal introduction to those slinking beasts.

—No, let me, he said. Give me my head. Let me try to remember what I was told.

—The hearts of these highland people, I've heard, are made of pure gold, I said. But they're inclined to be the tiniest bit suspicious of town-dressed strangers. As sure as God made smells and shotguns they think we're inspectors from some government department: weeds, or warble-fly or horror of horrors, rates and taxes. With equanimity they'd see us eaten. He laughed. His stride had a new elasticity in it. He was another man. The melancholy of the monastic summer dusk at Mount Melleray was gone. He was somebody else coming home. The white cloud had not moved. The silent dogs came closer. The unheeding people went on with their work.

—The office of rates collector is not sought after in these parts, I said. Shotguns are still used to settle vexed questions of land title. Only a general threat of excommunication can settle a major feud.

—This was the way he'd come home from the gambling cabin, the professor said, his pockets clinking with winnings. That night he fell he'd won the two bottles of whisky. He was only eighteen when he went away. But he was the tallest man in the glen. So he said. And lucky at cards.

The dogs were twenty yards away, silent, fanning out like soldiers cautiously circling a point of attack.

—He was an infant prodigy, I said. He was a peerless grandfather for a man to have. He also had one great advantage over us – he knew the names of these taciturn dogs and they knew his smell.

He took off his white hat and waved at the workers. One man at a haycock raised a pitchfork – in salute or in threat? Nobody else paid the least attention. The dogs were now at our heels, suiting their pace politely to ours. They didn't even sniff. They had impeccable manners.

—This sure is the right glen, he said. The old man was never done talking about the dogs. They were all black-and-white in his day, too.

He stopped to look at them. They stopped. They didn't look up at us. They didn't snarl. They had broad shaggy backs. Even for their breed they were big dogs. Their long tails were rigid. Fixing my eyes on the white cloud I walked on.

—Let's establish contact, I said, before we're casually eaten. All I ever heard about the dogs in these mountains is that their family tree is as old as the Red Branch Knights. That they're the best sheepdogs in Ireland and better than anything in the Highlands of Scotland. They also savage you first and bark afterwards.

Noses down, they padded along behind us. Their quiet breath was hot on my calves. High up and far away the nesting white cloud had the security of heaven.

—Only strangers who act suspiciously, the professor said.

—What else are we? I'd say we smell bad to them.

—Not me, he said. Not me. The old man told a story about a stranger who came to Kanareen when most of the people were away at the market. The house he came to visit was empty except for two dogs. So he sat all day at the door of the house and the dogs lay and watched him and said and did nothing. Only once, he felt thirsty and went into the kitchen of the house and lifted a bowl to go to the well for water. Then there was a low duet of a snarl that froze his blood. So he went thirsty and the dogs lay quiet.

—Hospitable people.

—The secret is touch nothing, lay no hand on property and you're safe.

—So help me God, I said, I wouldn't deprive them of a bone or a blade of grass.

Twice in my life I had been bitten by dogs. Once, walking to school along a sidestreet on a sunny morning and simultaneously reading in *The Boy's Magazine* about a soccer centre forward, the flower of the flock, called Fiery Cross the Shooting Star – he was redheaded and his surname was Cross – I had stepped on a sleeping Irish terrier. In retaliation, the startled brute had bitten me. Nor could I find it in my heart to blame him, so that, in my subconscious, dogs took on the awful heaven-appointed dignity of avenging angels. The other time – and this was an even more disquieting experience – a mongrel dog had come up softly behind me while I was walking on the fairgreen in the town I was reared in and bitten the calf of my leg so as to draw spurts of blood. I kicked him but not resenting the kick, he had walked away as if it was the most natural, legitimate thing in heaven and earth for a dog to bite me and be kicked in return. Third time, I thought, it will be rabies. So as we walked and the silent watchers of the valley padded at our heels, I enlivened the way with brave and trivial chatter. I recited my story of the four wild brothers of Adrigole.

—Once upon a time, I said, there lived four brothers in a

rocky corner of Adrigole in West Cork, under the mountain called Hungry Hill. Daphne du Maurier wrote a book called after the mountain, but divil a word in it about the four brothers of Adrigole. They lived, I heard tell, according to instinct and never laced their boots and came out only once a year to visit the nearest town which was Castletownberehaven on the side of Bantry Bay. They'd stand there, backs to the wall, smoking, saying nothing, contemplating the giddy market-day throng. One day they ran out of tobacco and went into the local branch of the Bank of Ireland to buy it and raised havoc because the teller refused to satisfy their needs. To pacify them the manager and the teller had to disgorge their own supplies. So they went back to Adrigole to live happily without lacing their boots, and ever after they thought that in towns and cities the bank was the place where you bought tobacco.

—That, said I with a hollow laugh, is my moral tale about the four brothers of Adrigole.

On a level with the stream that came from the lake and went down to join the valley's main river, we walked towards a group of four whitewashed, thatched farmhouses that were shining and scrupulously clean. The track looped to the left. Through a small triangular meadow a short-cut went straight towards the houses. In the heart of the meadow, by the side of the short-cut, there was a spring well of clear water, the stones that lined its sides and the roof cupped over it all white and cleansed with lime. He went down three stone steps and looked at the water. For good luck there was a tiny brown trout imprisoned in the well. He said quietly: That was the way my grandfather described it. But it could hardly be the self-same fish.

He stooped to the clear water. He filled his cupped hands and drank. He stooped again, and again filled his cupped hands and slowly, carefully, not spilling a drop, came up the moist, cool steps. Then, with the air of a priest, scattering hyssop, he sprinkled the five dogs with the spring-water. They backed away from him, thoughtfully. They didn't snarl or show teeth. He had them puzzled. He laughed with warm good nature at their obvious perplexity. He was making his own of them. He licked his wet hands. Like good pupils attentively studying a teacher, the dogs watched him.

—Elixir, he said. He told my father that the sweetest drink he ever had was out of this well when he was on his way back from a drag hunt in the next glen. He was a great hunter.

—He was Nimrod, I said. He was everything. He was the universal Kerryman.

—No kidding, he said. Through a thorn hedge six feet thick and down a precipice and across a stream to make sure of a wounded bird. Or all night long waist deep in an icy swamp waiting for the wild geese. And the day of this drag hunt. What he most remembered about it was the way they sold the porter to the hunting crowd in the pub at the crossroads. To meet the huntsmen halfways they moved the bar out to the farmyard. With hounds and cows and geese and chickens it was like having a drink in Noah's Ark. The pint tumblers were set on doors lifted off their hinges and laid flat on hurdles. The beer was in wooden tubs and all the barmaids had to do was dip and there was the pint. They didn't bother to rinse the tumblers. He said it was the quickest-served and the flattest pint of porter he ever saw or tasted. Bitter and black as bog water. Completely devoid of the creamy clerical collar that should grace a good pint. On the way home he spent an hour here rinsing his mouth and the well-water tasted as sweet, he said, as silver.

The white cloud was gone from the mountain.

—Where did it go, I said. Where could it vanish to?

In all the wide sky there wasn't a speck of cloud. The mountain was changing colour, deepening to purple with the approaching evening.

He grasped me by the elbow, urging me forwards. He said: Step on it. We're almost home.

We crossed a crude wooden stile and followed the short-cut through a walled garden of bright-green heads of cabbage and black and red currant bushes. Startled, fruit-thieving birds rustled away from us and on a rowan tree a sated, impudent blackbird opened his throat and sang.

—Don't touch a currant, I said, or a head of cabbage. Don't ride your luck too hard.

He laughed like a boy half hysterical with happiness. He said: Luck. Me and these dogs, we know each other. We've been formally introduced.

—Glad to know you dogs, he said to them over his shoulder.

They trotted behind us. We crossed a second stile and followed the short-cut through a haggard, and underfoot the ground was velvety with chipped straw. We opened a five-barred iron gate, and to me it seemed that the noise of its creaking hinges must be audible from end to end of the glen. While I paused to rebolt it he and the dogs had gone on, the dogs trotting in the lead. I ran after them. I was the stranger who had once been the guide. We passed three houses as if they didn't exist. They were empty. The people who lived in them were above at the hay. Towards the fourth thatched house of the group we walked along a green boreen, lined with hazels and an occasional mountain ash. The guardian mountain was by now so purple that the sky behind it seemed, by contrast, as silvery as the scales of a fish. From unknown lands behind the lines of hazels two more black-and-white dogs ran, barking with excitement, to join our escort. Where the hazels ended there was a house fronted by a low stone wall and a profusion of fuchsia. An old man sat on the wall and around him clustered the children of the four houses. He was a tall, broad-shouldered old man with copious white hair and dark side whiskers and a clear prominent profile. He was dressed in good grey with long, old-fashioned skirts to his coat – formally dressed as if for some formal event – and his wide-brimmed black hat rested on the wall beside him, and his joined hands rested on the curved handle of a strong ash plant. He stood up as we approached. The stick fell to the ground. He stepped over it and came towards us. He was as tall or, without the slight stoop of age, taller than the professor. He put out his two hands and rested them on the professor's shoulders. It wasn't an embrace. It was an appraisal, a salute, a sign of recognition.

He said: Kevin, well and truly we knew you'd come if you were in the neighbourhood at all. I watched you walking down.

I knew you from the top of the glen. You have the same gait my brother had, the heavens be his bed. My brother that was your grandfather.

—They say a grandson often walks like the grandfather, said the professor.

His voice was shaken and there were tears on his face. So, a stranger in the place myself, I walked away a bit and looked back up at the glen. The sunlight was slanting now and shadows were lengthening on mountain slopes and across the small fields. From where I stood the lake was invisible, but the ashwood on the slope above it was dark as ink. Through sunlight and shadow the happy haymakers came running down towards us; and barking, playing, frisking over each other, the seven black-and-white dogs, messengers of good news, ran to meet them. The great glen, all happy echoes, was opening out and singing to welcome its true son.

Under the hazels, as I watched the running haymakers, the children came shyly around me to show me that I also was welcome. Beyond the high ridge, the hard mountain the card-players used to cross to the cabin of the gambling stood up gaunt and arrogant and leaned over towards us as if it were listening.

It was moonlight, I thought, not sunlight, over the great glen. From house to house, the dogs were barking, not baying the moon, but to welcome home the young men from the card-playing over the mountain. The edges of rock glistened like quartz. The tall young gambler came laughing down the glen, greatcoat swinging open, waving in his hand the one bottle of whisky that hadn't been broken when he tumbled down the spink. The ghosts of his own dogs laughed and leaped and frolicked at his heels.

God's Own Country

THE PLUMP GIRL from Cork City who was the editor's
secretary came into the newsroom where the four of
us huddled together, and said, so rapidly that we had
to ask her to say it all over again: Goodness gracious, Mr.
Slattery, you are, you really are, smouldering.

She was plump and very pretty and enticingly perfumed
and every one of the four of us, that is everyone of us except
Jeremiah, would have been overjoyed to make advances to her
except that, being from Cork City, she talked so rapidly that we
never had time to get a word in edgeways. She said: Goodness
gracious, Mr. Slattery, you are, you really are, smouldering.

Now that our attention had been drawn to it, he really was
smouldering. He sat, crouched as close as he could get to the
paltry coal fire: the old ramshackle building, all rooms of no
definable geometrical shape, would have collapsed with
Merulius Lacrymans, the most noxious form of dry rot, the
tertiary syphilis of ageing buildings, if central heating had ever
been installed. Jeremiah nursed the fire between his bony
knees. He toasted, or tried to toast, his chapped chilblained
hands above the pitiful glow. The management of that small
weekly newspaper were too mean to spend much money on
fuel; and in that bitter spring Jeremiah was the coldest man in
the city. He tried, it seemed, to suck what little heat there was
into his bloodless body. He certainly allowed none of it to pass
him by so as to mollify the three of us who sat, while he
crouched, working doggedly with our overcoats and woollen

scarves on. The big poet who wrote the cinema reviews, and who hadn't been inside a cinema since he left for a drink at the intermission in *Gone With The Wind* and never went back, was typing, with woollen gloves on, with one finger; and for panache more than for actual necessity he wore a motor-cycling helmet with fleece-lined flaps over his ears. The big poet had already told Jeremiah that Jeremiah was a raven, a scrawny starved raven, quothing and croaking nevermore, crumpled up there in his black greatcoat over a fire that wouldn't boil an egg. Jeremiah only crouched closer to the fire and, since we knew how cold he always was, we left him be and forgot all about him, and he might well have gone on fire, nobody, not even himself, noticing, if the plump pretty secretary, a golden perfumed ball hopping from the parlour into the hall, hadn't bounced, warming the world, being the true honey of delight, into the room.

It was the turned-up fold of the right leg of his shiny black trousers. He extinguished himself wearily, putting on, to protect the fingers of his right hand, a leather motoring-gauntlet. He had lost, or had never possessed, the left-hand gauntlet. He moved a little back from the fire, he even tried to sit up straight. She picked up the telephone on the table before me. Her rounded left haunch, packed tightly in a sort of golden cloth, was within eating distance, if I'd had a knife and fork. She said to the switch that she would take that call now from where she was in the newsroom. She was silent for a while. The golden haunch moved ever so slightly, rose and fell, in fact, as if it breathed. She said: Certainly, your Grace.

—No, your Grace.

—To the island, your Grace.

—A reporter, your Grace.

—Of course, your Grace.

—And photographer, your Grace.

—An American bishop, your Grace.

—How interesting, your Grace.

—Confirmation, your Grace.

—All the way from Georgia, your Grace.

—Goodness gracious, your Grace.

—Lifeboat, your Grace.

—Yes, your Grace.

—No, your Grace.

—Next Thursday, your Grace.

—I'll make a note of it, your Grace.

—And tell the editor when he comes in from the nunciature, your Grace.

The nunciature was the place where the editor, promoting the Pope's wishes by promoting the Catholic press, did most of his drinking. He had a great tongue for the Italian wine.

—Lifeboat, your Grace.

—Absolutely, your Grace.

—Goodbye, your Grace.

The big poet said: That wouldn't have been His Grace you were talking to?

—That man, she said, thinks he's three rungs of the ladder above the Pope of Rome and with right of succession to the Lord himself.

She made for the door. The gold blinded me. She turned at the door, said to us all, or to three of us: Watch him. Don't let him make a holocaust of himself. Clean him up and feed him. He's for the Islands of the West, Hy-Breasil, the Isle of the Blest, next Thursday with the Greatest Grace of all the Graces, and a Yankee bishop who thinks it would do something for him to bestow the holy sacrament of confirmation on the young savages out there. Not that it will do much for them. It would take more than two bishops and the Holy Ghost...

She was still talking as she vanished. The door crashed shut behind her and the room was dark again, and colder than ever. Jeremiah was visibly shuddering, audibly chattering, because to his bloodlessness and to the chill of the room and of the harsh day of east wind, had been added the worst cold of all: terror.

—Take him out, the big poet said, before he freezes us to death. Buy him a hot whiskey. You can buy me one when I finish my column.

As he tapped with one gloved finger and, with a free and open mind and no prejudice, critically evaluated what he had not seen, he also lifted up his voice and sang: When the roses bloom again down by yon river, and the robin redbreast sings his sweet refrain, in the days of auld lang syne, I'll be with you sweetheart mine, I'll be with you when the roses bloom again.

In Mulligan's in Poolbeg Street, established 1782, the year of the great Convention of the heroic patriotic Volunteers at Dungannon when the leaders of the nation, sort of, were inspired by the example of American Independence, I said to Jeremiah: Be a blood. Come alive. Break out. Face them. Show them. Fuck the begrudgers. Die, if die you must, on your feet and fighting.

He said: It's very well for you to talk. You can eat.

—Everybody, for God's sake, can eat.

—I can't eat. I can only nibble.

—You can drink, though. You have no trouble at all with the drink.

His first hot whiskey was gone, but hadn't done him any good that you'd notice.

—Only whiskey, he said, and sometimes on good days, stout. But even milk makes me ill, unless it's hot and with pepper sprinkled on it.

I pretended to laugh at him, to jolly him out of it, yet he really had me worried. For he was a good helpless intelligent chap, and his nerves had gone to hell in the seminary that he had had to leave, and the oddest rumours about his eating or non-eating habits were going around the town. That, for instance, he had been seen in a certain hotel, nibbling at biscuits left behind by another customer, and when the waiter, who was a friend of mine, asked him in all kindness did he need lunch, he had slunk away, the waiter said, like a shadow that had neither substance nor sunshine to account for its being there in the first place. He was no man, I had to agree, to face on an empty stomach a spring gale, or even a half or a hatful of a gale, on the wild western Atlantic coast.

—And the thought of that bishop, he said, puts the heart across me. He's a boor and bully of the most violent description. He's a hierarchical Genghis Khan.

—Not half as bad as he's painted.

—Half's bad enough.

So I told some story, once told to me by a Belfast man, about some charitable act performed by the same bishop. It didn't sound at all convincing. Nor was Jeremiah convinced.

—If he ever was charitable, he said, be sure that it wasn't his own money he gave away.

—You won't have to see much of him, Jeremiah. Keep out of his path. Don't encounter him.

—But I'll encounter the uncandid cameraman who'll be my constant companion. With his good tweeds and his cameras that all the gold in the mint wouldn't buy. How do the mean crowd that run that paper ever manage to pay him enough to satisfy him? He invited me to his home to dinner. Once. To patronise me. To show me what he had and I hadn't. He ran out six times during dinner to ring the doorbell, and we had to stop eating and listen to the chimes. A different chime in every room. Like living in the bloody belfry. Searchlights he has on the lawn to illuminate the house on feast-days. Like they do in America, I'm told. Letting his light shine in the uncomprehending darkness. Some men in this town can't pay the electricity bill, but he suffers from a surplus. And this bishop is a friend of his. Stops with him when he comes to town. His wife's uncle is a monsignor in His Grace's diocese. Practically inlaws. They call each other by their Christian names. I was permitted and privileged to see the room the bishop sleeps in, with its own special bathroom, toilet seat reserved for the episcopal arse, a layman would have to have his arse specially anointed to sit on it. Let me tell you that it filled me with awe. When they have clerical visitors, he told me, they couldn't have them shaving in the ordinary bathroom. I hadn't the courage to ask him was there anything forbidding that in Canon Law, Pastoral Theology or the Maynooth Statutes. God look down on me between the two of them, and an American bishop thrown in for good luck. They say that in the United States the bishops are just bigger and more brutal.

—Jeremiah, I said severely, you're lucky to be out with that cameraman. He'll teach you to be a newsman. Just study how he works. He can smell news like, like...

The struggle for words went on until he helped me out. He was quick-witted; and even on him the third hot whiskey was bound to have some effect: to send what blood there was in his veins toe-dancing merrily to his brain.

—Like a buzzard smells dead meat, he said.

Then the poet joined us. Having an inherited gift for cobbling he had recently cobbled for himself a pair of shoes but, since measurement was not his might, they turned out to be too big even for him, thus, for any mortal man. But he had not given up hope of encountering in a public bar some Cyclopean for whose benefit he had, in his subconscious, been working, and of finding him able and willing to purchase those shoes. He carried them, unwrapped, under his arm. They always excited comment; and many were the men who tried and failed to fill them. That night we toured the town with them, adding to our company, en route, an Irish professor from Rathfarnham, a French professor from Marseilles, a lady novelist, a uniformed American soldier with an Irish name, who came from Boston and General Patch's army which had passed by Marseilles and wrecked it in the process. Outside Saint Vincent's hospital in Saint Stephen's Green a total stranger, walking past us, collapsed. He was a very big man, with enormous feet. But when the men from Boston and Marseilles, and the poet and myself, carried him into the hospital he was dead.

All that, as you are about to observe, is another story.

We failed, as it so happened, to sell the shoes.

On that corner of the western coast of Ireland the difference between a gale and a half-gale is that in a half-gale you take a chance and go out, in a gale you stay ashore.

The night before the voyage they rested in a hotel in Galway City. The wind rattled the casements and now and again blew open the door of the bar in which Jeremiah sat alone, until well after midnight, over one miserable whiskey. Nobody bothered to talk to him, not even in Galway where the very lobsters will welcome the stranger. The bar was draughty. He wore his black greatcoat, a relic of his clerical ambitions. It enlarged his body to the point of monstrosity, and minimised his head. Dripping customers came and drank and steamed and went again. When the door blew open he could see the downpours of rain hopping like hailstones on the street. The spluttering radio talked of floods, and trees blown down, and crops destroyed, and an oil-tanker in peril off the Tuskar Rock. The cameraman had eaten a horse of a dinner, washed it down with the best wine, said his prayers and gone to bed, to be, he said, fresh and fit for the morning. Jeremiah was hungry, but less than ever could he eat: with fear of the storm and of the western sea as yet unseen and of the bull of a bishop and, perhaps too, he thought, that visiting American would be no better. At midnight he drained his glass dry and afterwards tilted it several times to his lips, drinking, or inhaling, only wind. He would have ordered another whiskey but the bar was crowded by that time, and the barman was surrounded by his privileged friends who were drinking after hours. The wind no longer blew the door open for the door was double-bolted against the night. But the booming, buffeting and rattling of the storm could still be heard, at times bellowing like a brazen bishop, threatening Jeremiah. The customers kept coming and crowding through a dark passage that joined the bar and the kitchen. They acted as if they had spent all day in the kitchen and had every intention of spending all night in the bar. Each one of them favoured Jeremiah with a startled look where he sat, black, deformed by that greatcoat, hunched-up in his black cold corner. Nobody joined him. He went to bed, to a narrow, hard, excessively-white bed with a ridge up the middle and a downward slope on each side. The rubber hot-water bottle had already gone cold. The rain threatened to smash the window-panes. He spread his greatcoat over his feet, wearing his socks in bed, and, cursing the day he was born, fell asleep from sheer misery.

Early next morning he had his baptism of salt water, not sea-spray but rain blown sideways and so salty that it made a crust around the lips.

—That out there, said the cameraman in the security of his car, is what they call the poteen cross.

The seats in the car were covered with a red plush, in its turn covered by a protective and easily-washable, transparent plastic that Jeremiah knew had been put there to prevent himself or his greatcoat or his greasy, shiny pants from making direct contact with the red plush.

—Did you never hear of the poteen cross?

—No, said Jeremiah.

They had stopped in a pelting village on the westward road. The doors were shut, the windows still blinded. It was no morning for early rising. The sea was audible, but not visible. The rain came bellying inshore on gusts of wind. On a gravelled space down a slope towards the sound of the sea stood a huge bare black cross: well, not completely bare for it carried, criss-crossed, the spear that pierced, that other spear that bore aloft the sponge soaked in vinegar; and it was topped by a gigantic crown of thorns. The cameraman said: When the Redemptorist Fathers preached hellfire against the men who made the poteen, they ordered the moonshiners, under pain of mortal sin, to come here and leave their stills at the foot of the cross. The last sinner to hold out against them came in the end with his still but, there before him, he saw a better model that somebody else had left, so he took it away with him. There's a London magazine wants a picture of that cross.

—It wouldn't, said Jeremiah, make much of a picture.

—With somebody beside it pointing up at it, it wouldn't be so bad. The light's not good. But I think we could manage.

—We, said Jeremiah.

—You wouldn't like me, he said, to get up on the cross? Have you brought the nails?

He posed, nevertheless, and pointed up at the cross. What else could he do? We saw the picture afterwards in that London magazine. Jeremiah looked like a sable bloated demon trying to prove to benighted sinners that Christ was gone and dead and never would rise again. But it was undeniably an effective picture. Jeremiah posed and pointed. He was salted and sodden while the cameraman, secure in yellow oilskins and sou'wester, darted out, took three shots, darted in again, doffed the oilskins, and was as dry as snuff. They drove on westwards.

—That coat of yours, said the cameraman. You should have fitted yourself out with oilskins. That coat of yours will soak up all the water from here to Long Island.

—Stinks a bit too, he said on reflection. The Beeoh is flying. That was meant to be some sort of a joke and, for the sake of civility, Jeremiah tried to laugh. They crossed a stone bridge over a brown-and-white, foaming, flooded river, turned left down a byroad, followed the course of the river, sometimes so close to it that the floodwater lapped the edge of the road, sometimes swinging a little away from it through a misted landscape of small fields, thatched cabins dour and withdrawn in the storm, shapeless expanses of rock and heather, until they came to where the brown-and-white water tumbled into the peace of a little land-locked harbour. The lifeboat that, by special arrangement, was to carry the party to the island was there, but no lifeboatmen, no party. A few small craft lay on a sandy slope in the shelter of a breakwater. Jeremiah and the cameraman could have been the only people alive in a swamped world. They waited: the cameraman in the car with the heat on; Jeremiah, to get away from him for a while, prowling around empty cold sheds that were, at least, dry, but that stank of dead fish and were floored with peat-mould terrazzoed, it would seem, by fragments broken from many previous generations of lobsters. Beyond the breakwater and a rocky headland the sea boomed, but the water in the sheltered harbour was smooth and black as ink. He was hungry again but knew that if he had food, any food other than dry biscuits, he wouldn't be able to eat it. All food now would smell of stale fish. He was cold, as always. When he was out of sight of the cameraman he pranced, to warm himself, on peat-mould and lobsters. He was only moderately successful. But his greatcoat, at least, steamed.

The rain eased off, the sky brightened, but the wind seemed to grow in fury, surf and spray went up straight and shining into the air beyond the breakwater, leaped it and came down with a flat slap on the sandy slope and the sleeping small craft. Then, like Apache on an Arizona skyline, the people began to appear: a group of three suddenly, from behind a standing rock; a group of seven or eight rising sharply into sight on a hilltop on the switchback riverside road, dropping out of sight into a hollow, surfacing again, followed by other groups that appeared and disappeared in the same disconcerting manner. As the sky cleared, the uniform darkness breaking up into bullocks of black wind-goaded clouds, the landscape of rock

and heather, patchwork fields divided by grey, high, drystone
walls, came out into the light; and from every small farmhouse
thus revealed, people came, following footpaths, crossing
stiles, calling to each other across patches of light-green oats
and dark-green potatoes. It was a sudden miracle of growth, of
human life appearing where there had been nothing but wind
and rain and mist. Within three-quarters of an hour there
were a hundred or more people around the harbour, lean
hard-faced fishermen and small farmers, dark-haired laughing girls, old women in coloured shawls, talking Irish, talking
English, posing in groups for the cameraman who in his yellow
oilskins moved among them like a gigantic canary. They waved
and called to Jeremiah where he stood, withdrawn and on the
defensive, in the sheltered doorway of a fish-stinking shed.

A black Volkswagen came down the road followed by a red
Volkswagen. From the black car a stout priest stepped forth,
surveyed the crowd like a general estimating the strength of
his mustered troops, shook hands with the cameraman as if he
were meeting an old friend. From the red car a young man
stepped out, then held the door for a gaunt middle-aged lady
who emerged with an effort, head first: the local school-
teachers, by the cut of them. They picked out from the crowd
a group of twelve to twenty, lined them up, backs to the wall,
in the shelter of the breakwater. The tall lady waved her arms
and the group began to sing.

—Ecce sacerdos magnus, they sang.

A black limousine, with the traction power of two thousand
Jerusalem asses on the first Holy Thursday, came, appearing
and disappearing, down the switchback road. This was it,
Jeremiah knew, and shuddered. On the back of an open truck
behind the limousine came the lifeboatmen, all like the cameraman, in bright yellow oilskins.

—This is God's own country, said the American bishop, and
ye are God's own people.

Jeremiah was still at a safe distance, yet near enough to hear
the booming clerical-American voice. The sea boomed beyond
the wall. The spray soared, then slapped down on the sand,
sparing the sheltered singers.

—Faith of our fathers, they sang, living still, in spite of dungeon, fire and sword.

Circling the crowd the great canary, camera now at ease, approached Jeremiah.

—Get with it, Dracula, he said.

He didn't much bother to lower his voice.

—Come out of your corner fighting. Get in and get a story. That Yank is news. He was run out of Rumania by the Communists.

—He also comes, said Jeremiah, from Savannah, Georgia.

—So what?

—He doesn't exactly qualify as a Yankee.

—Oh Jesus, geography, said the cameraman. We'll give you full marks for geography. They'll look lovely in the paper where your story should be. If he came from bloody Patagonia, he's here now. Go get him.

Then he was gone, waving his camera. The American bishop, a tall and stately man, was advancing, blessing as he went, to the stone steps that went down the harbour wall to the moored lifeboat. He was in God's own country and God's own people, well-marshalled by the stout parish priest, were all around him. The Irish bishop, a tall and stately man, stood still, thoughtfully watching the approaching cameraman and Jeremiah most reluctantly plodding in the rear, his progress, to his relief, made more difficult by the mush of wet peat-mould underfoot, growing deeper and deeper as he approached the wall where sailing hookers were loaded with fuel for the peatless island. Yet, slowly as he moved, he was still close enough to see clearly what happened and to hear clearly what was said.

The bishop, tall and stately and monarch even over the parish priest, looked with a cold eye at the advancing cameraman. There was no ring kissing. The bishop did not reach out his hand to have his ring saluted. That was odd, to begin with. Then he said loudly: What do you want?

—Your Grace, said the great canary.

He made a sort of a curtsey, clumsily, because he was hobbled in creaking oilskins.

—Your Grace, he said, out on the island there's a nonagenarian, the oldest inhabitant, and when we get there I'd like to get a picture of you giving him your blessing.

His Grace said nothing. His Grace turned very red in the face. In increased terror, Jeremiah remembered that inlaws could have their tiffs and that clerical inlaws were well known to be hell incarnate. His Grace right-about-wheeled, showed to the mainland and all on it a black broad back, right-quick-marched towards the lifeboat, sinking to the ankles as he thundered on in the soft wet mould, but by no means abating his speed which could have been a fair five miles an hour. His long coat-tails flapped in the wind. The wet mould fountained up like snow from a snow-plough. The sea boomed. The spray splattered. The great canary had shrunk as if plucked. Jeremiah's coat steamed worse than ever in the frenzy of his fear. If he treats his own like that, he thought, what in God's holy name will he do to me? Yet he couldn't resist saying: That man could pose like Nelson on his pillar watching his world collapse.

The canary cameraman hadn't a word to say.

Once aboard the lugger the bishops had swathed themselves in oilskins provided by the lifeboat's captain, and the cameraman mustered enough of his ancient gall to mutter to Jeremiah that that was the first time that he or anybody else had seen canary-coloured bishops.

—Snap them, said Jeremiah. You could sell it to the magazines in Bucharest. Episcopal American agent turns yellow.

But the cameraman was still too crestfallen, and made no move, and clearly looked relieved when the Irish bishop, tall and stately even if a little grotesque in oilskins, descended carefully into the for'ard foxhole, sat close into the corner, took out his rosary beads and began to pray silently: he knew the tricks of his western sea. Lulled by the security of the land-locked sheltered harbour, the American bishop, tall and stately even if a little grotesque in oilskins, stood like Nelson on the foredeck. He surveyed the shore of rock, small fields, drystone walls, small thatched farmhouses, oats, potatoes, grazing black cattle, all misting over for more rain. Then he turned his back on the mainland and looked at the people, now marshalled all together by the parish priest and the two teachers in the lee of the harbour wall. The choir sang: Holy God, we praise thy name. Lord of all, we bow before thee.

An outrider of the squall of rain that the wind was driving inshore cornered cunningly around harbour wall and headland, and disrespectfully spattered the American bishop. Secure in oilskins and the Grace of State he ignored it. The cameraman dived into the stern foxhole. Jeremiah by now was so sodden that the squall had no effect on him. An uncle of his, a farmer in the County Longford, had worn the same heavy woollen underwear winter and summer and argued eloquently that what kept the heat in kept it out. That soaking salty steaming greatcoat could, likewise, stand upright on its own against the fury of the Bay of Biscay. It was a fortress for Jeremiah; and with his right hand, reaching out through the loophole of the sleeve, he touched the tough stubby oaken mast, a talismanic touch, a prayer to the rooted essence of the earth to protect him from the capricious fury of the sea. Then with the bishop, a yellow figurehead, at the prow, and Jeremiah, a sable figurehead, at the stern, they moved smoothly towards the open ocean; and, having withdrawn a little from the land, the bishop raised his hand, as Lord Nelson would not have done, and said: This is God's own country. Ye are God's own people.

The choir sang: Hail Glorious Saint Patrick, dear Saint of our isle.

From the conscripted and marshalled people came a cheer loud enough to drown the hymn; and then the sea, with as little regard for the cloth as had the Rumanian Reds, struck like an angry bull and the boat, Jeremiah says, stood on its nose, and only a miracle of the highest order kept the American bishop out of the drink. Jeremiah could see him, down, far down at the bottom of a dizzy slope, then up, far up, shining like the sun between sea and sky, as the boat reared back on its haunches and Jeremiah felt on the back of his head the blow of a gigantic fist. It was simply salt seawater in a solid block, striking and bursting like a bomb. By the time he had wiped his eyes and the boat was again, for a few brief moments, on an even keel, there were two bishops sheltering in the for'ard foxhole: the two most quiet and prayerful men he had ever seen.

—On the ocean that hollows the rocks where ye dwell, Jeremiah recited out as loudly as he could because no ears could hear even a bull bellowing above the roar and movement and torment of the sea.

—A shadowy land, he went on, has appeared as they tell. Men thought it a region of sunshine and rest, and they called it Hy-Breasil the Isle of the Blest.

To make matters easier, if not tolerable, he composed his mind and said to himself: Lifeboats can't sink.

On this harshly ocean-bitten coast there was the poetic legend of the visionary who sailed west, ever west, to find the island where the souls of the blest are forever happy.

—Rash dreamer return, Jeremiah shouted, oh ye winds of the main, bear him back to his own native Ara again.

For his defiance the sea repaid him in three thundering salty buffets and a sudden angled attack that sent the boat hissing along on its side and placed Jeremiah with both arms around the mast. In the brief following lull he said more quietly, pacifying the sea, acknowledging its power: Night fell on the deep amid tempest and spray, and he died on the ocean, away far away.

He was far too frightened to be seasick, which was just as well, considering the windy vacuum he had for a stomach. The boat pranced and rolled. He held on to the mast, but now almost nonchalantly and only with one arm. The sea buffeted him into dreams of that luckless searcher for Hy-Breasil, or dreams of Brendan the Navigator, long before Columbus, sailing bravely on and on and making landfall on Miami Beach. Secure in those dreams he found to his amazement that he could contemn the snubbed cameraman and the praying bishops hiding in their foxholes. He, Jeremiah, belonged with the nonchalant lifeboatmen studying the sea as a man through the smoke of a good pipe might look at the face of a friend. One of them, indeed, was so nonchalant that he sat on the hatch-roof above the bishops, his feet on the gunwale chain so that, when the boat dipped his way, his feet a few times went well out of sight in the water. Those lifeboatmen were less men

than great yellow seabirds and Jeremiah, although a landlub-
ber and as black as a raven, willed to be with them as far as he
could, for the moment, go. He studied on the crazy pattern of
tossing waters the ironic glint of sunshine on steel-blue hills
racing to collide and crash and burst into blinding silver. He
recalled sunshine on quiet, stable, green fields that he was
half-reconciled never to see again. He was on the way to the
Isle of the Blest.

Yet it was no island that first appeared to remind him, after
two hours of trance, that men, other than the lifeboat's crew
and cargo, did exist: no island, but the high bird-flight of a
dozen black currachs, appearing and disappearing, forming
into single file, six to either side of the lifeboat, forming a
guard of honour as if they had been cavalry on display in a
London park, to escort the sacerdotes magni safely into the
island harbour. Afterwards Jeremiah was to learn that lifeboats could sink and had done so, yet he says that even had he
known through the wildest heart of that voyage it would have
made no difference. Stunned, but salted, by the sea he arose a
new man.

The parish church was a plain granite cross high on a windy,
shelterless hilltop. It grew up from the rock it was cut from.
No gale nor half-gale, nor the gates of hell, could prevail
against it.

To west and south-west the land sank, then swept up dizzily
again to a high bare horizon, and beyond that there could be
nothing but monstrous seacliffs and the ocean. To east and
north-east small patchwork fields, bright green, dark green,
golden, netted by greystone walls, dotted by white and golden
cabins all newly limewashed and thatched for the coming of
the great priests, sloped down to a sea in the lee of the island
and incredibly calm. The half-gale was still strong. But the
island was steady underfoot. Far away the mainland, now a bit
here, now a bit there, showed itself, glistening, out of the
wandering squalls.

—Rock of ages cleft for me, he hummed with a reckless
merriment that would have frightened him if he had stopped
to reason about it, let me hide myself in thee. He was safe in

the arms of Jesus, he was deep in the heart of Texas. The granite cruciform church was his shelter from the gale, providing him, by the protection of its apse and right arm, with a sunny corner to hide in and smoke in. He was still giddy from the swing of the sea. He was also, being, alas, human and subject to frailty, tempted to rejoice at the downfall and humiliation of another. He hath put down the mighty, he began to chant but stopped to consider that as yet there was little sign of the lowly being exalted.

This corner of the cross was quiet. One narrow yellow grained door was securely shut. All the bustle, all the traffic was out around the front porch: white-jacketed white-jerseyed islanders sitting on stone walls, women in coloured shawls crowding and pushing, children hymn-singing in English, Irish and Latin, real Tower of Babel stuff, the cameraman photographing groups of people, and photographing the bishops from a safe distance, and the church from every angle short of the one the angels saw it from. He was no longer a great clumsy canary. He was splendid in his most expensive tweeds. He was, nevertheless, a cowed and broken man.

For back at the harbour, at the moment of disembarkation, it had happened again.

The two bishops, divested of oilskins, tall and black but not stately, are clambering up a ladder onto the high slippy quayside, and they are anything but acrobatic. Jeremiah, a few yards away, is struggling to tear from his body his sodden greatcoat, to hang it to dry under the direction of an islandman, in the lee of a boathouse where nets are laid to dry. The cameraman has jocosely snapped him. Then he directs the camera on the clambering bishops only to be vetoed by a voice, iron and Irish and clanging.

—Put away that camera, the Irish voice says, until the opportune time.

—Why Peter, says the American voice, that would make a fun picture.

—In Ireland we don't want or need fun pictures of the hierarchy. We're not clowns.

It is arguable, Jeremiah thinks. He recalls that archbishops, on their own territory and when in full regimentals, are entitled to wear red boots. But he keeps his back turned on the passing parade in sudden terror that his eyes might reveal his thoughts. He hears the cameraman say: Your Grace, there is on the island the oldest inhabitant, a nonagenarian. I'd like to...

But there is no response. The procession has passed on. Fickle, Jeremiah knows, is the favour of princes, particularly when, like the Grand Turk, they are related to you. But whatever or how grievous the cause of offence had been that led to these repeated snubs, Jeremiah feels for the first time, burning through empty belly and meagre body, the corpsspirit of the pressman. Who in hell, anyway, is a bishop that he won't stand and pose like any other mortal man? All men are subject to the camera. Face up to it, grin, watch the little birdie. Only murderers are allowed to creep past, faces covered. If he won't be photographed, then to hell with him. He will be scantily written about, even if he is Twenty Times His Grace. And to hell also with all American bishops and Rumanian Reds, and will all colour stories of confirmations and of simple island people who, more than likely, spend the long winter nights making love to their own domestic animals which, as far as Jeremiah is concerned, they have a perfect right to do.

So here in the corner of the granite cross he had found peace. He didn't need to see the nonsense going on out there. When the time came to type, as no doubt it would, the Holy Ghost would guide his fingertips. The moment on the quayside mingled with the moment in the shelter of the church and he realised, for the first time since anger had possessed him, that he had left his greatcoat still drying with the nets. He had been distracted by a call to coffee and sandwiches intended to keep them from collapsing until the show was over. But to hell, too, he decided with all greatcoats; a man could stand on his own legs. He smoked, and was content, and heard far away the voices of children, angels singing. Then the narrow yellow grained door opened, a great venerable head, a portion of surpliced body, appeared, a voice louder than the choirs of angels said: Come here, pressman.

Jeremiah went there.

—On the alert I'm glad to see, His Grace said. Waiting to see me. What can I do for you?

Jeremiah, to begin with, bent one knee and kissed his ring. That little bit of ballet enabled him to avoid saying whether he had or had not been on the alert, waiting for an interview.

—You must be starved, His Grace said. That was a rough journey.

They were in the outer room of the sacristy. The walls were mostly presses all painted the same pale yellow, with graining, as the narrow door. In an inner room the American bishop, head bowed, was talking to two tiny nuns. From one of the presses His Grace took a bottle and a half-pint tumbler and half-filled the tumbler with Jameson neat.

—Throw that back, he ordered. 'Twill keep the wind out of your stomach.

He watched benevolently while Jeremiah gasped and drank. The whiskey struck like a hammer. How was His Grace to know that Jeremiah's stomach had in it nothing at all, but wind? Jeremiah's head spun. This, he now knew, was what people meant when they talked about the bishop's bottle. His Grace restored bottle and glass to the press.

—We mustn't, he said, shock the good sisters.

He handed Jeremiah a sheaf of typescript. He said: It's all there. Names. History. Local lore. All the blah-blah, as you fellows say. Here, have a cigar. It belongs to our American Mightyship. They never travel without them. God bless you now. Is there anything else I can do for you?

Jeremiah's head had ceased to spin. His eyes had misted for a while with the warmth of the malt on an empty stomach, but now the mist cleared and he could see, he felt, to a great distance. The malt, too, had set the island rocking but with a gentle soothing motion.

—There's a man here, he said, the oldest inhabitant, a nonagenarian. The cameraman who's with me would like a picture.

—No sooner said than done, oh gentleman of the press. That should make a most edifying picture. I'll call himself away from the nuns. We'll just have time before the ceremony.

But, for reasons never known to me or Jeremiah, he laughed all the time as he led the way around the right arm of the cross to the front of the church; and brought with him another cigar for the cameraman, and shook hands with him, and offered him his ring to be kissed.

Apart from Jeremiah and the cameraman and the island doctor it was a clerical dinner, the island parish priest as host, a dozen well-conditioned men sitting down to good food, and wines that had crossed from Spain on the trawlers without paying a penny to the revenue.

—One of the best men in the business, said His Grace, although he'd sell us all body and soul to the *News of the World*.

He was talking about the cameraman, and at table, and in his presence. But he was laughing, and inciting the gathering to laughter. Whatever cloud there had been between the relatives had blown away with the storm, or with Jeremiah's diplomacy. So Jeremiah felt like Talleyrand. He was more than a little drunk. He was confirmed and made strong by the sea and the bishop's whiskey. He was hungry as hell.

—And Spanish ale, he muttered, shall give you hope, my dark Rosaleen.

His mutter was overheard, relayed around the table, and accepted as unquestionable wit. He was triumphant. He ate. He fell to, like a savage. He drank, he said afterwards – although we suspected that he had conned the names from a wine merchant's list, red and white Poblet, and red Rioja, and red Valdapenas, and another wine that came from the plain to the west of Tarragona where the Cistercians had a monastery: the lot washed down with Fundadór brandy which the American bishop told him had been the brandy specially set aside for the Conclave of Pope John the Twenty-third.

—Thou art Peter, said Jeremiah, and upon this rock.

Once again the remark was relayed around the table. Awash on the smuggled products of Spain, Jeremiah was in grave danger of becoming the life and soul of the party.

A boy-child had that day been born on the island. The American bishop had asked the parents could he baptise the child and name it after himself.

—Episcopus Americanus O'Flaherty, said Jeremiah.
Pope John's Fundadór circled the board. The merriment
knew no bounds. His Grace told how the great traveller,
O'Donovan, had dwelt among the Turkomans of ancient Merv,
whom he finally grew to detest because they wouldn't let him
go home, but who liked him so much they called all their
male children after him: O'Donovan Beg, O'Donovan Khan,
O'Donovan Bahadur, and so on.

—It was the custom in ancient Merv, said His Grace, to call
the newborn babes after any distinguished visitor who happened to be in the oasis at the time.

—It was not the custom in Rumania, said Jeremiah.

Renewed merriment. When the uproar died down, the
American bishop, with tears in his eyes, said: But this is God's
Own Country. Ye are God's Own People.

Jeremiah got drunk, but nobody minded. Later, outside a
bar close by the harbour, he was photographed feeding whiskey out of a basin to a horse. The horse was delighted. The
picture appeared in a London magazine, side-by-side with a
picture of the nonagenarian flanked by bishops.

—You got him to pose, said the cameraman, when he rusted
on me.

He meant, not the horse, but the bishop.

—Jer, he said, you'll make a newsman yet.

So, as Jer, a new man, eater of meat and vegetables, acknowledged gentleman of the press, he came back from the Isle of
the Blest, sitting on the hatch above the bishops, feet on the
gunwale chain. He was not beyond hoping that the swing of
the sea and the tilt of the boat might salt his feet. It didn't. The
easy evening sway would have lulled a child in the cradle.

—Episcopus Americanus O'Flaherty, he said to the lifeboatman who sat beside him and who had enough Latin to
clerk Mass.

—True for you, said the lifeboatman. Small good that chris-
tening will do the poor boy. As long as he lives on that island
he'll never be known as anything but An Teasbog Beag – the
Little Bishop. If he goes to the States itself, the name could
follow him there. His sons and even his daughters will be
known as the Little Bishops. Or his eldest son may be called

Mac an Easboig, the Son of the Bishop. They'll lose O'Flaherty and be called Macanespie. That's how names were invented since the time of King Brian Boru who bate the Danes.

Behind them the island stepped away into the mist: the wanderer, crazed for Hy-Breasil, would never find it. The rain would slant for ever on rocks and small fields, on ancient forts and cliffs with seabirds crying around them, on currachs riding the waves as the gulls do. Visitors would be enthralled by ancient ways, and basking sharks captured. But as long as winds rage and tides run, that male child, growing up to be a lean tanned young man in white jacket and soft pampooties, leaning into the wind as he walks as his forebears have always done, courteous as a prince but also ready to fight at the drop of a half-glass of whiskey, sailing with the trawlers as far away as the Faroes, will continue, because of this day, to be known as the Little Bishop.

In the foxhole underneath Jeremiah, the American bishop was telling the Irish bishop and the cameraman that in the neighbourhood of the Okefenokee Swamp, out of which the Suwannee River drags its corpse, and generally in the state of Georgia, there were many Southern Baptists with Irish Catholic names.

The water in the land-locked harbour was deadly still, and deep purple in the dusk. Sleepy gulls foraged on the edge of the tide, or called from inland over the small fields. Jer's greatcoat was still on the island, dry by now, and stiff with salt. He never wanted to see it again.

Shadowy people gathered on the harbour wall. The choir sang: Sweet Sacrament Divine, dear home of every heart.

—Ye are God's own people, said the American bishop. This is God's own country.

—Fuck, said the cameraman and in a painfully audible voice.

He had sunk over the ankles in soggy peat-mould, losing one shoe. But while he stood on one leg and Jer groped for the missing shoe, the bishops and the people and the parish priest and the choir, and the cameraman himself, all joked and laughed. When the shoe was retrieved they went on their way rejoicing.

In Galway City Jer ate a dinner of parsnips and rare roast meat and sauté potatoes that would have stunned an ox; and washed it down with red wine.

Far away the island gulls nested on his discarded greatcoat.

There Are Meadows in Lanark

THE SCHOOLMASTER IN Bomacatall or McKattle's Hut was gloved and masked and at his beehives when his diminutive brother, the schoolmaster from Knockata- tawn, came down the dusty road on his high bicycle. It was an Irish-made bicycle. The schoolmaster from Knockatatawn was a patriot. He could have bought the best English-made Raleigh for half the price, but instead he imported this edifice from the Twenty-six into the Six Counties and paid a mountain of duty on it. The bike, and more of its kind, was made in Wexford by a firm that made the sort of mowing-machine that it took two horses to pull. They built the bikes on the same solid principle. Willian Bulfin from the Argentine who long ago wrote a book about rambling in Erin had cycled round the island on one of them and died not long afterwards, almost certainly from over-exertion. There was a great view from the saddle. Hugh, who was the son of the schoolmaster from Bomacatall, once on the quiet borrowed the bike and rode into the side of a motor-car that was coming slowly out of a hedgy hidden boreen. He was tossed sideways into the hedgerow and had a lacework of scratches on his face. The enamel on the car was chipped and the driver's window broken. The bike was unperturbed.

The little man mounted the monster by holding the grips on the handlebars, placing his left foot on the extended spud or hub of the back wheel and then giving an electrified leap. This sunny evening he dismounted by stepping on to the top rail of the garden fence at Bomacatall. He sat there like a gigantic rook, the King Rook that you hear chanting base barreltone in the rookery chorus. He wore a pinstriped dark suit and a black wide-brimmed hat. He paid no attention to the buzzing and swarming of the bees. The herbaceous borders, the diamond-shaped beds at Bomacatall would blind you. There was a twisting trout stream a field away from the far end of the garden. To his brother who was six feet and more the little man said: I have a scheme in mind.

From behind the mask the big man said: Was there ever a day that God sent that you didn't have a scheme in mind?

—It would benefit the boy Hugh. *Cé an aois é anois?*

That meant: What age is he now?

—Nine, God bless him.

—Time he saw a bit of the world. Bracing breezes, silvery sands, booming breakers, lovely lands: Come to Bundoran.

That was an advertisement in the local newspaper.

—You could sing that if you had a tune to it, said the man behind the mask.

—The holiday would do him good, the King Rook said, and for three weeks there'd be one mouth less to feed.

That was a forceful argument. The master from Knockata-tawn, or the Hill of the Conflagrations, was a bachelor. Hugh was midways in a household of seven, not counting the father and mother.

The bees settled. The bee-keeper doffed the mask and wiped the sweat off a broad humorous face. He said: James, like St. Paul you're getting on. You want another to guide you and lead you where thou would'st not.

—John, said the man on the fence, in defiance of Shake-speare, I maintain that there are only three stages in a man's life: young, getting-on, and not so bad-considering. I've a sad feeling that I've got to the third.

The nine-year-old, as he told me a long time afterwards, was all for the idea of Bundoran except that, young as he was, he knew there was a hook attached. This was it. At home on the Hill of the Conflagrations there wasn't a soberer man than the wee schoolmaster, none more precise in his way of life and his teaching methods, more just and exact in the administering of punishments or rewards. But Bundoran was for him another world and he, when he was there, was another man. He met a lot of all sorts of people. He talked his head off, behaved as if he had never heard of algebra or a headline copy-book, and drank whisky as if he liked it and as if the world's stock of whisky was going to run dry on the following morning. Yet, always an exact man, he knew that his powers of navigation, when he was in the whisky, were failing, that – as Myles na Gopaleen said about a man coming home from a night at a boat-club dance in Islandbridge – he knew where he was coming from and going to, but he had no control over his lesser movements. He needed a pilot, he needed a tug, or both combined in one: his nephew. There was, also, this to be said for the wee man: he was never irascible or difficult in drink, he went where the pilot guided him and the tug tugged him. He was inclined to sing, but then he was musical and in the school in Knockatatawn he had a choir that was the terror of Féis Doire Cholmcille, the great musical festival held in Derry in memory of St. Colmcille. He even won prizes in Derry against the competition of the Derry choirs – and that was a real achievement.

So for one, two, three, four years the nephew-and-uncle navigational co-operation worked well. The nephew had his days on the sand and in the sea. He even faced up to it with the expert swimmers at Roguey Rocks and the Horse Pool. By night while he waited until his uncle was ready to be steered back to the doss he drank gallons of lemonade and the like, and saw a lot of life. With the natural result that by the time the fifth summer came around, that summer when the winds were so contrary and the sea so treacherous that the priest was drowned in the Horse Pool, the nephew was developing new interests: he was looking around for the girls. At any rate, Bundoran or no Bundoran, he was growing up. Now this was a special problem because the schoolmaster from Knockatatawn had little time for girls, for himself or anybody else and, least of all, for his nephew who, in the fifth summer, had just passed thirteen.

One of the wonders of the day on which they helped the schoolmaster from Knockatatawn to the hotel and happed him safely into bed by four o'clock in the afternoon was that Hugh saw a woman, one of the Scotchies, swimming at her ease in the pool where the priest had been drowned. She was a white and crimson tropical fish, more blinding than the handsomest perch in the lake at Corcreevy or the Branchy Wood: white for arms, shoulders, midriff and legs; crimson for cap and scanty costume. Women were not supposed to be in the Horse Pool on any account but so soon after the drowning, the usual people were shunning it, and that woman either didn't know or didn't care. The Scotchies who came to the seaside to Bundoran in the summer had a great name for being wild.

In the hotel bedroom the sun came in as muted slanted shafts through the cane blinds. The shafts were all dancing dust. Carpet-sweepers weren't much in use in that hotel. They helped the wee man out of his grey sober clothes and into a brutal pair of blue-and-white striped pyjamas. He was a fierce hairy wee fellow. Arms long like an ape and a famous fiddler when he was sober. The big purple-faced schoolmaster from Lurganboy said: Begod, you're like a striped earthenware jar of something good.

The little man waved his arms and tried to sing and once slipped off the edge of the bed and sat on the floor and recited word-perfect:

> *A Chieftain to the Highlands bound*
> *Cries: Boatman, do not tarry,*
> *And I'll give thee a silver crown*
> *To row me o'er the ferry.*

The lot of it, every verse, all about how the waters wild swept o'er his child and how Lord Ullin's daughter and her lover were drowned. The drowning of the priest must have put it into his mind. The purple-faced man from Lurganboy, rocking a little, listened with great gravity, his head to one side, his black bushy eyes glistening, his thick smiling lips bedewed with malt. He said: In the training college he was renowned for his photographic memory. And for the fiddle.

Hugh said nothing. He was sick with delight. His uncle was a blue-and-white earthenware jar of Scotch whisky, as full as it could hold. He always drank Scotch in Bundoran, out of courtesy, he said, to the hundreds of Scotchies who came there every year on their holidays and spent good money in the country. The music of hurdy-gurdies and hobby-horses and the like came drifting to them from the strand, over the houses on the far side of the town's long street. This blessed day the blue-and-white jar could hold no more. He would sleep until tomorrow's dawn and Hugh was a free man, almost fourteen, and the world before him.

—He'll rest now, said the red-faced master from Lurganboy.

They tiptoed out of the room and down the stairs.

—What'll you do now, boy?

—Go for a walk.

—Do that. It's healthy for the young.

He gave Hugh a pound, taken all crumpled out of a trouser pocket. Then nimbly, for such a heavy man, he sidestepped into a raucous bar and the swinging doors, glass, brass and mahogany, closed behind him. It was an abrupt farewell yet Hugh was all for him, and not only because of the crumpled pound, but because in him, man to man and glass for glass, the schoolmaster from the Hill of the Conflagrations had for once taken on more than his match. Several times as they helped the little man towards his bed the unshakeable savant from Lurganboy had said to Hugh: Young man, you are looking at one who in his cups and in his declining years can keep his steps, sir, like a grenadier guard.

He had the map of his day already worked out in his head. The Scotchy girl wouldn't be sitting on the high windowsill until seven o'clock. She was there most evenings about that time. She and God knew how many other Scotchies, male and female, lived in a three-storeyed yellow boarding-house at the east end of the town. There was a garden in front of it, a sloping lawn but no fence or hedge, and the two oval flower-beds were rimmed with great stones, smoothed and shaped by the sea, tossed up on the beach at Tullaghan to the west, gathered and painted and used as ornaments by the local people. This Scotchy girl was one that liked attention. The way she went after it was to clamber out of a bedroom window on the third floor and to sit there for an hour or more in the evening kicking her heels, singing, laughing, pretending to fall, blowing kisses, and shouting things in unintelligible Scottish at the people in the street below, throwing or dropping things, flowers, chocolates, little fluttering handkerchiefs and once, he had heard, a pair of knickers. He had only seen her once at those capers when one evening he navigated past, tug before steamship, with his uncle in tow. But a fella he knew slightly told him she was to be seen there at that time most evenings. She sure as God was there to be seen. It wouldn't have been half the fun if she'd worn a bathing-suit, but a skirt with nothing underneath was something to tell the fellas about when he got back to Bomacatall. Not that they'd believe him, but still.

Behind her in the room there must have been thirty girls. They squealed like a piggery. That was a hell of a house. A randyboo, the wee master called it. Bomacatall, Knockatatawn and Corcreevy all combined never heard the equal of the noise that came out of that house. On the ground floor the piano always going, and a gramophone often at the same time, and a melodeon and pipes, and boozy male voices singing *Bonny Doon* and *Bonny Charlie's Noo Awa'* and *Over the Sea to Skye* and *Loch Lomond* and *The Blue Bells of Scotland* and *Bonny Strathyre* and *Bonny Mary of Argyle* and, all the time and in and out between everything else:

> *For I'm no awa tae bide awa,*
> *For I'm no awa tae leave ye,*
> *For I'm no awa tae bide awa,*
> *I'll come back an' see ye.*

—They work hard all year, the wee master said. In the big factories and shipyards of Glasgow. Then they play hard. They're entitled to it. The Scots are a sensitive generous people and very musical.

This was the map that was in Hugh's mind when the red- or purple-faced master from Lurganboy left him outside the swinging doors of the saloon bar. That Lurganboy man was a wonder to see at the drink. When he moved, Hugh thought, he should make a sound like the ocean surf itself with the

weight of liquid inside him. He had also said something remarkable and given Hugh a phrase to remember. For as they'd
steered the Knockatatawn man round a windy corner from the
promenade to the main street, a crowd, ten or eleven, of
Scotchy girls had overtaken them, singing and shouting,
waving towels and skimpy bathing-suits, wearing slacks and
sandals, bright blouses, short skirts, sweaters with sleeves knot-
ted round their waists and hanging over rumps like britchens
on horses.

—This town, said the master from Lurganboy, is hoaching
with women.

That was the northern word you'd use to describe the way
fingerlings wriggle over and around each other at the shallow
fringes of pools on blinding June days.

—Hoaching. Hoaching with women, Hugh said to himself as
he set out to follow the map he had drawn in his mind that
would bring him back at seven o'clock to the place where the
daft girl kicked her heels and more besides on the windowsill.

From the house of glass to the Nuns' Pool by way of the harbour where the fishing boats are. It isn't really a house of
glass. This shopkeeper has a fanciful sort of mind and has
pebbledashed the front wall of his place with fragments of
broken glass. The shop faces east, catching the morning sun,
the whole wall then lives and dances like little coloured tropical
fish frisking, hoaching, in a giant aquarium. Hugh can look
down on it from his window which is right on top of the hotel
across the street. Some people say the wall is beautiful. Some
people say the man is crazy. The seer from Knockatatawn says
that's the way with people.

Westward the course towards the Nuns' Pool. Passing the
place where the sea crashes right into the side of the street,
no houses here, and only a high strong wall keeps it from
splattering the traffic. Here in the mornings when the tide is
ebbed and the water quiet a daft old lady in a long dress walks
out along rocks and sand, out and out until she's up to her
neck in the water, dress and all, and only her head and wide-
brimmed straw hat to be seen. Then she comes calmly out
again and walks home dripping. Nobody worries or bothers

about her. The bay is her bath tub. She lives here winter and summer.

This day the harbour is empty, a few white sails far out on the bay, pleasure boats. He sits on the tip of the mole for a while and looks down into the deep translucent water. On the gravelly bottom there are a few dead discarded fish, a sodden cardboard box, and fragments of lobster claws turned white. If he could clamber around that sharp rock headland and around two or three more of the same he could peep into the Nuns' Pool and see what they're up to. Do they plunge in, clothes and all, like the mad woman in the morning? It's hard to imagine nuns stripping like the Scotchy in the pool where the priest was drowned. Surely the priests and the nuns should share the one pool and leave Roguey Rocks and the Horse Pool to the men and the wild Scotchies. The strand and the surf are for children and after five summers he knows he's no longer a child.

But he's also alone and he knows it. Tugging and steering his mighty atom of an uncle has taken up all his time and cut him off from his kind. On the clifftop path by the Nuns' Pool there are laughing girls by the dozen, and couples walking, his arm as tightly around her as if she has just fainted and he is holding her up. In corners behind sod fences there are couples asprawl on rugs or on the naked grass, grappled like wrestlers but motionless and in deep silence. Nobody pays the least attention to him. Fair enough, he seems to be the youngest person present. Anyone younger is on the sand or in the surf. Or going for rides on donkeys. He is discovering that, unless you're the tiniest bit kinky, love is not a satisfactory spectator sport.

Steep steps cut in rock go down to the Nuns' Pool. Was it called after one nun or gaggles of nuns, season after season? It must have been one horse. But what was a horse ever doing out there on rocks and seaweed and salt water? He sees as he walks a giant nun, a giant horse. The steep steps turn a corner and vanish behind a wall of rock as big as Ben Bulben mountain. Only God or a man in a helicopter could see what goes on in there. Do they swim in holy silence, praying perhaps, making aspirations to Mary the Star of the Sea? He listens for the sort of shouts and music and screaming laughs that come from the house where the girl sits on the windowsill. He hears nothing but the wash of the sea, the wind in the cliffside grass, the crying of the gulls. What would you expect? It is ten minutes to five o'clock.

He has time to walk on to the place where the Drowes river splits into two and goes to the sea over the ranked, sea-shaped stones of Tullaghan, to walk back to the hotel by the main road, feast on the customary cold ham and tomatoes and tea, bread and butter, wash his hands and face and sleek his hair with Brylcreem and part it up the middle, and still be on good time and in a good place for the seven o'clock show. He does all this. He is flat-footed from walking and a little dispirited. On the stony strand of Tullaghan there isn't even a girl to be seen. If there was he could draw her attention to the wonderful way the sea forms and places the stones, rank on rank, the biggest ones by the water line and matted with seaweed, the smallest and daintiest right up by the sand and the whistling bent-grass. They are variously coloured. The tide has ebbed. Far out the water growls over immovable stones.

He rests for a while by the two bridges over the Drowes river. If there was a girl there he could tell her how the river flows down from Lough Melvin, and how the trout in the lake and the trout in the river have the gizzards of chickens and how, to account for that oddity, there's a miracle story about an ancient Irish saint. There is no girl there. A passing car blinds him with dust. Has the evening become more chilly or is that just the effect of hunger? He accelerates. He knows that while a Scotchy girl might show some interest in stones shaped and coloured into mantelpiece or dressing-room ornaments, she would be unlikely to care much about trout or ancient miracles. In the hotel the master is sound asleep in blue-and-white bars, the bed-clothes on the floor. He doesn't snore. Hugh eats four helpings of ham and tomatoes, two for himself, two for the recumbent fiddler from the Hill of the Conflagrations.

The evening is still ahead of him and the fleshpots delectably steaming. There is no glitter from the house of glass. The hot tea and ham, the thought of the kicking girl on the high

windowsill have done him a lot of good. In the evening most of
the children will be gone from the strand, the Palais de Danse
warming up, the hoaching at its best.

He wasn't the only one watching for the vision to appear, and
right in the middle, like a gigantic rugby-football forward
holding together a monumental scrum, was the purple-faced
man from Lurganboy. The Assyrian, Hugh thought, came
down like a wolf on the fold and his cohorts were gleaming in
purple and gold. He wasn't his uncle's nephew for nothing,
even if he wasn't quite sure what a cohort meant. As he told me
long afterwards in the Branchy wood, or Corcreevy, if his
literary education had then advanced as far as *Romeo and Juliet*
he would have been able, inevitably, to say: But soft what light
through yonder window etc. The man with the face as purple
as cohorts saw it differently. To the men that ringed him
round he said: Lads, I declare to me Jasus, 'tis like Lourdes
or Fatima waiting for the lady to appear. All we lack is hymns
and candles.

—We have the hymns, one voice said, she has the candles.

—*Ave ave*, said another voice.

The laughter wasn't all that pleasant to listen to. They were
a scruffy enough crowd, Hugh thought, to be in the company
of a schoolmaster that had the benefit of education and the
best of training; the master from Bomacatall, kind as he was,
would have crossed the street if he'd seen them coming. Shiny
pointy toes, wide grey flannels, tight jackets, oiled hair; the
man from Lurganboy must, at last, like the stag at eve, have
drunk his fill or he wouldn't, surely to God, be in the middle
of them. Hugh dodged. There was a fine fat flowering bush,
white blossoms, bursting with sparrows when the place was
quiet, right in the middle of the sloping lawn. He put it between himself and the waiting watching crowd. His back was to
the bush. He was very close to the high yellow house. The din
was delightful, voices male and female, a gramophone playing
a military march, somebody singing that there are meadows in
Lanark and mountains in Skye – and he was thinking what a
wonderful people the Scots were and what a hell and all of a

house that must be to live in, when the high window went up
with a bang and there she was, quick as a sparrow on a branch,
but brighter, much brighter.

He had heard of a bird of paradise but never had he, nor
has he up to the present moment, seen one. But if such a bird
exists then its plumage would really have to be something to
surpass in splendour what Hugh, in the dying western evening, saw roosting and swinging on the windowsill. Far and
beyond Roguey Rocks the sun would be sinking in crimson.
The light came over the roofs of the houses across the street,
dazzled the windows, set the girl on fire. Long red hair, red
dress, pink stockings, red shoes with wooden soles. She was so
high up, the angle was so awkward, the late sunlight so daz-
zling, that he could find out little about her face except that it
was laughing. The scrum around the Lurganboy man cheered
and whistled. He knew she was laughing, too, because he could
hear her. She was shouting down to the Lurganboy contingent,
the *caballeros*, but because of the noise from the house and the
street he couldn't pick out any words and, anyway, she would
be talking Scottish. Nor could he be certain that he had been
correctly informed as to what, if anything, she wore underneath the red dress although when he got home to his peers in
McKattle's Hut or Bomacatall he sure as God wouldn't spoil a
good story by unreasonable doubts.

All told it was an imperfect experience. She twisted and
tacked so rapidly, agile as a monkey, that a man could see
nothing except crimson. He couldn't even have known that her
red shoes had wooden soles if it hadn't been that, with the dint
of kicking, one of them came unstuck, and landed as surely as
a cricket-ball in his cupped palms where he stood in hiding
behind the bush. It was in the pocket of his jacket before he
knew what he was doing. Cinderella lost her slipper. He was
off through the crowd in a second and nobody but the girl saw
him go. The eyes of Lurganboy and his men were on the
vision. She screamed high and long. From the far end of the
crowd he glanced back and saw her pointing towards him. But
nobody bothered to look the way she was pointing. The map
of his evening was as clear in his mind as the strand before

him, as sure as the shoe in his pocket, and hunt-the-slipper was a game at which anything might happen.

The people in this place have, like the tides, their own peculiar movement. Evening, as he expected, draws most of the children away from the strand to a thousand boarding-house bedrooms. The promise of the moon draws the loving couples, the laughing and shouting groups away from the westward walk by the Nuns' Pool to dry sheltered nooks between strand and dunes, to the hollows in the grassy tops of the high cliffs above Roguey, to the place where later the drums will begin to feel their way in the Palais de Danse. Every night, including Sunday, in the palais there is not only a dance but a few brawls and a talent competition.

No moon yet. No drums yet. The last red rays are drowned in the ocean. The light is grey. The strand is pretty empty and a little chilly, the sea is far out. But as he runs, ankle deep in churned sand, down the slope from the now silent motionless hobby-horses and hurdy-gurdies, he sees a slow, silent procession of people coming towards him around the jagged black corner of Roguey Rocks. The sea washes up almost around their feet. They step cautiously across a shelf of rock, then more rapidly and boldly along the slapping wet sand by the water's edge. Four men in the lead are carrying something. He runs towards them, all girls forgotten. Whatever chance, anyway, he had of meeting a girl during the day he can only have less now in this half-desolate place. The red shoe will be his only souvenir, yet still something to show to the heathens in Bomacatall. Halfways across the strand a distraught woman in shirt and cardigan, hair blowing wild stops him. She says: Wee boy, see if it's a wee boy with fair hair. He's missing for an hour and I'm distracted. Jesus, Mary and Joseph protect him. I'm afraid to look myself.

But it isn't a wee boy with fair hair. It isn't even the crimson-and-white Scotchy girl who had been swimming in the Horse Pool and whom the sea might have punished for sacrilege, for surely a dead drowned priest must make some difference to the nature of the water.

What he sees is nothing that you could exactly put a name to. The four men carry it on a door taken off its hinges. It's very large and sodden. There's nothing in particular where the face should be – except that it's very black. A woman looks at it and gasps. Somebody says: Cover that up, for God's sake.

A tall red-headed man throws a plastic raincoat over the black nothing in particular. Hugh walks back to the woman in the skirt and cardigan. He tells her that it isn't a wee boy with fair hair. She thanks God.

—It's a big person that must have been a long time in the water.

But she has moved away and isn't listening. He falls in at the tail of the procession. People leave it and join it, join it and leave it. It's a class of a funeral. An ambulance comes screaming down the slope from the long town and parks beside the stabled silent hobby-horses. Two civic guards come running, a third on a bicycle. Behind on the strand one single man in a long black coat walks, fearing no ghosts, towards Roguey Rocks. No couples or laughing groups are to be seen, even on the grassy clifftops. He fingers the shoe in his pocket to remind him of girls. A drum booms, a horn blares from the Palais de Danse which is halfways up the slope towards the town. He gets in, and for free, simply by saying that he's singing in Irish in the talent competition.

The hall was already crowded because the evening had turned chilly and the threat of rain was in the air. He found a seat in a corner near the ladies where he could watch the procession coming and going. They came and went in scores and for all the attention any of them paid to him he might have been invisible. He was grateful for the anonymity. He was too weary to carry on with the hopeless chase and that grim vision on the beach had given him other things to think about. It was still fun to sit and watch the women, all shapes and sizes and colours, and moods, They went in demure and came out giggling. That was because most of them, he had heard, kept noggins of gin and vodka concealed in the cloakroom. It was a great world and all before him. The band was thunderous, the floor more and more crowded until somebody thumped a gong and everybody who could find a chair sat down: girls who couldn't sitting recklessly on the knees of strangers, nobody on his. So he stood up and gave his chair to a girl who didn't even say thanks. The band vanished. A woman sat at the piano, a man with a fiddle and a young fellow with a guitar stood beside her. This was the talent competition.

A grown man long afterwards in the Branchy Wood, or Corcreevy, he couldn't remember much of it. The time was after eleven, he had been on foot all day, his eyes were closing with sleep. A man with long brown hair and long – the longest – legs and big feet came out, sang in a high nervous tenor about the bard of Armagh, then tripped over the music stand and fell flat on his face. That act was much appreciated. A little girl in a white frock and with spangles or something shining in her hair, tiptoed out, curtsied, holding the hem of her skirt out wide in her hands, danced a jig to the fiddle, then sang a song in Irish that meant: There are two little yellow goats at me, courage of the milk, courage of the milk. This is the tune that is at the piper, Hielan laddy, Hielan laddy. And more of the same. A fat bald man sang: While I'm jog jog jogging along the highway, a vagabond like me. Then there were tin whistles and concertinas, six sets of Scottish and two of Irish or Uillean pipes, piano accordions, melodeons, combs in tissue paper and clicking spoons, cornet, fiddle, big bass, drum, something, something and euphonium. As the song says.

He lost interest. His insteps ached. He would unnoticed have slipped away only a crowd and girls hoaching was always better than a lonely room. Surveying the crowd from China to Peru he saw in the far corner the man from Lurganboy, like the old priest Peter Gilligan, asleep within a chair, his legs out like logs, hands locked over splendid stomach and watch-chain and velvet waistcoat, chin on chest, black hat at a wild angle but bravely holding on to his head. No angels, as in the case of Peter Gilligan, hovered over him, none that Hugh could see. Five other adults sat in a row beside him, all awake except Lurganboy. Angels that around us hover, guard us till the close of day. Singing that, the Knockatatawn choir had once won a first prize in Derry city.

As Hugh watched, Lurganboy awoke, pulled in his legs, raised his head, gripped the arms of his chair and hoisted himself to sit erect. The ballroom was silent. Was it the oddness of the silence made the sleeper awake? No, not that, but something, Hugh felt, was going to happen. The drummer was back on the stage. He struck the drum a boom that went round the room, echoing, shivering slowly away. Then the compère said: Ladies and gentlemen.

He said it twice. He held up his right hand. He said again: Ladies and gentlemen, while the judges, including our old, true, tried and stalwart friend from Lurganboy are making up their minds, adding up points, assessing the vast array of talent, not to mention grace and beauty, we will meet again an old friend, a man who needs no introduction, a man who many a time and oft has starred on this stage and who, in days gone by but well remembered has worn more laurels for music than——

The cheers hit the roof, and out on the stage like a released jack-in-the-box stepped the wee master from Knockatatawn, sober as a judge, lively as a cricket, dapper as a prize greyhound, fiddle in one fist, bow in the other. When the cheering stopped he played for fifteen minutes and even the gigglers, resurfacing after gin and vodka, kept a respectful silence. Lord God Almighty, he could play the fiddle.

It could be that the way to get the women is to be a bachelor and play the fiddle, and drink all day and pay no attention to them. For I declare to God, the schoolmaster from Corcreevy said long afterwards. I never saw anything like it before or since, flies round the honeypot, rats round a carcase, never did I see hoaching like that hoaching, and in the middle of it and hopping about on the stage like a wound-up toy, a monkey on a stick, the red Scots girl from the windowsill, and her shoe in my pocket. Radar or something must have told her where it was. She saw me, isolated as I was, standing like a pillar-box in the middle of the floor, for the crowd was on the stage or fighting to get on the stage, and the drum was booming and the compère shouting and nobody listening. She came towards me slowly and I backed away and then ran for the beach, and then stopped. The moon was out between clouds. There was a mizzle of rain.

He stopped running and looked at the moon and the moonlight on the water. This was destiny and he had no real wish to run from it. The moon shines bright, on such a night as this. As he is now, a moonlit beach always reminds him of loneliness, a crowded beach of faceless death. She was a little monkey of a girl and she crouched her shoulders and stooped when she talked. Her red hair was down to her hips. She said: Wee laddie, will ye no gie me back ma shoe?

He was learning the language.

—I'm as big as ye are, yersel.

—Will ye no gie me back ma shoe?

She wasn't pleading. She wasn't angry. He knew by her big eyes that it was all fun to her, all part of the holiday. She wasn't any taller than himself and her foot fitted into his pocket.

—It's no here. It's in ma room.

—You'll bring it tae me.

—For sure. It's no awa tae bide away.

—Guid laddie. Do ye dance?

—Thon's my uncle wi' the fiddle.

—Ye're like him. Ye were quick away wi' ma shoe. I'll no tell him ye're here.

The red shoe was his ticket of admission to the wild happy house. Nothing much, naturally, came of that except a lot of singing and some kisses in the mornings from a sort of elder sister. He learned to talk and understand Scots and to this day, and in his cups, can sing that he's no awa tae bide awa with the best Glaswegian that e'er cam doon frae Gilmour hill. Like his uncle he enjoyed his double life. Not for years, though, not until he had been through college and had his own school, in Corcreevy or the Branchy Wood, did he tell the tale to the old man who by that time was retired and able to drink as he pleased. The old fellow, mellow at the time, laughed immoderately and said: Seemuldoon, I always hold, is a land of milk and honey if you keep your own bees and milk your own cow.

That was a favourite and frequently irrelevant saying of his. Seemuldoon, meaning the dwelling-place of the Muldoons,

Suidhe Maoldúin?

was, in all truth, the place he came from, and not Knockatatawn. Nor did the man from Lurganboy really come from Lurganboy: I used the name just because I like it, and when people ask me to go to Paris and places like that I say no, I'll go to Lurganboy. Because you don't *go* to Lurganboy, you find yourself there when you lose the road going somewhere else.

The Weavers at the Mill

BAXBAKUALANUXSIWAE, she said to herself as she walked by the sea, was one of the odd gods of the Kwakiutl Indians, and had the privilege of eating human flesh. That pale-faced woman with the strained polite accent would devour me if her teeth were sharp enough. She even calls me, intending it as an insult, Miss Vancouver, although she knows damned well in her heart and mind, if she has a heart, that I don't come from Vancouver.

She loved the vast flat strand, the distant sea, the wraith-like outline of rocky islands that looked as if they were sailing in the sky, the abruptness with which a brook cradled by flat green fields became a wide glassy sheet of water spreading out over the sand.

A thatched cottage, gable end to the inshore gales, was palisaded against the sea by trunks of trees driven deep into the sand. On the sea-front road that curved around the shanty village, wind and water had tossed seaweed over the wall so regularly that it looked like nets spread out to dry. All the young men she met on the road wore beards they had grown for the night's pageant: not the melancholy, wishy-washy, desiccated-coconut pennants of artistic integrity but solid square-cut beards or shaggy beards that birds could nest in. To walk among them was a bit like stepping back into some old picture of the time of Charles Stewart Parnell: stern men marching home to beleaguered cabins from a meeting of the Land League.

That woman would say: They are all so handsome.

She was long-faced, pale and languid, the sort of woman who would swoon with craven delight at the rub of a beard. Yet she could never persuade the old man to abandon his daily careful ritual with cut-throat razor, wooden soap bowl, the strop worn to a waist in the middle, the fragments of newspaper splattered with blobs of spent lather and grey stubble.

—Eamonn, she would say to her husband, if you'd only grow a beard you'd look like Garibaldi with his goats on the island of Caprera.

—I have no knowledge of goats. I'm not on my own island any more.

To the girl she would say: If your bags are packed I'll run you at any time to the station.

—My bags are always packed. There's only one of them. A duffle-bag, she'd answer. But if it doesn't inconvenience you too much I'd like to stay another day. There are a few details I want to fill in.

It needed nerve to talk to a woman like that in her own house. But what could the girl do when the old man was plaintively urging her not to go, not to go, pay no heed to her, stay another day.

They had breakfast in bed every day and lunch in their own rooms, and all the time until four in the afternoon free. It was in some ways the most relaxed life the girl had ever known. She had been there for a week since she had come from London across England, Wales, the Irish Sea and a part of Ireland, to write one more article in the magazine series that kept her eating. It was a series about little-known heroes of our time.

The woman had met her at the train. She drove a station-wagon piled high in the back with hanks of coloured wool. They drove round the village, foam glimmering in the dusk to their right hand, then across a humped five-arched stone bridge and up a narrow, sunken, winding roadway to the old Mill House in the middle of gaunt, grey, eyeless ruins where – above the river foaming down a narrow valley – two hundred men had worked in days of a simple local economy. Four grass-grown waterwheels rusted and rested for ever.

—Only my weavers work here now, she said. That's what the wool's for. Aran sweaters and belts – criosanna, they call them here – and scarves and cardigans. We sell them in the States where you come from.

She sounded as friendly as her over-refined, Henley-on-Thames voice could allow her to sound.

—Canada, the girl said. British Columbia. My father worked among the Kwakiutl Indians.

—Can't say I ever heard of them. What do they do?

—They were cannibals once. For religious reasons. But not any longer. They catch salmon. They sing songs. They carve totem poles. They weave good woollens, too. With simplified totem designs.

—How interesting.

The car went under a stone archway topped by a shapeless mass that she was to discover had once represented a re-arising phoenix – until rain and salt gales had disfigured it to a death deeper than ashes. They were in a cobbled courtyard and then in a garage that had once been part of a stables.

—You want to write about my husband's lifeboat exploits when he was an islandman.

—The famous one. I was asked to write about it. Or ordered. I read it up in the newspaper files. It was heroic.

She slung the duffle-bag over her shoulder and they walked towards the seven-windowed face of the old stone house. From the loft above the garage the clacking of looms kept mocking time to their steps. The woman said: Do you always dress so informally?

—I travel a lot and light. Leather jacket and corduroy slacks. You need them in my business. A protection against pinchers and pawsey men.

—You're safe here, said the woman. The men are quiet. All the young ones have just grown lovely beards for a parish masque or a pageant or something. You mustn't tire him too much. Sometimes he can get unbearably excited when he remembers his youth.

His youth, the girl reckoned, was a long time ago.

She spread out her few belongings between the old creaking mahogany wardrobe and the marble-topped dressing-table, and tidied herself for dinner, and remembered that she had left her typewriter, smothered in wool, in the station-wagon. The newspaper that had told her about the rescue had been fifty years old; and Eamonn, the brave coxswain and the leader of the heroic crew, had been then a well-developed man of thirty. The newsprint picture had faded, but not so badly that she couldn't see the big man, a head taller than any of his companions, laughing under his sou'wester with all the easy mirth of a man who had never yet been afraid.

From her bedroom window she could look down into the courtyard and see girls in blue overalls carrying armfuls of wool from the wagon up an outside wooden stairway to the weaving shed. The thatched roofs of the village were, from her height, like a flock of yellow birds nestling by the edge of the sea and, far across the water, the outlines of the islands of Eamonn's origin faded into the darkness, as distant and lost for ever as his daring youth and manhood. Yet she knew so little, or had reflected so little, on the transfiguring power of time that she was ill-prepared for the gaunt, impressive wreck of a man who came slowly into a dining-room that was elaborately made up to look like a Glocamorra farmhouse kitchen. He sat down on a low chair by the open hearth and silently accepted a bowl of lentil soup with fragments of bread softening in it. He didn't even glance at the low unstained oak table where the girl sat most painfully, on a traditional three-legged wooden chair. Dressed in black, her black hair piled on her head, her oblong face, by lamplight, longer and whiter than ever, the woman sat aloof at the head of the table. Two girls, daytime weavers magically transformed by the touch of the creeping dusk into night-time waitresses, blue overalls exchanged for dark dresses, white aprons, white collars, served the table; and a third stood like a nurse behind the old man's chair. He slopped with a spoon, irritably rejecting the handmaiden's effort to aid him. He recited to himself what was to the girl an unintelligible sing-song.

—Merely counting, the woman said. In Gaelic. One, two, three, and so on. He says it soothes him and helps his memory, I told him what you want. He'll talk when he's ready.

Suddenly he said: She cracked right across the middle, that merchant vessel, and she stuffed as full as a fat pig with the costliest bales of goods and furniture and God knows what. I can tell you there are houses on this coast but not out on the islands where the people are honest and no wreckers, and those houses are furnished well to this day on account of what the waves brought in that night.

The voice came out like a bell, defying and belying time, loud and melodious as when he must have roared over the billows to his comrades the time the ship cracked. Then he handed the empty soup bowl to the nervous weaver-handmaiden, sat up high in his chair, bade the girl welcome in Gaelic, and said to the woman: She's not one of the French people from the hotel.

—From London, said the woman.

—There's a fear on the people in the village below that there won't be a duck or a hen or any class of a domestic fowl left alive to them with the shooting of these French people. The very sparrows in the hedges and God's red robins have no guarantee of life while they're about. They came over in the beginning for the sea-angling and, when they saw all the birds we have, nothing would satisfy them but to go home to France for their guns. They say they have all the birds in France shot. And the women with them are worse than the men.

—*Les femmes de la chasse*, said the woman.

—Patsy Glynn the postman tells me there's one six feet high with hair like brass and legs on her like Diana and wading boots up to her crotch. God, Pats said to me, and I agreed, the pity Eamonn, you're not seventy again, or that the Capall himself is dead and in the grave. He'd manipulate her, long legs and boots and all.

—Our visitor, said the woman, is not here to write about the Capall.

—Then, girl from London, 'tis little knowledge you have of writing. For there have been books written about men that weren't a patch on the Capall's breeches. A horse of a man and a stallion outright for the women. That was why we called him the Capall.

With a raised right hand and cracking fingers the woman had dismissed the three girls. This was no talk for servants to hear.

—That John's Eve on the island, the night of the bonfires and midsummer, and every man's blood warm with poteen and porter in Dinny O'Brien's pub. Dinny, the old miser that he was, serving short measure and gloating over the ha'pennies. But, by God, the joke was on him and didn't we know it. For wasn't the Capall in the barn-loft at the back of the house with Dinny's young wife that married him for money, for that was all Dinny had to offer. She had to lie down for two days in bed, drinking nothing but milk, after the capers of the Capall and herself in the loft. He walked in the back door of the bar, his shirt open to the navel, no coat on him and the sweat on him like oil. Two pints he drank and saw for the first time the new barmaid, a niece of Dinny, that had come all the way from Cork City, and the fat dancing on her and her dress thin. So he lifted the third pint and said: *Dhia! Is trua nach bhfuil dara bud ag duine.*

Feeling that she did understand, and close to coarse laughter, the girl said that she didn't understand. Coldly and precisely the woman said: To put it politely he regretted that he was merely one man, not two.

—But he saved my life did the Capall. For the gale swept us, and the eight men we took off the broken vessel, eastwards before it to a port in Wales. There was no turning back in the teeth of it. There we were trying to moor the boat by the mole in another country when, with weariness and the tossing of the water, didn't I slip and go down between the wall and the boat, to be crushed, sure as God, if the Capall hadn't hooked his elbow in mine and thrown me back into the boat the way a prize wrestler would. Remember that bit, girl, when you write the story, and thank God you never met the Capall on a lonely road. He came from a place called the Field of the Strangers that was the wildest place on the whole island. From the hill above it you could see the wide ocean all the way to Africa, and the spray came spitting in over the roofs of the little houses, and the salt burned the grass in the fields. There was no strand in it, no breakwater, no harbour or slip for boats. Nothing man ever built could stand against that ocean. You held the currach steady and leaped into it from a flat rock as you shot out to sea. But there were men of strength and valour reared there who could conquer valleys before them and throw sledge-hammers over high houses. Dried sea bream we ate, boiled or roasted over hot sods, the strongest sweetest food in the world. And rock birds taken in nets where they'd nest in the clefts of the cliffs. Bread and tea for a treat, and potatoes boiled or brusselled in the griosach.

The woman explained: Roasted in the hot peat ashes.

—Then a cow might break a leg in a split in the rocks and have to be destroyed. A black disaster in one way. But in another way a feast of fresh meat and liver with the blood running out of it, food for men. All out of tins nowadays, and nobody has his own teeth.

The woman said: You were, Eamonn, talking about the lifeboat.

—Good for its own purpose the lifeboat, he said. But you couldn't feel the heart of the sea beating in it as you could in the canvas currach. We had one fellow with us that night who always had ill luck with currachs. Three of them he lost, and once he nearly lost his life. So we put him in the crew of the lifeboat to break his ill-fortune, and the trick worked. It could be that the sea didn't recognise him in his new yellow oilskins. Three days in that Welsh town we sweated in kneeboots and oilskins, having nothing else to wear, and the gales blowing in against us all the time. But the welcome we got. Didn't a deputation of ladies come to us with a white sheet of cloth to draw our names on, so that they could embroider our names for ever on the flag of the town's football team. Didn't the Capall write himself down as Martin McIntyre the Horse. There was the laughing, I can tell you, when the ladies wanted us to tell them why we put the title of the horse on Martin. They made heroes out of us. It was a sea-going town and there wasn't a woman in it hadn't a son or a husband or a lover on the salt water.

The attendant girls had come back silently. His great head, shaggy with uncombed white hair, sank down. With a napkin one of the girls mopped a splatter of soup from the green leather zipper jacket and, startlingly, with the yeeow of a shout a young fellow would give at a country dance, he came awake and slapped her buttocks before she could leap, laughing and blushing, and seemingly well used to the horseplay, out of his reach. The woman looked at the servant and then at her food. She said: Don't tire yourself.

—Never saw the tired day, he said, that the smell of a young girl wouldn't put life into me.

—Tell me more, said the girl, about the sea.

—What would you want to know about the sea and you from the smoky heart of London?

—I'm not from London.

—From Canada, said the woman. Her girlhood companions were cannibalistic Indians.

—On an island, the girl said.

He was wide awake, and interested, and upright. How tall he was when he sat up straight.

—Tell me, he said, about your wild Indians and your island.

Because he had hard blue eyes with a compelling icy light in them, and because for her benefit he had so carefully dredged his memory, she wanted to tell him. She wanted to tell him even more because as soon as he showed interest she had sensed the first stirrings of antagonism in the woman.

—Eamonn, the woman said, our guest may be tired.

—Tell me a little, he said. It's lucky to begin a story by lamplight.

—Nothing much to tell, she said. Don't think of me as sitting in the middle of a pack of noble savages, chewing on a hunk of Tyee salmon while they ate long pig. I didn't grow up with drums and war chants throbbing around me. I was some miles distant, on the other side of the hill. Of course I had plenty of contact with the confused no-man's-land Indian that the white man has made. Studied their history and sociology at college. But when I was a little girl the closest I got to them was to run to the top of the hill and peep down through cedar branches at the noble Indians pulling the guts out of salmon. Sounds bitter I know. But beauty and nobility had left them for a long while. And in our village the groups were so divided that not even the minds of the children could meet. When I was a girl I remember trying to get a little Indian girl to tell me some of her words. She stayed sullen and very silent. Then finally she and her little friend giggled and spat out one word. Matsooie – that was what it sounded like. I found out later that she had simply been saying: what's the matter with you? It was a rebuff.

—It's sad, he said, when people don't understand you, no matter what you do or try to do. We'll talk more tomorrow, girl, when you've rested after your journey.

—I've talked too much, she said. I came to listen to you.

He rose alertly when she passed him and shook her hand in a solemn old-fashioned way. He belonged to a time when men shook hands elaborately at every meeting and parting.

Later – very much later – she thought drowsily that she heard his slow tread on the old creaking stairs, his coughing in the next room as he lay down on his bed; and far away the faint sound of the sea along the shore and around the islands.

She carried two notebooks always in the right-hand pocket of her leather jacket.

All women, said the hopeful man she had met on the Irish Mail, are lascivious.

One of the notebooks was paper-backed, spined with spiral wire, and with tear-out leaves. It was for ephemera and temporalities – in other words, her work. The other book was stiff-backed, with stable, ruled leaves for the recording of the experiences she would use when the day would come and she'd sit down really to write. The stiff-backed book had another quality: it kept the weaker member straight in her jacket pocket, for she found nothing more maddening than note-taking on a page that was bent like a crescent.

The people she met she divided into two classes: tear-outs or stiff-backs.

This wonderful old man, an aged hero recalling islands, immured here by a female dragon, was as notable a stiff-back as she had ever encountered.

When the clacking of looms awoke her in the morning, she sat up in bed and reached for ball-point and stiff-back where she had left them in readiness on the bedside table. Or was it the looms had awakened her, or the purring of the motor-car engine in the cobbled yard, or the morning coughing of the old giant in the next room? For an ancient stone house, she thought, the walls were thin. But then she studied the slant of the ceiling, and realised that her room was only half a room and that the sound of coughing came to her, not through old stone, but through a wooden partition. She went to the window and looked out at three of the blue weaving girls walking in single file from the station-wagon to the weaving shed and carrying hanks of coloured wool: obedient African kraal girls with burdens on their heads and disciplined by some wrinkled Zulu queen. Then the woman drove away under the faceless phoenix. When the girl was settled back in bed again, he spoke to her through the wall: I can hear you're awake. Has she driven off to do the shopping?

—Good morning, she said. She's driven off somewhere.

—Good morning to you, girl. Did you sleep well?

Her answer was lost in a fit of his coughing, and when his throat had cleared again, he said: No more rising with the lark for me. Nor the seagull itself. I'm old and lazy now. But I mind my father, the oldest day he was, walking barefoot in the dawn, the old greasy sailor's cap on his head, to the flagstone at the corner of the house, to look at the sea and the surf on the white strand, to sniff the wind and to tell the weather for the day to come. He had his own teeth to the age of ninety. If he was inland and far from the sea, he could tell by the smell of the wind whether the tide was ebbing or flowing. But it wasn't often he went inland, and he was never happy in an offshore wind.

This was the most wonderful way in the world to conduct an interview. The metallic voice came muted, but clear, through the timber. The looms, the sea, and the river made their noises. The wind muttered around grey stone. She could sit snug in bed, both notebooks open, and make notes at her ease without embarrassing her subject.

—Tell me more, she said.

He said: Tell me about your wild Indians.

So to entice him to talk, she talked about Quathiaski Cove at the mouth of the river, and about the wits among the Scots and Irish settlers who nicknamed it Quart of Whiskey Cove, about the great argonauts of salmon homing up the Campbell River, about people of many nations, Scots, Swedes, Irish, Indians, Chinese, Japanese, living in one way or another on the rich red body of the salmon.

—The very air in that place smells of salmon. When my mother first took me to visit Vancouver I thought there was something wrong with the place, something missing. Finally she told me I felt that way because I could no longer smell the salmon.

—Like myself, he said, when I came here with her. This far inland you can't sniff the salt properly.

—And tell me about their songs, he said. In my days on the island there were sweet singers and old men who could tell stories to last the night.

So, for his sake, she remembered that when she had been a little girl she had sneaked out one night to listen to the singing of the Indians. One song particularly stayed in her memory. Years afterwards, when she and her people had long left the place, she went north by boat with her father to revisit the haunts of her childhood. To one old noble chieftain she spoke of the songs – and of that special song. He answered her about all the forms of songs: morning songs, harvest songs, giving songs to be chanted at the potlatch when a man gave all he had to his neighbours, gambling songs, lullabies. And song after song he sang until she stopped him and said: That's it. That's the song I loved when I was a little girl.

Then, with tears in his eyes, the old chieftain said: That's my gambling song, written for me by my own songwriter.

Her story faded into coughing that rattled the partition between them. Later he said in a hoarse carrying whisper: Don't go away soon, girl. Stay as long as you can whether she wants you to or not.

It wasn't easy to think of any response.

—She doesn't like strangers about the place. She's cold, God help her, and has no failte in her. Even when I was married to my first wife, and herself only a stranger visiting the islands, she was always jealous to find me in the middle of a crowd.

—You were married before?

—To a woman of my own people. And year after year her-

self came as a tourist until my wife died. Then I went away
with her and we were married in London. A watery class of a
wedding they give you in cities. It wasn't love, as they call it.
She was too grand for that. But she was there always – and
willing. The islands do something to visiting women. And with
creams and perfumes and the best clothes out of the London
shops she was different from any woman I'd ever smelled or
seen. You know how it is with a strong imaginative young
fellow, and he only a few months married.

—I can guess, she said. Some minor poet said something
about white arms beckoning all around him.

—Minor or major he was poet enough to know what he was
talking about. We haven't slept heads on one pillow for twenty
years now, but in secret corners in those old days we'd play
hide and seek in our pelt on the bare rocks – when it was a sin
moreover. And look at me now, here, wrapped in coloured
wool, and broken in health, and surrounded by stupid women,
weaving.

Propped by pillows, and taking notes, she squatted like a
tailor, and made up her mind. She would stay a week if she
could, just to please the old man and – her blood warming to
the conflict – to spite that cold dried fish of a woman. In his
youth, to judge by his talk, the old man had eaten better.

When he heard the station-wagon returning he said: I'll
doze for a while now. She wouldn't like to hear us talking
through the wall. She was hinting last night she'd run you to
the station for the late train. But don't go, don't go, stay as long
as you can.

They had a week of mornings together talking through the
wall. Reading her notes afterwards she found that morning
mingled with morning. One morning, though, was distinct
because it had been a morning of gale and rain. The coy
red-and-purple blossoms were being whipped off the tormented fuchsia bushes, and when she stepped out for her
daily walk – the sea was too tossed for a swim – the sand and
salt were in her eyebrows and gritting between her teeth.
Bloated by a night of rain the brown mad river bellowed

around the dead millwheels and, for once, the clack, the mocking one-two-three of the looms couldn't be heard.

Through the wall and the frequent fits of coughing he had said to her: I've grown younger since you came. A gift to me from the god of the sea himself, a beautiful young girl from a far island.

As a clergyman's daughter, the object of as many jokes as an Aberdonian, she was calmly aware of her looks: neither better nor worse than they were. She laughed. She said: I've a nose like a pack saddle, and a square face and freckles, although they tell me I've honest eyes.

—But you're young, he said.

After a silence she heard his dry choking laughter: There's a lump on my own nose still where I had it broken and I no more than a boy. The way it happened is a story will tickle you. There was this free and easy girl, a rare thing on the islands I can tell you – with the close way we lived. She wasn't an island girl, whatever. She came from the mainland in the tourist season and, as the song says, her stockings were white and you'd love to be tickling her garter, even if she was no better than a servant-maid in a lodging-house. This evening weren't we lined up to see her, like penitents going to confession, at the bottom of the orchard behind the house she worked in, and when Pat's Jameseen stepped out of his fair place in the line to go ahead of me, I fought him and, although he cracked my nose, hammered him back.

The dry laughter went on, choking now not with phlegm but with remembered devilment.

—That was the way with me when I was young. A chieftain among my own people, like your fine Indian, and respected by all. Then when my first woman died I never wanted to see the islands again. The English woman had it easy to carry me to the smoke of London where, as God is my judge, I came near to choking. The islands pulled at me again, even though I got only this far and no farther. Old as I am, I think at times I'll take a boat and return. But they don't want me any more since I married a stranger, and grew grand, and left.

—It would be fun, said the girl, if we could go to an island I know in Spain. Life is simple and gentle there, and the food good, cooked over an open fire. Some rough wine, wild and coarse, but with a kind flavour. A little music and reading and story-telling by lamplight, and water all around.

—That would be a holiday to remember, he said.

With the gale that morning they didn't hear the station-wagon returning, and it was the woman opening the door of the old man's room that interrupted them. Afterwards, while the old man slept, she said, over black coffee, to the girl: Any time you're ready I'll run you to the station.

A conflict like this was, in some ways, worse than blows or eye-scratching. As steadily as she could the girl said: If it doesn't upset your arrangements too much I'd love to see the pageant. It would add colour to the story.

—Colour, the woman said. Well, the beards, yes. Please yourself. But don't talk to the girls so much. It holds them up at their work. They lose. I lose. They're paid by piece-work.

Walking out into the gale the girl, for the sake of peace and the old man, avoided the weaving-shed where, she had been glad to think, the sullen faces of the underpaid weavers brightened when she entered. She loved the soft coloured wool, the intricacies of warping mills and heddles, the careful spacing of the threads. When you looked at the process you were as much part of it as the wool winder and the sound of the looms was comforting, not mocking.

In the hotel bar the French hunters, driven in by the tempest that had also driven the birds to shelter, clustered around Diana who wore tight red pants and sneakers. Through a red beard like a burning bush the barman told her how five years ago the old man had run amok: Terrified the bloody country for a week. Wandering around with a loaded shotgun. Shooting and spearing salmon in the pool below the old mill. Then pleurisy laid him low and he was never the same again. Out on the islands they're savages. Half-crazy with inbreeding.

The raised wind-driven sea was sucking around the tree trunks that palisaded the white cottage. She walked, fighting the gale, along the thin line of sand the water had not devoured.

Baxbakualanuxsiwae, she recalled, shared his house with his

wife, Qominoqa, a frightful female who cooked his ghoulish meals. A female slave, Kinqalalala, rounded up victims and collected corpses, well-hung meat in the house of the gods.

The thunder of the waves made her want to run and shout. One Sunday morning the small, deep-toned drums of the potlatch had set the whole village vibrating, until her father was forced to abandon his pulpit and say with a good humour more than Christian: Let us marvel at the force of tradition which is also one of the works of the Lord.

Once, in one of the books in her father's library, she had read that the Dinka people of the southern Sudan had a special sort of priest known as Masters of the Fishing Spear. These men, if they had great names as heroes, could be honourably killed when old and failing, by being buried alive at their own request and before all their assembled kin.

The islands, lost in spume and low-running clouds, were not to be seen.

In the dusk the bearded young men came in twos and threes under the featureless phoenix, across the courtyard, out by another gateway at the back of the weaving-shed, and up the hill to the mounded rath that was to be the open-air, torch-lit stage for their pageant. They wore white shirts and saffron kilts, cowskin pampooties made on the islands and dyed all colours, and thick woollen stockings cross-gartered to the knees. Most of them carried long wooden spears with silvered cardboard heads, and cardboard shields bright with brassy tacks. Some of them carried and some of them even played the bagpipes.

The blue weaving girls gathered on the landing outside the door of the shed, and cat-called, and addressed the bearded heroes by their ordinary everyday names and nicknames. They asked with irony if the men were going to the wars or to stick flounder on the flat sands with the flowing tide. When one bandy-legged, hairy-kneed veteran tottered past carrying a huge harp, and preceded by the curate who was directing the pageant, the blue girls held each other up, embracing in paroxysms and pantomimes of suppressed mirth.

—Never yet, the old man said, did I hear tell of one of these pageants that wasn't a holy laugh in the end. The Orangemen in the North, they say, had a pageant about the landing of King Billy in Carrickfergus harbour. But the sea was choppy that day and the boat tilted and didn't his majesty land on his arse in the water. And in Straide in Mayo they had a pageant about the eviction of the family of Michael Davitt who founded the Land League. But they built the mock cabin so strong that all the guns of Germany, let alone the battering rams of the boys who were pretending to be the bailiff's men, couldn't knock it down. Still and all, for the laugh, we'll go up to the rath and drink porter and eat pork sausages with the rest. It'll be a fine night with a full moon.

—At your age, Eamonn, that's the worst thing you could do.

—At my age?

He tossed aside the blackthorn he leaned on and, on the flat flag at the door of the house, hopped, but stiffly, from one foot to the other.

—These days I'm a two-year-old. The Indian maiden here will lead me up the slope. Minnehaha.

The woman's eyelids came down – it seemed one after the other, and very deliberately – to hide her eyes.

—Please yourself, then. Those girls have wasted enough time. I'll go up later with coffee and sandwiches.

His arm was around the girl's shoulders as they walked up a twisting boreen towards bonfires reddening in the dusk.

—Kings lived on this high hill, he said. All gone now, and dead and buried, generations of ancient kings, but the mounds and the ramparts are as solid as the day they were raised.

For one night, she thought, the kings had returned. She sat beside him on a rug on the mound. They were sheltered by a blossoming whitethorn from the light seawind. She held his hand. A huge round moon was motionless in a cloudless sky. Under its influence, and in the glow of a dozen bonfires, the bearded, cross-gartered country boys, the one decrepit harper, were no longer comic.

It was a masque, not a pageant. In a hut in a forest a dozen old broken men, remnants of a beaten clan, waited sadly and with little hope for the fulfillment of a prophecy that told of the coming of a young hero to lead them back to victory.

—This, said the oldest of them, is the last day of the year of our foretold salvation, and the last hour of the last day, yet the prophecy still stands even if it was made by one of the faery women who make game of men.

Her own old man moved closer to her on the rug.

The blue girls were just ending the long day's weaving. The coffee and sandwiches, and the woman with them, were still a good hour away; and also the thought that her duffle-bag and typewriter had been stored, for simpler departure, in the hotel with the red-bearded barman. She felt a brute, but she had a job to do – such as it was – and an old man's dream couldn't go on for ever, nor could she any longer defy a woman who didn't want her about the place.

When he pressed her hand she returned the pressure. She felt the great bones from which the flesh had melted away. She could have wept.

—The pity, he said, I didn't meet you when I was a young blade.

—I wasn't born then.

—We'd have found our own island and lived on it.

—There was a Japanese poet, she said, who was born in 1911, the year after Halley's Comet. He reckoned with a sad heart that he'd never see the comet since it wouldn't come again until 1986. That it was the same case with human encounters. His true friend would appear after his death. His sweetheart had died before he was born.

—A fine young man there, he said.

For who should arrive at that moment but the red barman himself, striding from darkness into the glare of the fires. Spear on shoulder. With the firelight glinting in his bush of a beard he could only be the hero who was promised. The crowds, seated on the slopes of the rath, cheered him. He was a popular man. For the broken old men he brought venison from the forest, cakes impaled on spears, and rolling barrels of ale from an enemy fortress he had that day captured single-handed. Also a sackful of golden goblets, made out of cardboard, and all the tokens, including a severed head in a sack, to prove he was the man of destiny. The exigencies of the drama did not, mercifully, call for the production of the severed head.

Then the harper harped on his harp and, far away in the

shadows, the pipers played, slowly advancing towards the circle of fires to show that they were an army of young men following their unique leader. The watching crowds broke up into groups to eat sausages and pig's feet and to drink porter. The dancing began on the rough dry grass. Led by two of the pipers, the dancers moved to find a better surface between the weaving-shed and the millhouse. Then the woman was there, and the curate with her helping her to carry cups and sandwiches and the coffee pot.

—Not pig's feet, Eamonn. Not all that greasy fat.

—'Tisn't often now I have a night out under the moon.

—A midsummer night, she said. Madness.

—I could leap through bonfires, woman. I feel like twenty. Pour milk on the ground for the good people who lived here before kings were heard tell of. It's not lucky to let them go hungry.

—What silly waste, the woman said.

Slowly the girl tilted her cup and let the coffee drain down to the grass. She said: They might fancy coffee.

His great hand was in the bowl of brown sugar and the fistful he took he tossed into the air, scattering it over the crowd. Faces, some laughing, some curious, turned towards them in the firelight.

—The world knows, he said, that the good people have a sweet tooth. Halley's Comet, Minnehaha, will come again.

They laughed loudly together. She noticed that they were again hand in hand. The curate, pretending to answer a call from one of the bearded men, moved away. The woman poured more coffee. By the farthest fire the girl saw the red man standing and beckoning. He probably had notions above his state in life, but he could give her a lift to the nearest town, and her leather jacket was stout enough to resist even the paws and the pinches of a man mentioned in prophecy. When the barman moved off down the slope towards the millhouse, she excused herself.

—Come back soon Minnehaha, the old man called after her. Don't delay. It's a fine night for seeing comets.

—Eamonn, isn't it time you went in out of the night air?

Like in movies about Italy, the girl thought, everything ends with a carnival. She walked down the slope, taking his second youth with her, towing the sailing islands behind her. She was the sea receding for ever from a stranded master of the sea.

By torchlight in the cobbled courtyard blue weaving girls danced with bearded warriors who had cast aside their spears.

She walked on under the stone phoenix that could never arise again because it had merely decayed, never been purified by fire and burned to ashes.

With car, duffle-bag and typewriter, the red barman was waiting. She sat beside him and was driven off to find her next little-known hero.

Maiden's Leap

HE CIVIC GUARD, or policeman, on the doorstep was big, middle-aged, awkward, affable. Behind him was green sunlit lawn sloping down to a white horse-fence and a line of low shrubs. Beyond that the highway, not much travelled. Beyond the highway, the jetty, the moored boats, the restless lake-water reflecting the sunshine.

The civic guard was so affable that he took off his cap. He was bald, completely bald. Robert St. Blaise Macmahon thought that by taking off his cap the civic guard had made himself a walking, or standing, comic comment on the comic rural constable, in the Thomas Hardy story, who wouldn't leave his house without his truncheon: because without his truncheon his going forth would not be official.

Robert St. Blaise Macmahon felt like telling all that to the civic guard and imploring him, for the sake of the dignity of his office, to restore his cap to its legal place and so to protect his bald head from the sunshine which, for Ireland, was quite bright and direct. Almost like the sun of that autumn he had spent in the Grand Atlas, far from the tourists. Or the sun of that spring when he had submitted to the natural curiosity of a novelist, who was also a wealthy man and could afford such silly journeys, and gone all the way to the United States, not to see those sprawling vulgar cities, Good God sir no, nor all those chromium-plated barbarians who had made an industry out of writing boring books about those colossal bores, Yeats and Joyce, but to go to Georgia to see the Okefenokee Swamp which interested him because of those sacred drooping melancholy birds, the white ibises, and because of the alligators. Any day in the year give him, in preference to Americans, alligators. It could be that he made the journey so as to be able at intervals to say that.

But if he talked like this to the bald guard on the ancestral doorstep the poor devil would simply gawk or smirk or both and say: Yes, Mr. Macmahon. Of course, Mr. Macmahon.

Very respectful, he would seem to be. For the Macmahons counted for something in the town. His father's father had as good as owned it.

The fellow's bald head was nastily ridiculously perspiring. Robert St. Blaise Macmahon marked down that detail for his notebook. Henry James had so wisely said: Try to be one of those on whom nothing is lost.

Henry James had known it all. What a pity that he had to be born in the United States. But then, like the gentleman he was, he had had the good wit to run away from it all.

The bald perspiring cap-in-hand guard said: Excuse me, Mr. Macmahon. Sorry to disturb you on such a heavenly morning and all. But I've come about the body, sir.

Robert St. Blaise Macmahon was fond of saying in certain circles in Dublin that he liked civic guards if they were young, fresh from the country, and pink-cheeked; and that he liked Christian Brothers in a comparable state of development. In fact, he would argue, you came to a time of life when civic guards and Christian Brothers were, apart from the uniforms, indistinguishable. This he said merely to hear himself say it. He was much too fastidious for any fleshly contact with anybody, male or female. So, lightly, briefly, flittingly, trippingly, he now amused himself with looking ahead to what he would say on his next visit to town: Well if they had to send a guard they could have sent a young handsome one to enquire about the...

What the guard had just said now registered and with a considerable shock. The guard repeated: About the body, sir. I'm sorry, Mr. Macmahon, to disturb you.

—What body? Whose body? What in heaven's name can you mean?

—I know it's a fright, sir. Not what you would expect at all. The body in the bed, sir. Dead in the bed.

—There is no body in my bed. Dead or alive. At least not while I'm up and about. I live here alone, with my housekeeper, Miss Hynes.

—Yes, Mr. Macmahon, sir. We know Miss Hynes well. Very highly respected lady, sir. She's below in the barracks at the moment in a terrible state of nervous prostration. The doctor's giving her a pill or an injection or something to soothe her. Then he'll be here directly.

—Below in the barracks? But she went out to do the shopping.

—Indeed yes, sir. But she slipped in to tell us, in passing, like, sir. Oh it's not serious or anything. Foul play is not suspected.

—Foul what? Tell you what?

—Well, sir.

—Tell me, my good man.

—She says, sir, there's a man dead in her bed.

—A dead man?

—The very thing, Mr. Macmahon.

—In the bed of Miss Hynes, my housekeeper.

—So she says, sir. Her very words.

—What in the name of God is he doing there?

—Hard to say, Mr. Macmahon, what a dead man would be doing in a bed, I mean like in somebody else's bed.

With a huge white linen handkerchief that he dragged, elongated, out of a pants pocket, and then spread before him like an enveloping cloud, the guard patiently mopped his perspiration: Damned hot today sir. The hottest summer, the paper says, in forty years.

The high Georgian-Floridian sun shone straight down on wine-coloured swamp-water laving (it was archaic but yet the only word) the grotesque knobbly knees of giant cypress trees. The white sacred crook-billed birds perched gravely, high on grey curved branches above trailing Spanish moss, oh far away, so far away from this mean sniggering town and its rattling tongues. It was obvious, it was regrettably obvious, that the guard was close to laughter.

—A dead man, guard, in the bed of Miss Hynes, my house-keeper, and housekeeper to my father and mother before me, and a distant relative of my own.

—So she tells us, sir.

—Scarcely a laughing matter, guard.

—No, sir. Everything but, sir. It's just the heat, sir. Overcome by the heat. Hottest summer, the forecast says, in forty years.

That hottest summer in forty years followed them, panting, across the black and red flagstones of the wide hallway. A fine mahogany staircase went up in easy spirals. Robert St. Blaise Macmahon led the way around it, keeping to the ground floor. The guard placed his cap, open end up, on the hall stand, as reverently as if he were laying cruets on an altar, excusing himself, as he did so, as if the ample mahogany hall stand, mirrored and antlered, were also a Macmahon watching, or reflecting, him with disapproval. It was the first time he or his like ever had had opportunity or occasion to enter this house.

In the big kitchen, old-fashioned as to size, modern as to fittings, the hottest summer was a little assuaged. The flagstones were replaced by light tiles, green and white, cool to the sight and the touch. She had always held on to that bedroom on the ground floor, beyond the kitchen, although upstairs the large house was more than half empty. She said she loved it because it had french windows that opened out to the garden. They did, too. They would also give easy access for visitors to the bedroom: a thought that had never occurred to him, not once over all these years.

Earlier that morning she had called to him from the kitchen to say that she was going shopping, and had made her discreet escape by way of those windows. They still lay wide open to the garden. She was a good gardener as she was a good house-keeper. She had, of course, help with the heavy work in both cases: girls from the town for the kitchen, a healthy young man for the garden. All three, or any, of them were due to arrive, embarrassingly, within the next hour. Could it be the young man for the garden, there, dead in the bed? No, at least, thank God, it wasn't her assistant gardener, a scape-grace of a fellow that might readily tempt a middle-aged woman. She hadn't stooped to the servants. She had that much Macmahon blood in her veins. This man was, or had been, a stranger, an older man by far than the young gardener. He was now as old as he would ever be. The hottest summer was heavy and odorous in the garden, and flower odours and insect sounds came to them in the room. The birds were silent. There was also the other odour: stale sweat, or dead passion, or just death? The guard sniffed. He said: He died sweating. He's well tucked in.

Only the head was visible: sparse grey hair, a few sad pimples on the scalp, a long purple nose, a comic Cyrano nose. Mouth and eyes were open. He had good teeth and brown eyes. He looked, simply, surprised, not yet accustomed to wherever he happened to find himself.

—Feel his heart, guard.

—Oh dead as mutton, Mr. Macmahon. Miss Hynes told no lie. Still, he couldn't die in a better place. In a bed, I mean.

—Unhouselled, unappointed, unannealed.

—Yes, sir, the guard said, every bit of it.

—I mean he died without the priest.

With something amounting almost to wit – you encountered it in the most unexpected places – the guard said that taking into account the circumstances in which the deceased, God be merciful to him, had passed over, he could hardly have counted on the company of a resident chaplain. That remark could be adopted as one's own, improved upon, and employed on suitable occasions and in the right places, far from this town and its petty people.

—Death, said the guard, is an odd fellow. There's no being up to him, Mr. Macmahon. He can catch you unawares in the oddest places.

This fellow, by heaven, was a philosopher. He was, for sure, one for the notebook.

—Quite true, guard. There was a very embarrassing case involving a president of the great French Republic. Found dead in his office. He had his hands in the young lady's hair. They had to cut the hair to set her free.

—Do you tell me so, sir? A French president? 'Twouldn't be the present fellow, de Gaulle, with the long nose would be caught at capers like that.

—There was a Hemingway story on a somewhat similar theme.

—Of course, sir. You'd know about that, Mr. Macmahon. I don't read much myself. But my eldest daughter that works for the public libraries tells me about your books.

—And Dutch Schultz, the renowned American gangster, you know that he was shot dead while he was sitting, well in fact while he was sitting on the toilet.

—A painful experience, Mr. Macmahon. He must have been surprised beyond measure.

Far away, from the highway, came the sound of an automobile.

—That, said the guard, could be the doctor or the ambulance.

They waited in silence in the warm odorous room. The sound passed on and away: neither the doctor nor the ambulance.

—But that fellow in the bed, Mr. Macmahon, I could tell you things about him, God rest him.

—Do you mean to say you know him.

—Of course, sir. It's my business to know people.

—Try to be one of those on whom nothing is lost.

—Quite so, sir, and odd that you should mention it. For that fellow in the bed, sir, do you know that once upon a time he lost two hundred hens?

—Two hundred hens?

—Chickens.

—Well, even chickens. That was a lot of birds. Even sparrows. Or skylarks. He must have been the only man in Europe who ever did that.

—In the world, I'd say, sir. And it happened so simple.

—It's stuffy in here, Robert said.

He led the way out to the garden. The sound of another automobile on the highway was not yet the doctor nor the ambulance. They walked along a red-sanded walk. She had had that mulch red sand brought all the way from Mullachdearg Strand in County Donegal. She loved the varied strands of Donegal: red, golden or snow-white. To right and left her roses flourished. She had a good way with roses, and with sweetpea, and even with sunflowers, those lusty brazen-faced giants.

—He was up in Dublin one day in a pub, and beside him at the counter the mournfullest man you ever saw. So the man that's gone, he was always a cheery type, said to the mournful fellow: Brighten up, the sun's shining, life's not all that bad. The mournful one says: If you were a poultry farmer with two hundred hens that wouldn't lay an egg, you'd hardly be singing songs.

—The plot, said Robert St. Blaise Macmahon, thickens.

—So, says your man that's inside there, and at peace we may charitably hope, how much would you take for those hens? A shilling a hen. Done, says he, and out with two hundred shillings and buys the hens. Then he hires a van and a boy to drive it, and off with him to transport the hens. You see, he knows a man here in this very town that will give him half-a-crown a hen, a profit of fifteen pounds sterling less the hire of the van. But the journey is long and the stops plentiful at the wayside pubs, he always had a notorious drouth, and whatever happened nobody ever found out, but when he got to this town at two in the morning, the back doors of the van were swinging open.

—The birds had flown.

—Only an odd feather to be seen. And he had to pay the boy fifteen shillings to clean out the back of the van. They were never heard of again, the hens I mean. He will long be remembered for that.

—If not for anything else.

—His poor brother, too, sir. That was a sad case. Some families are, you might say, addicted to sudden death.

—Did he die in a bed?

—Worse, far worse, sir. He died on a lawnmower.

—Guard, said Robert, would you have a cup of tea? You should be writing books, instead of me.

—I was never much given to tea, sir.

—But in all the best detective stories the man from Scotland Yard always drinks a cup o' tea.

—As I told you, sir, I don't read much. But if you had the tiniest drop of whiskey to spare, I'd be grateful. It's a hot day and this uniform is a crucifixion.

They left the garden by a wicket-gate that opened through a beech-hedge on to the front lawn. The sun's reflections shot up like lightning from the lake-water around the dancing boats. Three automobiles passed, but no doctor, no ambulance, appeared. Avoiding the silent odorous room they reentered the house by the front door. In the dining-room Robert St. Blaise Macmahon poured the whiskey for the guard, and for himself: he needed it.

—Ice, guard?

—No thank you sir. Although they say the Americans are hell for it. In everything, in tea, whiskey, and so on.

Two more automobiles passed. They listened and waited.

—You'd feel, sir, he was listening to us, like for a laugh, long nose and all. His brother was the champion gardener of all time. Better even than Miss Hynes herself, although her garden's a sight to see and a scent to smell.

—He died on a lawnmower?

—On his own lawn, sir. On one of those motor mowers. It blew up under him. He was burned to death. And you could easily say, sir, he couldn't have been at a more harmless occupation, or in a safer place.

—You could indeed, guard. Why haven't I met you before this?

—That's life, sir. Our paths never crossed. Only now for that poor fellow inside I wouldn't be here today at all.

This time it had to be the doctor and the ambulance. The wheels came, scattering gravel, up the driveway.

—He was luckier than his brother, sir. He died in more comfort, in a bed. And in action, it seems. That's more than will be said for most of us.

The doorbell chimed: three slow cathedral tones. That chime had been bought in Bruges where they knew about bells. The guard threw back what was left of his whiskey. He said: You'll excuse me, Mr. Macmahon. I'll go and put on my cap. We have work to do.

When the guard, the doctor, the ambulance, the ambulance attendants, and the corpse had, all together, taken their departure, he sprayed the bedroom with Flit, sworn foe to the housefly. It was all he could think of. It certainly changed the odour. It drifted out even into the garden, and lingered there among the roses. The assistant gardener and the kitchen girls had not yet arrived. That meant that the news was out, and that they were delaying in the town to talk about it. What sort of insufferable idiot was that woman to put him in this way into the position of being talked about, even, in the local papers, written about, and then laughed at, by clods he had always regarded with a detached and humorous, yet godlike, eye?

He sat, for the sake of the experience, on the edge of the rumpled bed from which the long-nosed corpse had just been removed. But he felt nothing of any importance. He remembered that another of those American dons had written a book, which he had slashingly reviewed, about love and death in the American novel. To his right, beyond the open windows, was her bureau desk and bookcase: old black oak, as if in stubborn isolated contradiction to the prevalent mahogany. She had never lost the stiff pride that a poor relation wears as a mask when he or she can ride high above the more common servility. She was a high-rider. It was simply incomprehensible that she, who had always so rigidly kept herself to herself, should have had a weakness for a long-nosed man who seemed to have been little better than a figure of fun. Two hundred hens, indeed!

The drawers of the bureau-bookcase were sagging open, and in disorder, as if in panic she had been rooting through them for something that nobody could find. He had seldom seen the inside of her room but, from the little he had seen and from everything he knew of her, she was no woman for untidiness or unlocked drawers. Yet in spite of her panic she had not called for aid to him, her cousin-once-removed, her employer, her benefactor. She had always stiffly, and for twenty-five years, kept him at a distance. Twenty-five years ago, in this room. She would have been eighteen, not six months escaped from the mountain valley she had been reared in, from which his parents had rescued her. He closes his eyes and, as best he can, his nose. He remembers. It is a Sunday afternoon and the house is empty except for the two of them.

He is alone in his room reading. He is reading about how Lucius Apuleius watches the servant-maid, Fotis, bending over the fire: Mincing of meats and making pottage for her master and mistresse, the Cupboard was all set with wines and I thought I smelled the savour of some dainty meats. Shee had about her middle a white and clean apron, and shee was girdled about her body under the paps with a swathell of red silk, and shee stirred the pot and turned the meat with her faire and white hands, in such sort that with stirring and turning the same, her loynes and hips did likewise move and shake, which was in my mind a comely sight to see.

Robert St. Blaise Macmahon who, at sixteen, had never tasted wine except to nibble secretively at the altar-wine when he was an acolyte in the parish church, repeats over and over again the lovely luscious Elizabethan words of Adlington's translation from the silver Latin: We did renew our venery by drinking of wine.

For at sixteen he is wax, and crazy with curiosity.

Then he looks down into the garden and there she is bending down over a bed of flowers. She is tall, rather sallow-faced, a Spanish face in an oval of close, crisp, curling dark hair. He has already noticed the determination of her long lithe stride, the sway of her hips, the pendulum swish and swing of her bright tartan pleated skirt. For a girl from the back of the mountains she has a sense of style.

She has come to this house from the Gothic grandeur of a remote valley called Glenade. Flat-topped mountains, so steep that the highest few hundred feet are sheer rock-cliffs corrugated by torrents, surround it. One such cliff, fissured in some primeval cataclysm, falls away into a curved chasm, rises again into one cold pinnacle of rock. The place is known as the Maiden's Leap, and the story is that some woman out of myth – Goddess, female devil, what's the difference? – pursued by a savage and unwanted lover, ran along the ridge of the mountain, and when faced by the chasm leaped madly to save her virtue, and did. But she didn't leap far enough to save her beautiful frail body which was shattered on the rocks below. From which her pursuer may have derived a certain perverse satisfaction.

All through her girlhood her bedroom window has made a frame for that extraordinary view. Now, her parents dead, herself adopted into the house of rich relatives as a sort of servant-maid, assistant to the aged housekeeper and in due course to succeed her, she bends over a flower-bed as Fotis had bent over the fire: O Fotis how trimely you can stir the pot, and how finely, with shaking your buttocks, you can make pottage.

Now she is standing tall and straight snipping blossoms from a fence of sweetpea. Her body is clearly outlined against the multi-coloured fence. He watches. He thinks of Fotis. He says again: We did renew our venery with drinking of wine.

When he confronts her in this very room, and makes an awkward grab at her, her arms are laden with sweetpea. So he is able to plant one kiss on cold unresponding lips. The coldness, the lack of response in a bondswoman, surprises him. She bears not the slightest resemblance to Fotis. It was the done thing, wasn't it: the young master and the servant-maid? In the decent old days in Czarist Russia the great ladies in the landed houses used to give the maids to their sons to practise on.

The sweetpea blossoms, purple, red, pink, blue, flow rather than fall to the floor. Then she hits him with her open hand, one calm, deliberate, country clout that staggers him and leaves his ear red, swollen and singing for hours. She clearly does not understand the special duties of a young female servant. In wild Glenade they didn't read Turgenev or Saltykov-Schedrin. He is humiliatingly reminded that he is an unathletic young man, a pampered only child, and that she is a strong girl from a wild mountain valley. She says: Mind your manners, wee boy. Pick up those sweetpea or I'll tell your father and mother how they came to be on the floor.

He picks up the flowers. She is older than he is. She is also taller, and she has a hand like rock. He knows that she has already noticed that he is afraid of his father.

This room was not then a bedroom. It was a pantry with one whole wall of it shelved for storing apples. He could still smell those apples, and the sweetpea. The conjoined smell of flower and fruit was stronger even than the smell of the insect-killing spray with which he had tried to banish the odour of death.

That stinging clout was her great leap, her defiance, her declaration of independence but, as the case of the Maiden of Glenade, it had only carried her halfways. To a cousin once-removed, who never anyway had cared enough to make a second attempt, she had demonstrated that she was no chattel. But she remained a dependent, a poor relation, a housekeeper doing the bidding of his parents until they died and, after their death, continuing to mind the house, grow the roses, the sweetpea and the sunflowers. The sense of style, the long lithe swinging stride, went for nothing, just because she hadn't jumped far enough to o'erleap the meandering withering enduring ways of a small provincial town. No man in the place could publicly be her equal. She was part Macmahon. So she had no man of her own, no place of her own. She had become part of the furniture of this house. She had no life of her own. Or so he had lightly thought.

He came and went and wrote his books, and heard her and spoke to her, but seldom really saw her except to notice that wrinkles, very faint and fine, had appeared on that Spanish face, on the strong-boned, glossy forehead, around the corners of the eyes. The crisp dark hair had touches of grey that she had simply not bothered to do anything about. She was a cypher, and a symbol in a frustrating land that had more than its share of ageing hopeless virgins. He closed his eyes and saw her as such when, in his writings, he touched satirically on that aspect of life in his pathetic country. Not that he did so any more often than he could help. For a London illustrated magazine he had once written about the country's low and late marriage rate, an article that had astounded all by its hard practicality. But as a general rule he preferred to think and to write about Stockholm or Paris or Naples or Athens, or African mountains, remote from everything. His travel books were more than travel books, and his novels really did show that travel broadened the mind. Or to think and write about the brightest gem in an America that man was doing so much to lay waste: the swamp that was no swamp but a wonderland out of a fantasy by George MacDonald, a Scottish writer whom nobody read any more, a fantasy about awaking some morning in your own bedroom, which is no longer a bedroom but the heart of the forest where every tree has its living spirit, genial or evil, evil or genial.

At that moment in his reverie the telephone rang. To the devil with it, he thought, let it ring. The enchanted swamp was all around him, the wine-coloured water just perceptibly moving, the rugged knees of the cypress trees, the white priestly birds curved brooding on high bare branches, the silence. Let it ring. It did, too. It rang and rang and refused to stop. So he walked ill-tempered to the table in the hallway where the telephone was, picked it up, silenced the ringing, heard the voice of the civic guard, and then noticed for the first conscious time the black book that he carried in his right hand.

The guard said: She's resting now. The sergeant's wife is looking after her.

—Good. That's very good.

It was a ledger-type book, eight inches by four, the pages ruled in blue, the margins in red. He must, unthinkingly, have picked it up out of the disorder in which her morning panic had left the bureau-bookcase. For the first time that panic seemed to him as comic: it wasn't every morning a maiden lady found a long-nosed lover, or something, cold between the covers. It was matter for a short story, or an episode in a novel: if it just hadn't damned well happened in his own house. What would Henry James have made of it? The art of fiction is in telling not what happened, but what should have happened. Or what should have happened somewhere else.

The guard was still talking into his left ear, telling him that the doctor said it was a clear case of heart failure. Oh, indeed it was: for the heart was a rare and undependable instrument. With his right hand he flicked at random through the black book, then, his eye caught by some words that seemed to mean something, he held the book flat, focused on those words until they were steady, and read. The hand-writing was thick-nibbed, black as coal, dogged, almost printing, deliberate as if the nib had bitten into the paper. He read: Here he comes down the stairs in the morning, his double jowl red and purple from the razor, his selfish mouth pursed as tight as Mick Clinton, the miser of Glenade, used to keep the woollen sock he stored his money in when he went to the market and the horsefair of Manorhamilton. Here he comes, the heavy tread of him in his good, brown hand-made shoes would shake the house if it wasn't as solid on its foundations as the Rock of Cashel. Old John Macmahon used to boast that his people built for eternity. Thud, thud, thud, the weight of his big flat feet. Here he comes, Gorgeous Gussie, with his white linen shirt, he should have frills on his underpants, and his blue eyeshade to show to the world, as if there was anybody to bother looking at him except myself and the domestic help, that he's a writer. A writer, God help us. About what? Who reads him? It's just as well he has old John's plunder to live on.

The black letters stood out like basalt from the white, blue-and-red lined paper. Just one paragraph she wrote to just one page and, if the paragraph didn't fully fill the page, she made, above and below the paragraph, whorls and doodles and curlicues in inks of various colours, blue, red, green, violet. She was a lonely self-delighting artist. She was, she had been, for how long, oh merciful heavens, an observer, a writer.

The guard was saying: She said to the sergeant's wife that she's too shy to face you for the present.

—Shy, he said.

He looked at the black words. They were as distinct as that long-ago clout on the side of the head: the calloused hard hand of the mountainy girl reducing the pretensions of a shy, sensitive, effeminate youth.

He said: She has good reason to be shy. It is, perhaps, a good thing that she should, at least, be shy before her employer and distant relation.

—It might be that, sir, she might mean not shy, but ashamed.

—She has also good reason for being ashamed.

—She says, Mr. Macmahon, sir, that she might go away somewhere for a while.

—Shouldn't she wait for the inquest and the funeral? At any rate, she has her duties here in this house. She is, she must realise, paid in advance.

So she would run, would she, and leave him to be the single object of the laughter of the mean people of this town? In a sweating panic he gripped the telephone as if he would crush it. There was an empty hungry feeling, by turns hot, by turns cold, just above his navel. He was betraying himself to that garrulous guard who would report to the town every word he said. It was almost as if the guard could read, if he could read, those damnable black words. He gripped the phone, slippy and sweaty as it was, gulped and steadied himself, breathed carefully, in out, in out, and was once again Robert St. Blaise Macmahon, a cultivated man whose education had commenced at the famous Benedictine school at Glenstal. After all, the Jesuits no longer were what once they had been, and James Joyce had passed that way to the discredit both of himself and the Jesuits.

—Let her rest then, he said. I'll think over what she should do. I'll be busy all day, guard, so don't call me unless it's absolutely essential.

He put down the telephone, wiped his sweating hand with a white linen handkerchief, monogrammed and ornamented with the form of a feather embroidered in red silk. It was meant to represent a quill pen and also to be a symbol of the soaring creative mind. That fancy handkerchief was, he considered, his one flamboyance. He wore, working, a blue eyeshade because there were times when lamplight, and even overbright daylight, strained his eyes. Any gentleman worthy of the name did, didn't he, wear hand-made shoes?

On the first page of the book she had pasted a square of bright yellow paper and on it printed in red ink: Paragraphs.

In smaller letters, in Indian black ink, and in an elegant italic script, she had written: Reflections on Robert the Riter.

Then finally, in green ink, she had printed: By his Kaptivated Kuntry Kusin!!!

He was aghast at her frivolity. Nor did she need those three exclamation marks to underline her bitchiness, a withdrawn and secretive bitchiness, malevolent among the roses and the pots and pans, overflowing like bile, in black venomous ink. She couldn't have been long at this secret writing. The book was by no means full. She had skipped, and left empty pages here and there, at random as if she dipped her pen and viciously wrote wherever the book happened to open. There was no time sequence that he could discern. He read: He says he went all the way to the States to see a swamp. Just like him. Would he go all the way to Paris to see the sewers?

—But the base perfidy of that.

He spoke aloud, not to himself but to her.

—You always pretended to be interested when I talked about the swamp. The shy wild deer that would come to the table to take the bit out of your fingers when you breakfasted in the open air, the racoon with the rings round its eyes, the alligators, the wine-coloured waters, the white birds, the white sand on the bed of the Su'wannee River. You would sit, woman, wouldn't you, brown Spanish face inscrutable, listening, agreeing with me, oh yes, agreeing with me in words, but, meanly, all the time, thinking like this.

Those brief words about that small portion of his dream-world had wounded him. But bravely he read more. The malice of this woman of the long-nosed chicken-losing lover must be fully explored. She was also, by heaven, a literary critic. She wrote: Does any novelist, nowadays, top-dress his chapters with quotations from other authors? There is one, but he writes thrillers and that's different. Flat-footed Robert the Riter, with his good tweeds and his brass-buttoned yellow waistcoat, has a hopelessly old-fashioned mind. His novels, with all those sophisticated nonentities going nowhere, read as if he was twisting life to suit his reading. But then what does Robert know about life? Mamma's boy, Little Lord Fauntleroy, always dressed in the best. He doesn't know one rose from another. But a novelist should know everything. He doesn't know the town he lives in. Nor the people in it. Quotations. Balderdash.

He found to his extreme humiliation that he was flushed with fury. The simplest thing to do would be to let her go away and stay away, and then find himself a housekeeper who wasn't a literary critic, a secret carping critic, a secret lover too, a Psyche, by Hercules, welcoming by night an invisible lover to her bed. Then death stops him, and daylight reveals him, makes him visible as a comic character with a long nose, and with a comic reputation, only, for mislaying two hundred hens, and with a brother, a great gardener, who had the absurd misfortune to be burned alive on his own lawn. Could comic people belong to a family addicted to sudden death? Some-where in all this, there might be some time the germ of a story.

But couldn't she realise what those skillfully chosen quota-tions meant?

—Look now, he said, what they did for George MacDonald. A procession of ideas, names, great presences, marching around the room you write in: Fletcher and Shelley, Novalis and Beddoes, Goethe and Coleridge, Sir John Suckling and Shakespeare, Lyly and Schiller, Heine and Schleiermacher and Cowley and Spenser and the Book of Judges and Jean Paul Richter and Cyril Tourneur and Sir Philip Sidney and Dekker and Chaucer and the Kabala.

But, oh Mother Lilith, what was the use of debating thus with the shadow of a secretive woman who was now resting in the tender care of the sergeant's wife who was, twenty to one, relaying the uproarious news to every other wife in the town: Glory be, did you hear the fantasticality that happened up in Mr. Robert St. Blaise Macmahon's big house? Declare to God they'll never again be able to show their faces in public.

Even if she were with him, walking in this garden as he now was, and if he was foolish enough thus to argue with her, she would smile her sallow wrinkled smile, look sideways out of those dark-brown eyes and then go off alone to write in her black book: He forgot to mention the Twelve Apostles, the Clancy Brothers, and the Royal Inniskilling Fusiliers.

All her life she had resisted his efforts to make something out of her. Nor had she ever had the determination to rise and leap again, to leave him and the house and go away and make something out of herself.

He read: He's like the stuck-up high-falutin' women in that funny story by Somerville and Ross, he never leaves the house except to go to Paris. He doesn't see the life that's going on under his nose. He says there are no brothels in Dublin. But if Dublin had the best brothels in the long history of sin…

Do you know, now, that was not badly put. She has a certain felicity of phrase. But then she has some Macmahon blood in her, and the educational advantages that over the years this house has afforded her.

…long history of sin, he'd be afraid of his breeches to enter any of them. He says there are no chic women in Dublin. What would he do with a chic woman if I gave him one, wrapped in cellophane, for Valentine's Day? He says he doesn't know if the people he sees are ugly because they don't make love, or that they don't make love because they're ugly. He's the world's greatest living authority, isn't he, either on love or good looks? On another page: To think, dear God, of that flat-footed bachelor who doesn't know one end of a woman from the other, daring to write an article attacking the mountainy farmers on their twenty pitiful acres of rocks, rushes, bogpools and dunghills, for not marrying young and raising large families. Not only does he not see the people around him, he doesn't even see himself. Himself and a crazy priest in America lamenting about late marriages and the vanishing Irish. A fine pair to run in harness. The safe, sworn celibate and the fraidy-cat bachelor.

And on yet another page: That time long ago, I clouted him when he made the pass, the only time, to my knowledge, he ever tried to prove himself a man. And he never came back for more. I couldn't very well tell him that the clout was not for what he was trying to do but for the stupid way he was trying to do it. A born bungler.

The doodles, whorls and curlicues wriggled like a snake-pit, black, blue, green, red, violet, before his angry eyes. That was enough. He would bring that black book down to the barracks, and throw it at her, and tell her never to darken his door again. His ears boomed with blood. He went into the dining-room, poured himself a double whiskey, drank it slowly, breathing heavily, thinking. But no, there was a better way. Go down to the barracks, bring her back, lavish kindness on her, in silence suffer her to write in her book, then copy what she writes, reshape it, reproduce it, so that some day she would see it in print and be confounded for the jade and jezebel that she is.

With deliberate speed, majestic instancy, he walked from the dining-room to her bedroom, tossed the book on to her bed where she would see it on her return and know he had read it, and that her nastiness was uncovered. He had read enough of it, too much of it: because the diabolical effect of his reading was that he paused, with tingling irritation, to examine his tendency to think in quotations. Never again, thanks to her malice, would he do so, easily, automatically, and, so to speak, unthinkingly.

Coming back across the kitchen he found himself looking at

his own feet, in fine hand-made shoes, his feet rising, moving forwards, settling again on the floor, fine flat feet. It was little benefit to see ourselves as others see us. That was, merciful God, another quotation. That mean woman would drive him mad. He needed a change: Dublin, Paris, Boppard on the Rhine – a little town that he loved in the off-season when it wasn't ravished by boat-loads of American women doing the Grand Tour. First, though, to get the Spanish maiden of wild Glenade back to her proper place among the roses and the pots and pans.

The guard answered the telephone. He said: She's still resting, Mr. Macmahon, sir.

—It's imperative that I speak to her. She can't just take this lying down.

That, he immediately knew, was a stupid thing to say. On the wall before him, strong black letters formed, commenting on his stupidity.

There was a long silence. Then she spoke, almost whispered: Yes, Robert.

—Hadn't you better get back to your place here?

—Yes, Robert. But what is my place there?

—You know what I mean. We must face this together. After all, you are half a Macmahon.

—Half a Macmahon, she said, is better than no bread.

He was shocked to fury: This is nothing to be flippant about.

—No, Robert.

—Who was this man?

—A friend of mine.

—Do you tell me so? Do you invite all your friends to my house?

—He was the only one.

—Why didn't you marry him?

—He had a wife and five children in Sudbury in England. Separated.

—That does, I believe, constitute an impediment. But who or what was he?

—It would be just like you, Robert, not even to know who he was. He lived in this town. It's a little town.

—Should I have known him?

—Shouldn't a novelist know everybody and everything?

—I'm not an authority on roses.

—You've been reading my book.

She was too sharp for him. He tried another tack: Why didn't you tell me you were having a love affair? After all, I am civilised.

—Of course you're civilised. The world knows that. But there didn't seem any necessity for telling you.

—There must be so many things that you don't feel it is necessary to tell me.

—You were never an easy person to talk to.

—All your secret thoughts. Who could understand a devious woman? Far and from the farthest coasts...

—There you go again. Quotations. The two-footed gramophone. What good would it do you if you did understand?

—Two-footed, he said. Flat-footed.

He was very angry: You could have written it all out for me if you couldn't say it. All the thought hidden behind your brooding face. All the things you thought when you said nothing, or said something else.

—You really have been reading my book. Prying.

The silence could have lasted all of three minutes. He searched around for something that would hurt.

—Isn't it odd that a comic figure should belong to a family addicted to sudden death?

—What on earth do you mean?

Her voice was higher. Anger? Indignation?

—That nose, he said. Cyrano. Toto the Clown. And I heard about the flight of the two hundred hens.

Silence.

—And about the brother who was burned.

—They were kindly men, she said. And good to talk to. They had green fingers.

It would have gratified him if he could have heard a sob.

—I'll drive down to collect you in an hour's time.

—He loved me, she said. I suppose I loved him. He was something, in a place like this.

Silence.

—You're a cruel little boy, she said. But just to amuse you,

I'll give you another comic story. Once he worked in a dog kennels in Kent in England. The people who owned the kennels had an advertisement in the local paper. One sentence read like this: Bitches in heat will be personally conducted from the railway station by Mr. Dominic Byrne.

—Dominic Byrne, she said. That was his name. He treasured that clipping. He loved to laugh at himself. He died for love. That's more than most will ever do. There you are. Make what you can out of that story, you flat-footed bore.

She replaced the telephone so quietly that for a few moments he listened, waiting for more, thinking of something suitable to say.

On good days, light, reflected from the lake, seemed to brighten every nook and corner of the little town. At the end of some old narrow winding cobbled laneway there would be a vision of lake-water bright as a polished mirror. It was a graceful greystone town, elegantly laid-out by some Frenchman hired by an eighteenth-century earl. The crystal river that fed the lake flowed through the town and gave space and scope for a tree-lined mall. But grace and dancing light could do little to mollify his irritation. This time, by the heavenly father, he would have it out with her, he would put her in her place, revenge himself for a long-ago affront and humiliation. Body in the bed, indeed. Two hundred hens, indeed. Swamps and sewers, indeed. Bitches in heat, indeed. She did not have a leg to stand on. Rutting, and on his time, with a long-nosed yahoo.

The Byzantine church, with which the parish priest had recently done his damnedest to disfigure the town, struck his eyes with concentrated insult. Ignorant bloody peasants. The slick architects could sell them anything: Gothic, Byzantine, Romanesque, Igloo, Kraal, Modern Cubist. The faithful paid, and the pastor made the choice.

Who would ever have thought that a lawnmower could be a Viking funeral pyre?

The barracks, a square, grey house, made ugly by barred windows and notice-boards, was beside the church. The guard, capless, the neck of his uniform jacket open, his hands in his trouser pockets, stood in the doorway. He was still perspiring.

The man would melt. There was a drop to his nose: snot or sweat or a subtle blend of both. Robert St. Blaise Macmahon would never again make jokes about civic guards. He said: I've come for Miss Hynes.

—Too late, Mr. Macmahon, sir. The bird has flown.

—She has what?

—Gone, sir. Eloped. Stampeded. On the Dublin train. Ten minutes ago. I heard her whistle.

—Whistle?

—The train, sir.

—But the funeral? The inquest?

—Oh, his wife and children will bury him. We phoned them.

—But the inquest?

Her affidavit will do the job. We'll just say he dropped while visiting your house to look at the roses.

—That's almost the truth.

—The whole truth and nothing but the truth is often a bitter dose, sir.

—As I said, guard, you are a philosopher.

He remembered too late that he hadn't said that, he had just thought it.

—Thank you kindly, sir. Would you chance a cup of tea, sir? Nothing better to cool one on a hot day. Not that I like tea myself. But in this weather, you know. The hottest day, the forecast says.

Well, why not? He needed cooling. The bird had flown, sailing away from him, over the chasm, laughing triumphant eldritch laughter.

In the austere dayroom they sat on hard chairs and sipped tea.

—Nothing decent or drinkable here, sir, except a half-bottle of Sandeman's port.

—No thank you, guard. No port. The tea will suffice.

—Those are gallant shoes, sir, if you'll excuse me being so pass-remarkable. Hand-made jobs.

—Yes, hand-made.

—Costly, I'd say. But then they'd last for ever.

—Quite true, guard.

—He's coffined by now. The heat, you know.

—Don't remind me.

—Sorry, sir. But the facts of life are the facts of life. Making love one minute. In a coffin the next.

—The facts of death, guard. Alone withouten any company.

—True as you say, sir. He was a droll divil, poor Byrne, and he died droll.

—Among the roses, guard.

—It could happen to anyone, God help us. Neither the day nor the hour do we know. The oddest thing, now, happened once to the sergeant's brother that's a journalist in Dublin. This particular day he's due to travel to Limerick City to report on a flower show. But he misses the train. So he sends a telegram to ask a reporter from another newspaper to keep him a carbon. Then he adjourns to pass the day in the upstairs lounge bar of the Ulster House. Along comes the Holy Hour as they call it for jokes, when the pubs of Dublin close for a while in the early afternoon. To break up the morning boozing parties, you understand. There's nobody in the lounge except the sergeant's brother and a strange man. So the manager locks them in there to drink in peace and goes off to his lunch. And exactly halfways through the Holy Hour the stranger drops down dead. Angina. And there's me man that should be at a flower show in Limerick locked in on a licensed premises, the Ulster House, during an off or illegal hour, with a dead man that he doesn't know from Adam.

—An interesting legal situation, guard.

—Oh, it was squared, of course. The full truth about that couldn't be allowed out. It would be a black mark on the licence. The manager might lose his job.

—People might even criticise the quality of the drink.

—They might, sir. Some people can't be satisfied. Not that there was ever a bad drop sold in the Ulster House. Another cup, Mr. Macmahon, sir.

—Thank you, guard.

—She'll come back, Mr. Macmahon. Blood they say is thicker than water.

—They do say that, do they? Yet somehow, in spite of what they say, I don't think she'll be back.

On she went, leaping, flying, describing jaunty parabolas.

He would, of course, have to send her money. She was entitled to something legally and he could well afford to be generous beyond what the law demanded.

—So the long-nosed lover died, guard, looking at the roses.

—In a manner of speaking, sir.

—Possibly the only man, guard, who ever had the privilege. Look thy last on all things lovely.

But the guard was not aware of de la Mare.

—That's what we'll say, sir. It would be best for all. His wife and all. And no scandal.

—Days of wine and roses, guard.

—Yes, sir. Alas, that we have nothing here but that half-bottle of Sandeman's port. She was a great lady to grow roses, sir. That's how they met in the beginning, she told me. Over roses.

PART THREE

Make Straight for the Shore

BREAKFAST WAS perfunctory and the main meal of the day was taken at a place called the Continental Café or the Café Continental where we used to eat bangers and mash by the hundredweight and dance with the waitresses to a voice and a tune on the radio: There's a lovely lake in London where Rhododendrons grow.

It was a very popular tune at the time. I can't remember if that other song had then surfaced: At the Café Continental like a fool I fell in love.

Not one of the three of us did fall in love there. The waitresses were all as fat as fools: from snapping-up all day long unconsidered trifles of bangers and mash. Our ideal then was Ginger Rogers, the young Ginger Rogers, the Ginger Rogers of Roxy Hart: her dancing was different.

When there wasn't a lovely lake in London there were red sails in the sunset, way out on the sea. We picked up a lot of our current and popular music by hanging around bicycle shops: We'll build a nest way up in the west 'neath a sky of heavenly blue, a one-room flat and a two-pants suit and three square meals a day, I've told every little star just how sweet I think you are, with a carpet on the floor made of buttercups and clover. In more elevated moments we listened to John McCormack and Enrico Caruso and had strong controversy as to which of them was the greater. Caruso had, hadn't he, broken a wine-glass just by singing into it? But McCormack was one of our own.

Radio sets were scarce, so were the fourpences for the pit in the picture-house and scarcer still was the money to buy the records we coveted and not every household had a gramophone. So bicycle shops it had to be. We never even wondered: why bicycle shops? Why not confectioneries or groceries or newsagencies, where you might expect music to go with literature: or draperies or haberdasheries or hardware merchants?

Busto looked like this: I draw a circle supported by a larger circle supported by two stumpy rectangles. Lanko looked like this: I draw a small circle supported on two parallel lines. They were both Christian Brothers and both surnamed Burke, one from Dublin and the other from Tipperary, and because of them the three of us were in Belfast City dancing with the waitresses, walking the town like men of the town, watching the dark clouds of starlings around the gigantic but dignified Victorian city hall and in our leisure moments doing an entrance examination for the British civil service. In the late spring the clouds of starlings are a sight to see.

This day Lanko came to me after Latin class and said: Because of that arithmetic paper you haven't a hope in this world or the next of getting King's scholarship.

He was, as you may have guessed, a tall man, so tall he looked thin which he really wasn't, and he had a handsome blackavised face, a gentle musical Munster accent, and all the matrons in the town and a lot of the maidens were mad about him – the inaccessible, almost, in those days. He had played hurling for Tipperary, and the long black Christian Brothers' habit, especially long in his case, went very well with the easy athletic way he walked.

—No the arithmetic paper, he said, would be your Waterloo.

It was my final year in secondary school in an Ulster provincial town and, at that time and in those parts, the only future for the average secondary student was to go to training college for two years and resurface as a primary-school teacher so as to teach primary students to become secondary students. You could, if you were lucky, become an artisan, or dig holes in the street for the town council and nobody would ever see anything of you except the top of your head. As in greater towns like New York somebody was always digging holes in the street: constant employment. You could, of course, become a priest or a nun or, if your parents had the means, you could go to the university and follow one of the professions, or become a secondary teacher and teach other secondary students to become primary teachers, and so on. The United States produces every year, somebody told me, 30,000 doctors of philosophy and there can't be that many philosophers in the whole world: take a look at it, for God's sake.

But in 1936 about fifty percent of my class were doomed to sit for this examination called King's scholarship and to go, if they were successful, to a place in Twickenham, near London, called Strawberry Hill, sacred to the memory of Horace Walpole who had lived there and of Seán Ó Faoláin who had taught there, and to become primary-school teachers. The big hurdle in that examination was an arithmetic paper of four diabolical problems, and the way to take it was: if question one didn't provide an answer, to take a run at two and three and four so that, with the law of averages and good luck and one of them out of the way, there were fewer to bewilder you and your confidence was quadrupled. Or is quadrupled, I wonder, exactly what I mean?

A good friend of mine wouldn't or couldn't work that way: he'd stick with question one until the bell rang, with the result that he never became a primary-school teacher. Instead he became a wealthy businessman and still is one, and a credit to the country and a great benefit, I'm told, to the poor in the town he lives in.

As for myself, I never even attempted or was allowed to attempt King's scholarship. The thought of that arithmetic paper turned me off and subtraction was the only sort of arithmetic I was ever any good at, and Lanko said gently: No, dear boy, you'd never take that hurdle. But there is this exam for the British civil service if you don't mind serving the king, and it's becoming very popular nowadays, good conditions, good pay, you can rise to the top, no sectarianism across the water, and you could see a bit of the world into the bargain, beginning with Belfast where the exam is held.

Busto didn't put it so gently: Busto had a kind heart but blunter ways, picked up, perhaps, in the scrum when in his youth he had played rugby football for Blackrock; and about the kind heart I didn't find out until years later I met him in Dublin when he was ailing in health and wasn't even Busto any more, and his cheeks were hollow and his feet flat and his clothes had grown too big for him. But Busto he still assuredly was when he stopped me one day in the corridor outside the chemistry lab and told me of my prospects in the service of the King of England. He (Busto) had a deft way of lifting youths by their incipient sidelocks and occasionally booting them in the buttocks in a friendly but efficient fashion. For Blackrock, it was said, he had been the supremo among place-kickers.

He was the Brother Superior and students were sent to him for punishment, and they got it. One poor sniveller came in from a history class to meet his deserts and his whipping. So Busto says: What are you here for?

—Please sir, I forgot how a man died.

—Why, says Busto, didn't you say he forgot to draw his breath.

And lifted the non-historian with one well-placed boot.

But at the door of the stinks lab he merely tweaked my nose and said jovially: You can't put two and two together. You'll never get King's scholarship. You'll never be able to put two and two together. But there's the British civil service. To judge by the stupid things they do in Whitehall they'll never notice you in the crowd. Proceed and prosper and God save the king.

Unkicked, I proceeded.

And there we were, the chosen three, living on bangers and mash and dancing with fat waitresses to the tunes of a lovely lake in London and swift wings we must borrow, make straight for the shore, and more besides. As I said, we knew the tunes already from our regular scholarly attendance at a bicycle shop, one very special bicycle shop: and for the moment we were gentlemen on the town, three fine free right feet and fellows for them, truly at large and out of the reservation for the first time in our lives, living in an hotel at the back of the city hall and studying the black driving clouds of shrieking starlings. Have the bombs, I wonder, dispersed the starlings?

For the last time I was in that hotel the screaming birds were still blackening the sky but the bombs were just beginning. Thick as night or locusts the starlings were around the city hall and in the hotel there was no water in the taps. The hotel has changed its name now, or it may not, because of the bombs, be there any more; one new and neighbouring hotel was bombed nineteen times, room service how are you. But eight years ago it was still there and had then changed its name, and I sat sipping in the lounge, looking at a pop-group called the Necromancers and remembering the bright blonde hair of Trudi. Looking at, not listening to, I'm overjoyed to say, for the Necromancers were merely relaxing after their labours of the night before. A few of them were asleep or half asleep. There was little talk between them. They were possibly saving their breath for the night to come. An interestingly-mixed group: West Indian, Afro-American, European, which I could see for myself, Irish and English and German which I had been told. Two of them who were not slumbering ordered drinks, real drinks, which surprised me: who had always assumed that pop-groups and show-bands lived on cow's milk and pills. A slim young blonde girl from the hotel staff brought them a telegram. O the blonde head of my Trudi long ago when Rhododendrons grew around the lovely lake in London. As she bent to deliver the telegram the girl blushed to the backs of her mini-skirtless thighs at having been chosen for the honour of carrying a message that came through the air, to the corner where the gods reposed: no harpers those to learn their songs and melodies in bicycle shops, red sails in the sunset I'm trusting in you.

Later as I sat at dinner with a BBC ballad-singer and a Dublin political, both convivial men, we heard a great sound. At first we thought that a large part of Belfast had been blown up. But later still it was reported that a meteorite had splashed down, hitting nobody as far as was known – the heavens were harmless – in a peat-bog in County Down.

The ballad-singer said: At all times of crisis and calamity there are signs in the sky.

The political said: Rockets from Russia.

The hotel was full of pressmen. Rumour, painted all over with tongues, was running wild to tell us that, for instance, the papishes were to march on Sandy Row at ten o'clock when the pubs closed.

To prove what?

Why, to prove to the Protestant Sandy Rowers that the IRA did not blow up the aqueduct near the big reservoir in the Silent Valley in the Mountains of Mourne: which was why there was no water in the taps in the hotel nor in the hospitals nor anywhere else, almost, in Belfast.

That demonstration would have made a lot of sense: just as much as when the Holy Rollers of Dayton, Tennessee, proved to their own satisfaction, by rolling all together on the ground, that man was not descended from the monkey.

Trudi I could see quite plainly, although the dining-room, which we three students long ago hadn't much frequented, had been altered and redecorated and, anyway, her sort of hotel-work didn't bring her into the dining-room.

Later still we heard that the rumour was false and that the demonstration was not to take place. But the pressmen who, because of the unhappy nature of their calling, are obliged to give at least a friendly nod to every rumour, were already on the way to Sandy Row, just to see.

We had an excellent dinner and much wine. Later still we heard that the meteorite had splashed down not in County Down but in County Derry: and jocose speculation continued about the nature of the great sound.

The Holy Ghost descending at long last on the collapsing parliament in Stormont Castle.

Dr. Ian Paisley ascending from the Crumlin Road Jail in a flaming flying saucer and all the trumpets sounding for him from the other side as they did for Mr. Standfast. For Dr. Paisley was that night in Pauline chains for disturbing the peace outside the Presbyterian assembly building five minutes walk away in Fisherwick Place: in which pinnacled, dark-stone, ice-cold building Bill and Fuzzy-Wuzzy and myself had long before sat, more or less, for that civil service examination.

The evening papers had reported that Dr. Paisley's aide-de-camp, the Rev. Mr. Foster, who had just been released, said that Dr. Paisley was the happiest man in the prison, happier even than the governor, because Dr. Paisley was with God.

The ballad-singer wondered if governors of prisons were necessarily happy.

The political wondered if governors of prisons were of necessity not with God.

We sipped our brandy and I remembered Trudi.

Later still I tried to tell the manager, a brusque, busy fellow, how a female member of the staff of that hotel had, away before his time, kept me out of the Second World War and thus may, by several years, have postponed the German defeat. But he seemed in too much of a hurry to try or to bother to understand.

There she was on the very first morning the three of us woke up in that hotel. We had a room each, small rooms and not over-elegant but independent and our own. Belfast we had often visited, on the lead with parents or led by teachers, to rugby games in Ravenhill, but this was different. What could a man have done or said to Trudi if he had been sandwiched between parents or crocodiled on the sporting road to Raven-hill? O, the long bright blonde hair of Trudi, and Easter sun dancing over a new-arisen world. In the hometown I knew two sisters, one called Deborah, the other Rachel, Presbyterians, naturally, with names like that, but never a girl called Trudi and never a girl so blonde.

—Trudi, I said, is your name really and truly Trudi.

—That's what my father and mother call me, and my brothers and sisters all seven of them, and the neighbours, who speak to me. Where I come from everybody doesn't speak to everybody.

She was a wit. She had to be, she was so beautiful.

—Do you come from Germany? Or Switzerland?

Switzerland was all hotels and mountains.

Her accent should have told me but I hadn't travelled much at the time and all beautiful women spoke with the same accent. She was, at that moment, stripping my bed preparatory to re-making it: the lass that made the bed to me, I knew my Burns, it was the closest that poetry had brought us to such matters. She wore a grey dress and white apron and a funny white little hat all lost and unbalanced and loveable and comic

on the crown of that shining head: her hair was like the links
o' gowd, her teeth were like the ivorie, her cheeks like lilies
dipped in wine.

—Germany, she said. Switzerland, she said. I couldn't spell
Switzerland if you paid me. Germany I can manage.

She did, haltingly, all seven letters, music to mine ears her
voice was.

No, she was from Castledawson in County Derry, not too far
from where, thirty-three years later, the meteorite was to
splash down, and her family name was Beatty and Trudi came
out of a magazine called *Peg's Paper* that her mother read. Her
father kept an unlicensed bull that was worth a fortune, he
worked so hard, even at half the legal price, but it was cash
down for if it wasn't some of them wouldn't pay you at all,
you had no legal way of getting at them, and that was about
the meanest thing she ever heard of. Cash and carry, her
father, who was a joker, said. That was the name of one of
those new-fangled supermarkets. On the first morning she
told me about Castledawson and Beatty and *Peg's Paper* but it
was the third morning, we were rapidly growing closer, before
she told me about the unlicensed bull, and laughed like a
music box when she told me: You should see him, the solemn
face of him.

She was lovelier than the lovely lake in London, lovelier than
red sails in the sunset although Fuzzy-Wuzzy would never
agree with that and disapproved of Trudi: jealous, I thought at
first, but no, I knew after a while that he was just shy of
women. It was the red sails in the song that enchanted him, not
the loved one that the red sails were to carry home safely to the
singer. Bill, a big affable man whose longest speech about
anything was a grunt of good-natured assent, was neutral
although he did whisper to Fuzzy-Wuzzy to whisper to me that
there'd be hell to pay when Busto found out, as find out he
sure as hell would, that time was spent helping the lass that
made the bed to me that should have been spent in the Presbyterian assembly building in Fisherwick Place outside which,
thirty-three years later, Dr. Paisley was picked up for disturbing the peace.

As for Fuzzy-Wuzzy, everywhere he went he must have seen
red sails in the sunset. He hummed the tune of it all the time,

or something not unlike the tune. He never could make any fist of the words although, God knows, he tried very hard. He was six feet two inches when he was seventeen and he walked on his toes, bouncing a bit, and always leaned forward a little as if he were eager to fly or take off like a rocket for the moon. His real name was Patrick Ignatius O'Kane and his people were far-out relations of my mother, and he wore grey tweed trousers and a serge navy-blue jacket, the jacket always too big for him and the trousers always too small. In the village he came from, we reckoned, there must be a very special tailor, either that or his father had a very large family of boys all older than Fuzzy-Wuzzy. Some in navy-blue serge, others in grey tweed.

Most of our last year at school he spent in Peter Sloper McAleer's bicycle shop trying to learn the words and music of Red Sails in the Sunset. He could, as I've said, make a stab at the music but never, no, no never, he could never get the words right. He cycled into the town to school from his village twelve miles away, so that he had a legitimate reason for being in Peter Sloper's where he parked his bike: and Peter Sloper with his tan shopcoat all marked with streaks of oil, and his small, exactly-oval gold-rimmed spectacles, and his wrinkled monkey-face and his five ribs of grey hair plastered straight across his bald crown, was a man to reckon with. He walked out young nurses from the county hospital until he was the age of eighty, nurses, only nurses: the nurses, he used to say with great solemnity, the nurses are the worst, they know it all. My cousin Brigid who was a great deal older than me and who was hospital matron for a time said that it was on the records that Peter Sloper had started walking out nurses when he was eighteen, that was sixty-two years of young nurses, and never proposed matrimony to one of them which was why he was called Sloper. He was mean, too, or at least tight or careful about money, and never had it been heard of that he bought a drink for anybody except once when a telegram came to him that he had won £50,000 in the Irish Hospitals Sweepstake, and he went crazy and toured the town and bought drinks for one and all and everybody in every pub, to find out too late that the telegram had come from his best friend, a greengrocer, who was noted for practical jokes. It was the same greengrocer who, when Peter Sloper died, suggested that on his tombstone the words should be cut: The nurses were the worst. But the parish priest put a stop to that.

Well anyway, there in the middle of a maze and a pop-art swirl of bicycles was a gramophone with a high green horn playing music that could be heard two blocks away and Fuzzy-Wuzzy, his head half up the horn, trying in vain to learn the words of Red Sails in the Sunset, way out on the sea, oh carry my swift wings straight home to the shore. Never, oh never could he get the words right: and he was called Fuzzy-Wuzzy because his hair was black as coal-tar and bristly and closely clipped.

Bulky affable Bill with a voice like a bugle was such a genius at Latin composition that his themes or exercises were in constant demand for what we called cogging and American students rather grandly called plagiarization. Shakespeare and Eliot plagiarized. We grimly cogged in the early morning-oh – so that, by popular request, Bill had to be up early and into the classroom before our teachers were astir to trouble the air. One morning the demand for pure Ciceronian Latin was so brisk that a fight began and the golden book of Bill's themes was torn to shreds. A day of sharp questioning, discoveries and retribution followed.

—*Festina lente,* Bill said on the third morning in Belfast.

He blushed and looked the other way when he said that. It was the only attempt he made to reproach me. No, warn me, guide me, save me, counsel me. He couldn't have reproached anybody: but dancing with fat waitresses was one thing, dallying in bedrooms and dereliction of duty that might land the three of us in the stockade, another. My companions were rattled. Fuzzy-Wuzzy repeated: *Festina lente.*

But with a sort of shy, awkward half-laugh. And I marvelled that he was able to get the two words in their right order.

For myself and the blonde belle of Castledawson were into the straight and ahead of the field, and little was I seeing of the cold, stone, high-windowed hall where on solemn occasions pious Presbyterians assembled. At one history paper to which I went because I liked history, and knew how men died and even when, and Trudi was not that morning available, the man at the next desk to mine had an epileptic fit and desks and papers and inkwells went flying. That can't much have affected me: my history marks turned out to be the best I had when I had any at all.

She taught me to make beds. She taught me to mitre sheets as neatly as any young nurse ever did in any hospital. She taught me as the woman lovely in her bones taught the poet: Turn and Counter-turn and Touch and Stand. The outlaw bull, benevolent, beneficent in his secret Castledawson meadow, bellowed his blessing: and I taught her a lot about King Charles and Robert Burns. Not the Charles who lost his head, I assured her, but the Charles who held on to his head and had all the women he could count. Like Rudolf Valentino.

—The blackguard.

—Who?

—Both of them. Easy for him and he a king.

—Valentino wasn't a king.

—He was a film-star.

—He died from sleeping with women.

That was a gentlemanly way of putting what we then happily and enviously believed.

—He should have slept on his own, so.

But it wasn't often that we argued seriously. King Charles on the run from the Roundheads and the lass who, according to the legend and the poem that Robert Burns based on the legend, made the bed for the fugitive king were better company for us than Valentino who had it all too easy: I bow'd fu' low unto this maid, And thank'd her for her courtesie; I bow'd fu' low unto this maid, And bade her mak a bed to me . . .

Loftily, and with the style of a man who was a scholar when he hadn't better things to occupy his mind, I told her: Some people say that it wasn't about King Charles at all but Robbie Burns writing about himself and remembering some girl he met in some inn. He met a lot of girls and wrote a lot of poems about them.

—He was a bit of a playboy, she said. My uncle who's a teacher near Limavady knows a lot about Burns. He was standing in a gateway with a girl, Burns was . . .

She was turning the upper sheet, patting down pillows.
. . . and a wee fellow came by. Eating a bun. And stopped to
look. And Robert there and then made a poem: Walk on my
son and munch your bun. The works of nature maun be done.

In our places Burns was as much part of the folklore as he
was in the land he was born in.

We laughed over the story. We tackled the bed in the next
room. Once only had I to run and hide when a stout, supervis-
ing, old lady came along. Trudi, while I stood mute in a
built-in wardrobe, sang, sweetly and with a Scot's accent as
good as real, that her love was like a red red rose. In the
darkness I thought: She took her mither's holland sheets, and
made them a' in sarks to me. Blythe and merry may she be, the
lass that made the bed to me.

Burns and the lass and the king, perhaps, were with us in
whatever room we happened to be in. They didn't intrude.
They encouraged us in happiness and folly. Long afterwards I
read a translation from some Spanish (I think) poet, and knew
then what we were up to and, because I couldn't put it better
myself, memorised the words: My chosen part to be with a girl
and alone with her secret and her gift.

Morning after morning the real true scholars marched off
with pen, pencil, ruler, box of mathematical instruments and
the accumulated wisdom of the ages to the grim assembly hall.
Some of the times I went with them but my heart wasn't in it,
my mind wasn't on it. Trudi, whether present or not, was a
dream of my early morning and, as I've said, breakfast was
perfunctory and the main meal of the day, a very late lunch,
was eaten in the Café Continental or the Continental Café
when the regulars were fed and back in their shops and
offices, and the floor and the air clear for dancing and music.
Our examination papers of the day were disposed of by that
time and we were free to roam the town, men of the town, and
one night even so reckless and led by the great lover who for
love had given up learning, as to accost a woman of the town.
Not an easy thing to do for the first time, as every gentleman
knows. Fuzzy-Wuzzy loitered in the rear, dreaming of red sails,
and was useless in the action. Bill, imperturbable, all good

nature and prepared to be at least polite, came two paces
behind me and I, in the van, pondered on the best, most
telling words to begin with. All I could think of was: Miss,
could you show us the way to the Great Northern station?

It was past ten o'clock and all the trains long gone.

She didn't even alter her stride. She said: Wee fella, could
you show me the way to the Albert Clock.

And walked on. It wasn't a question, or a pretended question. The Albert Clock, high on the most prominent tower
in Belfast and beaming like the moon, was thirty yards away
from us.

One evening, after music and dancing and bangers and
mash, we did the bookstalls and the curio shops in Smithfield
market, a Persian bazaar sort of a place, and I bought
Johnson's *Lives of the Poets* and Adam Smith's *The Wealth of
Nations*. In one of my history text-books I had read that the
younger Pitt had read *The Wealth of Nations* and anything the
younger Pitt could do I could do better: it was not recorded in
the text-book that he had ever tried to accost a girl under the
most prominent tower in London, whichever it then was. The
Tower, I suppose.

One evening we came out from Eddie Cantor's *Roman Scan-
dals* and saw, in the queue waiting to get in – it was our last day
but one in Belfast – Trudi and a young man arm-in-arm and
smiling into each other's eyes. They didn't see us. Fuzzy-Wuzzy
blushed and said nothing. Oh, carry my loved one home safely
to me, we'll marry tomorrow and go sailing no more. Bill said
sadly that women were women and it might be that I was her
beau only in the early morning. Even for then, beau was a
curiously Edwardian word to use. Next morning she told me
that it was her cousin from Castledawson and surely to God it
was no sin to go to the cinema with her cousin and that,
moreover, I'd never asked her out in the evening. Which I had
to admit was the bare truth. She had been so much a part of
the morning that it had never occurred to me that she might
be free in the evening and what, without me, would Bill and
Fuzzy-Wuzzy have done, parading the town and lacking their
natural leader? We made it up and made the beds and that was
the last time but one I saw her.

The starlings may still be there but the Old Persian markets are gone, destroyed by bombs. The black news never mentions the starlings.

Lanko was gentle about it when the results came out and Bill and Fuzzy were called and I was not. But he seemed a trifle puzzled, a trifle hurt. There were, after all, three quite inexplicable zeros. Busto huffed and puffed but to my amazement and relief made little comment, and not one place-kick, not one attack on my hair style. But I knew that he knew that something out of the ordinary had happened, that God had saved the king from my services: and he hoped that, for me, something else would turn up.

Those zeros? Well, not quite inexplicable. At least with audacity, *De l'audace, et encore de l'audace, et toujours l'audace,* as the man said who died by the guillotine, with audacity and the aid of friends they could be explained away.

Because three months previously, flogging a mountain stream for trout, in my brother's company and with a triple-hooked bait-tackle that was just about legal, I'd gone in ass first, fished all day in wet clothes and caught one trout, spent three weeks in bed, tossing and turning, my brain tormented, as the brain of man coming out of a bad attack of alcohol might be, by a turning and turning repetition: I would that we were, my beloved, white birds on the foam of the sea.

Over and over and over again. Turning, turning, turning, turning, turning.

Perhaps that had set me in the mood for Trudi, and Bill and Fuzzy-Wuzzy may not have been so far out when they lied like heroes about the flushed and feverish state I'd been in on three Belfast mornings. As heroes I gratefully remember them.

Busto said: Watch it. First in one exam. Twenty-first in the next. Up and down, up and down, watch it, boy.

He may have been a bit of a prophet. For the moment all were happy except my mother who worried about her delicate boy. For a while.

Twice I wrote to Trudi, once to Belfast and once to Castle-dawson and never had an answer. She couldn't spell Switzerland so that she mightn't have been so good at the writing. Better by far at the making of beds and the mitring of sheets: Her bosom was the drifted snaw, twa drifted heaps sae fair to see; her limbs the polish'd marble stane, the lass that made the bed to me.

And it came to pass that Bill was called to the civil service of the King of England to the city of Carlisle, and then to the army in 1939. After the war (that onc) he went into the Palestine police and, after that, to somewhere farther east of Suez and never came home again. Fuzzy-Wuzzy, being called, went to London and its lovely lake and then to the royal navy and, in 1941, sank with a minesweeper in the Channel: oh carry my loved one home safely to me. He never could get the words right.

Flat on my back in a Dublin hospital I heard the news of his death and saw him with his head up the green horn in Peter Sloper's and wondered where I'd be at that moment if Trudi hadn't come between me and the assembly hall: and saw red sails in the sunset and the Rhododendrons round the lovely lake and, through misted eyes, two student nurses mitring my sheet at the corners of my bed: the nurses are the best.

An authority on such things – a man who wrote a book on John McCormack – tells me that the reason why we studied music in bicycle shops was this: the sale of push-bikes in Edwardian times was seasonal, you sold them in the summer. The sale of phonographs and, before them, of the primitive wax cylinders was also seasonal; you sold them in the winter. Bicycle sales, he tells me, thrived during the summer and slumped in winter. Phonographs sold well coming up to Christmas and hardly at all after the festive season. So that, if you were, like Peter Sloper, into both bicycles and phonographs you prospered all the year round and walked the student nurses in your leisure moments.

Where I came from, Edwardian days lasted until 1939.

A Room in Linden

ONE DAY IN the dark maze of the yew-hedges Sister Lua, who has arthritis, looks up at him from her wheelchair which he's pushing, and says: Tell me the truth. Don't be modest about it. Are you Nanky Poo?

Since he is a bookish young man it is an exciting thing for him to have history living along the corridor. The poet he's reading just before he leaves his room writes that there's a wind blowing, cold through the corridor, a death-wind, the flapping of defeated wings from meadows damned to eternal April. The poet has never seen it, but he could have been writing about this corridor. On its dull green walls, a mockery of the grass and green leaves of life, the sun never shines. All day and all night the big windows at the ends of the corridor, one at the east wing of the house and one at the west, are wide open, and from whichever airt the wind does blow it always blows cold. The rooms on the north side of the corridor are, as one might expect, colder and darker than the rooms on the south side, or would be if their light and heat depended totally on the sun.

Before the nuns got here and turned the place into a convalescent home it was lived in by a family famous for generations for a special brand of pipe tobacco. The old soldier who is reluctantly, vociferously fading away in a room on the north side of the corridor, says: This house was built on smoke. Just think of that. Smoke.

The old soldier himself belongs to some branch of the fam-

ily that emigrated to South Africa and made even more money
out of burgundy than the people who stayed at home made
out of smoke, and there was always as much soldiering as
smoke in the family; and big-game hunting, too, to judge by
the fearful snarling mounted heads left behind and surviving,
undisturbed by nuns or convalescents, in the entrance hall.

—You'll be nice to the old man, won't you, Mother Polycarp
had said to him. He'll bore you to death. But he needs somebody to listen to him. He hasn't much longer to talk, in this
world at any rate.

So he talks to the old soldier in the evenings and, in the
afternoons, to the old priest and historian, dying as methodically and academically as he has lived, checking references,
adding footnotes, in a room on the south side of the corridor.
At other times he reads in his own room, or has visitors,
or wheels Sister Lua's wheelchair in the ample bosky grounds,
or leaves the grounds on his own and goes through quiet
suburban roads to walk slowly, tapping his stick, in the public
park that overlooks, across two walls and a railway, the flat
sand and the bay. It is not an exciting life, but it's not meant
to be.

He wheels Sister Lua round and round the dark cloisters
of the yew-hedge maze from the corner where Jesus is condemned to death to the central circle where he is laid in the
tomb. He tells her that he is not Nanky Poo.

—Well, I heard you had poems in that magazine. And I
didn't see your name. And there is this poet called Nanky Poo.
And he's very good. About the missions.

—Not me, alas, sister. I was never on the missions.

—Know you weren't. A university student.

Although she is always sitting down and being wheeled she
is also always breathless and never quite begins or finishes a
sentence, and it is necessary to fill in her words and meanings
as she goes along. Bird-like, he knows, isn't much of a description, but she is bird-like, little hands like claws because of the
arthritis, of course, a little nose like a beak peeking out from
under the nun's pucog. To the left corner of her pale unvar-
nished little mouth, so often twisted with patience in pain,

there's a mole with two hairs. She loves the dark green maze that grew up, like the house, out of smoke and was used by the nuns as a setting for a via dolorosa with life-size figures; and backgrounds of good stone columns and arches robbed from the wreckage of some eighteenth-century mansion. His first faux pas with the old historian had to do with those stations of the cross. One dull evening when the talk wasn't going so well he had, just to make chat, said: Don't they have a big day here once a year? People coming in hundreds to do the stations of the cross. What day does that happen on?

The old man pulls the rug more tightly around his long legs. His feet are always cold. In large bodies, Edmund Burke held, circulation is slower at the extremities, but the coldness of the old man's feet is just the beginning of death. He snuffs black snuff expertly from the hollow between thumb and forefinger, he sneezes, he says with crushing deliberation: Good Friday, my good young man. Even the younger generation should be aware that the Lord was crucified on Good Friday.

He's a carnaptious old bastard and even for the sake of Mother Polycarp, the kindly reverend mother, who is always thanking God for everything, it's sort of hard to suffer him at times. But he has both made and written history, and poems, too, of a learned sort, and collected folksong, and the best people have written about him and discovered an old-world courtesy and all the rest of that rot behind his rude exterior: the old-world courtesy of a Scandinavian sea-rover putting the full of a monastery of shaven-pated monks to the gory hatchet. By comparison the old soldier who has actually killed his man in far-away wars, is a gentleman. But then the old soldier is simply fading away, all battles fought and won, all comrades gone before him, all trumpets sounding from the other side. The old priest, still trying to work, has his last days aggravated by a mind that remembers everything and by the pain of a stomach cancer.

He leaves Sister Lua in the charge of a big red-headed nurse and walks down the main avenue towards suburbia and the park by the sea. The old white-haired vaudeville entertainer who has some sort of shaking paralysis, which he says is an occupational disease, waves to him from his seat by the grotto under the obelisk and gives him three letters to post at the postbox outside the gate. They are, he notices, all addressed to well-known celebrities of screen, stage and television: one in Dublin, one in London, one in New York. Out there is the world of healthy living people.

Life and playing children are, of course, all around him in the park by the sea but it isn't quite the same thing. There isn't enough of life there to help him to stop thinking of old men dying. He is very much on his own either because of his sullenness, or because he thinks that while he may be of interest to himself he couldn't possibly be of interest to anybody else. Nothing humble about that, though. In that park he's really a visitor from a special sort of world, from a cold green corridor damned to eternal December: sort of exclusive, though, a rich old soldier, a famous old historian, the artist who is still in touch with the best people; and only the best die in that corridor.

One old man who sits on a green wooden seat, close to the play-hall where the children run when it rains, talks to him as if he would gladly talk longer. He discourages that old man with abrupt sentences for he has, at the moment, enough of old men. He walks on beyond him and along by the tennis courts. A stout bespectacled girl with strong tanned legs plays awkwardly with a tall blond handsome fellow who wins every set and enjoys his superiority, while she seems to enjoy being beaten. A stranger from a strange land, he enjoys, as he passes or rests for a while on a seat and watches, the leaping of her legs. So everybody is happy and the park is beautiful. The blond boy isn't even good at the game and he, the stranger, knows that if it wasn't for the stiff hip, still slowly recovering, he could challenge him and beat him easily. But then the stout girl, legs excepted, isn't really interesting.

He himself is blond and doesn't take too well to the sun. So his favourite seat is in a shady corner under dark horsechest-nuts whose white candles are fading. He likes the place also because nobody else sits there. Strollers seem to accelerate as they walk past. Once in a while children run shouting, hooting through the dark tunnel, from one shire of sunshine into another. Through a fence of mournful laurels and copper beeches he sees the glitter of the sun on the lake. Out of the corner of his left eye he sees a well-built girl in white shorts flat on her back on the sunny grass. Sometimes she reads. Sometimes she raises her legs and, furiously with flashing thighs, pedals an invisible bicycle, faster and faster until it seems as if she has seven or seventeen legs, until the flash of her thighs takes the shape of a white circle. Her belly muscles must be jingling like springs. The joints in her hips, unlike his own, must be in perfect lubricated condition. She is at the moment one of the five women in his life: Polycarp thanking God for the rain and the sunshine, for the hail and the snow; Lua, twisted in her chair; she who, nameless, cycles on her back on the grass; the strong-legged tennis player whose name, he has heard the blond fellow shout, is Phyllis; and A.N. Other.

To the rear of his shady corner there is a privet hedge and a high wooden fence and a gate with a notice that says no admission except on business. That's exactly the way he feels. Adam in Eden must have had just such a corner where he kept his tools and experimented with slips and seeds. But then before Adam and Eve made a pig's ass out of a good arrangement the garden must have looked after itself and needed none of that sweat-of-the-brow stuff. What would old Thor the thunderer, brooding in his room, biting on his cancer, think of that?

Belloc, says the old priest, was a big man who looked as if all his life he had eaten too much and drunk too much. The best way to learn French is to read cowboy and injun stories. They hold the interest better than Racine.

Aware of his own inanity, he says: translations.

Before that face, oblong, seemingly about twelve feet long, like a head cut out of the side of some crazy American mountain, he is perpetually nonplussed into saying stupidities.

—Cowboys and injuns, my good young man, are not indigenous to the soil of France.

—There's a city called Macon in Georgia, U.S.A.

—There's a city called everything somewhere in the States. Naturally they mispronounce the names. So it goes on. You can't win with the old bastard.

—Darlington, he says, used to call on Hopkins to take him out for walks. Hopkins was for ever and always complaining of headaches. What else can you expect, Darlington would say to him, immured up there in your room writing rubbish. I'm not so sure that Darlington wasn't right.

He is at that time just entering his Hopkins phase and if he wasn't afraid of that granite face, eyes sunken and black and burning, jawbones out rigid like a forked bush struck by lightning, he would defend the poet, quoting his sonnet about the windhover which, with some difficulty, he has just memorised. Yet it still is something to hear those names tossed about by a man who knew the men, and was a name himself. He feels grateful to Mother Polycarp who, as a friend of his family, has invited him to this place for a while, after his year in orthopaedic, so that he can read his books and learn to walk at his ease. In all that green cold corridor, which is really a place for old men, he is the only person who is going to live. He searches for something neutral to say: Wasn't Hopkins always very scrupulous about marking students' papers?

—He was a neurotic Englishman, my good fellow. They never could make up their minds between imperialism and humanitarianism. That's what has them the way they are. Darlington was English, too, of course, the other sort, the complacent Englishman, thinking that only what is good can happen to him, and that all his works are good. Then a young upstart called Joyce put him in a book. That should have been a lesson to Darlington, if they have books in heaven or wherever he went to.

He should, as Mother Polycarp says, be taking notes, thank God, except he feels that if he did so, secretly even in his room, the old lion might read his mind and take offence. The old man laughs seldom, but he's laughing now, perhaps at some memory of two English Jesuits marooned in Ireland, or at some other memory surfacing for a second in the dark crowded pool behind his square forehead. He has kept his hair, a dirty grey, standing up and out as if it had never encountered a comb. The long bony hands tighten the rug about his knees. The cold is creeping upwards.

In the green corrider he kneels for a while at the prie-dieu before the shrine, not praying, just thinking about age and death, and looking up at the bearded face of St. Joseph, pure and gentle, guardian of the saviour child. With a lily in his hand. Another old man and, by all accounts, very patient about it. What in hell is St. Joseph, like Oscar Wilde or somebody, always doing with a lily in his hand? An awkward class of a thing for a carpenter to be carrying.

Before his hip betrayed him he has had a half-notion of being a priest, but a year in orthopaedic, bright nurses hopping all around him, has cured him by showing him that there are things that priests, in the ordinary course of duty, are not supposed to have.

—You're too young, the old soldier says, to be in this boneyard.

He's a small man with a red boozy face, a red dressing-gown, a whiskey bottle and a glass always to his right hand. The whiskey keeps him alive, thank God, Mother Polycarp says. He is, like St. Joseph, gentle but not so pure, rambling on about dirty doings in far-away places, Mombasa and Delhi are much mentioned, about Kaffir women, and about blokes who got knocked off in the most comical fashion. He laughs a lot. He doesn't need a considered answer or a balanced conversation, just a word now and then to show he's not alone. He shares the whiskey generously. He has bags of money and, when he dies, he'll leave the perishing lot to the nuns.

—They do good, you know. Keep perky about it, too. Who else would look after the likes of me? Ruddy boneyard, though. Elephant's graveyard. Get out of here and get a woman. Make sons. Before it's too late. Would get out myself only nobody would have me any more, and I couldn't have them. Only whiskey left. But I had my day. When I was your age I laid them as quick as my batman could pull them out from under me. Three women shot under me at the battle of

Balaclava and all that. Fit only for the boneyard now and the
nuns. They don't want it and I can't give it. But there's always
whiskey, thank God, as the mother says. A field behind the
barracks where old wind-broken cavalry mounts went on grass
with the shoes off until they died. At least we didn't eat them
like the bloody Belgians. Smell of slow death around this place.

He sniffs the whiskey and laughs and then coughs. By night
the coughing is constant. Lying awake and listening, the young
man has a nightmarish feeling that they are all in prison cells,
all dying, which is true, all the living are dying, and after one
night the sun will never rise again on the park, and every time
the cycling girl spins her legs she's another circle nearer to the
grave. His own healthy youth has already collapsed in illness.
Life is one collapse after another. The coughing goes on and
on. To be a brave soldier and to end up coughing in a lonely
room. Let me outa here. No, Sister Lua, I am not Nanky Poo.

—But every day that passes, Mother Polycarp tells him, brings
you a day nearer to getting back to your studies, thank God.
You made a great recovery in orthopaedic.

She is a tall woman with a long flat-footed step and more
rattlings of keys and rosary beads than seem natural even in a
nun. When he tells her that, she laughs and says, of course,
that she has the keys of the kingdom, thank God. She has a
good-humoured wrinkled mannish face, and she is famous
everywhere for her kindness and her ability to gather money
and build hospitals.

Does she say to the old men: Every day that passes brings
you a day nearer heaven, thank God?

She naturally wouldn't mention death as the gate of heaven.

He has a feeling that none of them want to go any farther
forward, they look backward to see heaven: on the day a new
book was published or a new woman mounted or a new show
went well. Heaven, like most things, doesn't last, or could only
be an endless repetition of remembered happiness, and would
in the end be, like dying, a bloody bore.

In her chair as he wheels her, Sister Lua, chirping like the
little robin that she is, prays a bit and chats a bit and, because

of her breathlessness and the way she beheads her sentences and docks the tails off them, he has to listen carefully to know whether she is chatting or praying. The life-size figures in the maze of dark yews – fourteen Christs in various postures, with attendant characters from jesting Pilate to the soldiers by the tomb – have acquired a sombre existence of their own. Do they relax at night, yawn, stretch stiff limbs, mutter a curse, light a cigarette, say to hell with show business? He must try that one out on the vaudeville man, shaking his way to the grave, on the seat by the grotto under the obelisk.

—Weep not for me, Sister Lua prays, but for yourselves and for your children.

The lord is talking to the weeping women of Jerusalem and not doing a lot to cheer them up. Some anti-semitical Irish parish priest must have written the prayers that Lua reels off. He didn't think much either of the kind of recruitment that got into the Roman army: These barbarians fastened him with nails and then, securing the cross, allowed him to die in anguish on this ignominious gibbet.

From the prayer book she has learned, by heart, not only the prayers but the instructions that go with them. She says, as the book instructs: Pause a while.

He pauses. The yew-hedges are a dark wall to either hand. Twenty paces ahead, the lord, in an arbour, is being lowered from the cross. The dying has been done.

—Nanky Poo. Nanky Poo.

—Sister, I am not Nanky Poo.

—But I call you Nanky Poo. Such a lovely name.

—So is Pooh Bah.

—Pooh Bah is horrible. Somebody making mean faces. Nanky Poo, you must write a poem for Mother Polycarp's feast-day. So easy for you. Just a parody. Round Linden when the sun was low, Mother Polycarp the Good did go.

—There's a future in that style.

—You'll do it, Nanky Poo?

—At my ease, sister. Whatever Nanky Poo can do, I can do better.

By the laying of the lord in the tomb they encounter A.N. Other. She tries to escape by hiding behind the eighteenth-century cut-stone robbed from the old house, but Sister Lua's birds-eye is too quick and too sharp for her.

—Nurse Donovan, Nurse Donovan, the French texts have arrived.

—Yes, Sister Lua.

—When can you begin, Nanky Poo?

—Any time, sister.

—So useful to you, Nurse Donovan, French, when you're a secretary.

She is a small well-rounded brunette who has nursed in the orthopaedic hospital until something happened to her health. He is in love with her, has been for some time. Nothing is to come of it. He is never to see her again after he leaves the convalescent home. The trouble is that Sister Lua has decided that the girl must be a secretary and that Nanky Poo must teach her French, and it is quite clear from the subdued light in the girl's downcast dark eyes that she doesn't give a fiddler's fart about learning anything, even French, out of a book. Worse still: on the few occasions on which he has been able to corner the girl on her own he hasn't been able to think of a damn thing to talk about except books. How can he ever get through to her that pedagogy is the last thing in his mind?

She wheels Sister Lua away from him to the part of the house where the nuns live. Between the girl and himself Sister Lua has thrown a barbed-wire entanglement of irregular verbs. No great love has ever been so ludicrously frustrated.

A white blossom that he cannot identify grows copiously in this suburb. Thanks be to God for the thunder and lightning, thanks be to God for all things that grow.

No, Sister Lua, I am not Nanky Poo, am a disembodied spirit, homeless in suburbia, watching with envy a young couple coming, white and dancing, out of a house and driving away to play tennis, am a lost soul blown on the blast between a green cold corridor of age and death, and the children running and squealing by the lake in the park.

Beyond the two walls and the railway line the sea is flat and purple all the way to Liverpool. He envies the young footballers in the playing fields close to where the cycling girl lies flat on her back and rides to the moon on her imaginary bicycle. He envies particularly a red-headed boy with a superb left foot, who centres the ball, repeating the movement again and again, a conscious artist, as careless as God of what happens to the ball next, just so that he drops it in the goalmouth where he feels it should go. The footballer is on talking terms with the cycling girl. He jokes and laughs with her when the ball bounces that way. She stops her cycling to answer him. From his shadowy corner under the chestnuts Nanky Poo watches and thinks about his latest talk with the vaudeville man on his seat by the grotto under the obelisk.

The obelisk has also been built on smoke to celebrate the twenty-first birthday of a son of the house who would have been the great-grand-uncle of the old soldier.

—Vanished somewhere in India, the poor fellow. There was a rumour to the effect that he was eaten by wild beasts. A damn hard thing to prove unless you see it happen. Anyway he did for a good few of them before they got him. Half of the heads in the hallway below are his.

The obelisk stands up on a base of a flowering rockery, and into the cave or grotto underneath the rockery the nuns have, naturally, inserted a miniature Lourdes: the virgin with arms extended and enhaloed by burning candles, Bernadette kneeling by a fountain of holy water that is blessed by the chaplain at its source in a copper tank.

—The candles, says the vaudeville man, keep my back warm.

He wears a faded brown overcoat with a velvet collar. His white hair is high and bushy and possibly not as well trimmed as it used to be. The skin of his shrunken face and bony Roman nose has little purple blotches and, to conceal the shake in his hands, he grips the knob of his bamboo walking-cane very tightly. When he walks his feet rise jerkily from the ground as if they did so of their own accord and might easily decide never to settle down again. The handwriting on the envelopes is thin and wavery as if the pen now and again took off on its own.

—You know all the best people.

—I used to.

He is never gloomy, yet never hilarious. Somewhere in

between he has settled for an irony that is never quite bitter.

—You still write to them.

—Begging letters, you know. Reminders of the good old days. They almost always work with show people. I never quite made it, you know, not even when I had the health. But I was popular with my own kind. This one now.

He points to a notable name on one envelope.

—We met one night in a boozer in London when I wasn't working. He stood me a large Jameson straight away, then another, then another. He asked me to dine with him. We talked about this and that. When we parted I found a tenner in the inside breast pocket of my overcoat. While we were dining he had slipped into the cloakroom. No note, no message, just a simple tenner to speak for itself. He wasn't rich then, mark you, although as the world knows he did well afterwards. But he remembers me. He promises to come to see me. Do you know, now that I think of it, this was the very overcoat.

The cycling girl has stopped cycling and is talking to the red-headed footballer. He stands above her, casually bouncing the ball on that accurate left foot. Whatever he's saying the girl laughs so loudly that Nanky Poo can hear her where he sits in gloom and broods on beggary. She has a good human throaty sort of a laugh.

The night there is no coughing, but only one loud single cry, from the next room, he knows that the old soldier has awakened for a moment to die. He rises, puts on slippers and dressing-gown, and heads down the corridor to find the night nurse. But Mother Polycarp is there already, coming stoop-shouldered, beads and keys rattling, from the old man's room.

—Thank God, she says, he died peacefully and he had the blessed sacrament yesterday morning. He wandered a lot in his time but he came home in the end.

He walks down the stairway to the shadowy main hall. Do the animals in the half-darkness grin with satisfaction at the death of a man whose relative was eaten by one or more of their relatives? The front door is open for the coming of the doctor and the priest. Above the dark maze of yew-hedge the obelisk is silhouetted against the lights of the suburb. The place is so quiet that he can hear even the slight noise of the sea over the flat sand. This is the first time he has been out of doors at night since he went to orthopaedic. Enjoying the freedom, the quiet, the coolness, he walks round and round in the maze until his eyes grow used to the blackness and he is able to pick out the men and women who stand along the via dolorosa. They are just as motionless as they are during the day. When he comes back Mother Polycarp is waiting for him in the hallway.

—Now you're bold, she says. You could catch a chill. But every day that passes brings you nearer to freedom, thank God, and you can walk very well now.

She crosses herself as she passes the shrine in the corridor. She says: One thing that you could do now that you are up, is talk to himself. Or listen to him. He's awake and out of bed and lonely for somebody to talk to.

He is out of bed but not fully dressed; and, in a red dressing-gown that must have been presented to him by Mother Polycarp, he doesn't seem half as formidable as in his black religious habit. There is an open book on the rug that, as usual, covers and beats down the creeping cold from his thighs and knees. He is not reading. His spectacles are in their case on the table to his right hand. Above the light from the shaded reading-lamp his head and shoulders are in shadow. For once, since he is red and not black and half invisible, Nanky Poo feels almost at ease with him.

From the shadows his voice says: Credit where credit is due, young man. The first Chichester to come to Ireland was certainly one of the most capable and successful robbers who ever lived. He stole most of the north of Ireland not only from its owners but even from the robbers who stole it from its owners. Twice he robbed his royal master, James Stuart, the fourth of Scotland and the first of England. The man who did that had to rise early in the morning. For although King James was a fool about most things he was no fool about robbery: it was he who got the Scots the name for parsimony. Chichester stole the entire fisheries of Lough Neagh, the largest lake in the British

Isles, and nobody found out about it until after he died. *Age quod agis*, as the maxim says. Do what you do. At his own craft he was a master. I dealt with him in a book.

—I read it.

—Did you indeed? A mark in your favour, young man.

—As a matter of fact, sir, the copy of it I read had your name on the flyleaf. Father Charles from your monastery loaned it to me when I was in orthopaedic.

As soon as the words are out he knows he has dropped the biggest brick of his career, and prays to Jesus that he may live long and die happy and never drop a bigger one. He has never known silence to last so long and be so deafening. Even the bulb in the reading-lamp makes a sound like a big wind far away. Blood in the ears?

—They're not expecting me back, so.

—What do you mean, sir?

—You know damned well what I mean. In a monastery when they know you're dead and not coming back they empty your room. There's another man in it now. They were kind and never told me. That room was all I had, and my books. They have sent me to the death-house as they so elegantly say in the United States. This here is the death-house. What do you do here, young man?

He is asking himself that question. So far no easy answer has offered itself.

—Books you build around you, more than a house and wife and family for a layman, part of yourself, flesh of your flesh, more than furniture for a monk's cell, a shell for his soul, the only thing in spite of the rule of poverty I couldn't strip myself of, and my talents allowed me a way around the rule, but man goeth forth naked as he came, stripped of everything, death bursts among them like a shell and strews them over half the town, and yet there are men who can leave their books as memorials to great libraries...

Sacred Heart of Jesus, he thinks, up there in the shadows there may be tears on that granite face.

—I'm sorry, sir.

—You didn't know, young man. How could you know?

—You will be remembered, sir.
—Thank you. The old must be grateful. Go to bed now. You have reason to rest. You have a life to live.
In his room he reads for what's left of the night. He has a life to live.

Through a drowsy weary morning he feels he wants to leave the place right away. Never again will he see the old soldier. Never again can he face the old scholar.
—Nanky Poo, Nanky Poo, you won't see your old friend again.
—No, sister. He died last night.
—Not him. Your old friend on the seat by the grotto.
Flying from French, A.N. Other cuts across their path through the maze. But she's moving so fast that not even Lua can hail her. Somewhere in the maze and as quietly as a cat she is stealing away from him for ever. Dulled with lack of sleep his brain is less than usually able to keep up with the chirpings of Lua.
—Is he dead too?
Let them all die. Let me outa here. I am not Nanky Poo.
—A stroke, not fatal yet, but, alas, the final one.
—I'll go to see him.
But Mother Polycarp tells him there's no point in that: all connection between brain and tongue and eyes is gone.
—He wouldn't know whether you were there or not.
—Couldn't he see me?
—We don't know. The doctor says, God bless us, that he's a vegetable.
—I wondered had he any letters to send out. I used to post them for him.
—He can't write any more.
A silence. So he can't even beg.
—It's a blow to you, she says. You were his friend. He used to enjoy his talks with you. But it'll soon be over, thank God. Pray for him that he may pray for us. For some of us death isn't the worst thing and, as far as we can tell, he's content.
A vegetable has little choice. Refusing to lie down and rest in that green place of death he walks dumbly through the

suburb. The white blossoms blind him. When he leaves this place he will do so with the sense of escape he might have if he was running on a smooth hillside on a sunny windy day. But later he knows that the place will be with him for ever: the cry in the night, the begging letters sent to the stars, the pitiful anger of an old man finding another man living in his room. Crucified god, there's life for you, and there's a lot more of it that he hasn't yet encountered. He expects little, but he will sit no longer expecting it alone in any dark corner.

He would like to be able to tell the cycling girl a really good lie about how he injured his hip. The scrum fell on me on the line in a rather dirty game, just as I was sneaking away and over: that's how it happens, you know.

Or: An accident on a rockface in Snowdonia, a bit of bad judgment, my own fault actually.

Or: You've heard of the parachute club that ex-air force chap has started out near Celbridge.

He would prefer if he had crutches, or even one crutch, instead of a stick which he doesn't even need. A crutch could win a girl's confidence for no harm could come to her from a fellow hopping on a crutch unless he could move as fast as, and throw the crutch with the accuracy of, Long John Silver.

There he goes, thinking about books again. He'd better watch that.

The red-headed footballer is far-away and absorbed in the virtues of his own left foot. For the first time Nanky Poo notices the colour of her hair, mousy, and the colour of her sweater, which today is mauve, because when she lay flat on the grass and he watched from a distance, she was mostly white shorts and bare circling thighs.

He sits down, stiffly, on the grass beside her. She seems not in the least surprised. She has a freckled face and spectacles. That surprises him.

He says: I envy the way your hips work.

If he doesn't say something wild like that he'll begin talking about books and his cause is lost.

—Why so?

—I was laid up for a year with a tubercular hip. I'm in the convalescent over there.

—Oh I know who you are. Sister Lua told me. You're Nanky Poo. You write poetry.

He is cold all over.

You know Sister Lua?

—She's my aunt. I write poetry too. Nobody has ever printed it though. Yet. Sister Lua said that some day she'd ask you to read some of it.

—I'd be delighted to.

—I watched you sitting over there for a long time. But I didn't like to approach you. Sister Lua said you were stand-offish and intellectual.

She walks back with him as far as the obelisk and the grotto. They will meet again on the following day and take a bus into a teashop in the city. They may even go to a show if Mother Polycarp allows him – as she will – to stay out late.

He suspects that all this will come to nothing except to the reading of her poetry which as likely as not will be diabolical. He wonders if some day she will, like her aunt, be arthritic, for arthritis, they say, like a stick leg, runs in the blood. But with one of his three friends dead, one estranged and one a vegetable, it is something to have somebody to talk to as you stumble through suburbia. He has a life to live. Every day that passes brings him a day nearer to somewhere else.

So thanks be to God for the rain and the sunshine, thanks be to God for the hail and the snow, thanks be to God for the thunder and lightning, thanks be to God that all things are so.

A Ball of Malt
and Madame Butterfly

O N A WARM but not sunny June afternoon on a crowded Dublin street, by no means one of the city's most
elegant streets, a small hotel, a sort of bed-and-
breakfast place, went on fire. There was pandemonium at first,
more panic than curiosity in the crowd. It was a street
of decayed Georgian houses, high and narrow, with steep
wooden staircases, and cluttered small shops on the ground
floors: all great nourishment for flames. The fire, though,
didn't turn out to be serious. The brigade easily contained and
controlled it. The panic passed, gave way to curiosity, then to
indignation and finally, alas, to laughter about the odd thing
that had happened when the alarm was at its worst.

This was it.

From a window on the top-most floor a woman, scantily-
clad, puts her head out and waves a patchwork bed coverlet,
and screams for help. The stairway, she cries, is thick with
smoke, herself and her husband are afraid to face it. On what
would seem to be prompting from inside the room, she calls
down that they are a honeymoon couple up from the country.
That would account fairly enough for their still being abed on
a warm June afternoon.

The customary ullagone and ullalu goes up from the crowd.
The fire-engine ladder is aimed up to the window. A fireman begins to run up the ladder. Then suddenly the groom

appears in shirt and trousers, and barefooted. For, to the horror of the beholders, he makes his bare feet visible by pushing the bride back into the room, clambering first out of the window, down the ladder like a monkey although he is a fairly corpulent man; with monkey-like agility dodging round the ascending fireman, then disappearing through the crowd. The people, indignant enough to trounce him, are still too concerned with the plight of the bride, and too astounded to seize him. The fireman ascends to the nuptial casement, helps the lady through the window and down the ladder, gallantly offering his jacket which covers some of her. Then when they are halfways down, the fireman, to the amazement of all, is seen to be laughing right merrily, the bride vituperating. But before they reach the ground she also is laughing. She is brunette, tall, but almost Japanese in appearance, and very handsome. A voice says: If she's a bride I can see no confetti in her hair.

She has fine legs which the fireman's jacket does nothing to conceal and which she takes pride, clearly, in displaying. She is a young woman of questionable virginity and well known to the firemen. She is the toast of a certain section of the town to whom she is affectionately known as Madame Butterfly, although unlike her more famous namesake she has never been married, nor cursed by an uncle bonze for violating the laws of the gods of her ancestors. She has another, registered, name: her mother's name. What she is her mother was before her, and proud of it.

The bare-footed fugitive was not, of course, a bridegroom, but a long-established married man with his wife and family and a prosperous business in Longford, the meanest town in Ireland. For the fun of it the firemen made certain that the news of his escapade in the June afternoon got back to Longford. They were fond of, even proud of, Butterfly as were many other men who had nothing at all to do with the quenching of fire.

But one man loved the pilgrim soul in her and his name was Pike Hunter.

Like Borgnefesse, the buccaneer of St. Malo on the Rance,

who had a buttock shot or sliced off in action on the Spanish Main, Pike Hunter had a lopsided appearance when sitting down. Standing up he was as straight and well-balanced as a man could be: a higher civil servant approaching the age of forty, a shy bachelor, reared, nourished and guarded all his life by a trinity of upper-middle-class aunts. He was pink-faced, with a little fair hair left to emphasise early baldness, mild in his ways, with a slight stutter, somewhat afraid of women. He wore always dark-brown suits with a faint red stripe, dark-brown hats, rimless spectacles, shiny square-toed brown handmade shoes with a wide welt. In summer, even on the hottest day, he carried a raincoat folded over his arm, and a rolled umbrella. When it rained he unfolded and wore the raincoat and opened and raised the umbrella. He suffered mildly from hay fever. In winter he belted himself into a heavy brown overcoat and wore galoshes. Nobody ever had such stiff white shirts. He favoured brown neckties distinguished with a pearl-headed pin. Why he sagged to one side, just a little to the left, when he sat down, I never knew. He had never been sliced or shot on the Spanish Main.

But the chance of a sunny still Sunday afternoon in Stephen's Green and Grafton Street, the select heart or soul of the city's south side, made a changed man out of him.

He had walked at his ease through the Green, taking the sun gratefully, blushing when he walked between the rows of young ladies lying back in deck-chairs. He blushed for two reasons: they were reclining, he was walking; they were as gracefully at rest as the swans on the lake, he was awkwardly in motion, conscious that his knees rose too high, that his sparse hair – because of the warmth he had his hat in his hand – danced long and ludicrously in the little wind, that his shoes squeaked. He was fearful that his right toe might kick his left heel, or vice versa, and that he would fall down and be laughed at in laughter like the sound of silver bells. He was also alarmingly aware of the bronze knees, and more than knees, that the young ladies exposed as they leaned back and relaxed in their light summer frocks. He would honestly have liked to stop and enumerate those knees, make an inventory – he was in the Department of Statistics; perhaps pat a few here and there.

But the fearful regimen of that trinity of aunts forbade him even to glance sideways, and he stumbled on like a winkered horse, demented by the flashing to right and to left of bursting globes of bronze light.

Then on the park pathway before him, walking towards the main gate and the top of Grafton Street, he saw the poet. He had seen him before, but only in the Abbey Theatre and never on the street. Indeed it seemed hardly credible to Pike Hunter that such a man would walk on the common street where all ordinary or lesser men were free to place their feet. In the Abbey Theatre the poet had all the strut and style of a man who could walk with the gods, the Greek gods that is, not the gods in the theatre's cheapest seats. His custom was to enter by a small stairway, at the front of the house and in full view of the audience, a few moments before the lights dimmed and the famous gong sounded and the curtain rose. He walked slowly, hands clasped behind his back, definitely balancing the prone brow oppressive with its mind, the eagle head aloft and crested with foaming white hair. He would stand, his back to the curtain and facing the house. The chatter would cease, the fiddlers in the orchestra would saw with diminished fury. Some of the city wits said that what the poet really did at those times was to count the empty seats in the house and make a rapid reckoning of the night's takings. But their gibe could not diminish the majesty of those entrances, the majesty of the stance of the man. And there he was now, hands behind back, noble head high, pacing slowly, beginning the course of Grafton Street. Pike Hunter walked behind him, suiting his pace to the poet's, to the easy deliberate rhythms of the early love poetry: I would that we were, my beloved, white birds on the foam of the sea. There is a queen in China or, maybe, it's in Spain.

They walked between the opulent windows of elegant glittering shops, doors closed for Sunday. The sunshine had drawn the people from the streets: to the park, to the lush green country, to the seaside. Of the few people they did meet, not all of them seemed to know who the poet was, but those who did know saluted quietly, with a modest and unaffected reverence, and one young man with a pretty girl on his arm stepped off the pavement, looked after the poet and clearly whispered to the maiden who it was that had just passed by the way. Stepping behind him at a respectful distance Pike felt like an acolyte behind a celebrant and regretted that there was no cope or cloak of cloth-of-gold of which he could humbly carry the train.

So they sailed north towards the Liffey, leaving Trinity College, with Burke standing haughty-headed and Goldsmith sipping at his honeypot of a book, to the right, and the Bank and Grattan orating Esto Perpetua, to the left, and Thomas Moore of the Melodies, brown, stooped and shabby, to the right; and came into Westmoreland Street where the wonder happened. For there approaching them came the woman Homer sung: old and grey and, perhaps, full of sleep, a face much and deeply lined and haggard, eyes sunken, yet still the face of the queen she had been when she and the poet were young and they had stood on the cliffs on Howth Head, high above the promontory that bears the Bailey Lighthouse as a warning torch and looks like the end of the world; and they had watched the soaring of the gulls and he had wished that he and she were only white birds, my beloved, buoyed out on the foam of the sea. She was very tall. She was not white, but all black in widow's weeds for the man she had married when she wouldn't marry the poet. Her black hat had a wide brim and, from the brim, an old-fashioned veil hung down before her face. The pilgrim soul in you, and loved the sorrows of your changing face.

Pike stood still, fearing that in a dream he had intruded on some holy place. The poet and the woman moved dreamlike towards each other, then stood still, not speaking, not saluting, at opposite street corners where Fleet Street comes narrowly from the east to join Westmoreland Street. Then still not speaking, not saluting, they turned into Fleet Street. When Pike tiptoed to the corner and peered around he saw that they had walked on opposite sides of the street for, perhaps, thirty paces, then turned at right angles, moved towards each other, stopped to talk in the middle of the street where a shaft of sunlight had defied the tall overshadowing buildings. Apart from themselves and Pike that portion of the town seemed to be awesomely empty; and there Pike left them and walked in a daze by the side of the Liffey to a pub called The Dark Cow. Something odd had happened to him: poetry, a vision of love?

It so happened that on that day Butterfly was in the Dark Cow, as, indeed, she often was: just Butterfly and Pike, and Jody with the red carbuncled face who owned the place and was genuinely kind to the girls of the town, and a few honest dockers who didn't count because they had money only for their own porter and were moral men, loyal to wives or sweethearts. It wasn't the sort of place Pike frequented. He had never seen Butterfly before: those odd slanting eyes, the glistening high-piled black hair, the well-defined bud of a mouth, the crossed legs, the knees that outclassed to the point of mockery all the bronze globes in Stephen's Green. Coming on top of his vision of the poet and the woman, all this was too much for him, driving him to a reckless courage that would have flabbergasted the three aunts. He leaned on the counter. She sat in an alcove that was a sort of throne for her, where on busier days she sat surrounded by her sorority. So he says to Jody whom he did not yet know as Jody: May I have the favour of buying the lady in the corner a drink?

—That you may, and more besides.

—Please ask her permission. We must do these things properly.

—Oh there's a proper way of doing everything, even screwing a goose.

But Jody, messenger of love, walks to the alcove and formally asks the lady would she drink if the gentleman at the counter sends it over. She will. She will also allow him to join her. She whispers: Has he any money?

—Loaded, says Jody.

—Send him over so. Sunday's a dull day.

Pike sits down stiffly, leaning a little away from her, which seems to her quite right for him as she has already decided that he's a shy sort of man, upper class, but shy, not like some. He excuses himself from intruding. She says: You're not inthrudin'.

He says he hasn't the privilege of knowing her name.

Talks like a book, she decides, or a play in the Gaiety.

—Buttherfly, she says.

—Butterfly, he says, is a lovely name.

—Me mother's name was Trixie, she volunteers.

—Was she dark like you?

—Oh, a natural blonde and very busty, well developed, you know. She danced in the old Tivoli where the newspaper office is now. I'm neat, not busty.

To his confusion she indicates, with hands moving in small curves, the parts of her that she considers are neat. But he notices that she has shapely long-fingered hands and he remembers that the poet had admitted that the small hands of his beloved were not, in fact, beautiful. He is very perturbed.

—Neat, she says, and well-made. Austin McDonnell, the fire-brigade chief, says that he read in a book that the best sizes and shapes would fit into champagne glasses.

He did wonder a little that a fire-brigade chief should be a quotable authority on female sizes and shapes, and on champagne glasses. But then and there he decided to buy her champagne, the only drink fit for such a queen who seemed as if she came, if not from China, at any rate from Japan.

—Champagne, he said.

—Bubbly, she said. I love bubbly.

Jody dusted the shoulders of the bottle that on his shelves had waited a long time for a customer. He unwired the cork. The cork and the fizz shot up to the ceiling.

—This, she said, is my lucky day.

—The divine Bernhardt, said Pike, had a bath in champagne presented to her by a group of gentlemen who admired her.

—Water, she said, is better for washing.

But she told him that her mother who knew everything about actresses had told her that story, and told her that when, afterwards, the gentlemen bottled the contents of the bath and drank it, they had one bottleful too many. He was too far gone in fizz and love's frenzy to feel embarrassed. She was his discovery, his oriental queen.

He said: You're very oriental in appearance. You could be from Japan.

She said: My father was, they say. A sailor. Sailors come and go.

She giggled. She said: That's a joke. Come and go. Do you see it?

Pike saw it: He giggled with her. He was a doomed man.

She said: Austin McDonnell says that if I was in Japan I could be a geisha girl if I wasn't so tall. That's why they call me Butterfly. It's the saddest story. Poor Madame Butterfly died that her child could be happy across the sea. She married a sailor, too, an American lieutenant. They come and go. The priest, her uncle, cursed her for marrying a Yank.

—The priests are good at that, said Pike who, because of his reading allowed himself, outside office hours, a soupçon of anticlericalism.

Touched by Puccini they were silent for a while, sipping champagne. With every sip Pike realised more clearly that he had found what the poet, another poet, an English one, had called the long-awaited long-expected spring, he knew his heart had found a time to sing, the strength to soar was in his spirit's wing, that life was full of a triumphant sound and death could only be a little thing. She was good on the nose, too. She was wise in the ways of perfume. The skin of her neck had a pearly glow. The three guardian aunts were as far away as the moon. Then one of the pub's two doors – it was a corner house – opened with a crash and a big man came in, well drunk, very jovial. He wore a wide-brimmed grey hat. He walked to the counter. He said: Jody, old bootlegger, old friend of mine, old friend of Al Capone, serve me a drink to sober me up.

—Austin, said Jody, what will it be?

—A ball of malt, the big man said, and Madame Butterfly.

—That's my friend, Austin, she said, he always says that for a joke.

Pike whose face, with love or champagne or indignation, was taut and hot all over, said that he didn't think it was much of a joke.

—Oh, for Janey's sake, Pike, be your age.

She used his first name for the first time. His eyes were moist.

—For Janey's sake, it's a joke. He's a father to me. He knew my mother.

—He's not Japanese.

—Mind your manners. He's a fireman.

—Austin, she called. Champagne. Pike Hunter's buying champagne.

Pike bought another bottle, while Austin towered above them, swept the wide-brimmed hat from his head in a cavalier half-circle, dropped it on the head of Jody whose red carbuncled face was thus half-extinguished. Butterfly giggled. She said: Austin, you're a scream. He knew Trixie, Pike. He knew Trixie when she was the queen of the boards in the old Tivoli.

Sitting down, the big man sang in a ringing tenor: For I knew Trixie when Trixie was a child.

He sipped at his ball of malt. He sipped at a glass of Pike's champagne. He said: It's a great day for the Irish. It's a great day to break a fiver. Butterfly, dear girl, we fixed the Longford lout. He'll never leave Longford again. The wife has him tethered and spancelled in the haggard. We wrote poison-pen letters to half the town, including the parish priest.

—I never doubted ye, she said.

—Leave it to the firemen, I said.

—The Dublin Fire Brigade, Austin said, has as long an arm as the Irish Republican Army.

—Austin, she told Pike, died for Ireland.

He sipped champagne. He sipped whiskey. He said: Not once, but several times. When it was neither popular nor profitable. By the living God, we was there when we was wanted. Volunteer McDonnell, at your service.

His bald head shone and showed freckles. His startlingly blue eyes were brightened and dilated by booze. He said: Did I know Trixie, light on her feet as the foam on the fountain? Come in and see the horses. That's what we used to say to the girls when I was a young fireman. Genuine horsepower the fire-engines ran on then, and the harness hung on hooks ready to drop on the horses as the firemen descended the greasy pole. And where the horses were, the hay and the straw were plentiful enough to make couches for Cleopatra. That was why we asked the girls in to see the horses. The sailors from the ships, homeless men all, had no such comforts and conveniences. They used to envy us. Butterfly, my geisha girl, you should have been alive then. We'd have shown you the jumps.

Pike was affronted. He was almost prepared to say so and take the consequences. But Butterfly stole his thunder. She stood up, kissed the jovial big man smack on the bald head and then, as light on her feet as her mother ever could have been, danced up and down the floor, tight hips bouncing, fingers clicking, singing: I'm the smartest little geisha in Japan, in Japan. And the people call me Rolee Polee Nan, Polee Nan.

Drowning in desire, Pike forgot his indignation and found that he was liking the man who could provoke such an exhibition. Breathless, she sat down again, suddenly kissed Pike on the cheek, said: I love you too. I love champagne. Let's have another bottle.

They had.

—Rolee Polee Nan, she sang as the cork and the fizz ascended.

—A great writer, a Russian, Pike said, wrote that his ideal was to be idle and to make love to a plump girl.

—The cheek of him. I'm not plump. Turkeys are plump. I love being tall, with long legs.

Displaying the agility of a trained high-kicker with hinges in her hips she, still sitting, raised her shapely right leg, up and up as if her toes would touch the ceiling, up and up until stocking-top, suspender, bare thigh and a frill of pink panties, showed. Something happened to Pike that had nothing at all to do with poetry or Jody's champagne. He held Butterfly's hand. She made a cat's cradle with their fingers and swung the locked hands pendulum-wise. She sang: Janey Mac, the child's a black, what will we do on Sunday? Put him to bed and cover his head and don't let him up until Monday.

Austin had momentarily absented himself for gentlemanly reasons. From the basement jakes his voice singing rose above the soft inland murmur of falling water: Oh my boat can lightly float in the heel of wind and weather, and outrace the smartest hooker between Galway and Kinsale.

The dockers methodically drank their pints of black porter

and paid no attention. Jody said: Time's money. Why don't
the two of you slip upstairs. Your heads would make a lovely
pair on a pillow.

Austin was singing: Oh she's neat, oh she's sweet, she's a
beauty every line, the Queen of Connemara is that bounding
barque of mine.

He was so shy, Butterfly said afterwards, that he might have
been a Christian Brother and a young one at that, although
where or how she ever got the experience to enable her to
make the comparison, or why she should think an old Christian Brother less cuthallacht than a young one, she didn't say.
He told her all about the aunts and the odd way he had been
reared and she, naturally, told Austin and Jody and all her
sorority. But they were a kind people and no mockers, and
Pike never knew, Austin told me, that Jody's clientele listened
with such absorbed interest to the story of his life, and of his
heart and his love-making. He was something new in their
experience, and Jody's stable of girls had experienced a lot,
and Austin a lot more, and Jody more than the whole shebang,
and all the fire-brigade, put together.

For Jody, Austin told me, had made the price of the Dark
Cow in a basement in Chicago. During the prohibition, as they
called it, although what they prohibited it would be hard to say.
He was one of five brothers from the bogs of Manulla in the
middle of nowhere in the County of Mayo. The five of them
emigrated to Chicago. When Al Capone and his merry men
discovered that Jody and his brothers had the real true secret
about how to make booze, and to make it good, down they
went into the cellar and didn't see daylight nor breathe fresh
air, except to surface to go to Mass on Sundays, until they left
the U.S.A. They made a fair fortune. At least four of them
did. The fifth was murdered.

Jody was a bachelor man and he was good to the girls. He
took his pleasures with them as a gentleman might, with the
natural result that he was poxed to the eyebrows. But he was
worth more to them than the money he quite generously paid
after every turn or trick on the rumpled, always unmade bed
in the two-storeyed apartment above the pub. He was a kind

uncle to them. He gave them a friendly welcome, a place to sit down, free drink and smokes and loans, or advances for services yet to be rendered, when they were down on their luck. He had the ear of the civic guards and could help a girl when she was in trouble. He paid fines when they were unavoidable, and bills when they could no longer be postponed, and had an aunt who was reverend mother in a home for unmarried mothers, and who was, like her nephew, a kindly person. Now and again, like the Madame made immortal by Maupassant, he took a bevy or flock of the girls for a day at the seaside or in the country. A friend of mine and myself, travelling into the granite mountains south of the city, to the old stone-cutters' villages of Lackan and Ballyknockan where there were aged people who had never seen Dublin, thirty miles away, and never wanted to, came upon a most delightful scene in the old country pub in Lackan. All around the bench around the walls sat the mountainy men, the stone-cutters, drinking their pints. But the floor was in the possession of a score of wild girls, all dancing together, resting off and on for more drink, laughing, happy, their gaiety inspired and directed by one man in the middle of the floor: red-faced, carbuncled, oily black hair sleeked down and parted up the middle in the style of Dixie Dean, the famous soccer centre-forward, whom Jody so much admired. All the drinks were on generous Jody.

So in Jody's friendly house Pike had, as he came close to forty years, what he never had in the cold abode of the three aunts: a home with a father, Austin, and a brother, Jody, and any God's amount of sisters; and Butterfly who, to judge by the tales she told afterwards, was a motherly sort of lover to him and, for a while, a sympathetic listener. For a while, only: because nothing in her birth, background, rearing or education had equipped her to listen to so much poetry and talk about poetry.

—Poor Pike, she'd say, he'd puke you with poethry. Poethry's all very well, but.

She had never worked out what came after that qualifying: But.

—Give us a bar of a song, Austin. There's some sense to

singing. But poethry. My heart leaps up when I behold a
rainbow in the sky. On Linden when the sun was low. The lady
of Shalott left the room to go to the pot. Janey preserve us
from poethry.

He has eyes, Jody told Austin and myself, for no girl except
Butterfly. Reckon, in one way, we can't blame him for that. She
sure is the smartest filly showing in this paddock. But there
must be moderation in all things. Big Anne, now, isn't bad, nor
her sister, both well-built Sligo girls and very co-operative, nor
Joany Maher from Waterford, nor Patty Daley from Castle-
island in the County Kerry who married the Limey in Brum
but left him when she found he was as queer as a three-
dollar bill. And what about little Red Annie Byrne from Kil-
kenny City, very attractive if it just wasn't for the teeth she
lost when the cattleman that claimed he caught gonorrhoea
from her gave her an unmerciful hammering in Cumberland
Street. We got him before he left town. We cured more than
his gonorrhoea.

—But, Austin said, when following your advice, Jody, and
against my own better judgment, I tried to explain all that to
Pike, what does he do but quote to me what the playboy of the
Abbey Theatre, John M. Synge, wrote in a love poem about
counting queens in Glenmacnass in the Wicklow mountains.

—In the Wicklow mountains, said Jody. Queens? With the
smell of the bog and the peat smoke off them.

Austin, a great man, ever, to sing at the top of his tenor voice
about Dark Rosaleen and the Queen of Connemara and the
County of Mayo, was a literary class of a fireman. That was one
reason why Pike and himself got on so well together, in spite of
that initial momentary misunderstanding about the ball of
malt and Madame Butterfly.

—Seven dog days, Austin said, the playboy said he let pass,
he and his girl, counting queens in Glenmacnass. The queens
he mentions, Jody, you never saw, even in Chicago.

—Never saw daylight in Chicago.

—The Queen of Sheba, Austin said, and Helen, and Maeve
the warrior queen of Connacht, and Deirdre of the Sorrows
and Gloriana that was the great Elizabeth of England and

Judith out of the Bible that chopped the block of Holofernes.

—All, said Jody, in a wet glen in Wicklow. A likely bloody story.

—There was one queen in the poem that had an amber belly.

—Jaundice, said Jody. Or Butterfly herself that's as sallow as any Jap. Austin, you're a worse lunatic than Pike.

—But in the end, Jody, his own girl was the queen of all queens. They were dead and rotten. She was alive.

—Not much of a compliment to her, Jody said, to prefer her to a cartload of corpses.

—Love's love, Jody. Even the girls admit that. They've no grudge against him for seeing nobody but Butterfly.

—They give him a fool's pardon. But no doll in the hustling game, Austin, can afford to spend all her time listening to poetry. Besides, girls like a variety of pricks. Butterfly's no better or worse than the next. When Pike finds that out he'll go crazy. If he isn't crazy already.

That was the day, as I recall, that Butterfly came in wearing the fancy fur coat – just a little out of season. Jody had, for some reason or other, given her a five-pound note. Pike knew nothing about that. And Jody told her to venture the five pounds on a horse that was running at the Curragh of Kildare, that a man in Kilcullen on the edge of the Curragh had told him that the jockey's wife had already bought her ball dress for the victory celebration. The Kilcullen man knew his onions, and his jockeys, and shared his wisdom only with a select few so as to keep the odds at a good twenty to one.

—She's gone out to the bookie's, said Jody, to pick up her winnings. We'll have a party tonight.

Jody had a tenner on the beast.

—She could invest it, said Austin, if she was wise. The day will come when her looks will go.

—Pike might propose to her, said Jody. He's mad enough for anything.

—The aunts would devour him. And her.

—Here she comes, Jody said. She invested her winnings on her fancy back.

She had too, and well she carried them in the shape of pale

or silver musquash, and three of her sorority walked behind her like ladies-in-waiting behind the Queen of England. There was a party in which even the dockers joined, but not Pike, for that evening and night one of his aunts was at death's door in a nursing home, and Pike and the other two aunts were by her side. He wasn't to see the musquash until he took Butterfly on an outing to the romantic hill of Howth where the poet and the woman had seen the white birds. That was the last day Pike ever took Butterfly anywhere. The aunt recovered. They were a thrawn hardy trio.

Pike had become a devotee. Every day except Sunday he lunched in Jody's, on a sandwich of stale bread and leathery ham and a glass of beer, just on the off-chance that Butterfly might be out of the doss and abroad, and in Jody's, at that, to her, unseasonable hour of the day. She seldom was, except when she was deplorably short of money. In the better eating places on Grafton Street and Stephen's Green, his colleagues absorbed the meals that enabled higher civil servants to face up to the afternoon and the responsibilities of State: statistics, land commission, local government, posts and telegraphs, internal revenue. He had never, among his own kind, been much of a mixer: so that few of his peers even noticed the speed with which, when at five in the evening the official day was done, he took himself, and his hat and coat and umbrella, and legged it off to Jody's: in the hope that Butterfly might be there, bathed and perfumed and ready for wine and love. Sometimes she was. Sometimes she wasn't. She liked Pike. She didn't deny it. She was always an honest girl, as her mother, Trixie, had been before her – so Austin said when he remembered Trixie who had died in a hurry, of peritonitis. But, Janey Mac, Butterfly couldn't have Pike Hunter for breakfast, dinner, tea and supper, and nibblers as well, all the livelong day and night. She still, as Jody said, had her first million to make, and Pike's inordinate attachment was coming between her and the real big business, as when, say, the country cattle men were in town for the market. They were the men who knew how to get rid of the money.

—There is this big cattle man, she tells Austin once, big he is in every way, who never knows or cares what he's spending. He's a gift and a godsend to the girls. He gets so drunk that all you have to do to humour him is play with him a little in the taxi going from pub to pub and see that he gets safely to his hotel. The taximen are on to the game and get their divy out of the loot.

One wet and windy night, it seems, Butterfly and this philanthropist are flying high together, he on brandy, she on champagne, for which that first encounter with Pike has given her a ferocious drouth. In the back of the taxi touring from pub to pub, the five pound notes are flowing out of your man like water out of a pressed sponge. Butterfly is picking them up and stuffing them into her handbag, but not all of them. For this is too good and too big for any taximan on a fair percentage basis. So for every one note she puts into her handbag she stuffs two or three down into the calf-length boots she is wearing against the wet weather. She knows, you see, that she is too far gone in bubbly to walk up the stairs to her own room, that the taximan, decent fellow, will help her up and then, fair enough, go through her bag and take his cut. Which, indeed, in due time he does. When she wakes up, fully clothed, in the morning on her own bed, and pulls off her boots, her ankles, what with the rain that had dribbled down into her boots, are poulticed and plastered with notes of the banks of Ireland and of England, and one moreover of the Bank of Bonnie Scotland.

—Rings on my fingers, she says, and bells on my toes.

That was the gallant life that Pike's constant attendance was cutting her off from. She also hated being owned. She hated other people thinking that she was owned. She hated like hell when Pike would enter the Dark Cow and one of the other girls or, worse still, another man, a bit of variety, would move away from her side to let Pike take the throne. They weren't married, for Janey's sake. She could have hated Pike, except that she was as tender-hearted as Trixie had been, and she liked champagne. She certainly felt at liberty to hate the three aunts who made a mollycoddle out of him. She also hated, with a hatred that grew and grew, the way that Pike puked her with poethry. And all this time poor Pike walked in a dream that he never defined for us, perhaps not even for himself, but that certainly must have looked higher than the occasional trick on Jody's rumpled bed. So dreaming, sleep-walking, he persuaded Butterfly to go to Howth Head with him one dull hot day when the town was empty and she had nothing better to do. No place could have been more fatally poetic than Howth. She wore her musquash. Not even the heat could part her from it.

—He never let up, she said, not once from the moment we boarded the bus on the quays. Poethry. I had my bellyful.

—Sure thing, said Jody.

—Any man, she said, that won't pay every time he performs is a man to keep a cautious eye on. Not that he's not generous. But at the wrong times. Money down or no play's my motto.

—Well I know that, Jody said.

—But Pike Hunter says that would make our love mercenary, whatever that is.

—You're a great girl, said Austin, to be able to pronounce it.

—Your middle name, said Jody, is mercenary.

—My middle name, thank you, is Imelda. And the cheek of Pike Hunter suggesting to me to go to a doctor because he noticed something wrong with himself, a kidney disorder, he said. He must wet the bed.

—Butterfly, said Austin, he might have been giving you good advice.

—Nevertheless. It's not for him to say.

When they saw from the bus the Bull Wall holding the northern sand back from clogging up the harbour, and the Bull Island, three miles long, with dunes, bent grass, golfers, bathers and skylarks, Pike told her about some fellow called Joyce – there was a Joyce in the Civic Guards, a Galwayman who played county football, but no relation – who had gone walking on the Island one fine day and laid eyes on a young one, wading in a pool, with her skirts well pulled up; and let a roar out of him. By all accounts this Joyce was no addition to the family for, as Pike told the story, Butterfly worked out that the young one was well under age.

Pike and Butterfly had lunch by the edge of the sea, in the Claremont Hotel, and that was all right. Then they walked in the grounds of Howth Castle, Pike had a special pass and the flowers and shrubs were a sight to see if only Pike had kept his mouth shut about some limey by the name of Spenser who landed there in the year of God, and wrote a poem as long as from here to Killarney about a fairy queen and a gentle knight who was pricking on the plain like the members of the Harp Cycling Club, Junior Branch, up above there in the Phoenix Park. He didn't get time to finish the poem, the poet that is, not Pike, for the Cork people burned him out of house and home and, as far as Butterfly was concerned, that was the only good deed she ever heard attributed to the Cork people.

The Phoenix Park and the Harp Club reminded her that one day Jody had said, meaning no harm, about the way Pike moped around the Dark Cow when Butterfly wasn't there, that Pike was the victim of a semi-horn and should go up to the Fifteen Acres and put it in the grass for a while and run around it. But when, for fun, she told this to Pike he got so huffed he didn't speak for half an hour, and they walked Howth Head until her feet were blistered and the heel of her right shoe broke, and the sweat, with the weight of the musquash and the heat of the day, was running between her shoulder-blades like a cloudburst down the gutter. Then the row and the ructions, as the song says, soon began. He said she should have worn flat-heeled shoes. She said that if she had known that he was conscripting her for a forced march over a mountain she'd have borrowed a pair of boots from the last soldier she gave it to at cut-price, for the soldiers, God help them, didn't have much money but they were more open-handed with what they had than some people who had plenty, and soldiers didn't waste time and breath on poetry: Be you fat or be you lean there is no soap like Preservene.

So she sat on the summit of Howth and looked at the light-house and the seagulls, while Pike walked back to the village to have the broken heel mended, and the sweat dried cold on her, and she was perished. Then when he came back, off he was again about how that white-headed old character that you'd see across the river there at the Abbey Theatre, and Madame Gone Mad McBride that was the age of ninety and looked it, and known to all as a roaring rebel, worse than Austin, had

stood there on that very spot, and how the poet wrote a poem
wishing for himself and herself to be turned into seagulls, the
big dirty brutes that you'd see along the docks robbing the
pigeons of their food. Butterfly would have laughed at him,
except that her teeth by this time were tap-dancing with the
cold like the twinkling feet of Fred Astaire. So she pulled her
coat around her and said: Pike, I'm no seagull. For Janey's
sake take me back to civilisation and Jody's where I know
someone.

But, God sees, you never knew nobody, for at that moment
the caveman came out in Pike Hunter, he that was always so
backward on Jody's bed and, there and then, he tried to flatten
her in the heather in full view of all Dublin and the coast of
Ireland as far south as Wicklow Head and as far north as
where the Mountains of Mourne sweep down to the sea.

—Oh none of that, Pike Hunter, she says, my good musquash will be crucified. There's a time and a place and a price
for everything.

—You and your musquash, he tells her.

They were wrestling like Man Mountain Dean and Jack
Doyle, the Gorgeous Gael.

—You've neither sense nor taste, says he, to be wearing a fur
coat on a day like this.

—Bloody well for you to talk, says she, with your rolled
umbrella and your woollen combinations and your wobbly ass
that won't keep you straight in the chair, and your three
witches of maiden aunts never touched, tasted or handled by
mortal man, and plenty of money and everything your own
way. This is my only coat that's decent, in case you haven't
noticed, and I earned it hard and honest with Jody, a generous
man but a monster on the bed, I bled after him.

That put a stop to the wrestling. He brought her back to the
Dark Cow and left her at the door and went his way.

He never came back to the Dark Cow but once, and Butterfly
wasn't on her throne that night. It was the night before the
cattle-market. He was so lugubrious and woebegone that Jody
and Austin and a few merry newspaper men, including myself,
tried to jolly him up, take him out of himself, by making jokes

at his expense that would force him to come alive and answer back. Our efforts failed. He looked at us sadly and said: Boys, Beethoven, when he was dying, said: Clap now, good friends, the comedy is done.

He was more than a little drunk and, for the first time, seemed lopsided when standing up; and untidy.

—Clap now indeed, said Jody.

Pike departed and never returned. He took to steady drinking in places like the Shelbourne Hotel or the Buttery in the Hibernian where it was most unlikely, even with Dublin being the democratic sort of town that it is, that he would ever encounter Madame Butterfly. He became a great problem for his colleagues and his superior officers in the civil service, and for his three aunts. After careful consultation they, all together, persuaded him to rest up in Saint Patrick's Hospital where, as you all may remember, Dean Swift died roaring. Which was I feel sure, why Pike wasn't there to pay the last respects to the dead when Jody dropped from a heart attack and was waked in the bedroom above the Dark Cow. The girls were there in force to say an eternal farewell to a good friend. Since the drink was plentiful and the fun and the mourning intense, somebody, not even Austin knew who, suggested that the part of the corpse that the girls knew best should be tastefully decorated with black crepe ribbon. The honour of tying on the ribbon naturally went to Madame Butterfly but it was Big Anne who burst into tears and cried out: Jody's dead and gone forever.

Austin met her, Butterfly not Big Anne, a few days afterwards at the foot of the Nelson Pillar. Jody's successor had routed the girls from the Dark Cow. Austin told her about Pike and where he was. She brooded a bit. She said it was a pity, but nobody could do nothing for him, that those three aunts had spoiled him for ever and, anyway, didn't Austin think that he was a bit astray in the head.

—Who knows, Butterfly? Who's sound or who's silly? Consider yourself for a moment.

—What about me, Austin?

—A lovely girl like you, a vision from the romantic east, and think of the life you lead. It can have no good ending. Let me

tell you a story, Butterfly. There was a girl once in London, a
slavey, a poor domestic servant. I knew a redcoat here in the
old British days who said he preferred slaveys to anything else
because they were clean, free and flattering.

—Austin, I was never a slavey.

—No Butterfly, you have your proper pride. But listen: this
slavey is out one morning scrubbing the stone steps in front of
the big house she works in, bucket and brush, carbolic soap
and all that, in one of the great squares in one of the more
classy parts of London Town. There she is on her bended
knees when a gentleman walks past, a British army major in
the Coldstream Guards or the Black Watch or something.

—I've heard of them, Austin.

—So this British major looks at her, and he sees the naked
backs of her legs, thighs you know, and taps her on the shoulder or somewhere and he says: Oh, rise up, lovely maiden and
come along with me, there's a better life in store for you
somewhere else. She left the bucket and the brush, and the
stone steps half-scrubbed, and walked off with him and
became his girl. But there were even greater things in store for
her. For, Butterfly, that slavey became Lady Emma Hamilton,
the beloved of Lord Nelson, the greatest British sailor that ever
sailed, and the victor of the renowned battle of Trafalgar.
There he is up on the top of the Pillar.

—You wouldn't think to look at him, Austin, that he had
much love in him.

—But, Butterfly, meditate on that story, and rise up and get
yourself out of the gutter. You're handsome enough to be the
second Lady Hamilton.

After that remark, Austin brought her into Lloyd's, a famous house of worship in North Earl Street under the shadow
of Lord Nelson and his pillar. In Lloyd's he brought her a drink
and out of the kindness of his great singing heart, gave her some
money. She shook his hand and said: Austin, you're the nicest
man I ever met.

Austin had, we may suppose, given her an image, an ideal.
She may have been wearied by Pike and his sad attachment to
poetry, but she rose to the glimmering vision of herself as a
great lady beloved by a great and valiant lord. A year later she

married a docker, a decent quiet hard-working fellow who had slowly sipped his pints of black porter and watched and waited all the time.

Oddly enough, Austin told me when the dignity of old age had gathered around him like the glow of corn-stubble in the afterwards of harvest.

He could still sing. His voice never grew old.

—Oddly enough, I never had anything to do with her. That way, I mean. Well you know me. Fine wife, splendid sons, nobody like them in the world. Fine daughters, too. But a cousin of mine, a ship's wireless operator who had been all round the world from Yokohama to the Belgian Congo and back again, and had had a ship burned under him in Bermuda and, for good value, another ship burned under him in Belfast, said she was the meanest whore he ever met. When he had paid her the stated price, there were some coppers left in his hand and she grabbed them and said: give us these for the gas-meter.

But he said, also, that at the high moments she had a curious and diverting way of raising and bending and extending her left leg – not her right leg which she kept as flat as a plumb-level. He had never encountered the like before, in any colour or in any country.

PART FOUR

The Night We Rode
With Sarsfield

HAT WAS THE house where I put the gooseberries back on the bushes by sticking them on the thorns. It wasn't one house but two houses under one roof, a thatched roof. Before I remember being there, I was there.

We came from the small village of Dromore to the big town of Omagh, the county town of Tyrone, in the spring of 1920, bad times in Ireland (Violence upon the roads/Violence of horses) particularly bad times in the north-east corner of Ulster. There have been any God's amount of bad times in the north-east corner of Ulster. There were no houses going in the big town and the nearest my father could find to his work was three miles away in the townland of Drumragh and under the one roof with Willy and Jinny Norris, a Presbyterian couple, brother and sister. They were small farmers.

That was the place then where I put the gooseberries back on the bushes by impaling them on the thorns. But not just yet because I wasn't twelve months old, a good age for a man and one of the best he's ever liable afterwards to experience: more care is taken of him, especially by women. No, the impaling of the gooseberries took place seven to eight years later. For, although we were only there six or so months until my father got a place in the town – in the last house in a laneway over-looking the green flowery banks of the serpentine Strule – we went on visiting Willy and Jinny until they died, and my father walked at their funeral and entered their church and knelt with the congregation: a thing that Roman Catholics were not by no means then supposed to do. Not knelt exactly but rested the hips on the seat and inclined the head: Ulster Presbyterians don't kneel, not even to God above.

It was a good lasting friendship with Willy and Jinny. There's an Irish proverb: *Nil aitheantas go haontigheas.* Or: You don't know anybody until you've lived in the one house with them.

Not one house, though, in this case but two houses under one roof which may be the next best thing.

Willy and Jinny had the one funeral because one night the house burned down – by accident. Nowadays when you say that a house or a shop or a pub or a factory burned down, it seems necessary to add – by accident. Although the neighbours, living next door in our house, did their best to rescue them and to save the whole structure with buckets of water from the spring-well which was down there surrounded by gooseberry bushes, they died, Willy from suffocation, Jinny from shock, the shock of the whole happening, the shock of loneliness at knowing that Willy was dead and that the long quiet evenings were over. However sadly and roughly they left the world, they went, I know, to a heaven of carefully-kept harvest fields, and Orange lilies in bloom on the lawn before the farmhouse, and trees heavy with fruit, and those long evenings spent spelling-out, by the combined light of oil-lamp and hearth fire, the contents of *The Christian Herald.* My three sisters who were all older than me said that that was the only literature, apart from the Bible, they had ever seen in the house but, at that time, that didn't mean much to me.

The place they lived in must have been the quietest place in the world. This was the way to get there.

The Cannonhill road went up from the town in three steps but those steps could only be taken by Titans. Halfways up the second step or steep hill there was on the right-hand side a tarred timber barn behind which such of the young as fancied, and some as didn't, used to box. My elder brother, there, chopped one of the town's bullies, who was a head-fighter, on the soft section of the crown of his head as he came charging like a bull, and that cured him of head-fighting for a long time. Every boy has an elder brother who can box.

The barn belonged to a farmer who would leave a team of horses standing in the field and go follow a brass band for the length of a day. Since the town had two brass bands, one military, one civilian, his sowing was always dilatory and his harvests very close to Christmas. He owned a butcher shop in the town but he had the word, Butcher, painted out and replaced by the word, Flesher, which some joker had told him was more modern and polite but which a lot of people thought wasn't exactly decent.

If you looked back from Cannonhill the prospect was really something: the whole town, spires and all, you could even see clear down into some of the streets; the winding river or rivers, the red brick of the county hospital on a hill across the valley, and beyond all that the mountains, Glenhordial where the water came from, Gortin Gap and Mullagharn and the high Sperrins. Sometime in the past, nobody knew when, there must have been a gun-emplacement on Cannonhill so as to give the place its name. Some of the local learned men talked vaguely about Oliver Cromwell but he was never next or near the place. There were, though, guns there in 1941 when a visit from the Germans seemed imminent and, indeed, they came near enough to bomb Belfast and Pennyburn in Derry City and were heard in the darkness over our town, and the whole population of Gallowshill, where I came from, took off for refuge up the three titanic steps of the Cannonhill road. It was a lovely June night, though, and everybody enjoyed themselves.

If any of those merry refugees had raced on beyond the ridge of Cannonhill they would have found themselves, Germans or no Germans, in the heart of quietness. The road goes down in easy curves through good farmland to the Drumragh River and the old graveyard where the gateway was closed with concrete and stone long before my time, and the dead sealed off forever. There's a sort of stile made out of protruding stones in the high wall and within – desolation, a fragment of a church wall that might be medieval, waist-high stagnant grass, table tombstones made anonymous by moss and lichen, a sinister hollow like a huge shellhole in the centre of the place where the dead, also anonymous, of the great famine of the 1840s were thrown coffinless, one on top of the other. A man who went to school with me used to call that hollow the navel of nothing and to explain in gruesome detail why and how the earth that once had been mounded had sunk into a hollow.

That same man ran away from home in 1938 to join the British navy. He survived the sinking of three destroyers on which he was a crew member: once, off the Faroes; once, for a change of temperature, in the Red Sea; and a third time at the Battle of Crete. It may be possible that the crew of the fourth destroyer he joined looked at him with some misgiving. A fellow townsman who had the misfortune to be in Crete as a groundsman with the RAF when the Germans were coming in low and dropping all sorts of unpleasant things to the great danger of life and limb, found a hole in the ground where he could rest unseen, and doing no harm to anybody, until he caught the next boat to Alexandria.

When he crawled into the hole who should be there but the thrice-torpedoed sailor reading *The Ulster Herald*. He said hello and went on reading. He was a cool one, and what I remember most about him is the infinite patience with which he helped me when, impelled by a passion for history, I decided to clean all the table tombstones in old Drumragh and recall from namelessness and oblivion the decent people who were buried there. It was a big project. Not surprisingly it was never completed, never even properly commenced, but it brought us one discovery: that one of the four people, all priests, buried under a stone that was flat to the ground and circled by giant yews, was a MacCathmhaoil (you could English it as Campbell or McCarvill) who had in history been known as the Sagart Costarnocht because he went about without boots or socks, and who in the penal days of proscribed Catholicism had said Mass in the open air at the Mass rock on Corra Duine mountain.

For that discovery our own parish priest praised us from the pulpit. He was a stern Irish Republican who had been to the Irish college in Rome, had met D'Annunzio and approved of

him and who always spoke of the Six Counties of north-east
Ulster as *Hibernia Irredenta.* He was also, as became his calling,
a stern Roman Catholic, and an antiquarian, and in honour of
the past and the shadow of the proscribed, barefooted priest,
he had read the Mass one Sunday at the rock on Corra Duine
and watched, in glory on the summit like the Lord himself, as
the congregation trooped in over the mountain from the seven
separate parishes.

This ground is littered with things, cluttered with memories
and multiple associations. It turns out to be a long three miles
from Gallowshill to the house of Willy and Jinny Norris. With
my mother and my elder sisters I walked it so often, and later
on with friends and long after Willy and Jinny were gone and
the house a blackened ruin, the lawn a wilderness, the gooseberry bushes gone to seed, the Orange lilies extinguished –
miniature suns that would never rise again in that place
no more than life would ever come back to the empty mansion
of Johnny Pet Wilson. That was just to the left before you
turned into the Norris laneway, red-sanded, like a tunnel with
high hawthorn hedges and sycamores and ash trees shining
white and naked. My father had known Johnny Pet and afterwards had woven mythologies about him: a big Presbyterian
farmer, the meanest and oddest man that had ever lived in
those parts. When his hired men, mostly Gaelic speakers from
West Donegal, once asked him for jam or treacle or syrup or,
God help us, butter itself, to moisten their dry bread, he said:
Do you say your prayers?
—Yes, boss.
They were puzzled.
—Do you say the Lord's prayer?
—Yes, boss.
—Well, in the Lord's prayer it says: Give us this day our
daily bread. Damn the word about jam or treacle or syrup or
butter.
When he bought provisions in a shop in the town he specified:
So much of labouring man's bacon and so much of the good
bacon.

For the hired men, the imported long-bottom American bacon. For himself, the Limerick ham.

He rose between four and five in the morning and expected his men to be already out and about. He went around with an old potato sack on his shoulders like a shawl, and followed always by a giant of a gentleman goat, stepping like a king's warhorse. The goat would attack you if you angered Johnny Pet, and when Johnny died the goat lay down and died on the same day. Their ghosts walked, it was well known, in the abandoned orchard where the apples had become half-crabs, through gaps in hedges and broken fences, and in the roofless rooms of the ruined house. Nobody had ever wanted to live there after the goat and Johnny Pet died. There were no relatives even to claim the hoarded fortune.

—If the goat had lived, my father said, he might have had the money and the place.

—The poor Donegals, my mother would say as she walked past Johnny Pet's ghost, and the ghost of the goat, on the way to see Willy and Jinny. Oh, the poor Donegals.

It was a phrase her mother had used when, from the doorstep of the farmhouse in which my mother was reared, the old lady would look west on a clear day and see the tip of the white cone of Mount Errigal, the Cock o' the North, sixty or more miles away, standing up and shining with shale over Gweedore and the Rosses of Donegal and by the edge of the open Atlantic. From that hard coast, a treeless place of diminutive fields fenced by drystone walls, of rocks, mountains, small lakes, empty moors and ocean winds the young Donegal people (both sexes) used to walk eastwards, sometimes barefoot, to hire out in the rich farms along the valley of the Strule, the Mourne and the Foyle – three fine names for different stages of the same river.

Or the young people, some of them hardly into their teens, might travel as far even as the potato fields of Fifeshire or Ayrshire. They'd stand in the streets at the hiring fairs to be eyed by the farmers, even by God to have their biceps tested to see what work was in them. The last of the hiring fairs I saw in Omagh in the early 1930s but by that time everybody was well dressed and wore boots and the institution, God be praised, was doomed. There was a big war on the way and the promise of work for all. But my mother, remembering the old days and thinking perhaps more of her own mother than of the plight of the migratory labourers, would say: The poor Donegals. Ah, the poor Donegals.

Then up the sheltered red-sanded boreen or laneway – the Gaelic word would never at that time have been used by Ulster Presbyterians – to the glory of the Orange lilies and the trim land and, in the season, the trees heavy with fruit. Those gooseberries I particularly remember because one day when I raided the bushes more than somewhat, to the fearful extent of a black-paper fourteen-pound sugar-bag packed full, my sisters (elder) reproved me. In a fit of remorse I began to stick the berries back on the thorns. Later in life I found out that plucked fruit is plucked forever and that berries do not grow on thorns.

Then another day the three sisters, two of them home on holidays from Dublin, said: Sing a song for Jinny and Willy.

Some children suffer a lot when adults ask them to sing or recite. There's never really much asking about it. It's more a matter of get up and show your paces and how clever you are, like a dancing dog in a circus, or know the lash or the joys of going to bed supperless. Or sometimes it's bribery: Sing up and you'll get this or that.

Once I remember – can I ever forget it? – the reverend mother of a convent in Dublin gave me a box of chocolates because in the presence of my mother and my cousin, who was a nun, and half the community I brazenly sang:

> *Paddy Doyle lived in Killarney*
> *And he loved a maid named Bessy Toole,*
> *Her tongue I know was tipped with blarney,*
> *But it seemed to him the golden rule.*

But that was one of the exceptionally lucky days. I often wondered, too, where the reverend mother got the box of chocolates. You didn't expect to find boxes of chocolates lying around convents in those austere days. She dived the depth of her right arm for them into a sort of trousers-pocket in her habit, and the memory of them and of the way I won them ever after braced me in vigour (as the poet said) when asked to give a public performance.

—Up with you and sing, said the eldest sister.

Outside the sun shone. The lilies nodded and flashed like bronze. You could hear them. On a tailor's dummy, that Jinny had bought at an auction, Willy's bowler hat and sash were out airing for the Orange walk on the twelfth day in honour of King William and the battle of the Boyne. The sash was a lovely blue, a true blue, and the Orangemen who wore blue sashes were supposed to be teetotallers. Summer and all as it was the pyramid of peat was bright on the hearth and the kettle above it singing and swinging on the black crane, and Jinny's fresh scones were in three piles, one brown, one white, one spotted with currants and raisins, on the table and close to the coolness of the doorway.

—Sing up, said the second sister. Give us a bar.

—Nothing can stop him, said the third sister who was a cynic.

She was right. Or almost. Up I was and at it, with a song learned from another cousin, the nun's brother, who had been in 1920 in the IRA camp in the Sperrin mountains:

We're off to Dublin in the green and the blue,
Our helmets glitter in the sun,
Our bayonets flash like lightning
To the rattle of the Thompson gun.
It's the dear old flag of Ireland, boys,
That proudly waves on high,
And the password of our order is:
We'll conquer or we'll die.

The kettle sputtered and spat and boiled over. Jinny dived for it before the water could hit the ashes and raise a stink, or scald the backs of my legs where I stood shouting treason at Willy and the dummy in the bowler and the teetotaller's blue sash. It may have been a loyal Orange kettle. Willy was weeping with laughter and wiping the back of his left hand sideways across his eyes and his red moustache. In the confusion, the eldest sister, purple in the face with embarrassment, said: If you recited instead of singing. He's much better at reciting.

So I was – and proud of it. Off I went into a thundering galloping poem learned by heart from the *Our Boys*, a magazine that was nothing if not patriotic and was produced in Dublin by the Irish Christian Brothers.

The night we rode with Sarsfield out from Limerick to meet
The waggon-train that William hoped would help in our defeat.
How clearly I remember it though now my hair is white
That clustered black and curly 'neath my trooper's cap that night.

This time there was no stopping me. Anyway Willy wouldn't let them. He was enjoying himself. With the effrontery of one of those diabolical little children who have freak memories, even when they don't know what the words mean, I let them have the whole works, eight verses of eight lines each, right up to the big bang at Ballyneety on a Munster hillside at the high rock that is still called Sarsfield's Rock.

It is after the siege of Derry and the battle of the Boyne and the Jacobite disaster at the slope of Aughrim on the Galway road. The victorious Williamite armies gather round the remnants of the Jacobites locked up behind the walls of Limerick. The ammunition train, guns, and wagons of ball and powder, that will end the siege rumble on across the country. Then Sarsfield with the pick of his hard-riding men, and led by the Rapparee, Galloping Hogan, who knows every track and hillock and hollow and marsh and bush on the mountains of Silver Mine and Keeper and Sleive Felim, rides north by night and along the western bank of the big river:

'Twas silently we left the town and silently we rode,
While o'er our heads the silent stars in silver beauty glowed.
And silently and stealthily well led by one who knew,
We crossed the shining Shannon at the ford of Killaloe.

On and on from one spur of the mountains to the next, then silently swooping down on the place where, within a day's drag from the city's battered walls, the well-guarded wagons rest for the night. For the joke of it the Williamite watchword is Sarsfield:

The sleepy sentry on his rounds perhaps was musing o'er
His happy days of childhood on the pleasant English shore,
Perhaps was thinking of his home and wishing he were there
When springtime makes the English land so wonderfully fair.
At last our horses' hoofbeats and our jingling arms he heard.
'Halt, who goes there?' the sentry cried. 'Advance and give
   the word.'
'The word is Sarsfield,' cried our chief, 'and stop us he who
   can,
'For Sarsfield is the word tonight and Sarsfield is the man.'

Willy had stopped laughing, not with hostility but with excitement. This was a good story, well told. The wild riders ride with the horses' shoes back to front so that if a hostile scouting party should come on their tracks, the pursuit will be led the wrong way. The camp is captured. Below the rock a great hole is dug in the ground, the gun-powder sunk in it, the guns piled on the powder, the torch applied:

We make a pile of captured guns and powder bags and stores,
Then skyward in one flaming blast the great explosion roars.

All this is long ago – even for the narrator in the poem. The hair is now grey that once clustered black and curly beneath his trooper's cap. Sarsfield, gallant Earl of Lucan, great captain of horsemen, is long dead on the plain of Landen or Neerwinden. Willy is silent, mourning all the past. Jinny by the table waits patiently to pour the tea:

For I was one of Sarsfield's men though yet a boy in years
I rode as one of Sarsfield's men and men were my compeers
They're dead the most of them, afar, yet they were Ireland's sons
Who saved the walls of Limerick from the might of William's
   guns.

No more than the sleepy sentry, my sisters never recovered from the shock. They still talk about it. As for myself, on my way home past the ghosts of Johnny Pet and the gentleman goat, I had a vague feeling that the reason why the poor girls were fussing so much was because the William that Sarsfield rode to defeat must have been Willy Norris himself. That was why the poem shouldn't be recited in his house, and fair play to him. But then why had Willy laughed so much? It was all very puzzling. Happy Ulster man that I then was I knew as little about politics and the ancient war of Orange and Green as I knew about the way gooseberries grew.

It wasn't until after my recital that they found out about the black-paper fourteen-pounder of a sugar-sack stuffed full of fruit. The manufacturers don't do sacks like that any more in this country. Not even paper like that any more. It was called crib-paper, because it was used, crumpled-up and worked-over and indented here and bulged out there to simulate the rock walls of the cave of Bethlehem in Christmas cribs.

For parcelling books I was looking for some of it in Dublin the other day, to be told that the only place I'd come up with it was some unlikely manufacturing town in Lancashire.

Bluebell Meadow

WHEN SHE CAME home in the evening from reading in the park that was a sort of an island the sergeant who had been trounced by the gipsies was waiting to ask her questions about the bullets. He had two of them in the cupped palm of his right hand, holding the hand low down, secretively. His left elbow was on the edge of the white-scrubbed kitchen table. The golden stripes on his blue-black sleeve, more black than blue, were as bright as the evening sunshine on the old town outside. He was polite, almost apologetic, at first. He said: I hate to bother yourself and your aunt and uncle. But it would be better for everybody's sake if you told me where you got these things. People aren't supposed to have them. Least of all girls in a convent school.

There had been six of them. The evening Lofty gave them to her she had looked at them for a whole hour, sitting at that table, half-reading a book. Her uncle and aunt were out at the cinema. She spread the bullets on the table and moved them about, making designs and shapes and patterns with them, joining them by imaginary lines, playing with them as if they were draughts or dominoes or precious stones. It just wasn't possible that such harmless mute pieces of metal could be used to kill people. Then she wearied of them, put them away in an old earthenware jug on the mantelpiece and after a while forgot all about them. They were the oddest gifts, God knew, for a boy to give to a girl. Not diamonds again, darling. Say it with bullets.

This is how the park happens to be a sort of an island. The river comes out of deep water, lined and overhung by tall beeches, and round a right-angled bend to burst over a water-fall and a salmon leap. On the right bank and above the fall a sluice-gate regulates the flow of a millrace. A hundred yards downstream the millrace is carried by aqueduct over a rough mountain stream or burn coming down to join the river. Between river and race and mountain stream is a triangular park, five or six acres, seats by the waterside, swings for children, her favourite seat under a tall conifer and close to the corner where the mountain stream meets the river. The place is called Bluebell Meadow. The bluebells grow in the woods on the far side of the millrace.

When the river is not in flood a peninsula of gravel and bright sand guides the mountain stream right out into the heart of the current. Children play on the sand, digging holes, building castles, sending flat pebbles skimming and dancing like wagtails upstream over the smooth water. One day Lofty is suddenly among the children just as if he had come out of the river which is exactly what he has done. His long black waders still drip water. The fishing-rod which he holds in his left hand, while he expertly skims pebbles with the right, dips and twiddles above him like an aerial. The canvas bag on his back is sodden and heavy and has grass, to keep the fish fresh, sticking out of the mouth of it. One of the children is doing rifle-drill with the shaft of his net. She has never spoken to him but she knows who he is.

When she tires of reading she can look at the river and dream, going sailing with the water. Or simply close her eyes. Or lean back and look up into the tall conifer, its branches always restless and making sounds, and going away from her like a complicated sort of spiral stairway. She has been told that it is the easiest tree in the world to climb but no tree is all that easy if you're wearing a leg-splint. She is looking up into the tree, and wondering, when Lofty sits beside her. His waders are now dry and rubbery to smell. The rod, the net and the bag are laid on the grass, the heads of two sad trout protruding, still life that was alive this morning. Her uncle who keeps greyhounds argues that fishing is much more cruel than coursing: somewhere in the happy river are trout that were hooked and got away, hooks now festering in their lovely speckled bodies. She thinks a lot about things like that.

Lofty sits for five minutes, almost, before he says: I asked Alec Quigley to tell you I was asking for you.

—He told me.

—What did you say?

—Did he not tell you?

—He said you said nothing but I didn't believe him.

—Why not?

—You had to say something.

—If I said anything Alec Quigley would tell the whole town.

—I daresay he would.

—He's the greatest clatter and clashbag from hell to Omagh.

—I didn't know.

—You could have picked a more discreet ambassador.

The words impress him. He says: It's a big name for Alec Quigley. I never thought of him as an ambassador.

—What then? A go-between? A match-maker? A gooseberry?

They are both laughing. Lofty is a blond tall freckled fellow with a pleasant laugh. He asks her would she like a trout.

—I'd love one. Will we cook it here and now?

—I can roll it in grass for you and get a bit of newspaper in McCaslan's shop up at the waterfall.

—Who will I tell my aunt and uncle gave me the trout?

—Tell them nothing. Tell them you whistled and a trout jumped out at you. Tell them a black man came out of the river and gave you a trout.

He left his bag and rod where they were and walked from the apex of the triangular park to the shop at the angle by the waterfall. He came back with a sheet of black parcelling paper and wrapped up the trout very gently. He had long delicate hands, so freckled that they were almost totally brown. The trout, bloody mouth gaping, looked sadly up at the two of them. Lofty said: I'd like to go out with you.

—I'm often out. Here.

So he laughed and handed her the trout and went on upstream towards the falls, casting from the bank at first, then wading knee-deep across a shallow bar of gravel and walking on across a green hill towards the deeps above the falls. She liked his long stride, and the rod dipping and twiddling above him, and the laden bag – even though she knew it was full of dead gaping trout. She knew he was a popular fellow in the town. Yet she didn't tell her aunt and uncle who exactly it was had made her a gift of the trout. She said it was an elderly man and she wasn't quite sure of his name, but she described him so that they'd guess he was a well-known fisherman, a jeweller by trade and highly respected in the town. Not that Lofty and his people were disrespectable.

The gipsies who trounced the sergeant hadn't been real romany gipsies but tinkers or travelling people from the west of Ireland, descendants, the theory was, of broken people who went on the roads during the hungry years of the 1840s and hadn't settled down since. Five of them, wild, ragged, rough-headed fellows came roaring drunk out of a pub in Bridge Lane. The pub was owned by a man called Yarrow and the joke among those literate enough to appreciate it was about Yarrow Visited and Yarrow Revisited. There was also an old English pishroge about girls putting Yarrow, the plant, between two plates and wishing on it and saying: Good morrow, good morrow, good yarrow, thrice good morrow to thee! I hope before this time tomorrow thou wilt show my true love to me.

One of the five fell with a clatter down the three steps from the door of the pub. In their tottering efforts to pick him up two of the others struck their heads together and began to fight. The remaining two joined in and so, when he was able to stand up, did the fellow who had fallen down the steps. The sergeant was walking past and was fool enough to try to stop them. In the west of Ireland the civic guards had more sense and stood as silent spectators until the tinkers had hammered the fight out of each other.

The five of them, united by foreign invasion, gave the sergeant an unmerciful pounding. He had just enough breath left to blow his whistle. More police came running. More tinkers came shouting, men, women and children, out of the pub, out of dark tunnels of entryways between houses, out of holes in the walls. The battle escalated. More police came. The tinkers made off on two flat carts. One old man was so drunk he fell helpless off a cart and was arrested. The police followed in a tender.

At their encampment of caravans a mile outside the town the tinkers abandoned the carts and took in the darkness to the fields and the hedgerows and even, it was said, to the tops of the trees. The police wisely did not follow, but set a heavy guard on the camp, caravans, carts, horses, scrap metal and everything the tinkers owned. Sober and sheepishly apologetic they reappeared in the morning and gave themselves up and half a dozen of them went to jail. But for a long time afterwards when the sergeant walked the town the wits at the street-corner would whistle: Oh, play to me gipsy, the moon's high above.

Thanks to Arthur Tracy, known as the Street Singer, it was a popular song at the time.

In spite of all that, the sergeant remained an amiable sort of man, stout, slow-moving, with a large brown moustache and a son who was a distinguished footballer.

Yarrow is a strong-scented herb related to the daisies. It has white or pink flowers in flat clusters.

One Sunday in the previous June in an excursion train to Bundoran by the western sea she had overheard Lofty's mother telling funny stories. As a rule Protestants didn't go west to Bundoran but north to Portrush. The sea was sectarian. What were the wild waves saying: At Portrush: Slewter, slaughter, holy water, harry the papishes every one, drive them under and bate them asunder, the Protestant boys will carry the drum. Or at Bundoran: On St. Patrick's day, jolly and gay, we'll kick all the Protestants out of the way, and if that won't do we'll cut them in two and send them to hell with their red, white and blue.

Nursery rhymes.

She sat facing her aunt in the train and her uncle sat beside her. They were quiet, looking at all the long beauty of Lough

Erne which has an island, wooded or pastoral, for every day in the year. Her aunt, a timid little woman, said now and again: Glory be to God for all his goodness.

Her uncle said just once: You should see Lake Superior. No end to it. As far as the human eye can see.

Then they were all quiet, overhearing Lofty's mother who had no prejudices about the religion of the ocean and who, with three other people, sat across the corridor from them, and who had a good-natured carrying voice and really was fun to listen to. She was saying: I'm a Protestant myself, missus dear, and I mean no disrespect to confession but you must have heard about the young fellow who went to the priest to tell him his sins and told him a story that had more women in it than King Solomon had in the Bible and the goings-on were terrible, and the priest says to him, Young man are you married?, and the young fellow says back to him, dead serious and all, Naw father but I was twice in Fintona.

The train dived through a tunnel of tall trees. The lake vanished. Sunlight flashing and flickering through leaves made her close her eyes. Everybody on the train, even her aunt, seemed to be laughing. A man was saying: Fintona always had a bit of a name. For wild women.

Lofty's mother said: I was born there myself but I never noticed that it was all that good, nobody ever told me.

She opens her eyes and the sunlight flickers down on her through the spiralling branches of the great conifer. There's a book in the public library that has everything, including pictures, about all the trees of Great Britain and Ireland. Lofty is on the very tip of the peninsula of sand and gravel, demonstrating fly-casting to half a dozen children who are tailor-squatting around his feet. She is aware that he's showing off to impress her and the thought makes her warm and pleased, ready to laugh at anything. But to pretend that she's unimpressed she leans back and looks up into the tree in which the sunlight is really alive, creeping round the great bole, spots of light leaping like birds from one branch to another. She thinks of the omú tree which grows on the pampas of

South America. Its trunk can be anything up to forty or fifty feet thick. The wood is so soft that when cut it rots like an over-ripe melon and is useless as firewood. The leaves are large, glossy and deep green like laurel leaves – and also poisonous. But they give shade from the bare sun to man and beast, and men mark their way on the endless plains by remembering this or that omú tree. She has read about omú trees. Her own tree is for sure not one of them. She sits up straight when her book is lifted from her lap. Lofty is sitting by her side. The children are pointing and laughing. He must have crept up on hands and knees pretending to be a wild animal, a wolf, a prowling tiger. He's very good at capers of that sort. His rod and net lie by the side of the burn.

It was April when he first sat beside her. It is now mid-June. Her school will close soon for the holidays and she will no longer be compelled to wear the uniform: black stockings, pleated skirt of navy-blue serge, blue gansey, blue necktie with saffron stripes, blue blazer with school crest in saffron on breast-pocket, blue beret, black flat-heeled shoes. Even Juliet, and she was very young, didn't have to wear a school uniform. If she had had Romeo wouldn't have looked at her.

Not that they are star-crossed lovers or Lofty any Romeo. They haven't even crossed the millrace to walk in the bluebell woods as couples of all ages customarily do. She isn't shy of walking slowly because of the leg-splint but she knows that Lofty hasn't asked her because he thinks she might be: that makes her feel for him as she might feel, if she had one, for a witless younger brother who's awkward. And a bit wild: for a lot of Lofty's talk doesn't go with the world of school uniforms mostly blue for the mother of God. What the saffron is for, except variety of a sort, she can't guess. Lofty's rattling restless talk would lift Mother Teresa out of her frozen black rigidity.

Lofty with great good humour fingers the saffron stripes and says that, in spite of everything, she's a wee bit of an Orange-woman. They hold hands regularly. Lofty can read palms, a variant reading every time. They have kissed occasionally, when the children who are always there have been distracted by a water-hen or rat or leaping fish or a broken branch or an iceberg of froth from the falls.

—Don't look now, he says one day, but if you swivel round slowly you'll see my three sisters in action.

Beyond the millrace and against the fresh green of woods she can see the flash of coloured frocks, the glint of brass buttons and pipe-clayed belts. In those days it was only the wild ones who went with the soldiers: it wasn't money and security they were after.

—They're hell for soldiers, he says, between the three of them they'd take on the Germans.

Lofty himself reads a lot of military books, campaigns and generals, Napoleon and Ludendorf, all the way from Blenheim to the Dardanelles. When he doodles as he often does on the writing-pad she always carries with her – to make notes on her reading, to transcribe favourite poems – he doodles uniforms, every detail exact. Yet he listens to her when she reads poetry or the splendid prose of a volume of selected English essays, Caxton to Belloc.

—They're advancing on us, he says. They have us surrounded, enfiladed, debouched and circumnavigated.

—We'll tell Maryanne, the three sisters say, that you're with another.

Two of them, Mildred and Rosemary, are plump, laughing, blonde girls, and Mildred who is the youngest is as freckled as her brother. Gertie, the eldest, is olive-faced, with jet-black hair, wrinkles on the forehead and around the eyes like her mother. She is never to see the father of the family but the gossip of the town is to tell her that he's away a lot in Aldershot and India and that Lofty's mother, that merry woman, is friendly with more soldiers than the one she's married to.

The three British soldiers who are with the sisters are, one of them from Sligo, one from Wexford and one actually from Lancashire, England. They all talk and laugh a lot and she likes them. The Lancashire lad climbs right up to the top of the tree and pretends to see everything that's going on in the town and tells them about it: he has a lurid imagination. Then they go away towards the waterfall, still laughing, calling back about telling Maryanne. She asks him who Maryanne is. Lofty who clearly likes his sisters is not in the least embarrassed by the suggestion that he has another woman.

—Oh Maryanne's nobody or nobody much.

—She has a name. She must be somebody.

She's not really jealous, just curious.

—Maryanne's a girl I met one day on the road beyond McCaslan's shop.

—You met nobody on the road?

—She was wheeling a pram.

—She's married to Mr. Nobody?

—It wasn't her pram. She's the nursemaid in Mooney's, the fancy-bread bakery. There was a lovely smell of fresh bread.

—Had you a good appetite, apple-jelly, jam-tart?

But since the rest of that rhyme to which children, Protestant and Catholic, rope-skip on the streets, is tell me the name of your sweetheart, she doesn't finish it and finds herself, to her annoyance, blushing. Lofty doesn't seem to notice.

—There were twins in the pram. I pushed it for her up the hill to the main road. Then she said I bet you wouldn't do that for me if it was in the town on the court-house hill where everybody could see you. I said why not and she said Christian Brothers' boys are very stuck-up, I've met some that would do anything they could or you'd let them if they had a girl in the woods or in the dark, but that wouldn't be seen talking to her on the street, maids aren't good enough for them. I didn't tell her I was a Presbyterian and went to the academy.

—Why not?

—She mightn't like a Presbyterian pushing her pram.

They laugh at that until the playing children turn and look and laugh with them. Cheerful voices call from beyond the millrace where soldiers and sisters are withdrawing to the woods.

—We have girls at the academy, on the house, what Harry Cassidy and Jerry Hurst and the boys don't have at the Brothers. Harry and the boys are mad envious when we tell them about the fun we have feeling Daisy Allen under the desk at school. All lies of course.

—I hope Daisy Allen doesn't hear that.

—Och Daisy, she's well handled anyway, she's going about with a bus-driver and he's a married man as well, he ruined a doctor's daughter in Dungannon. Harry and the Catholic boys think the Protestant girls are wilder because they don't have to tell it all in confession. That isn't true either.

One other funny story she had heard Lofty's mother telling that day as the train in the evening left Bundoran station and the great romantic flat-topped mountains diminished into the distance. This time the story-teller faced her aunt and sat beside her uncle who had been talking about jerry-building in a new housing estate. Lofty's mother agreed with him. She had a shopping-bag of sugar to smuggle back into the Six Counties where it cost more. The sugar was tastefully disguised under a top-dressing of dulse. With content and triumph Lofty's mother sang a parody popular at the time: South of the border down Bundoran way, that's where we get the Free State sugar to sweeten our tay.

She was great fun. She had bright blue eyes and a brown hat with a flaring feather, and a brown crinkly face. She said: Those houses are everything you say and worse. Fancy fronts and ready to fall. When you flush the lavatory in them the noise is heard all over the town. Only the other day the lady who lives in number three sent down to River Row for old Mr. Hill, the chimney-sweep, and up he came and put the brush up the chimney and then went out, the way sweeps do, to see if the brush was showing out of the top of the chimney. No brush. In he went and screws on another length of handle on the brush and pushes for dear life, and out again to look, but no brush. In again and screws on the last bit of handle he has, and he's pushing away when the lady from number eleven knocks on the door. Have you the sweep in, missus dear, she says. I have, missus dear, says the lady from number three. Then please ask him to be careful, missus dear, she says, that's twice now he's upset our wee Rosy from the lavatory seat.

Because of her happy carrying voice passers-by in the corridor stop to join the fun. The smuggled sugar is safely across the border.

Remembering Lofty's laughing mother makes it easier still to like Lofty. The three sisters also look as if they'd be good for a lot of laughs.

Her uncle is a tall broad-shouldered man with a good grey

suit, a wide-brimmed hat, two gold teeth and a drawl. Years ago he was in the building trade in the United States and knows a lot about jerry-building. He gets on very well with Lofty's mother.

It was well on towards the end of August when the black man sat on the bench beside her. She was looking sideways towards the bridge over the millrace, and laughing: because two big rough young fellows were running like hares before Mr. McCaslan's boxer dog. Mr. McCaslan who owned the shop was also water-bailiff and park-keeper. The rough fellows had been using, brutally, one of the swings meant for small children, so brutally that the iron stays that supported it were rising out of the ground. Mr. McCaslan had mentioned the matter to them. They had been offensive, even threatening, to the old rheumatic man so he hobbled back to his shop and sent the boxer dog down as his deputy. The pair took off as if all hell were behind them. It was funny because the dog didn't bark or growl or show hostility, didn't even run fast, just loped along with a certain air of quiet determination and wouldn't (as far as she knew) savage anybody. But he was a big dog even for a boxer and the retreat of the miscreants was faster than the Keystone Cops. She laughed so much that the book fell on the grass. The black man picked it up and sat down beside her.

She thought of him as a black man not because he was a Negro but because her uncle had told her that he was a member of the black preceptory which was a special branch of the Orange Order. She had seen him walking last twelfth of July in the big parade in memory of the battle of the Boyne, which happened a long time ago, and in honour of King William of Orange who was a long time dead and had never been in this town. He had worn the black sash, with shining metallic esoteric insignia attached, as had the other men who marched beside him. The contingent that followed wore blue sashes and were supposed to be teetotallers but her uncle said that that was not always so. One of the blue men, a red-faced red-headed fellow was teetering and might have fallen if he hadn't been holding on to one of the poles that supported a banner.

The drums drummed, the banners bellied in the breeze, the pipes and fifes and brass and accordions played:

It is old but it is beautiful
And its colours they are fine,
It was worn at Derry, Aughrim,
Enniskillen and the Boyne.
My father wore it in his youth,
In bygone days of yore,
And on the Twelfth I'll always wear
The sash my father wore.

The name of the black man who sat beside her was Samuel McClintock and he was a butcher. It was said about him for laughs that if the market ran out of meat the town could live for a week on McClintock's apron: blue, with white stripes. That August day and in the public park he naturally wasn't wearing the apron. He had a black moustache, a heavy blue chin, a check cloth-cap, thick-soled boots, thick woollen stockings and whipcord knee-breeches. The Fomorians, the monsters from stormy seas had, each of them, one arm, one leg and three rows of teeth. He said: The dog gave those ruffians the run.

The way he said it took the fun out of it. She said: Yes, Mr. McClintock.

She wished him elsewhere. She half-looked at her book. She was too well-reared to pick it up from her lap and ostentatiously go on reading. The river was in a brown fresh that day, the peninsula of sand and gravel not to be seen, nor Lofty, nor the children. The black man said: Plenty water in the river today.

She agreed with him. It was also a public park in a free-and-easy town and everyone had a right to sit where he pleased. Yet this was her own seat under the tall tree, almost exclusively hers, except when Lofty was there. The black man said: The Scotchies have a saying that the salmon's her ain when there's water but she's oors when it's oot.

He explained: That means that often they're easier to catch when the water's low.

He filled his pipe and lighted it. The smell of tobacco was

welcome. It might have been her imagination but until he pulled and puffed and sent the tobacco smell out around them she had thought that the resinous air under the tree was polluted by the odours of the butcher's shop and apron. He said that the salmon were a sight to see leaping the falls when they went running upstream. She said that she had often watched them.

—I'm told you're very friendly with a well-known young fisherman of my persuasion.

—Who, for instance?

—You know well. That's what I want to talk to you about. It's a serious matter.

—Being friendly with a fisherman?

—Don't play the smarty with me, young lassie. Even if you do go to the convent secondary school. Young people now get more education than's good for them. Lofty at the academy and you at the convent have no call to be chumming it up before the whole town.

—Why not?

But it occurred to her that they hadn't been chumming-up or anything else before the whole town. What eyes could have spied on them in this enchanted island?

—His uncle's a tyler, that's why.

—I never knew he had an uncle.

—His mother's brother is a tyler and very strict.

—What's a tyler?

—I shouldn't repeat it, lassie. But I will, to impress on you how serious it is. A tyler he is and a strict one. Wasn't it him spoke up to have Lofty let into the B Specials?

—Don't ask me. I never knew he was a B Special.

But one day for a joke, she remembered, he had given her a handful of bullets.

—The nuns wouldn't tell you this at school but the B Specials were set up by Sir Basil Brooke to hold Ulster against the Pope and the Republic of Ireland.

The nuns, for sure, hadn't told her anything of the sort: Mother Teresa who was very strong on purity and being a lady and not sitting like a man with your legs crossed had never once mentioned the defensive heroisms of the B Specials who, out in country places, went about at night with guns and in black uniforms, holding up Catholic neighbours and asking them their names and addresses – which they knew very well to begin with. The Lofty she knew in daylight by this laughing river didn't seem to be cut out for such nocturnal capers.

—If his uncle knew that the two of you and you a Catholic girl were carrying-on there'd be hell upon earth.

—But we're not carrying-on.

—You were seen kissing here on this bench. What's that but carrying-on?

—What does he level?

—What does who level?

—The uncle who's a leveller or whatever you called him.

—Speak with respect, young lassie. A tyler, although I shouldn't tell you the secret, is a big man in the Order at detecting intruders. His obligation is this: I do solemnly declare that I will be faithful to the duties of my office and I will not admit any person into the lodge without having first found him to be in possession of the financial password or without the sanction of the Worshipful Master of the Lodge.

Then after a pause he said with gravity: And I'm the worshipful master.

He was the only one of the kind she had ever met or ever was to meet and she did her best, although it was all very strange there by the river and the rough stream and under the big tree, to appear impressed, yet all she could think of saying was: But I'm not interfering with his tyling.

Then she was angry and close to tears, although it was also funny: For all I care he can tile the roofs and floors and walls of every house in this town.

The big man hadn't moved much since he sat down, never raised his voice, but now he shouted: Lassie, I'll make you care. The B Specials are sworn to uphold Protestant liberty and beat down the Fenians and the IRA.

—I'm not a Fenian nor an IRA.

—You're a Roman Catholic, aren't you? And there isn't any other sort. Sir Basil Brooke says that Roman Catholics are one hundred percent disloyal and that he wouldn't have one of them about the house.

—Sir Who's It?

—No cheek, lassie. Didn't he sit up a tree at Colebrook all night long with a gun waiting for the IRA to attack his house? Didn't he found the B Specials to help the police to defend the throne and the Protestant religion?

What was it to her if Sir Somebody or Other spent all his life up a tree at Colebrook or anywhere else? The Lancashire soldier had climbed her tree and been as comic as a monkey up a stick. The black man calmed himself: Your own clergy are dead set against mixed marriages.

—We weren't thinking of marriage.

—What of then? Silliness and nonsense. The young have no wit. What would Mother Teresa say if she heard you were keeping company with a Protestant?

—Who would tell her?

—I might. For your own good and for Lofty.

He knocked the ash out of his pipe and put it away. The pleasant tobacco smell faded. She smelled blood and dirt and heard screams and knew, with a comical feeling of kindness, that she had been wrongly blaming him for bringing with him the stench of the shambles. There was a piggery at the far end of the field beyond the river and the wind was blowing from that direction.

—That's the piggery, she said. It's a disgrace.

—Time and again I've said that on the town council. You must have read what I said in the papers. It's a sin, shame and scandal to have a piggery beside a beauty spot. Not that I've anything against pigs, in my business, in their own place.

He stood up and patted her on the shoulder. He was really just a big rough friendly man: You don't want him put out of the Specials or the Lodge itself.

—Why should he be?

—These are deep matters. But they tell me you read a lot. You've the name for being one of the cleverest students in this town, Protestant or Catholic. So I'll talk to you, all for the best, as if you were a grown-up and one of my own. It is possible but very difficult for a convert to be accepted as a member of the Orange Order.

He was as good as standing to attention. He was looking over her head towards the waterfall.

—A convert would have to be of several years standing and his background would have to be carefully screened. His admission would have to be authorized by the Grand Lodge. They'd have to go that high, like Rome for the Catholics. No convert can get into the Black Preceptory if either of his parents is still living, in case the Roman Catholic Church might exert pressure on a parent.

He was reciting. Like the sing-song way in which in school the children learned the Catechism.

Q: *What are the seven deadly sins?*
A: *Pride, covetousness, lust, gluttony, envy, anger and sloth.*
Q: *What are the four sins that cry to heaven for vengeance?*
A: *Wilful murder, sodomy, oppression of the poor and defrauding the labourer of his wages.*

Dear Sacred Heart it was a cheery world.

—A convert who was even a Protestant clergyman was blacked-out because one of his parents was still living, and there is automatic expulsion for dishonouring the Institution by marrying a Roman Catholic.

The great tree creaked its branches above them. The brown water tumbled on towards the town.

—You see what I mean, lassie.

She supposed she saw. In a way she was grateful. He was trying to help. He shook her hand as if they were friends forever. He went off towards the waterfall so that, without turning around, she could not see him walking away and he could not, thank God, see her face laughing, laughing. For, sweet heart of Jesus fount of love and mercy to thee we come thy blessings to implore, but it was comic to think of him marching up the convent grounds (he should wear his black sash and have a fife and drum before him), holy white statues to left and right and a Lourdes grotto as high as Mount Errigal, to relate all about the love-life of Lofty and herself to Mother Teresa who had a mouth like a rat-trap – and a mind. A worshipful master and a most worshipful reverend mother and never, or seldom, the twain shall meet. She was an odd sort of a girl. She sat around a lot and had read too many books. It was funny, also, to think of his daughter, Gladys, a fine good-natured brunette with a swinging stride, a bosom like a Viking prow, and a dozen boy friends of all creeds and classes. Nothing sectarian about Gladys who was one of his own kind and the daughter of a worshipful master. Somebody should tell the tyler to keep an eye on her. But she was too clever to be caught, too fast on her feet, too fast on her feet.

Walking slowly past the Orange hall on the way home she thought that the next time she met him she would have a lot to tell to lazy, freckled, lovable Lofty. The Orange hall was a two-storeyed brownstone building at a crossroads on the edge of the town. High on its wall a medallion image of William of Orange on an impossibly white horse rode forever across the Boyne. The two old cannon-guns on the green outside had been captured from the Germans in the Kaiser war. In there, Lofty's lodge met and it was a popular joke that no man could become a member until he rode a buck goat backways up the stairs. Sometimes in the evenings bands of music played thunderously in there, practising for the day in July when they marched out, banners flying. It was crazy to think that a man on a white horse, riding across a river two hundred years ago could now ride between herself and Lofty. Or for that matter – although Mother Teresa would have a fit if she thought that a pupil of hers could think of such things – another man on a chair or something being carried shoulder-high in the city of Rome.

All this she meant to mention to Lofty the next time he came to the seat under the tree. But all she could get around to saying was: Lofty, what's a tyler?

He had no rod and net and was dressed, not for fishing, in a new navy-blue suit. The children called to him from the gravel but he paid no attention to them. At first he didn't pretend to hear her, so she asked him again. He said that a tyler was a man who laid tiles. That was the end of that. Then it was winter. One whole week the park was flooded. She couldn't exactly remember when it was that Lofty had given her the bullets.

It was also crazy to think that Lofty's laughing mother could have a brother who went about spying on people and nosing them out. What eyes had spied on Lofty and herself on the enchanted island? What nosy neighbour had told somebody who told somebody who told the sergeant that she had bullets in the earthenware jug?

—If you don't tell me, the sergeant says, it will be awkward for all concerned. What would Mother Teresa think if she thought you had live bullets in an earthenware jug?

It wasn't possible to control the giggles. What, in the holy name of God, would Mother Teresa think, if the sergeant and the worshipful master descended on her simultaneously, what would she say, how would she look? Keeping live bullets in a jug must be one of the few things that she had not warned her girls against.

—You'll have to come down to the barracks with me. I'll walk ahead and you follow just in case the people are passing remarks. They might think I'm arresting you.

—What are you doing?

—Och, I'd just like you to make a statement. It's not a crime to have bullets. Not for a young lady like you who wouldn't be likely to be using them. But we have a duty to find out where they came from. My son Reggie speaks highly of you, Reggie the footballer you know.

She knew. It was a town joke that the sergeant couldn't speak to anybody for ten minutes without mentioning Reggie who parted his hair up the middle, wore loud scarves and played football very well: it was clear that the sergeant thought that to be thought well of by Reggie was a special distinction.

Old low white houses line the hill that goes up from the brook and the co-operative creamery to the centre of the town. The sergeant plods on, twenty yards ahead of her. The town is very quiet. His black leather belt creaks and strains to hold him together. The butt of his pistol, his black baton case shine. She has never noticed before that Lofty has a stutter. Another sergeant sits behind a desk in the dayroom and makes notes. Two young constables are laughing in the background. The black man comes in and says: I warned the two of them.

Her own sergeant says: There wasn't much harm in it.

—Not for the girl, says the man behind the desk. But for him a breach of discipline.

Lofty has surely never stuttered when he talked to her by the meeting of the waters.

—Did you tell them I gave you the bullets?

—Dear God, it wasn't a crime to give me bullets.

—Did you tell them?

—I did not.

—They said you did.

—So.

Her own sergeant looks ashamed and rubs his moustache. The other sergeant says: Case closed.

Then her uncle walks in, and so hopping mad that he seems to have a mouthful of gold teeth. He talks for a long time and they listen respectfully because he's a famous man for keeping running dogs which he feeds on brandy and beef. He says over and over again: You make a helluva fuss about a few bullets.

—A breach of discipline, says the man behind the desk.

—My ass and yours, says her uncle. A helluva fuss.

And repeats it many times as they walk home together.

—But all the same they'll put him out of the Specials, he says. And I dare say he shouldn't have been assing around giving away government issue.

Over the supper table he remembers the time he had been a policeman in Detroit: Some Negro trouble then and this rookie policeman from Oklahoma was on patrol with a trained man. The rookie has no gun. So they're rushed by twenty black men and the first rock thrown clobbers the trained man unconscious. But the Oklahoma guy he stoops down, takes the pistol out of the other man's holster and shoots six times and kills six black men, one, two, three, four, five, six. He didn't waste a bullet.

—Sacred Heart have mercy, says her aunt.

—What did the other black men do, uncle?

—They took off for home and small blame to them. He was a cool one, that rookie, and a damned good shot. Here in this place they make a helluva fuss over a few bullets. I told them so.

Lofty came never again to the tall tree. They met a few times on the street and spoke a few words. She left the town after a while and went to work in London. Once, home on holidays, she met Lofty and he asked her to go to the pictures, and she meant to but never did. The Hitler war came on. She married an American and went to live in, of all places, Detroit. Her uncle and aunt and the sergeant and the worshipful master and the tyler and, I suppose, Lofty's mother and McCaslan and his dog died.

Remembering her, I walked, the last time I was in the town to revisit Bluebell Meadow. The bridge over the millrace was broken down to one plank. Rank grass grew a foot high over most of the island. The rest of it was a wide track of sand and gravel where the river in fierce flood had taken everything before it. The children's swings and all the seats were gone, smashed some time before by reluctant young soldiers from the North English cities doing their national service. Repair work had been planned but then the bombings and murders began.

No laughing Lancashire boy in British uniform will ever again climb the tall tree. For one thing the tree is gone. For another the soldiers go about in bands, guns at the ready, in trucks and armoured cars. There are burned-out buildings in the main streets – although the great barracks is unscathed – and barricades and checkpoints at the ends of the town. As a woman said to me: Nowadays we have gates to the town. Still, other towns are worse: Strabane which was on the border and easy to bomb is a burned-out wreck. And Newry, where the people badly needed shops and factories, and not ruins. And Derry is like Dresden on the day after.

When I wrote to her about this she said, among other things, that she had never found out the name of that tall conifer.

Down Then by Derry

T HE FIRST TIME Tom Cunningham ever saw Sadie Law's brother, Francie, that brother was airborne between the saddle of a racing bicycle and a stockade filled with female lunatics. Francie is not the chief part of this story, nor is his sister, but since he has been mentioned, it might be fair to his fame and memory to say who he was and what he was doing in the air in that odd place.

A resident medical officer in the district's mental hospital had, years before, been a believer in athletics as curative therapy for the crazy: running and jumping and the lord knows what. So he set those who were out of cells and strait-jackets, and otherwise capable, at the running and jumping, barring, for good reasons the throwing of the hammer or the discus, or the tossing of the caber – which can be dangerous occupations even for the sane. Then the medical officer, to introduce a sanative, competitive spirit, organised an annual sports meeting, with cups, shields and lesser prizes. The thing grew and grew. That medical officer died and went to Valhalla. The annual meeting continued to grow until it was one of the most notable sporting events in that part of the country. Professionals competed. The crazy men and women, those of them who could be out and about, were now only two small corralled sections among the spectators. They had been pushed back into the shouting or gibbering shadows where everybody, except the man in Valhalla, thought they belonged.

Francie Law was a famous track cyclist. That was how he came to be there in the air. There was one bad corner on the packed cinder track. This day there was a pile-up and

Francie was catapulted clean, to land among the lunatic ladies. He survived. It was as a hero-worshipper bearing grapes to Francie's hospital bedside – Francie, wherever he was, always smelled of embrocation – that Tom Cunningham first met Francie's sister, Sadie, who was almost as famous as her brother, but not for track-cycling.

—She's Number One, according to all the talk, Tom said to his favourite friend who was five years younger than him.

Tom was nineteen.

—And she liked me, Tom said. We have a date. She wore a black leather coat with a belt. There was a good warm smell off it. Like the smell of the plush seats at the back of the cinema where all the feeling goes on. Hot stuff, boy. Also the smell of embrocation. Rub it up good. Frank Mullan told me she was okay and easy to get, if you once got to know her. And the May devotions are on the way. Long evenings. Warm grass. And Frank Mullan should know. He knows them all.

Of course it goes without saying that the devotions on May evenings in the parish church, with the high, limping, Gothic spires, went away back to something far before the worship of holy purity and the blessed virgin, to some pagan festival of the rites of spring. This he found out afterwards by reading, and by much dull talk, in more sophisticated places, heaven help us, than his own native town. But in the spring of that year he neither knew nor worried about such things, as he knelt beside Tom Cunningham in the side aisle to the left hand of the high altar.

Oh, those brown angels cut in wood of a slightly lighter colour than the wood of the beams to which they provided a figurehead finish. They swooped out towards each other over the nave and eyed the praying people. Once he had tried to write a poem about them:

> *In church the angels cut in wood,*
> *In row on row arranged,*
> *Stand always as before they stood,*
> *And only I am changed.*

But it wouldn't work. The angels weren't standing, for God's sake, they had no legs or feet to stand on, or, if they had, those legs were buried in the wood of the beams from which winged torsos and long-haired oaken heads seemed to have instantaneously, ecstatically, emerged. Times, he still saw those angels in his dreams, soaring, in a sort of a way, over altar, incense, monstrance, praying priest, responding mumbling people, over Tom Cunningham in the side aisle making cute sideways eyes and secret signs at Sadie Law who knelt with her favourite friend directly under the angels in the nave. Whatever about bullshit talk and the rites of spring, the devotions on May evenings was where you met people for good or evil; and all around the church, high on a hill with its hopalong spires, the rolling country was rich in deep grass and the birds were making mocking calls along hidden lovers' lanes. The high grassy embankments along the railways that went out of the town to the Donegal sea at Bundoran, or to Dublin or Belfast, or down then by Derry to the northern sea, were a sort of secret world where only lovers went in the long evenings. No respectable girl would be seen walking along the railway. The art was in not being seen.

His daughter, who was eighteen years of age, said to his mother who admitted to being eighty-five: Dad must have been happy here in this town in his schooldays. He's always singing a song. Well, not singing exactly. It has no particular tune. No beat. Dad's a bit of a square. It goes more like an African chant.

—Wallawalla boom boom, said his son who was fourteen.

—John, said the daughter, mind your manners. Granny doesn't dig Swahili. No granny. The song begins like this. Thrice happy and blessed were the days of my childhood and happy the hours I wandered from school, by green Mountjoy's forest, our dear native wildwood, and the green flowery banks of the serpentine Strule.

—Mountjoy forest, he said, was part of the estate of Lord and Lady Blessington. Back in the days of the great Napoleon. That was an old song.

—He was a good scholar, his mother said. He was very fond of reading poetry out loud. In the mornings after breakfast. Before he went to school.

As if he wasn't there at all. His daughter giggled.

He was accustomed to his mother rhapsodising in this way, talking about him to other people in his presence. Once she had said to a friend of his: He would be the best man in Ireland if it wasn't for the little weakness.

Afterwards his friend had said with great good humour: with you standing there I couldn't very well ask her which weakness she meant.

Another time and under similar circumstances she had said to the same friend: His father, God rest him, put on some weight when he passed forty, but he never swelled like that.

Pointing to him. As if, by God, the son, had had a dropsical condition.

To her grand-daughter and grandson she said: He read Shelley. If Winter comes can Spring be far behind. I liked that. Shelley was a good poet. Although my own mother could never understand about Tennyson and the brook. She used to say: Poor fellow, could nobody stop him. I think she thought it was about some unfortunate man that had something astray with his bowels. Then there was one poet that droned on and on about Adam and Eve and the fall of Satan.

She spat mildly and politely towards the fireplace where, winter or summer, there was always a fire. She preserved many old country customs. One was to spit when, by inadvertence or necessity, one mentioned a name of the devil – and his names were legion.

Twenty-eight years later he was still a little ashamed that he had inflicted on his mother's patient ears the monotony of Milton, even to the utter extremity of the Latin verses.

—Milton, he said, a bit of a bore.

But nobody paid the least attention to him. So he closed his eyes and his mind to the lot of them: the mother, old, wrinkled, wearing a battered old felt hat that looked like a German helmet, but with an eye as bright and inquisitive as it must have been when she was a lively singing country girl, and the man she was to marry was walking round and round the South African veldt; and he himself wasn't even a fragment of an imagination, or a gleam or a glint in his father's eye; the daughter, pert, small, lively, endlessly talkative; the son, tall, easy-going, slouching when he walked – as his grandfather had done. It was uncanny to observe such resemblances.

Since not one of the three of them paid any attention to him he shut his eyes and his mind to them and went on his own through the town, and back to the past that had made the town and him.

The two tall limping Gothic spires rose high above the hilly narrow streets. Those two spires and the simple plain spire of the Protestant church – that would be Church of Ireland, for the Methodists and Presbyterians did not rise to spires – could be seen for a distance of ten miles. They soared, they were prayers of a sort, over the riverine countryside.

The taller spire was all of two hundred and thirty feet high, thirty of that being for the surmounting cross. To climb up the inside of that spire you went first by a winding stone stairway to the organ loft, then by a steep straight wooden stairway to the shaky creaky platform where the sexton stood when he pulled the bell-rope, then up a series of perpendicular ladders to the place where the two bells were hung, sullen and heavy, but ready at the twitch of a rope to do their duty. From that eminence, one hundred and fifty feet up, you could look down on everything. The town was almost flat, no longer all humps and hills and high ridged roofs and steep narrow streets. Down there was the meeting place of two rivers, the Camowen and the Drumragh: a sparkling trout-water, a sullen pike-water. Who could comprehend the differences there were between rivers, not to speak now of the Amazon and the Seine and the Volga and the Whang-ho and the Ohio, but even between neighbouring rivers destined to marry and to melt into one? United, the waters of Drumragh and Camowen went on under the name of the Strule, sweeping in a great horse-shoe around the wide holm below the military barracks, tramping and tossing northwards to meet yet another river, the Fairywater, then to vanish glistening into a green-and-blue infinity.

Except you were the sexton, or some lesser person authorised by him, you were not, by no means, supposed to be up there at all. Dusty boards, with crazy, dizzy gaps between them, swayed and bent under your feet. Vicious jackdaws screeched.

The blue-and-green infinity into which the sparkling water vanished was the place where Blessington's Rangers had once walked, speaking Gaelic, great axes on shoulders. They cut down the trees to make timber for war against Bonaparte, and money to keep Lord and Lady Blessington, their daughter, and the ineffable Count D'Orsay gallivanting.

One day coming home from school alone – that was a time of the day when it wasn't easy to be alone but, with cunning, it could be managed – he had found the door at the foot of the stone stairway open and had taken the chance that it was open by accident. It was. He made the climb. He saw the world. He was alone with the jackdaws and the moan of the wind. Then on the way down the perpendicular ladders he had missed a rung, slipped, screamed with the jackdaws, grabbed desperately and held on. Just about where the sexton would stand to pull the bell-rope he had vomited a sort of striped vomit that he had never seen before. Even in boyhood there was the fear of death.

Nobody, thank God, had ever found out who had thus paid tribute, made offertory, in the holy place. For weeks afterwards he had felt dizzy even when climbing the stairs to his bedroom.

When the war was over and Boney beaten, the gallivanting lords and ladies had no more use for the woodsmen of Mountjoy. For the last time they walked down there below in the old Flax Market that hadn't changed much since 1820: in their rough boots and frieze coats, axes on shoulders, speaking a guttural language that was doomed almost to die, singing, drinking, fighting among each other, but standing shoulder to shoulder or axe to axe against the world. The paltry townsmen and shopkeepers must have breathed easily when the woodsmen went north to Derry to board the American boat.

As a boy he had known of them and walked among their shadows in the Old Market: No more will we see the gay silver trouts playing, or the herd of wild deer through its forest be straying, or the nymph and gay swain on its flowery bank straying, or hear the loud guns of the sportsmen of Strule.

On those May evenings the steeplejacks were swinging on the spires, tiny black dwarfs sitting in wooden chairs at the ends of ropes. They were pointing the stones, which meant that they smeared in fresh cement, netted the soaring prayers in nets of new white. Snug and secure in deep warm grass on a railway embankment from which there was a view both of the tips of the roofs of the town and of one deep curve of the slow pike-infested Drumragh River, Tom and Sadie, Tom's friend and Sadie's friend, lay on their backs and watched the dwarfs on the steeples.

—Why, Angela said, did they not build one steeple as long as the other?

—As high, he said, you mean.

—High or long, she said, what's the difference?

She had a wide humorous mouth that, some evening, with the help of God, he would get around to kissing.

—It all depends, Tom said, on which way you're going. Like up or down or sideways.

—Why, she repeated.

She was a stubborn girl. He held her hand.

—In this life, Tom said, there is nothing perfect.

—No, he said.

Because he knew.

—Two men were killed on the smaller steeple. So they stopped.

—Brian, said Tom, always has a better story. Say us a poem, Brian.

—That's no story. It's gospel truth.

Tom and Sadie were kissing, gurgling. Angela tickled his palm.

—That's a job, he said, I wouldn't have for all the tea in China.

He meant being a steeplejack.

Tom surfaced. He said: I'm not so sure. I wouldn't mind being able to get up as high as that.

Sadie said: You could always try.

With her left hand she gently massaged Tom's grey-flannelled crotch.

He watched Sadie's small moving hand. He wondered how many people within a ten-mile radius, in the town, in villages, from farmhouse doorways, walking along laneways, or fishing, or lying on grass, were watching the steeplejacks on the spires.

For no reason that he could explain he thought it would be exciting to see that face again, the wide humorous mouth, the brown hair that curled like two little brown horns over her temples, the plump fresh cheeks. The hair, though, wouldn't be brown any more. Don't forget that. Look for something older. Three years older than yourself: a reasonable gap of years, once upon a time, for a girl who could teach and a boy who was willing, even afraid, to learn.

—That woman, his daughter said, who writes you those letters from Indiana. What part of this town did she live in? When she was a girl, I mean.

The three of them were walking down the steep High Street. Behind and above them, where two narrower streets met to form the High Street, was the eighteenth-century courthouse, high steps before it and Doric columns, dominating the long undulations of High Street and Campsie Avenue until the houses ended and the point of vision was buried in deep trees.

He told them that there had once been in the town a police-man so lazy that he hated to walk. So he sat all day, when the day was sunny, on the courthouse steps. When his superior officers asked him what he thought he was at, he defended himself by saying that he had the whole town under observation.

This grey day, the last sad day but one of the old year, would have been no day for sitting on the steps.

They laughed at the memory of the lazy policeman, and descended the steep street. The daughter said: You never met her, all the times you were in the States?

—I never even met her, I only saw her, when we were young together here in this town. She's a shadow, a memory.

—Shadows, she said precisely, don't write letters. Memories might.

—One time last year, he said, I had hoped to meet her. I was, so to speak, passing that way. That is, within a few hun-dred miles or so of where she lives. That's not far, out there.

—Just next door, his son said.

—It was in March, he said, and I was on the way north to give a lecture in Minnesota. I crossed Indiana.

—See any Injuns dad, said the son.

—No, what I mostly remember about Indiana is big barns

and ducks, the big ducks that we call Muscovy ducks. Never saw so many Muscovy ducks, anywhere else in the world.

—But then dad, his daughter said, you never were in Muscovy.

—Or if he was, said the son, he never told us.

In March in Indiana the endless flat brown land still shivered. The harness-racing tracks by the roadside were soggy and empty. The last of the snow lay here and there in sordid mounds. Cattle, with a certain guilty look about them, foraged among the tall battered corn-stalks of last year's harvest. There was ice at the fringes of creeks and rivers that looked far too small to negotiate such interminable expanses of flat land. Great round-roofed barns stood aloof from, yet still dwarfed, the neat houses. Flat and sombre the land went every way to a far horizon...

—A small American penny, his daughter said, for your wandering thoughts.

He told her that in one small field near the city of Lafayette he had seen a flock of more than two hundred Muscovy ducks. The field had been between a railway and a line of power pylons.

—Nothing, he explained, more emphasises distance in flat land than a line of pylons striding on and on for ever, giants marching, carrying cables on their shoulders, until they vanish east or west.

—Or north or south, his son said.

—Now, she said sweetly, we know all about electricity. Dad, you're such a dear old bore. We couldn't care less about ducks or pylons. We want to know about the woman who writes you those marvellous letters from Indiana.

—She was an orphan, he said. In an orphanage. In Derry City.

—So far so good, his son said.

—She was taken out of the orphanage by this woman and reared in this town. She suffered a lot from illness. She wore a leg-splint when she was a child. She grew up. She read books. My father used to talk a lot about her. He used to say: You should meet that young woman. She's a wonder.

—But I was in college in Dublin, by that time, coming and going and somehow or other I never did get the opportunity of speaking to her. My memory is of a rather long beautiful face, sort of madonna, and fair hair. Framed like an old picture in glass and wood, against a background of coloured magazines and paperbacked books. Because my last recollection of her is that she was working in the bookstall in the railway station. During the war she went off to London, married an American. Then seven or eight years ago she read something I'd written and wrote to me. That's the whole story.

She had written: You may have a vague recollection of who I am when you read my name. Then again you may not. It's been a long time. About thirty years. But I remember you very well, indeed: on your way to school, to church, walking the roads around our town, always, it seemed to me, alone.

That would be a romantic young girl confusing an average sullen lout of a fellow with her private image of Lord Byron.

—We rarely said more than hello. We lived in the same town all our growing years. We walked the same roads, knew the same people, and didn't meet at all. We might have shared a common interest. I loved books, poetry, music, but had little opportunity to enjoy any of them. I did manage to read quite a lot, and to remember poetry, and get a little music on an old radio. I walked, and thought of the books I'd read, and repeated the poetry to myself, and could hear the music again along the quiet roads. Thus I survived the town I was born in. Though mostly I remember it with love, because of Margaret, the woman who reared me. She was gentle, poor, uneducated, but with a lively mind and kind to all things living – especially to me when she took me from the nightmare of the orphanage in Derry, haunting me even now with its coldness, the crooked hilly streets of Derry, the jail, the Diamond, the wide Foyle which is really our own Strule, and the ships.

—Another penny for your thoughts, his daughter said. Or a measly nickel.

They turned right from the Market Street along the Dublin Road, past a filling station and a Presbyterian church, a toy-like gasworks, the old white houses of Irishtown. Beyond

Irishtown, he told them, was the Drumragh River and the old humped King's Bridge where James Stuart, falling back from the walls of Derry, had watched the town burn behind him.

Then they were ascending through a pleasant affluent suburb.

—No, he said, this wasn't the part of the town she lived in. We're not going that way just at the moment.

They were, in fact, walking to say a prayer at his father's grave. Everywhere he went he carried with him for luck a white stone from the grave. A white stone from the grave of a kind man would have to be lucky, wouldn't it, if there was the least pick of reason in the universe? But in a drunken moment in Dublin City he had loaned the stone to a man who ran greyhounds, and this particular greyhound had won, and the man had begged to be allowed to keep the stone. Today he would say his prayer and take away with him another white stone.

The Protestants lay to the left of the cemetery's main avenue, the Catholics to the right, and between them, on a slight rise, the stone oratory, cold and draughty, where on harsh days the last prayers were said over the coffins. He never remembered the wind around the corners of that oratory as being, even in summer, anything but bitterly cold. This last dead day, but one, of the year it was unbearable. Bravely the boy and girl knelt on the damp earth and prayed. He knelt with them, not praying, talking without words to the man under the clay, or somewhere in the air around him, and around him wherever in the world he went: the dead hover for ever over the living.

Low dark clouds travelling, or being forced to travel, fast, bulged with rain. To the lee of the empty oratory the three of them stood and looked over the forest of obelisks and Celtic crosses, Sacred Hearts and sorrowing mothers, at the distant sweep of the flooded Drumragh, at where the railway line used to cross it by a red metal bridge. The bridge was gone and the railway too – sold for scrap. But three hundred yards to the east of the river, there was still the stone bridge under the embankment – it looked like a gateway into an old walled city – and the lovers' lane that led into the fields, and across the fields to the wooden brambly slope above one of the deepest, most brooding of the river's pike-pools.

Would it be sin or the beginning of living to touch the hidden flesh of Angela? His dream of fair women was all about the creeping hand, the hair, the warmth. That was all that Tom and the other boys talked about.

She lay on her back in the brambly wood – the pike hovering in the pool below them – and he fumbled fearfully, and tickled her, his hand timidly outside her dress. But when she reached for him he rolled away. She laughed for a longer time than seemed necessary. From the far side of a clump of bushes he heard Tom say to Sadie: There must be nothing in Brown's house that doesn't smell of embrocation.

—The grave was very weedy, the daughter said.

—So I noticed. Your grandmother pays good money to have it kept clean and covered with white stones. On the way out I'll call to the caretaker's house and talk to him.

The clay in the centre of the grave had sunk. He was glad that neither son nor daughter had noticed that. It would be so painful to have to explain to young people, or even to oneself, that clay sank so when the coffin underneath had collapsed.

The hotel they stopped in was a mile outside the town, a domed mid-nineteenth-century house, miscalled a castle, on a hill top with a view of the heathery uplands the Camowen came from, and quite close to a park called the Lovers' Retreat, but known to the soldiers in the barracks as Buggers' Den.

The aged mother was safely at home in bed, in her small house across the narrow street from those gigantic limping spires. She liked to be close to the quietness of the church, the glowing red circle around the sanctuary lamp where she remembered and prayed for and to the dead man.

Leaving her in peace they had walked through the lighted crowded town, along a quiet dim suburban road, over a bridge that crossed the invisible talkative Camowen – there was a good gravelly trout pool just below that bridge. They dined late in a deserted dining-room. Along a corridor there was the noise of merriment from the bar. His son asked him which room had been the haunted room in the days when the hotel had been a castle.

—For the sake of the ghost, the daughter said, let's hope it wasn't where the bar is now.

—Ghosts, he told her, might like company.

—Not mine I pray, she said.

—Fraidy cat, the son said. A ghost couldn't hurt you.

—That ghost, he told them, couldn't hurt anyone. The story was that the people who lived here called in the priest and he blessed the room and put the ghost in a bottle.

—Poor ghost, she said.

—But where, she wondered, did the priest put the bottle.

—On the river, the son said. And it floated over the sea, to England, and somebody found it and opened it, and got a ghost instead of a message.

He saw them to their rooms. No ghost could survive in such up-to-date comfort. No ghost could rest in peace in any of the coloured bottles in the bar. The noisy local drinkers had gone home, taking their din with them. A few commercial men, talking of odds and ends, drinking slowly but with style, sat in an alcove. He joined them.

—Did you like it out there, they asked him.

—You were a friend of Tom Cunningham, they said.

—It's good out there. Fine people. Hospitable. The sort of people I meet.

—Tom went into the Palestine police after the war, they said. Then he went farther east. Never heard of since.

—Chasing the women in China, they said.

—But the crime in America, they said. Did you ever come up against that?

—It's there. But I never came up against it. Except in the newspapers.

—By God, they said, they have picturesque murders out there. We never have anything here except an odd friendly class of a murder. But out there. That fellow in Chicago and the nurses. And the young fellow that made the women in the beauty parlour lie down like the spokes of a wheel and then shot the living daylights out of them.

—The one that sticks most in my mind...

They were all attention.

...was the girl in the sump. This sump is an overflow pond at the back of a dry-cleaning plant. One morning a man walking by sees a girl's leg standing up out of the water.

—Clothed in white samite, they said. Mystic, wonderful.

—Seems she had been by day a teller in a bank and by night a go-go dancer in a discotheque. One day she walks out of the bank with a bagful of thousands of dollars. She is next encountered in the sump, one leg surfacing, her hands tied behind her back, her throat cut, the bag and the dollars gone. A barman from the discotheque is also missing.

—All for love, they said.

The long cold day, the search for the past, the drink, the warm company, had made him maudlin.

—When I read the newspapers today there are times I think I was reared in the Garden of Eden.

—Weren't we all, they said.

But it hadn't been the Garden of Eden for one waif of a girl, now a woman in far-away Indiana. From Atlanta, Georgia, where he had been for two years he had remailed to her the local newspapers that had come to him from this town.

She had written: That photograph of the demolition of the old stone railway bridge at Brook Corner saddened me. I recall that bridge with affection. When I'd spent about fourteen months flat on my back in the County Hospital, and was at last permitted up on crutches, I headed, somewhat shakily, under that bridge to begin the first of many walks. I still remember the bridge framing the road beyond like a picture, and the incredible green of the fields, the flowering hedges, the smell of hawthorn. The bridge became for me a gateway: to happy solitude. When I had trachoma and thought I might go blind my bitterest thought was that I might never again see the world through that bridge. Margaret's brother, Fred, was my companion and consolation in those dark days. He had been hired out at the age of six to work with a farmer and Margaret remembered seeing the golden-curly-haired child going off in the farmer's trap.

—Perhaps that was why Fred never cared to work. He hadn't,

for about twenty-five years before he died, not because he couldn't but simply because he didn't want to. Oh, on a number of occasions he worked, briefly, for farmers at harvest time, was rarely paid in cash but in kind; and only on condition that his dog, Major, could accompany him. Major barked all day, every day, as though indignant at his master's labours, and much to the chagrin of the other workers and the farmer. But since, when he wanted to, Fred could work as well as the others, his services were always desired and he was permitted to stay, dog and all.

—He was a strange silent man who sat by the fire all day with a far-off look in his eyes. He had very blue eyes. He rarely spoke to anybody outside the house. He was my sole companion during many long hours when I was confined to bed. I would read to him and ask him to spell and he would deliberately mis-spell and would be delighted when I would sharply correct him. I never knew how much I loved him until he died.

—Margaret housekept for Morris, the lawyer, who lived in the Georgian house beside the church with the high spires, and that left Fred and me a lot alone, and Fred would cook for me. Once, after I had been with Margaret several months, some sadistic neighbour woman told me that I was being sent back to the orphanage. So terrified was I that I hobbled up to the church and stood for hours across the street from the lawyer's house, waiting, the wind moaning away up in the spires in the darkness, until Margaret came and comforted me, led me home by the hand to Fred and Major and numerous cats, and a one-legged hen who had a nest in the corner and who was infuriated if another hen ever came to the back door in search of scraps.

His room was haunted, sure enough. He had sat too late, drunk too much, perhaps released the ghosts from the bottles. Oaken angels sang from the ceiling. A tearful crippled girl waited in the darkness at the foot of spires lost also in the windy darkness, no longer magic towers from which one could see the world. The leg of a girl who had stolen for love stood up like a stump of wood out of stagnant water.

Very cautiously he had asked his mother: Do you remember a family called Law? Are they still in the town? One of them, I think, was a famous racing cyclist.

Cautiously: because in her eyes there were times when he was still fourteen or less and there were people that he wasn't supposed to know.

—Oh, I remember the Laws. They were famous, indeed.

Around the house she had a fancy for dressing as if she were a pirate chief. Or perhaps it was a gipsy queen. Sometimes instead of the helmet-shaped hat she wore a white gipsy head-handkerchief; and a long red dressing-gown and Galway shawl with the corners tucked back under her oxters and pinned behind.

—One of them called in to see me one morning after Sunday mass. A Law or a half-Law or a quarter-Law or a by-Law. You wouldn't have much time for the like of them. Not condemning anyone for the weakness, but there were more distant cousins in that clan than was natural. Or godly.

That seemed to be that.

—You wouldn't have expected much of the Laws, she said. But it's heartrending to see the fate of some families that had every chance that God and man could give them.

—Like who, for instance?

—Like many I've seen. Like the Glenshrule family, for one.

The red bull of Glenshrule roared through his haunted dreams.

—Glenshrule's sold, she said, and in the hands of strangers.

The bull, he supposed, had been sold to make bovril.

Two private roadways led into the old house at Glenshrule, one from the steep by-road along which the crippled girl had hobbled to find peace, one from the road that led west to the Donegal sea. To either hand on either road it was all Glenshrule land, green, bountiful, a little unkempt, cattle country, little tillage. The three bachelor brothers of Glenshrule were gentlemen farmers: which meant whipcord breeches and booze and hunter horses. But they were frank, reckless, generous, easy in their money and good breeding, and made no objection to the townspeople using their private roads for circular walks on Sunday afternoons. Roving boys used those roads all the time, and the fields around them, and the only prohibiting notice to be seen told you to beware of the red bull.

—Christ, look at the size of him, Tom cried with an artist's enthusiasm. Boy, if you were built like that you'd be welcome anywhere.

They sat on a five-barred iron gate. Between them and the bull's private meadow was the additional fortification of a strong wooden gate. He was an unruly bull. His red coat shone. He had a head near as big as the head of the mouldy bison they had seen in the Old Market in Bostock and Wombell's travelling menagerie. He rooted at the ground with one fore-foot. The great head rose and fell. He didn't roar. He rumbled all the time like a train, far away, going into a tunnel.

—There's a lot to be said, Tom said, for being a bull.

—Everybody puts up with your tantrums.

—There's more to it than that.

Then the lady of Glenshrule, the one single sister of the three bachelor brothers, rode by on a bay mare. To acknowledge that they existed she raised her riding-crop, she smiled and said: Don't tempt him. Don't enter the meadow. Bulls eat boys.

—Boys, Tom muttered.

He was very bitter.

—There's also a lot to be said, he said, for being a bay mare.

She was bareheaded. She was blonde. She was twenty-five. She was blonde, she was blonde, she was blonde and calm-faced, and all the officers in the barracks pursued her. Years afterwards – altering the truth, as memory always does – he thought that he had then thought about queen and huntress, chaste and fair. But he hadn't. He had been too breathless to think of anything except, perhaps, that Sadie and Angela, lively and provoking as they could be, were still only in the servant-maid class.

She rode on towards the Donegal road. The sound of the hooves died away. The red bull, calmed, had lain down on the grass.

—One Sunday evening I sat beside her in the church, Tom said. My right leg against her left. It burned me. I can feel it still.

He rubbed his right thigh slowly, then sniffed his hand.

—I swear to God, he said, she pressed her thigh against mine. It made short work of the holy hour.

That was the year Tom and himself had been barred from the town's one cinema because Tom, ever an eager and enquiring mind, had discovered the anti-social use of hydrogen sulphide. A few sizzling test-tubes planted here and there in the darkness could have tumultuous effects on the audience. Old Mr. Pritchard – he was so old that it was suspected he had fought in the Zulu war – was heard to say in a barracks-square voice that some bloke here needed a purge of broken bottles. But three burly ushers simply purged Tom and his companion from the audience, two of them to hold Tom, the other to herd the companion before him.

Such a splendid deed and its consequences gave the two of them the glory of outlaws among their contemporaries. And to be barred from the delights of Eddy Cantor's Rome, or of Broadway with its gold-diggers, or of Wallace Beery's Big House, meant more nights in the Old Flax Market. That was fair enough, because the Old Flax Market was the place for outlaws. Black-uniformed constables patrolled the streets but, unless there was very audible drunken disorder, they left the Old Flax Market alone. No flax was ever sold there any more.

—The ghosts of the woodsmen are still here, he told Tom. This was their place when they came to town.

—You and those bloody woodsmen. You're a haunted man.

The unpaved three acres of the Old Market were sodden and puddled. A sharply-defined half-moon cut like a cleaver through wispy running clouds. He shouted at the moon: No more will the fair one of each shady bower hail her dear boy of that once happy hour, or present him again with a garland of flowers that they oft times selected and wove by the Strule.

—And poetry, boy, will be your ruination. Poetry will get you nowhere with Angela. Move in man. Angela demands action.

The moon, even if it was only half a moon, was useful to outlaws in a land of outlaws. For there were only three gas-lamps in the whole of the Old Flax Market and gas-lamps were little use on windy nights or when somebody, for fun or hellery, wished to quench them. One lamp was on a wall-bracket at the corner of a rowdy dance hall. It lighted, when it was allowed to, the wooden stairway to the door of the dance hall, and the people ascending or descending or standing in groups making noise. One lamp lighted the covered cobbled entry-way from the High Street. The third lighted the muddy uncovered exit to a dark riverside walk from which an irate lover had, about that time, heaved his fancy into the river.

—Let's have a look, Tom said, at the Jennett's corner. You'd see things there you never saw at the pictures.

—But look, he said, there goes the Bluebottle, her legs like elevenpence marked on a new bucket.

The drum boomed, the horn blared from the dance hall. The half-moon coldly shone on the Strule waters that flowed by one side of the Old Market.

—If your woodsmen ever walked here you can bloody well guess what they were after.

A tall thin girl in a blue coat was being eased into the shadows by a drunken man.

—Would you believe it, Tom said, she fought like a cat here one night with one of the Fighting McDermotts. The one with the dinge in his temple where some decent man brained him with a bottle of port-wine. When she wouldn't go with him he shouted he'd tell her father that sent her out for money, and her uncle that broke her in. She tore the red face off him.

—He rings the bell, her uncle.

—They say he rang the bell for her when she was thirteen.

There then was the terror of the dark walk by the river. The uncle who rang the bell as one of the last town-criers was a figure out of a German fairy-tale, a pied piper, tall hard hat, tailed coat, long grey moustache, a small man with a voice of thunder, swinging his handbell, shouting out fragments of news: that a group of strolling players would perform in the town hall, that the water supply would be turned off – for repairs to pipes in this or that part of the town, that such and such a house property would be auctioned. Was it credible that a comic fairy-tale figure should also be a part of some sniggering story? The Bluebottle vanished ahead of them into some riverside bushes. Where the river made an elbow bend a group of smoking muttering men waited at the Jennet's corner. Her shady bower was a wooden shelter put there by the town council to protect Sunday walkers from sudden showers. The council had not intended to cater for the comfort of the Jennet and her customers. She was a raw-boned red-headed country girl whose husband was in the mental hospital.

—Good natured and charges very little, Tom said.

Some of the shadowy courtiers called after them.

—But, boy, a little bit too open to the general public for men of taste like ourselves. Take me back to sweet sinful Sadie. Or the lady of Glenshrule on her bay mare.

She rode on to Donegal road, the hooves dancing clippetyclop, and the bull lay down in the meadow.

—What went wrong there, he said to his mother. They had everything.

—What would go wrong but debt and drink and the want of wit. The three brothers fled to Canada.

—They followed the woodsmen.

His mother didn't hear him.

—And my, she said, she looked lovely when she rode out astraddle on that bay mare.

—Tom Cunningham would have agreed with you.

—Oh, Tom Cunningham was a rare one. Very freckled when he was a little boy. And curly-haired. I'm amazed you remember him. He went to the war and never came back when it was over. But then you always had a good memory.

—I always had.

—She lived alone after the brothers left, and she never married, and went on drinking. There was a bit of scandal, too. But I never paid much attention to that sort of talk. She died in the ambulance on the way to hospital. But not, thank God, without the priest. For one of the curates was driving past just at that moment.

On the road she had ridden over on the bay mare.

—The Lord, his mother said, has everything mixed with mercy.

—He must have a lot of mercy for orphans, he said.

—Tell granny that story, dad, about the girl in the rain. The woman who writes to you. When she was a child, I mean.

She could still be outside there, the ghost of a frightened child, standing in the darkness at the foot of the spires. But one day in the orphanage playground she had broken out in rebellion.

—A sudden storm came up. The nuns called us in. We were to shelter, cold and miserable, in a sort of arcade or cloister. I started in with the rest, but suddenly I stopped and ran back to the playground. It was pouring. I was alone. The nuns called me. I wouldn't come. I danced around that playground in my bare feet, hair and dress soaking wet. Repeated calls failed to move me. Two nuns came after me. I ran and danced from one side to the other, dodging the hands that tried to clutch me. I laughed and danced in the wind and rain. I'd wait until they got close and then I'd run like the wind. Their long robes were heavy with water. They were exhausted. But I was exhilarated. Until suddenly I collapsed and was dragged inside. Mute and terrified and expecting to be lashed. I don't know why, but my defiance was forgiven.

—It was a ballet, his daughter said. The truant in the rain.

— Nuns on the run, said the son.

The German poet, long ago, went walking in the botanical gardens, saw plants, that elsewhere he had seen only in pots or under glass, growing cheerfully under the open sky. Might he not discover among them, the original plant from which all others are derived? After all, the poet thought, it must exist, the innermost nucleus.

A crazy idea. A wise old woman dressed like a gipsy or a pirate chief. A pert young girl curious about the American woman who had once been an orphan child in this town. Sadie Law with her leather coat and the smell of embrocation. A blonde horse-riding queen and huntress dying of drink in the back of an ambulance. Two sad creatures, nicknamed, one for the colour of her only coat and the hard meagre shape of her body, the other because it was said, with sniggers, that she was hopeless of progeny and disreputable in her ancestry. Angela

running hand in hand with him on a wet Saturday afternoon
through the Old Flax Market.

The place was empty that day. Not even the ghosts of the
woodsmen walked in the grey light and the rain. He couldn't
remember where Sadie and Tom had been at that time. The
Jennet's corner was also empty. In the wooden shelter, hacked
with names and odd obscenities and coy references to local
love affairs, they sat on a creaky seat and kissed and fumbled.
Then around a corner of the shelter came the Jennet herself,
leading a staggering cattle-drover, his ash-plant in his hand.

—Wee fellow, he said with great camaraderie, I suppose
you're at the same game as myself.

—He's too bashful, Angela said.

—He'll live to learn, the Jennet said. They all do.

The rain ran down her bony face. Wet yellow hair stuck out
from under a red tam o'shanter. Her eyes were of such a
bright blue as to make her seem blind.

—The good book, the drover said, says that the wise man
falls seven times. And, as sure as my name is Solomon, I'm
going to fall now.

So the wee fellow retreated from the shelter, dragging
Angela with him for a little way until she dug her heels into the
muddy ground. The river was in a brown fresh, taking with it
broken branches and hay from flooded meadows, sweeping
on, down then by Derry our dear boys are sailing. Now he
remembered that that day Angela had been wearing a
sou'wester and Sadie's black coat, a little big for her but a
stronghold against the rain.

—What do we need to run for? You might learn something.
He said nothing.

—Wee boy, she said. I'm going back for a peep.

He stood alone looking at the turbulent river, looking across
the river at the limping spires, one proud and complete, one
for ever unfinished, a memory of defeat and death. What
would a wild woodsman have done? Down along the river
valley it was said that there were trees on which the woodsmen,
just before they left, had carved their names so strongly that
the letters could still be read. But that must be a fable, a
memory out of the old song: Their names on the trees of the

rising plantation, their memories we'll cherish, and affection ne'er cool. For where are the heroes of high or low station that could be compared with the brave boys of Strule?

—That was as good as a circus, Angela said. You've no idea in the world what you missed.

At breakfast in the hotel in the morning the chatty little waitress shook his belief in himself by saying to him and his children that she had never heard of anybody of his name coming from this town.

—The great unknown, his daughter said.

—Fooling us all the time, the son said. He came from Atlanta, Georgia.

But then it turned out that the waitress came from a smaller town twenty miles away and was only eighteen years of age.

—Off we go now, said the daughter, to see where granny came from.

—Bring no whiskey to Claramore, his mother said. There was always too much whiskey in Claramore. Returned Americans coming and going.

The son and the daughter wished her a happy new year.

—Drive down the town first, she said. I owe a bill I must pay.

—Won't it wait?

She was dressed in high style: widow's black coat, high hat and veil, high buttoned boots for walking in country places.

—Never begin the new year in debt was a good maxim. I'll stick to it while I have breath.

Her grand-daughter, sitting beside her in the back of the hired car, giggled. Sourly he accepted the comments, one unconscious, one conscious, of two other generations on his own finances.

He drove down the High Street. They waited for her outside a hardware shop. The sky was pale blue, cloudless, and last night's unexpected white frost lay on the roofs and spotted the pavements. His daughter said: Granny never heard of a credit card.

More sordidly the son said: Nor hire purchase. Nor a post-dated cheque.

—It was a different world, mes enfants. They paid their way or went without.

But he knew that he had never worked out where – in the world that he had grown into – that terrifying old-fashioned honesty had gone: no debt, no theft, no waste. Beggars were accepted, because Joseph and Mary and the Child Jesus had gone homeless into Egypt. But debt was a sort of sin.

—Eat black bread first, she would say. But let no man say you're in his debt.

He had never taken to black bread. He hadn't told her that in a briefcase in the boot he had two bottles of Jack Daniels as a gift for his cousin – and for himself. A decent man could not with empty hands enter a decent house, and two bottles of American whiskey would be a fit offering to a house that had sent so many sons and daughters to the States.

She was back in the car again, settling herself like a duchess, her small red-headed grand-daughter helping her to tuck a rug around her knees. She refused to believe that a moving vehicle could be heated like a house.

It was a twelve-mile drive, first down the Derry road, over the steep hill that, in spite of all the miracles of macadam, was called, as it had been called in the eighteenth century, Clabber Brae. Then west, over the Drumquin railway crossing. There was no longer any railway to cross. Once upon a time the crossing-keeper's daughter had been as famous as Sadie Law. Then by Gillygooley crossroads where, one June day, Tom and himself, coming tired from fishing perch in the Fairywater, had seen Angela climbing a gate into a ripe meadow just opened for the mower. Her companion was a stocky-shouldered blackavised soldier. That much they could see. A hundred yards ahead, Tom rested from his cycling and was silent for a long time. Then he said: Boy, I'd leave that one alone for the future.

—She's leaving me alone. Who's she with?

—The worst in the barracks. Fusilier Nixon. And he'll never rank higher.

—Why so?

—Four years ago when he came back from India he was all but drummed out for raping a slavey in the soldier's holm.

—There's a great view of the holm from the tall spire.

—If you had been up there you could have seen the fun. His bacon was saved by a major whose life he saved, or something, in India. And God help the slaveys. The offspring of that bit of love at first sight is now toddling around Fountain Lane. I'll point him out to you some day. You'd have something in common.

They cycled on.

—I'll tell Sadie, Tom said, what we saw. Sadie has some sense. She wouldn't want to be seen in the company of Fusilier Nixon.

Their bicycles bumped over the railway crossing. The keeper's daughter waved, and called: Hello, Tom Cunningham.

—Cheer up, boy. You'll get another girl.

—I suppose I will.

—From here to China the world's full of them.

—I liked Angela.

He found it hard not to sob. Angela peeping around a corner at the animals in the circus. Angela in the clutches of a black-chinned brute. He had, too, really liked her. More than thirty years later he foolishly looked for her face on the streets of the old town and the face he looked for could not, in reason, ever be there. He would see, instead, a Madonna – whom, also, he had never known – against a background of the coloured covers of magazines.

Now as he drove on, he looked at the gate that Angela had climbed into the meadow. But one gate was very like another and, under white frost, all meadows were the same. Although this valley to him would always be summer holiday country. Every mile of it he had walked or cycled. A hay-shed by a prosperous farmhouse meant for him mostly the sultry July hush before the rain came, the smell of sheds and barns, heavy rain on tin roofs, or soda bread and strong tea by peat fires on open hospitable hearths.

There now across the stilled, white fields was the glint of water at the pool where Tom and himself would first strike the Fairywater. The road climbed here, up over the stony place of Clohogue, then switchbacked for miles in and out of hazel glens, over loud rough brooks, then on to a plateau, high, very high; and visible in such clear frosty air, and a good seventy miles away by the edge of the Atlantic, the pigback of Muckish Mountain, the white cone of Mount Errigal, the Cock of the

North. Claramore was just below the plateau. It was a place of
its own, in a new valley.

From the Barley Hill beyond the old long white farmhouse
you could also see those two far-away mountains and, in the
other direction and looking down the valley of the Fairywater,
the tips and crosses of the two limping Gothic spires, but not
the smaller plain spire of the Protestant church.

—On a calm evening, his cousin said, they seem so close that
you'd imagine you could hear the bell ringing for the May
devotions.

He asked his cousin: Do the young people still climb
Drumard in autumn to pluck the blayberries?

—We've heard a lot about those same blayberries, his daughter said. To pluck and eat them, dad says, was a memory of
some ancient pagan feast.

—The young people, his cousin said, have their own pagan
feasts.

The four of them walked on the boreen that crossed the
Barley Hill to the place where the men were building a house
for his cousin's son and the bride he would bring home with
him in three months' time. Hard frost had slowed up the
building work. Among the men, half-loitering, working just
enough to keep warm, keeping as close as possible to an open
brazier, his cousin passed round one of the bottles of bourbon.
They drank from cracked cups and tin mugs, toasted the
health of the visitors, of the bride-to-be, wished luck for ever
on the house they were building. High above a jet plane,
westward-bound out of Prestwick, made its mark on the cold
pale blue.

—They'll be in New York before you, his son said.

The drinking men, circling the brazier, saluted the travellers
in the sky and raised a cheer. It was only a few hours to
New York from the Barley Hill or the pagan blayberries
of Drumard. Breath ascended in puffs as white as the jet's
signature. On the far side of the hill from the long farmhouse the Fairywater, glittering black, looped through frosted
bottom-land.

—Phil Loughran, that used to work for you, he said. He was
about my age. Where did he go?

The Black Stepping Stones were at that bend of the Fairy-water, the seventh bend visible from where they stood; and above the Black Stones the pool where the country boys went swimming. Willows drooped over it. The bottom was good yellow sand. The water had the brown of the peat and was nowhere more than four feet deep. It was an idyllic place, had been an idyllic place until the day he had that crazy fight with Phil Loughran.

—He went to Australia, his cousin said. We hear he's doing well. The family, what's left of them, are still living here on my land.

Even to this day, and in the frosty air, he blushed to think of the lies he had told to Phil Loughran down there by the Black Stones – blushed all the more because, country boys being so much more cunning than towny boys, Phil almost certainly hadn't believed a word he said. Phil as he listened would have secretly laughed.

—So her name is Angela, he said.

Phil was a squat sallow-faced young fellow, dressed in rough corduroys and heavy nailed boots, his brown hair short-cropped, his eyes dark brown and close together. There was always a vague smell of peat smoke, or stables or something, from those corduroys.

—Angela the walking angel, he said.

They were dressing after a swim. Three other boys splashed and shouted in the pool. A fourth hung naked from a trailing willow, swinging like a pendulum, striking the water with his feet.

—So you tell us, Phil, you had the little man out of sight.

He made a sideways grab, as Angela had done on the wooded brambly slope above the pike-pool on the Drumragh. He was laughing. He said: Little man, you've had a busy day.

Then the two of them were rolling on the grass, swiping at each other, Phil still laughing, he sobbing, with temper, with the humiliation of having his tall tales of conquest made mockery of. Four naked dripping boys danced and laughed and shouted around them. It was the last day but one that he had been at the Black Stones. He had come second best out of that fight but he had a mean miserable sort of vengeance on his very last visit to the place.

Phil in his best corduroys – since it was Sunday – is crossing the water, stepping carefully from stone to stone, in his right hand the halter with which he is leading a love-stricken Claramore cow to keep her date with a bull on the farm on the far side of the river. So he calls to Phil to mind his Sunday-go-to-meeting suit and Phil, turning round to answer, is off his guard when the restive beast bolts. It is, fair enough, his turn to laugh, sharp, clear and cruel, as Phil, bravely holding on to the halter is dragged through the shallow muddy water below the stones. There are seventeen in Phil's family, and he is the eldest, and those corduroys will not be easily replaced.

Over the hard frosted fields his own laughter came back to him.

—I'm glad to hear he did well in Australia.

—They were a thrifty family, his cousin said. A sister of his might visit us this evening, the youngest of the breed, a goddaughter of mine.

The trail of the jet was curdling in the cold sky. The men had gone back to work. For penance he told his cousin and son and daughter how he had laughed on the day the cow dragged Phil through the muddy water. They stood by a huge sycamore a little down the slopes from the unfinished house. Icicles hung from bare branches. He said nothing about how James had mocked his boasting.

—Weren't you the beast, dad, his daughter said.

—But it was funny, the son said.

—The young, his cousin said, can be thoughtless. Present company excepted.

For the daughter, the face of a good mimic distorted with mock fury, was dancing towards the cousin to stab him with an icicle broken from the sycamore.

—No, but seriously, he said when they had played out their pantomime of fury and terror: a grey man over sixty with a restful singing sort of voice and a pert little girl of sixteen.

—Seriously. Look at the sycamore. It was planted here more than a hundred years ago by an uncle of mine who was a priest. He died young, not long after ordination. He planted this tree on the day he was ordained, and blessed the earth and the sapling. You may recall, when you were young yourselves, some of his books were still about the house. Mostly Latin.

Theology. Some novels. I told you about one of them and you rushed to get it. The *Lass of the Barns,* you thought I said. But, man alive, were you down in the mouth when you discovered it was the *Last of the Barons.*

—Oh dad, his daughter said.

—But I know the age of this tree by checking on the date on the priest's tombstone in Langfield churchyard. And my son says to me: We'll cut it down. It'll spoil the view from the new house. So I said: The house may fall, but this tree will stand while I do. The old have a feeling for each other.

—Lucky tree, the daughter said, that has somebody to stand up for it.

They went, laughing, back down the Barley Hill towards the warmth of the great kitchen of the farmhouse. Under the pall of the white frost it seemed as if nothing here would ever change: not the sycamore, not his cousin, nor the ancient sleeping land. Nothing would change, no matter how many airliners swept westwards up there, leaving nothing behind them but a curdling dissolving mark on the sky. All the ships that had carried all those people westwards, even so many sons and daughters of this house, and the ocean was still unmarked and the land here as it had been. It was elsewhere in the world the changes happened.

—But this fatal ship to her cold bosom folds them. Wherever she goes our fond hearts shall adore them. Our prayers and good wishes will still be before them, that their names be remembered and sung by the Strule.

The pond at the corner of the avenue was frozen over. He had fallen into it once, climbing the fence above and beyond it to chase a wandering bullock out of a field of young oats. The fence-post he had been holding on to had broken. The water, he had always imagined, had tasted of duck-dirt. But then how in hell would one be expected to know what duck-dirt tasted like? The fence-post, he noticed, was now made of iron, and that might be some indication, even here, of change. But not much.

The ash-grove to the left before you came to the stables – in that grove he had once criminally broken a young sapling to make a fishing rod – was now a solid wall of grown strong trees, a windbreak on days of south-westerly gales.

Would the horses in the stables be the same, with the same names, as they had been thirty years ago? He was afraid to ask, to be laughed at, to be told what he knew: that even here, even loved familiar farmhorses didn't live for ever. The dogs seemed the same – collies, with more sprawling pups underfoot than had ever seemed natural. The pattern of farming though, had changed somewhat, he had been told: more barley, more pigs fed on the barley, less oats, less root crops, more sucking calves bred in season on the open pasture, taken early from their mothers and sold to be fattened somewhere in confinement, and slaughtered.

In the house ahead of them somebody was playing a melodeon, softly, slowly, and that was something that hadn't changed, because in the past in that house there had been great country dances to pipe, fiddle and melodeon. That was before so many of his cousins, all much older than himself, had gone to the States.

His mother had enjoyed herself. She was red in the face and moist-eyed from sitting by the open hearth with its high golden pyramid of blazing peat; from remembering, for the instruction of a younger generation, the comic figaries of her dear departed dowager of a sister, Kate, who as a widow in her thirties, had ruled not only Claramore but half the countryside; and from, let it be admitted, sipping at the bourbon. For while she was a great one to lecture about the dangers of drink, she was liable the next minute to take from her sideboard a bottle of brandy and a bottle of whiskey, to ask what you were having, and to join you herself, and she instinctively thought the worst of a man who neither smoked, drank, swore, nor rode horses.

—The young people, she said, are growing up well, God bless them. They haven't forgotten the old ways. That house was never without music and dancing.

The Claramore people had stood around the car, under a frosty moon, and sang Auld Lang Syne as their guests departed.

—That Loughran girl was a good hand at the melodeon. Did you all see her making up to the widow man, the returned American?

She poked him between the shoulder-blades as he drove slowly over the icy plateau.

—She sat on your knee, dad, the daughter said.

He could still feel the pressure of the underparts of the girl's thighs. She was conventionally slim and dark and handsome, with wide brown eyes; in appearance most unlike her eldest brother. She had sat on his knee in the dancing kitchen to tell him that Phil, in every letter he wrote from Australia, enquired about him. She stayed sitting there while his cousin sang: There was once a maid in a lonely garden when a well-dressed gentleman came passing by.

—Was that story true granny, the son asked. The one about the lone bush.

—Would I tell it if it wasn't.

They descended into the first hazel glen. Over the rushing of its brook they could hear the roaring of another jet, out of Prestwick, bound for New York.

—They're lining up to get into America, the son said.

—To get out of it too, son.

Six hours or so to the bedlam of Kennedy airport: But now our bold heroes are past all their dangers. On America's shores they won't be long strangers. They'll send back their love from famed Blessington's Rangers to comrades and friends and the fair maids of Strule.

People who travelled by jet left no shadows in old market-places. Generations would be born to whom the ache and loneliness in the old songs of exile would mean nothing.

—Jordan Taggart the cobbler, as I said, had his house on the road from Claramore to Carrickaness, and a small farm to boot. Against the advice of all, even against Father Gormley the priest that cured people, he cut down a whitethorn that grew alone in the middle of his meadow and, at nightfall, he dragged it home behind him for kindling. In the orchard before his house he saw two small children, dressed in white, and he spoke to them but they made no answer. So he told his wife and his three sons, who were also cobblers, that there were two shy children waiting, maybe for mended shoes in the orchard. But when two of the sons went out and searched they saw nothing. Then Jordan ate the supper of a healthy man and went to bed and died in his sleep.

—But he wasn't really dead, the son said.

—No, the white children took him. God between us and all harm.

In the darkness in the car she spat, but slightly and politely, and into her handkerchief.

The daughter said nothing.

They were back again in the meadow country where Angela had climbed the gate and, except for one last meeting, had climbed out of his life for ever. They bumped over the Drumquin crossing where there was no longer any railway to cross, no easy girl to call longingly after Tom Cunningham who was chasing girls in China and never wrote to enquire about anybody.

The daughter was alert again. She was giggling. She said: Dad, Granny wants to do something about the way you dress.

—I was only thinking about his own good, his mother said.

Although he was carefully driving the car over Clabber Brae, he knew by the way she talked that he was no longer there.

—But when I was by the seaside at Bundoran I saw these young fellows wearing loose coloured patterned shirts outside their trousers. I was told it was an American fashion, and I was sure that he would be wearing one of them when he came home.

He said: I'm no young fellow.

—What I thought was that it would cover his middle-aged spread.

As they descended by the military barracks into the town the daughter's giggles rocked the car.

—A maternity shirt, she said.

—For how could he expect anyone to look at him at his age and with a stomach like that.

Castle Steet went up so steeply that it seemed as if it was trying to climb those dark grotesque spires.

—A young one, for instance, like that Loughran girl who sat on his knee because the chairs were scarce.

—That one, he said. All that I remember about the

Loughrans is that her bare-footed elder brothers were always raiding Aunt Kate's cherry trees and blaming the depredation on the birds.

In the hotel bar only two of the commercial men were left. They said: What do you think now of your happy home town?
—How do you mean?
—Last night's tragic event, they said. Didn't you hear? Didn't you read the paper?
—I was in the country all day.
Back in the past where one didn't read the newspapers.
—A poor man murdered, they said. What your American friends would call a filling-station attendant.
—Robbed and shot, they said. Just when we were sitting here talking about murder.
The grandfather clock in the hallway chimed midnight.
—The New Year, he said. May it be quiet and happy.
In the ballroom in the far wing of the hotel the revellers were clasping hands and singing about old acquaintance.
—We should be there singing, he said.
—The second murder here this year, they said. The other was a queer case, two young men, a bit odd. Things like that usen't to happen. This town is getting to be as bad as Chicago.
—It isn't as big or as varied.
They laughed. They agreed that the town was still only in a small way of business. He asked them was the park called the Lovers' Retreat still where it had been.
—If that's the way you feel, it is.
More laughter.
—But it's gone to hell, they told him. It's not kept as it used to be. The young compulsory soldiers in national service wreck everything. They haven't the style of the old Indian army, when the empire was in its glory. Children's swings uprooted now. Benches broken. One of the two bridges over the millrace gone completely. The grass three feet long.
—Nothing improves, they said.
When they left him he sat on for a long time, drinking alone. Was it imagination, or could he really hear the sound of the Camowen waters falling over the salmon leap at the Lovers'

Retreat? That place was one of the sights of the town when the salmon were running: the shining curving bodies rising from the water as if sprung from catapults – leaping and struggling upwards in white foam and froth. But one year the water was abnormally low, the salmon a sullen black mass in the pool below the falls – a temptation to a man with Tom Cunningham's enterprise. The water-bailiff and his two assistants and his three dogs came by night and caught Tom and his faithful companion with torch and gaff and one slaughtered salmon. But since the bailiff, a bandy-legged amiable man, was also the park-keeper he said not a word to the police on condition that the two criminals kept the grass in the park mowed for a period of six months.

—Hard labour, by God, boy. He has us by the hasp. The Big House with Wallace Beery. You be Mickey Rooney.

The bad news travelled and was comic to all except the two mowers. Then one day from the far side of the millrace that made one boundary to the park they heard the laughter of women, and saw Sadie and Angela, bending and pointing.

—Two men went to mow, they sang, went to mow the meadow.

—Grilled salmon for all, they called.

Tom crossed the millrace by leaping on to the trunk of a leaning tree that was rooted on the far bank. Sadie, laughing, screaming in mock terror, and Tom in pursuit, vanished into the bluebell woods. Tom's companion crossed the millrace prosaically by one of the wooden footbridges. Was it the one that the wild young resentful compulsory soldiers had destroyed? She didn't run. She wasn't laughing any more. Her brown hair no longer curled in little horns on her temples but was combed straight back. But the wide mouth, in spite of the black fusilier, was to him as inviting as ever. She said: You're a dab-hand at mowing. You've a future in cutting grass.

He said: I never see you any more.

—Little boys should take what's offered to them, when it's offered. Go back to your scythe.

—Go back to the fusilier, he said.

He went back to his scythe by climbing along the trunk of the leaning tree and leaping the millrace. The grass that fell before his scythe was crimson in colour and swathed in a sort of mist. The swing of the scythe moved with the rhythm of the falling water sweeping on to meet the Drumragh, to become the Strule, to absorb the Fairywater and the Derg and the Owenkillew, to become the Mourne, to absorb the Finn, to become the Foyle, to go down then by Derry to the ocean, taking with it the shadows of the woodsmen, the echoes of the brass and pipes and tramping feet of the army of a vanished empire, the stories of all who had ever lived in this valley.

He knew he was drunk when he heard the woman's voice speak respectfully to him and saw her through the crimson mist through which long ago he had seen the falling grass. She said: You wouldn't remember me, sir.

He didn't. She wore the black dress, white collar and cuffs of the hotel staff. She would be sixtyish. She said: We saw you on the teevee one night and I said to Francie who you were. But he said he didn't know you. He knew your elder brother better.

—My brother was well known.

—Francie's my brother. You might remember he used to ride racing bicycles. I saw you in the dining-room. I work in the kitchen. I knew it was you when I saw your son, and from the teevee.

—You're Sadie Law.

—I didn't like to intrude on you and the children.

He said there was no intrusion. They shook hands. He asked her how her brother was.

—He's in a chair all the time. He broke his back at the tomfool cycling. But he does woodcarving, and I work here. We manage. I never married.

Her face did not remind him of Sadie Law, but then he found that he could not remember what Sadie Law's face had looked like.

—Nobody, he said, could replace Tom Cunningham.

She neither smiled nor looked sorrowful. Her face remained the same. She said: Oh, Tom was a card. He went away.

Some revellers from the ballroom came in, drunk, singing, wearing paper hats. She said: I must be off.

—I'll see you in the morning.

—I'm off duty then. Because of the late dance tonight. But we hope you'll come back often to see the old places.

—Do you ever remember, he asked, a Fusilier Nixon, a wild fellow.

She thought: No. But there were so many fusiliers. A lot of them we'll never see again.

—We'll look out for you on the teevee, she said.

They shook hands again.

They said goodbye to his mother and drove away. His daughter said: Dad, this isn't the Dublin road.

—There's a place I want to see before we leave.

It was the place that Tom and himself used to go to when they considered that the mental strain of school was too much for them. For it was an odd thing that in all the comings and goings of that railway station nobody ever thought of asking a pair of truants what they were doing there. Everybody thought that everybody else was waiting for somebody else, and there were always porters and postmen who knew what you were at, but who kept the knowledge to themselves, and would share talk and cigarettes with runaway convicts, let alone reluctant schoolboys. No police hunted for drifters or loiterers as in American bus stations; and the sights were superb and you met the best people. They had spent several hours one day with Chief Abidu from southern Nigeria and his Irish wife and honey-coloured brood. He danced on broken glass and swallowed fire in a wooden booth in the Old Market, and beating on his breast, made the most wonderful throaty noises; and came, most likely, from Liverpool.

—I understand, she had written, that the railway station is closed now. Only the ghosts of those who passed through it abide there. Some were gentle, some were violent men, morose or gay, ordinary or extraordinary. I had time to watch them passing by. It is pain that they died so young, so long ago.

The tracks were gone, the grass and weeds had grown high through the ballast. The old stone buildings had been turned into warehouses. Two men in dusty dungarees kept coming and going, carrying sacks of meal, at the far end of the platform. But if they spoke to each other they were too far away for their voices to be heard, and the cold wind moved as stealthily in grass and weeds as if it were blowing over some forlorn midland hillside. Where the bookstall had been there was just a scar on the granite wall, where she had stood, framed against coloured books and magazines, and watched the soldiers coming and going.

—The young English poet you mention, I knew briefly. He came to buy books. At first he had little to say, simply polite, that's all. Then one day he and another young man began to talk. They included me. But mostly I listened. It was fascinating. After that, when he came he talked about books. He asked questions about Ireland. He was uneasy there, considered it beautiful but alien, felt, I think, that the very earth of Ireland was hostile to him, the landscape had a brooding quality as though it waited.

—He was five or six months garrisoned in our town. They told me he could be very much one of the boys, but he could also be remote. He treated me kindly, teased me gently. But he and a brilliant bitter Welshman gave me books and talked to me. Sometimes they talked about the war.

—It was only after he was reported missing in Africa that I learned he was a poet. But I think I knew anyway.

—I never heard if the Welshman survived. I had several long letters from him and that was all.

Ghosts everywhere in this old town.

—Now I have a son who may pass through a railway station or an airport on his way to war.

He said to his daughter: That's where the bookstall was.

—Will you go to see her, dad? In the States, I mean.

—In a way I've seen her.

He was grateful that she didn't ask him what on earth he was talking about.

—As the song says, I'll look for her if I'm ever back that way.

The ghost of his father stood just here, waving farewell to him every time he went back after holidays to college in Dublin.

They walked through the cold deserted hall, where the ticket offices had been, and down the steps, grass-grown, cracked, to the Station Square, once lined with taxis, now empty except for some playing children and the truck into which the dusty men were loading the sacks. From the high steeple the noonday angelus rang.

—How high up is the bell? his son asked.

He told him, and also told him the height of the spire and of the surmounting cross, and why one spire was higher than the other, and how he had once climbed up there, and of the view over the valley, and of how he had almost fallen to doom on the way down, and of the vertigo, the fear of death, that followed.

—And a curious thing. Once, on top of the Eiffel Tower, that vertigo returned. And once over the Mojave desert when I thought the plane was going to crash. But I didn't see Paris or the Mojave desert. I saw that long straight ladder.

The bell ceased. The spires were outlined very clearly in the cold air, looked as formidable as precipices. Around them floated black specks, the unbanishable jackdaws.

—Once I got a job from the parish priest because I was a dab hand with a twenty-two. The job was to shoot the jackdaws, they were pests, off the spires. It was going fine until the police stopped me for using a firearm too close to a public highway. The sexton at the time was a tall man in a black robe down to his feet, more stately than a bishop. One day, when he was watching me at work, a bird I shot struck one of those protruding corner-stones and came soaring, dead, in a wide parabola, straight for the sexton. He backed away, looking in horror at the falling bird. But he tripped on his robe, and the bird, blood, feathers, beak and all got him fair in the face. At that time I thought it was the funniest thing I had ever seen.

—Grisly, his daughter said.

—But once upon a time I laughed easily. It was easy to laugh here then.

High Street, Market Street, the Dublin Road. A stop at the grave where the caretaker's men had already done their job. The weeds were gone, the sad hollow filled, new white stones laid.

Then on to Dublin, crossing the Drumragh at Lissan Bridge where, it was said, Red Hugh O'Donnell had passed on his way back from prison in Dublin Castle to princedom in Donegal and war with Elizabeth of England. The wintry land brooded waiting, as it had always done, and would do for ever.

He sang at the wheel: There was once a maid in a lonely garden.

—Oh dad, his daughter said.

So he thought the rest of it: Oh, do you see yon high high building? And do you see yon castle fine? And do you see yon ship on the ocean? They'll all be thine if thou wilt be mine.

PART FIVE

Proxopera

In Memory of the Innocent Dead

SEA-LIONS AND SHARKS, *alligators and whales with mouths that would swallow a truck...*
       That lake would never be the same again.
...oh the sights that we saw as we waited for death on the treacherous waves of Lough Muck.
Yet the birds, they say, sang around Dachau.

The waterfowl now swim on the still surface or fly around and cry around the circle of hills, harvest-coloured. The holidays are over and the dry rustle this year is early in the leaves. A dozen or more waterhens are in convention in a reedy corner near a sagging black boathouse. Only in one bay on the far shore is the silence disturbed by two black boats, moving slowly, men just barely using the oars or standing up and sitting down again. The sound of voices comes faintly across the water. He says to his son: the lake will never be the same again.

—The water never knew what was happening.

—I doubt that. Water may know more than we think. And grass. And old rocks. Think of all those old rocks that were around us in Donegal for the last three weeks. The lake looked as if it knew what was happening on the day of the water-skiing.

His son's wife who is a tall handsome red-headed girl with slightly prominent teeth, daring breasts and the faintest hint of an incipient double chin – very voluptuous, although he shouldn't be thinking along those lines – says that on the day of the water-skiing the lake was bright and dancing. On the night that thing happened the lake was dark and still. Wouldn't that make a difference?

He pats her on the shoulder affectionately as he climbs out from the back of the car where he has been sitting with the two children and a large glass jar containing two morose crabs rudely torn away from their homes on the Donegal shore.

She is an amusing imaginative girl.

—But no, he says, still waters run deep and all that. Water doesn't need light in order to see. Water is a sort of a god. Or at any rate a goddess. That's what people thought long ago, they called rivers after goddesses.

The lake for sure had been a goddess on the day of the water-skiing. Never had he thought that he would see on his own lake the sort of thing you saw on the movies or television: Californian or Hawaiian beaches, galloping rollers, bouncing speed-boats, naked young women on surfboards, Arion on the dolphin's back, rising and falling, vanishing, reappearing through jewels of flying spray, spirits at one moment of the air and the water, marred by no speck of sordid earth. Was it better or worse to be young now than it was, say, forty-five years ago?

For him in his boyhood that lake had always been asleep. He lived in those days in the town three miles away. The walk from the town to the lake switchbacked over rolling farmland, root crops and oats, heavy black soil, solid square slated farmhouses, a well-planted Presbyterian countryside. After the first mile it was the custom for himself and his comrades to slither down an embankment where the road crossed the railway to the west and the ocean, to walk a hundred yards into a dank rock-cutting, to drink there from a spring that came on an iron spout out of the naked rock. That, for him, had been the well at the world's end mentioned in the old stories. No water had ever tasted like that water. One of the best meals he had ever eaten had been eaten there: raw turnips taken from a neighbouring field, cleaned at the spring and sliced, washed down by the clear ice-cold water. There was also the delight and danger of being caught there by a train, of crushing close to the dripping rock until the roaring belching monster passed.

Half a mile further on, the road went up a steep hill and into a tunnel of tall beeches. In the autumn and right on into January the leaves stayed so russet the road seemed warm. On the hilltop to the right hand and dominating the countryside stood a square, white, three-storeyed house inhabited then by an amazing family: strong, red-cheeked, flaxen-haired brothers and sisters, a dozen or more of them, he was never quite sure how many. They came, carrying bibles, to church in the town but never all of them at the same time. The popular report was that under that roof brothers and sisters knew each other as brothers and sisters conventionally shouldn't: it was a fascinating idea.

From the top of the hill you had a choice of routes: to the right the longer one, uphill, down dale, passing a place where there was a wooden bridge over the bend of a river, going round the world for sport, by fifty farms, a corrugated-iron-roofed Orange hall where there had been a bloody row one night because some guileless, love-deludhered young Orange man had brought a Catholic girl to a dance, and by half-a-hundred ridges and bridges to rejoin the shorter route at a cross-roads and go on the level to the lakeshore.

The shorter road ran straight along a spine of sandy, heath-ery, esker-land where once the glaciers had stopped. Below, in a hollow of quaking bog was a small lake, surrounded by sallies and bog-birch, in which demented old ladies and others were continually drowning themselves. There was an almost vocal sadness about the place. Association? Or had it been melan-choly to begin with: right from the beginning of time, from the melting of the glaciers? That little lake as far as he knew had never had a name.

From the crossroads where the two routes rejoined, the road went again under splendid beech trees, the lake, a white light, widening and brightening at the end of a tunnel until it burst on you in all its delight, only a few miles all round but an almost perfect oval, a black boat-house to the right and boats dancing attendance in a semi-circle in front of it, a half-mile around the gravelly lakeshore road the bright red timber of the jetty and diving-boards at the swimming-club.

These dark days the swimming-club didn't function any more. The water-skiing had been a heroic attempt to give that sort of life back to the lake. The last attempt? The lake would never be the same again.

The murmur of voices still comes across the water from the men searching and searching in a bay among the reeds, in a bay that had been the best place of all for perch on those long-lost sunny days.

July was the best month for perch and the best day was the twelfth. It was folklore that the Orangemen always got a sunny day for their procession of bands and banners in honour of King William of Orange and the Battle of the Boyne. Up to the age of twelve or so the band and the banners were what the Americans called fun things: fifes and pipes and brass and melodeons, kettle drums, big drums, and giant drums beaten – merely to make a rolling rhythmical bedlam that might bring down rain on the Sahara – with bamboo canes by sweating coatless men with bleeding knuckles. Often it took two men to carry one of those drums, one fore, the actual drummer (naturally) aft. The best drummer was the man who smashed the most canes, even the most hides. Odd as the jungle it all was, bongo, bongo, bongo, I don't want to leave the Congo! but what the hell? The marching men wore coloured sashes. On the silken picture-banners King William on a white horse went splashing across the Boyne, or Queen Victoria sat on a throne and handed a bible to a kneeling negress and the legend said: The secret of England's greatness.

Then after twelve or so you began to think and the thing wasn't funny any more, wasn't just parade and pantomime, and the giant drums were actually saying something. Like: To hell with the Pope, Croppies Lie Down, We'll kick Ten Thousand Papishes right over Dolly's Brae, Slewter, slaughter, holy water, harry the Papishes every one, drive them under and cut them asunder the Protestant boys will carry the drum.

What it was all about was hate which, as always, bred hate, and suddenly you were sick of the town on that day and the lake was paradise.

Like the Orangemen the perch shoaled and were lively in the heat and the sunshine – and hungry for bait. Heat haze clouded the sun. Ripening oats on hills around the lake stood motionless as sheets of bronze. From green hills cattle stam-

peded to the shore to wade in until the water lipped their
bellies, to stand lashing hopelessly with their tails against
relentless clegs. The surface of the lake was dark and quiet
except that once in a while an arc of little ripples would move
on it, coming from nowhere, vanishing suddenly; and a breeze
like a quick kiss from a ghost would touch a sweaty forehead
and be gone again; and after that the perch would move, mad
as mackerel, tearing the water as if the low hot skies were
raining rocks, and all you had to do was pull them in, big and
little, striped black and green and orange, fine fighters, big
dorsal fins opening and closing, in outrage and despair, like
Japanese fans.

The best corners in the lake were in there beyond the boat-
house where the reeds were so high you were almost but not
quite cut off from the rest of the world: or over there where
men in black boats were still probing and dredging. Almost but
not quite. For through a gap in the reeds you could, as you
waited for the perch, look across the waters at the white house.
Reeds made one frame for the picture. Beech trees set back
from the avenue that led up to the house made another. There
were other houses, Orange and Green or Protestant and Catholic, on the hills around the lakeshore, but they were simple
thatched cottages and nothing at all in the bay-windowed, wide-
fronted style of the white house. He had always envied the
people who owned it, the lawn and flower-beds before it, the
barns and varied outbuildings behind it. He had missed strikes
and earned mockery from his companions by sitting heed-
lessly, absorbed in envy of the people who lived in that house,
long and white, an air of aristocratic age about it: and, the
most beautiful thing of all, cutting across a corner of the lawn
a small brook tumbling down to join the lake. To have your own
stream on the lawn was the height of everything.

In reveries now between sleeping and waking, relaxed in a
deck chair on a sunny lawn and looking at the lake through
half-closed eyes, he liked to tell himself that he had always
known he would own and live in that house. That wasn't so. He
may have wished that he one day would, but however could he
have known. Premonitions were notions you had after the
event.

Here they all were now, his son and son's wife and their two children, all happy after their Donegal holiday, the children tired but still talkative, the displaced crabs motionless as the rocks they came from: and himself. All being driven slowly by his daughter-in-law between deep banks and hedges into the farmyard, home again, and out of the car now, the children suddenly energetic again and racing in circles around the yard like hounds released from kennels, running to this and that corner to see if everything is as they had left it.

Behind the hayshed the three great sycamores are dark and motionless in the evening. Not one of the party seems as yet to have a premonition about anything. Well, perhaps the sycamores, perhaps the crabs.

All the way back from Dungloe in Donegal the streams they crossed had been in a brown foaming fresh. The rains and tempest of last week, the Lammas floods coming early this year; and now sunshine that by the texture of it would last until Christmas. Countless bees are still hard at it in the pink-oxalis borders that his son's wife loves so well because of the radiance that opens to the sun, because she has her flourishing apiary in the orchard beyond the hayshed. And the benefit of heather-blossom into the bargain from a small patch of turbary within beesflight and on the lakeshore.

The bees in the pink blossoms, the breeze in the sycamores make the only sound. There is suddenly something too much about the silence.

The pink borders, living with bees, go all round the yard, backed by the white barns and byres and stables, doors and windows outlined in red. Nothing moves but the bees. He stands alone, ten paces from the car, and breathes in the peace and is inexplicably perturbed.

The little boy runs towards the hayshed where three weeks ago there was a litter of cocker pups. The little girl dances towards the back porch of the house. She calls: Minnie, Minnie Brown, we're home again from Dungloe town.

On the journey home he has composed that rhyme for her. Minnie is the housekeeper and it is odd in a way that she hasn't been out in the yard to meet them.

His broadbacked son walks towards the red half-door of one of the stables. The harriers ride no more in these times but he still keeps and pastures two amiable hacks. A stout quick-tempered man who too early, and much to his own chagrin, has gone completely bald and whose jacket never buttons without obvious strain. The back of his eggshaped head is comic.

His wife, a full-bodied red wine, goes gracefully after her little daughter.

He stands where he is, simply looking at his house, at his people, at the sycamores, at the last fifty years. Time stands still. The little boy comes running back from the hayshed. Trotting rather. His head down and sideways as if he were playing ponies. He pulls, pulling a bellrope, at his granda's jacket. He says: Granda, there's a funny man in the hayshed.

Granda already knows. The man has stepped out into the open. He has a shotgun. He wears a felt-brimmed hat and a gasmask. The mask has been slashed at the mouth for the sake of sound but the effect still is as if somebody with laryngitis were trying to talk through tissue paper and a comb. He says: Freeze. Everybody freeze.

As in the best or the worst gangster films except that the hoodlums talk and act cool and this fellow seems to be nervous: All of you freeze.

Granda says: Including the children?

He picks the boy up in his arms. The man advances, pointing the shotgun. The wheezes say, almost as if the creator of the wheezes had a cleft palate: One false step. Into the house. All of you. We're all inside.

They walk towards the house. He comes behind them. Not all inside the house. Because another masked man steps out from the laurels and rhododendrons to the right. He has a sock or something over his face. Carries a pistol. Wears a workman's tin hat.

His son walks before him, the back of his neck now red with anger. Even his egghead seems to be changing colour. He says: Who are you? What the hell is this?

—We'll let you know a chara, the second man says.

He has a sharp clear voice and something like a Cork accent: Inside, everybody inside.

This is the first time that I have ever been ordered into my own house. He is for a moment paralysed with anger. He watches his daughter-in-law carrying her daughter and bending under the lintel, the doorway is low, then his son, the back of his neck on fire with fury and the mark of Donegal sunburn, then Gasmask waving the shotgun. The ass of Gasmask's trousers is shiny and hangs low. There's something familiar-looking about his feet. Holding the little boy whose heart beats like the heart of a captive bird he stands stiffly on his own threshold.

—Keep it moving, old man.

That's Corkman speaking.

—Why should I? What hell right has a lout like you to order me about in my own house?

—This right.

It is, of course, the gun poking into the small of his back. This is cowboy country.

—I'm hardly worth shooting. Or kneecapping. The knees anyway aren't working as well as they used to.

—You're an old fellow, we know. But don't make things hard for anybody else. Children can be kneecapped.

—You would too. All for Ireland. Or is it Orange Ulster? But then you're from Cork.

—Less talk. Inside. Deliver the goods. That's all you have to do.

With a child in his arms and a pistol at his back he hasn't much choice. From the kitchen, as he walks a tiled corridor and across the wide scullery, he hears the sound of the television: whizzes, bangs, the clanking of machinery. So that the coloured screen is, ludicrously, the first thing to catch his eye. Against a blue sky a fighter-plane is falling, twisting, leaving behind it a spiral of black smoke. The Battle of Britain. Then he sees Minnie, stiff as a stick in a high wooden armchair. Gagged and bound. In a rough Belfast accent the third man says: Wizard prangs. And the bastards of Brits wouldn't even give us the credit for Paddy Finnucane. They say no Irishman was killed in the Battle of Britain.

Corkman says: Fuck you and Paddy Finnucane. Turn that bloody thing off. What do you think you're on? Your holidays?

Gasmask twists the knob. The plane hasn't yet touched earth. What is it about Gasmask's feet?

—Uncork the old dame. She can't do any damage now.

The third man, wearing a black felt mask that covers all his face, and an old-style British soldier's peaked cap, steps forward from the window bay: with no gun showing but with a hunting-knife at his belt. He unsheathes the knife, hacks away the gag, and the ropes that bind Minnie to the chair. They lie where they fall. Minnie moves her arms stiffly. Given time her tongue will get going.Not even the odd terrifying feeling of talking to a mask will keep Minnie mute.

—You're welcome home all of you and God bless you, she says, even if it wasn't much of a reception you got.

She slobbers a little. Her jaws and tongue are still stiff from the gag. She is a tall, brown-faced, wrinkled witch of a woman who always dresses in black for the husband who deserted her when they were three years married and that was forty years ago. The story as she tells it at Christmastime, or on the few other occasions when her memory is unfrozen by festivity, always follows the same formula: We tracked him everywhere, even as far as Newcastle-on-Tyne where he vanished without trace. We heard he joined the British army under a false name. But I know to God that even if he called himself Montgomery he wouldn't be taken in the Coldcream Gurkhas.

She stands up stiffly. She says: You'll want some refreshment after the long journey. At any rate you had a happy holiday. I got all the postcards you sent me. And Catherine, how are you? and Gary boy, don't be frightened. It's just that I wasn't that well able to greet ye when ye came in. But I'll make it up to ye when these blackguards are gone.

The children go to her silently and stand holding on to the long black skirt that recalls treachery and desertion and a man too worthless to be taken in an imaginary regiment, named contemptuously.

—Sit down old lady, Corkman says. Keep the children with you if you like.

—Thank you for nothing, Paddy from Cork. And who are you to tell me to sit down in my own kitchen?

—Sit down, for Christ's sake, and don't try my patience. You can cook everything in the house in half an hour. First, I've something to say.

—If you speak as well as you look you should be worth listening to.

—If you don't sit down we'll knock you on the head and tie you up again.

The voice behind the sock has risen an octave. She says: You're a hero. A grown man with a gun in his fist isn't afraid of any old woman.

But she is herself afraid and the children sense it. They cling to her. Catherine begins to sob.

—Oh Jesus, says Gasmask, I hate to hear children cry.

Corkman says: You should be running a creche. Suffer the little children. Sit down, you old hag, while your kneecaps still allow you to bend your knees.

—Wait a minute, his son says.

And takes a step forward. But Corkman tilts the pistol upwards and there is a silence broken only by the little girl's sobs; and that seems to last for a long time until Corkman laughs, a rich, hearty, surprisingly good-natured laugh. He says: There's many a fat farmer whose heart would break in two if he could see the townland that we are riding to. Dear gracious old lady would you for the last time, and for the love and honour of Almighty God, sit down and shut up and keep the children quiet?

She's frightened, more by the masks he'd say than by any horrors that she, at her age and coming out of another time, can readily imagine. Even though she reads the papers every day and clucks her tongue and says Sacred Heart of Jesus over outrage after outrage she has not yet fully realised the nature of the deeds now being done – for Ireland or what they call Ulster. Masks and queer faces and painted devils she can understand and she knows that they are evil: Lucifer looked like that once upon a time with the addition of horns and tail and a cow's foot. Yet, frightened or not, she does not give up easily: I'll sit down when Mr. Binchey asks me to sit down. Either of them. They are the masters in this house. And gentlemen into the bargain.

Under the sock Corkman hisses like a serpent. Binchey

senior realises with guilt that he has been enjoying or at least studying this struggle of wills between an old woman and a madman in a mask. Binchey junior, isolated and furious and helpless where the pistol has halted him in the middle of the floor, says hoarsely and so unexpectedly that it sounds like a startled shout: Sit down, Minnie. We'll hear what the man has to say.

The hissing ceases. It has been a most deliberate performance. Corkman says: Well said, Mr. Binchey Two. *Ex ore infantium* or out of the mouths of babes and sucklings. Thanks for consenting to listen. I don't want to be forced to show you who for the moment is master in this house. But I want you two men to listen carefully. If everybody plays ball nobody will get hurt.

The children, silent again, are together between Minnie's long legs, faces to her midriff like frightened sheep at a fair.

—If the three of you would sit together on that couch for the sake of concentration like, we could get down to business. What time is it now?

Gasmask tells him. He pulls a chair close to the couch and sits looking at an angle at father and son and the woman between them. He says: We'll have a wait but it can't be helped. The stuff isn't here yet. We can't move until light, tomorrow morning, when the good people are going to Sunday mass.

—What in hell do you mean? You're telling us nothing.

That was Binchey Two.

—Patience brother. I'll explain. I want Binchey One here to do a little milk delivery. To one of two spots in the town. He'll even have a choice. This is a free democratic society.

—My father-in-law, she says, can't drive any more.

Binchey Two says: I'll do it.

Corkman is hissing again, steam escaping. What sort of a mind is in there behind the sock?

—Jesus, give us credit for some savvy. We know you're suspended for dangerous and drunken driving. The first Royal Ulster cunt of a constable that saw you would pull you in. The town wouldn't get its milk delivery.

—It's a proxy bomb.

—How bright you are, fat farmer.

—Afraid to do your own dirty work.

—Stuff it. Too many pigs spoil the breath. They say that when you were in college you used to go to the cattle-market in the morning to get dung on your boots to let the world know you were doing agriculture.

Soldier's Cap, who sits straddle on a chair, his back to the low bay-window, the light fading through the blood-red leaves of Virginia creeper, and who is honing his hunting knife on the heel of his hand, laughs hoarsely, Gasmask stands by the door, butt of his shotgun grounded, at attention almost, a soldier of the Republic. What the hell is it about his feet? Gasmask says nothing. Binchey Two is very red in the face and in the bald head: The smell was better in the cattle-market, and that goes for you. Put down the gun and step outside and we'll see how much pigshit you contain.

—Easy, easy, fat man. We're here on business.

—Keep it that way.

Minnie whoops and cackles: It was a fair gentleman's challenge.

The hissing must make the sock uncomfortably damp. Gasmask shifts his feet and gun-butt: behind the mask he could be alarmed. The woman says: Take it easy, everybody. My father-in-law has been forbidden to drive. He has a heart condition.

—The police don't know that.

—He could drop at the wheel.

—He can drive carefully. Lady, we all have heart conditions.

Binchey senior says that nowadays a man is lucky to have any sort of a condition, or a heart to tick or a knee to bend: What do you want me to drive and where?

—You'll do it.

—I don't have much choice.

—You're a reasonable man.

—I wouldn't count on it.

The woman says: The people will wonder if they see him driving.

—They will like fuck, Soldier's Cap says. They'll just think he's so mean he can't keep his hands off the wheel.

Again the coarse laugh. He has a gravelly recognisable voice. With the exception of Corkman these are local people, for Gasmask's feet are as familiar as fireirons. Soldier's Cap knows that he still has an interest in the hackney-car business that his father, who was also a saddler, founded. Corkman walks slowly, blowing into his pistol, to where Soldier's Cap sits straddle in the bay of the window. They wait uneasily for blows and discipline. The children have not moved. Minnie murmurs to them and strokes their heads. Corkman stoops and whispers, hissing, and Soldier's Cap leaps up as if he had been electrocuted, sheathes the hunting-knife, stands rigid as a guardsman. The last light is dying behind the red creepers. Binchey Two sullenly repeats to Corkman: I can easily do the driving. Who'll stop me on a Sunday morning?

—Your licence is suspended.

—Like you don't want to do anything illegal. My father has bad sight as well as a weak heart.

—He can drive slow and wear his glasses. Look, farmer boy, we've been over this.

The woman says: I drove back from Donegal.

—Lady, we can't send a woman out with the goods.

—Chivalry, says Binchey One.

—Dear Christ, Corkman hisses, we have enough to do fighting the Brits, without listening to your bullshit.

—Fight the Brits, says Binchey Two, to the last Catholic shop in the village of Belleek or the town of Strabane. Man, you love the Brits, you couldn't exist without them. The nickname is affectionate. They give you the chance to be Irish heroes. They give you targets you can easily see.

In a low strained voice, controlling hysteria, the woman says: Stop it, all of you. Let's get this over with. There are the children.

—Sense, lady, says Corkman. I could do biz with you.

Before her man can again explode, she says: The occasion won't arise. But tell us, for God's sake, what the drill is.

—Simple. Sometime during the night a creamery can will be delivered here. All you have to do is drive it into the town and leave it in one of two places.

—What happens to the car?

—You're well insured, farmer boy.

Soldier's Cap says: Commandeered by the freedom fighters. But the silence that Corkman allows to settle for a while

after that remark indicates to Soldier's Cap that his words are
unwanted.

—Suppose, says Binchey One, that we all refuse to do it.

—You won't. There are children. And the women. We don't
want to be rough.

There's an even longer silence and then Minnie's voice, low
and hoarse: Harm a hair on their heads and I'll pray prayers
on you and yours.

—Jesus, Gasmask says.

But Corkman tells the old woman to be quiet: Pray not for
me nor on me but for yourselves and for your children.

—You mock God's words, Minnie says.

—Jesus, Gasmask says, I don't like this.

He shuffles uneasily from one familiar foot to another.

—It'll be a nice quiet time, says Corkman. But plenty people
on the roads going to mass and meeting. The Brits and the
R.U. cunts will be keeping a low profile. Put the children to
bed, old woman. You (he means Soldier's Cap) go with her and
keep your big mouth shut. One place is the entryway between
the town hall and the post office. But if the security there is too
tight the next best place is the avenue between Judge Flynn's
house and the golf-club. Very close to the Judge. We have the
women and the children and your fine fat son. Remember
that.

—I'll remember. I'll remember it for a long time.

—No threats, old man. You're in no fucking position.

—Judge Flynn is one of the best men in the north.

—The more reason he shouldn't be where he is. He lends
credit to the system.

Soldier's Cap, who has returned, ventures to say that Judge
Flynn is a tool of imperialism. No comment from Corkman.

—So you kill a man more readily because he's a good man.
And blow up the town hall and post office. What's the point?

—You could call it a reprisal, Corkman says, for what they
found in the lake.

And the lake would never be the same again.

The undulating movement of the skiers, the sweeping

curves made by the speed-boats, the wash and the perturbation of the waters could have brought the body up from the depths. Over there in that corner where, now that twilight has fallen, the men in the black boats have suspended their search for the murder weapon.

The body was badly decomposed. Forensic scientists said that it had been in the water for some time. You'd hardly need to be a forensic scientist to guess that much. Never knew before that we had a forensic scientist in the town or district. They could, though, have brought them from Belfast. Or the army may bring a truckload of them with it wherever it goes. Badly needed nowadays.

But with or without them it was a fair guess that the body might have been in the lake from the night of the evening on which the man who owned it didn't come home from work. Lying weighted down there in the dark until the movement of life on the day of the water-skiing drew it up from the mud at the roots of the reeds.

That water-skiing would be the lake's last effort to laugh. *Sea-lions and sharks, alligators and whales.* A man I know wrote a good comic song about that lake and that line was part of the chorus.

An early-morning fisherman, idling in one of those black boats, saw the floating body in that quiet corner among the reeds. A wire that had come unwound led to a fifty-six pound weight sunk deep in the mud. The man had been in his thirties and was the father of four children. Last seen alive when he locked his public-house in the town to drive his white Mazda car the three miles to his rural home. When he didn't get home at his usual time his wife raised the alarm. Bloodstains and shirt-buttons were discovered in the laneway leading to his house. A neighbour said he had heard five shots fired in the dusk.

For two weeks after, hundreds of people walked with the police and their tracker dogs scouring the country. Nobody seemed to suspect the lake because it was far away in another direction. So the water-skiing went happily ahead. But murderers in the dark had made the sleeping lake their accomplice. The innocent lake had been forced to share the guilt. The lake, out there and fading into another dusk, the lake knew. It could never be the same again.

Corkman is speaking: They killed him because some of us used his pub. He wasn't one of us. But he was with us. We'll get them.

—They say ye shot him because he spoke against murder gangs at a town council meeting.

—Mind your manners, old man.

—Manners, says Binchey Two.

—Anyway, it's a fucking lie. We'll get them.

—You'll get who, Binchey One asks. The town hall. The post office? Judge Flynn who sure as God had nothing to do with it?

—We'll show them we're active. That we can plant bombs where we like.

—Big deal. When my father does it for you.

—Stuff it, farmer.

His hand, a long bony pale hand, has tightened on the pistol. It could also be a damp hand.

The women and children have been locked into Minnie's basement bedroom. They have been told that their men's lives depend on their conduct. But as an extra precaution Soldier's Cap has been ordered outside to watch the bedroom window, to watch the world around them. He clearly doesn't like the detail but he goes. The dishonoured lake lies uneasily in the darkness: *Oh the sights that we saw as we waited for death on the treacherous waves of Lough Muck.*

Binchey One says: Judge Flynn stands for justice and peace.

—Old man, for an old man who was a famous teacher you've no head on your shoulders. They'll blame the people who put the body in the lake. Who wants peace?

—Logic, says Binchey Two. We. They. Them. Us. Who, in Christ's name, is who? Everybody wants peace except the madmen.

—Big words, farmer boy. We're not dealing with logicians. Let me tell you a story.

Seated on a chair by the door that leads to the night outside, and the lake and the town, Gasmask crosses his legs and, dear God, I know now what's familiar about his feet, his father's feet, poor civil shambling sod. In the corner on the floor behind him there's a child's tricycle, red with green wheels, and a doll's pram, the doll sitting upright and staring, lonely for three weeks while her playmate was in Donegal, still lonely, and surprised that no hugs and kisses have come her way for the homecoming.

—The little girl, he says, may need her doll.

—See to it, Corkman says.

And Gasmask stands up on his father's awkward feet and, with his shotgun trailing, wheels the pram out the other door and along the corridor to Minnie's room. The severed ropes and gag still lie where they fell. What has happened to the two crabs in the jar? The dead have peace but they don't know it.

—Let me tell both of you a story to show you the sort of animals we're dealing with.

Binchey Two says: Public relations.

Corkman ignores him. He tells his story.

—There were three U.V.F. men came over from the murder triangle by Portadown to kill a Catholic in Newtownstewart. Two hit men and one man to finger the subject. When they got there the man's away in Dublin. They go into a pub in Newtownstewart and start to drink. Then the fingerman says he knows another papish who would be better dead. They set out to get him. But he has emigrated to Canada. Feeling very bad they go back to the pub in Newtownstewart. On the way home, well drunk, they stop in Gortin Gap for a piss and the gunmen shoot the fingerman because he couldn't find anybody for them to shoot. One of their own. Think of that, old man.

—Quite right they were, says Binchey Two. He wasted a whole day on them. Time's money in your business.

—You'll push me too far, farmer boy.

—Go out and tar and feather a few girls. To keep your hand in.

—Jesus, I'll kneecap you just for the fun of it.

—Kneecaps are up in the Tam Ratings, the popularity polls. You don't know who you are until you look at your knees. I made you a fair offer. Put down the gun and step outside.

—Jesus.

Corkman is on his feet, the pistol coming up. Binchey One steps in front of him.

—Enough. Both of you. One shot and I'm through.

And to his son: Keep it cool. This will all be over by noon. Think of the women.

Corkman says: You should have whipped sense into him before he went bald. Men have been shot for less.

They are all seated again except Gasmask who stands shifting from one awkward foot to the other, his back to the wide window. Corkman orders him to pull the curtains. And to Binchey One: Get what rest you can. I want you fresh for the morning.

The curtains are drawn. Gasmask hisses: The shades of night are falling fast.

—A poet, says Binchey Two, by God a poet.

—As regards the men in Gortin Gap, Binchey One says, it makes more sense than to murder Judge Flynn because he's a good man. More of you should kill each other. Go to the Greenland Cap and settle whatever it is between ye and leave normal people alone.

Bearing the bomb, an angel of death, he will in the morning drive past the graveyard in which his wife is buried. *Soles occidere possunt et redire.* The back of the couch is hard against his spine. This is a rare way to keep a vigil. St. Ignatius, turning his back on the sword and vowing himself to Christ and to Christ his mother, had, in the mad manner of the man from La Mancha, watched all night over his armour. *Nobis cum semel occidit brevis lux.* There would be no time to stop to say a prayer at the graveside. The urgent business of Ireland did not nowadays allow time for prayer. *Nox est perpetua, una dormienda. Da mihi basia mille.*

No time to walk crunching up the gravel path, past the graves of men and women who were still alive in his memory. The tall tweedy jeweller, a great man to fish trout and salmon, prematurely bald like my pugnacious son, who had married such a handsome brunette, much younger than himself, from another town, that he was the envy of every man. Mysteriously, she died young and the tall lean man fished no more, spoke little and only to few and, among his jewels and trinkets and chimney clocks, withered away.

The two main paths in the graveyard are cruciform, Protestants to the left as you enter, Catholics to the right, the cross that had divided them in life divided them also in death: on one arm of the cross the grave of my father and mother and beside it my wife, a controversial placing perhaps, since she had been born and died a Protestant; and beside her the grave of that big happy companion of my youth, six years older than me, with whom I used to go shooting and fishing. He taught me the ways of guns and the ways of women, and became a military doctor and, in some dark night in the early days of the Hitler war, shot himself in his rooms in Aldershot camp in Britain. *Soles occidere possunt et redire.* Catullus also was a great friend to me in those days, when I, as people used to say, wooed her and won her, one day in the High Street her father halting me, at the beginning of my summer holidays in my second year in college, and asking me would I grind his daughter in Latin for her senior certificate.

That lovely old thatched farmhouse, pointed eaves, and dormer windows cowled in the thatch, apple-orchards all around it, at a crossroads a mile north-east of the town: can't remember who lives in it now. Happy hours, heads together over Allen's Latin grammar or Ritchie's Latin composition, and Livy and Tacitus and Virgil and Horace, and Catullus, my favourite, who naturally was not on any secondary-school course but, *da mihi basia mille.* I could even quote a lot of Catullus in those days and I had a good voice. The evening the hem of her school uniform skirt caught on her case of books as she lifted it from the floor to table, and the skirt came up with the case and my breath caught a bit as I saw for the first time the perfections of that body, her burning innocence. Standing behind her where she sat and quoting Catullus and looking down on the white northern slopes of her breasts and thinking of the warm south, the true, the blushful Hippocrene: and one breast in time was to be cut away for cancer leaving behind it a strange, chaste champain about which she used to make jokes, almost lewd for her. But even that sacrifice could not halt the cancer.

The evening I asked her father could I marry her, and he

said yes, he walked with me to the edge of the town where the roads meet and he talked with melancholy about what was to come on Europe and the world. A tall handsome man with a Roman profile and dark hair, not a rib of grey in it, parted up the middle. He was a tea and whiskey salesman, and ineluctable war would ruin his livelihood. He said: We lived through one big war. We won't be able to stand a second. The world will never be the same again.

He was dead in six months. Coronary? Melancholy? He lies buried with his wife and a son who died of wounds after Dunkirk. On the other arm of the cross. There will be no time, either, to pray at his grave.

Corkman sits, his elbows on the kitchen table, the pistol on the board before him. He is silent but very much awake. His son, with his head in his hands, seems asleep – but restlessly. Gasmask is snoring in Minnie's rocking-chair. Through the slit in the mask the snores make a sound that was never heard before. For sure and certain these distorted faces are out of a nightmare. Soldier's Cap is making out as well as he may in the shrubbery, with the cold promise that the watch will be changed at three in the morning. Corkman's tin hat has tilted and the sock-or-something, misshapen over his face, makes him like a Guy Fawkes or that Colonel Lundy the Orangemen used to burn annually in effigy in happy memory of the siege of Derry. *From Antrim crossing over in sixteen eighty-eight, a plumed and belted lover came to the Ferry Gate.* That was the Earl of Tyrconnel. *She summoned to defend her, our sires, a beardless race. With shouts of No Surrender, they slammed it in his face.*

The Apprentice Boys of Protestant Derry, the Maiden City, close the gate before Tyrconnel and the troops of James Stuart. The long memory lives on. With riots and ructions and bombs and bloody Sundays as much a maiden now as Dresden on the morning after.

All this he says to Corkman. No comment. Gasmask creaks and rocks in the chair. The snores ride on like advancing shingly waves.

—The Cambridge rapist, he says, had a better mask than any of you. More imagination. You must have seen a picture of it in the papers. Like a great black pointy bonnet with a long zipper where the mouth should be. He had sewn hair all around the bottom of it so that it looked as if he had long hair and a beard.

No comment from Corkman.

—And white eyebrows painted above the eyeholes. And painted in white on the forehead or what covered it the simple word: Rapist. He wasn't, do you see, ashamed of his craft, trade or profession. When a girl woke up and looked up and read that in the middle of the night she knew right away what was in store for her.

No comment.

—What could you write on your forehead?

From behind his cupped clutched hands Binchey Two says: Cain.

No comment.

—The chief constable in Cambridge blamed the case on the prevalence of unchecked porn. A dangerous word to use. It could have been misprinted.

—Old man, you talk too much.

—It's an old man's privilege.

—You don't have any privileges until you deliver the goods.

—After that, says Binchey Two, you could send him a 1916 medal.

No comment.

Binchey One says that according to Irenaeus in Edmund Spenser's Viewe of the State of Ireland the kerns and gallowglasses oppressed all men, spoiled their own people as well as the enemy, stole, were cruel and bloody and full of revenge, delighted in deadly execution, were licentious, swearers and blasphemers, common ravishers of women and murderers of children.

—He didn't like the Irish, old man. We know you taught Latin and history and English literature. It had to be English. We know what your history was like.

—You know a lot for a stranger to these parts.

—I do my homework.

Gasmask's snores trample onwards towards a gravelly coast.

He is wandering through London streets with his wife. They are planning a trip by water to the country but they fall asleep in a pub or in a flat and can't get to the boat. We meet a young official who asks me to telephone Mary Cluskey that in my youth I rolled in the ditches with, on the expert advice of that big happy man who died in Aldershot by his own hand. And when I'm talking to Mary on the 'phone I can still hear my wife's voice in the background. I keep asking Mary to pass the 'phone on to her but when she tries to, my wife is gone. Then she re-appears, walking along Kensington High Street and carrying two travelling bags. She says she won't go to wherever it was we were going because I would only torment myself and her. Kensington High Street becomes a clay road between shambles of outhouses. We meet a crowd of boys playing with dogs and ask them the way to Hampstead. We have been going the wrong way, and an adult, a dwarf, Dickens' Daniel Quilp, redirects us. We sit down to eat at a rough wooden table and in the open air. My son is there as a boy, and his sister, grown-up, the image of her mother. In a dry, deep-sunken dyke to my left are bundles of antique books, weather-stained, mouldering. Then a girl at a little table, also to my left, produces tickets for a raffle and I am sharing a room with an Old Christian Brother who taught me in secondary school and had slight homosexual tendencies. There are two beds in the room, hospital screens, the floor slopes steeply down from one wall to the other, my bed is behind a screen in the corner farthest from the door. The old brother's pupils are doing exams and doing badly and in the dusk there is the slapping of buttock-flogging (he was an adept) and wailing from an adjacent building. In his bed I fall asleep but, perhaps wisely, go to my own bed when he comes in, and Mary Cluskey is there. Then the room is full of autumn leaves blown in through a window and the door, which is swinging open in the wind. Mary is picking up the leaves. She is pleasantly naked. The door slams shut.

And Gasmask has snored and rocked himself out of the chair and is picking himself up from the floor. The whole room is awake. Corkman says: Go out, for God's sake, and relieve Charlie Chaplin. Keep awake. Don't frighten the birds.

He has for a long time had recurrent nightmares about

books left to rot and decay in the open air, sometimes in heaps or bound bundles, sometimes, even more crazily, on orderly shelves. He was also at the deathbed of that old Christian Brother in Baldoyle in Dublin. The old man had had a happy and holy death. On the Chinese mission he had picked up the passion for boys and buttock-whipping. He had had two brothers in the flesh who committed suicide and to the end, almost, he had a fear that he would go that way.

His son, yawning, stretching himself, says out of nowhere: It was simply that I preferred the cattle-market, to the college. There was more brains there. And, believe it or not, less shit.

No comment from Corkman.

Then knocks and footsteps round the house, whistles after dark. Corkman gives his pistol to Soldier's Cap: Watch this pair. Your life's on it. That's the milk delivery.

There has been no sound of a car engine. That could mean that the milk delivery has been prepared in and carried from somewhere close by. Or did the car stop a distance away so as not to draw attention to the house? It would be odd to think that somebody in a neighbouring cottage could all the time have been plotting and preparing this. His son says: One day when I was in primary school I was walking home through Fountain Lane where the soldiers' girls lived. Two of them were having an argy-bargy and one of them called the other a hoor. So being all of eight years of age I went right home and asked my mother what was a hoor? She laughed until she cried. She said: You'll find out soon enough. There's a fair share of them in this town.

—Next morning I'm on my way back through Fountain Lane and one of the pair is leaning out over the half-door, red in the face, hair in the eyes. She shouted at me: Wee fella, did you pass many worms this morning?

—That puzzled me for a long time. You see I couldn't recall seeing or overtaking any worms.

Something's going on outside. The gentlemen go by. Five and twenty ponies trotting through the dark, brandy for the parson, baccy for the clerk, laces for a lady, letters for a spy, watch the wall my darling...

—That's life for you, his son says. Or a lot of it. Hoors and worms. Worms and hoors.

No comment from Soldier's Cap. Corkman has come back. He says: That was the milk delivery, the creamery can. Brace yourself old man. You might yet be the first of your breed to die for Ireland.

Standing with one foot in the stone-flagged corridor and one in the basement bathroom, holding his shotgun as if he were behind a covered wagon and waiting for Indians, Gasmask hisses: Be careful Mr. Binchey. And good luck.

Binchey One is in shirt and trousers, and washing and shaving. This is a job he needs to be fresh for: Oh weep, my own town, for after all these years of love I carry death to your threshold.

Carefully he combs back his plentiful silver hair. It changed colour after she died but it stayed with me. When he. was younger and drank more than was good for him he always had a fancy that if your hair was combed you looked sober. He soaks a face-cloth in cold water and swabs his face, particular attention to the ears so that I'll hear the bomb if it goes off prematurely. Do you hear the bomb that kills you? On the western front the old sweats said that you didn't hear the whistle of the shell that had your name on it. Yet how could anybody know if nobody lived to tell the tale? He says: That's the oddest bloody wish I ever heard, Bertie.

He hadn't meant to use the name but the harm's done now, if it is harm. Gasmask doesn't move. Or Bertie. He may be seeing Indians. He hisses: Search me. Silence is golden.

With those temporary speech-defects he should eschew sibilants.

—Your father's feet, Bertie.

—I'm saying nothing.

—I'd know them anywhere.

—For God's sake don't let him know you know me.

—Are you afraid of him?

—He's hell on wheels. He might hear us.

—He can't with the sound of the rashers frying.

And also the voices of children who seem blessedly to have

adapted, accepted painted devils and funny faces so as now in the morning to be able to dance around Minnie, Minnie Brown, we're home again from Dungloe town, and to tell her in a pattering hail-shower of words in two voices about Donegal and the ocean and the crabs in the glass-jars and the golden and white strands of the Rosses. Soldier's Cap has been detailed to carry the crabs into the kitchen. Corkman says: Anything to keep them quiet.

He sits by the outer door, pistol in hand, back to the wall. Soldier's Cap has been sent out again to watch the world and the loaded car. Binchey Two sits on the couch, his head in his hands, brooding, his father fears, violence. The two women cook breakfast. It is Sunday morning and callers are unlikely and it is the custom of the house to pick up the Sunday papers in the town after mass. So there will be no newsboy. For all the townspeople know, they are still in Donegal.

—He's all ears, Gasmask hisses. He's one of the big ones.

—Who? That half-educated gutty from Cork. He's big when he's out like the prick of a jackass.

—Holy God, Mr. Bee, be careful. Keep your voice down.

—In my own house.

—It's his house now. For the cause. You were good to my father, Mr. Bee, my father always says.

—The son repays me.

—It's the cause, Mr. Bee. We must get the Brits out of Ireland. They want our oil.

—Our hairoil. I never knew we had oil.

—We will have offshore oil.

—You won't see much of it, Bertie boy, where you're going. You'll have more need of luck than I'll have.

—Not my name, Mr. Bee. Walls have ears. The trees outside have ears.

—You really are a poet, Bertie. Your father was a decent man. Your father's son shouldn't be mixed up in this.

—I'm a soldier of the Republic.

—You're an ass. You could give me that gun. Mad Eyes Minahan has only a knife.

—Jesus, Mr. Bee, you know him too.

—No mask could hide those mad eyes.

He hadn't recognised the eyes. He had just guessed. If I survive this, will I pass the names to the police?

Carefully he knots his dark-green tie, Dublin poplin. He could do with a clean shirt: and suddenly his care for such things at such a time seems crazily comic. Yet he dusts the broad shoulders of his pin-striped jacket, carefully polishes and sets his pince-nez: she had always liked them.

—You could give me that gun.

—Dear God, Mr. Bee, talk sense. You were a teacher. He'd kill us all. Even if he didn't get me, they would. There's no way out. Sorry, Mr. Bee.

The elbow of his left arm, slightly crooked, pains a little as it has done most mornings since he broke it in a boxing bout in college and, after my time, my son was shaping well on the college team but he lost interest and gave all his heart to farming: and perhaps Bertie, as stupid as his father before him, is right and there's no way out, and Corkman is calling from the kitchen to say that time is ticking away and the milk may be boiled over.

His son still sits with his head in his hands. The empty doll's pram is under the table. The doll is asleep in Minnie's bed. The crabs stare out from their jar on the wide windowsill. Rashers and eggs and tea laced with brandy, good for the ticking of the heart. There's a double naggin of brandy in the back of the car and he hopes they haven't found out about that. The family sit and eat, and Corkman and Bertie guard the doors, they'll eat, Corkman says, when the milk is safely on the road. His son's strong hands, now marmalading bread for the children, are matted with dark hair, none on his head, the fingers are thick and flat-tipped, brutal. He is dangerously silent. Could have been a champion in the ring but it was nature for him to find his content on the land, among cattle and horses, behind him generations of strong farmers who had survived the famine of the 1840s and grown stronger in a new and better world. Branching out into saddlery which also belonged to the land, then into a fleet of hackney cars which seemed to be a natural successor to saddlery. Or unnatural? Over the tea laced with brandy, Franco-Irish courage, gallant

France, indomitable Ireland, the noble name of Hennessy, he sniffs the wax-end and leather and daubing in the saddlery, then the gasolene in the garages, another new world, old Ford cars, tin lizzies, that stood high and stilted and quivered like thoroughbreds when you set the engine running, and had never been perverted to carry bombs. Proxy or otherwise. Looking back at it now it was a lost lyrical innocent place in which gasolene smelled sweet as the rose and droppings of spilled gasolene reflected all the colours of the rainbow. Corkman says: Let's take a look at the goods.

His son's wife picks up from the floor the severed ropes and gag, puts them in a plastic trash-bag and hopes out loud that they'll never be used in this house again. Then sits on the couch, her arms around her children. The little girl, golden as her mother with the promise of wine, wears a leprechaun's navy-blue jacket and slacks, remembers, and hides her face against her mother and whimpers a little. It could, except for the whimpering, be an idyllic picture. They look at her in silence. But do masks or the minds in them really look? What can they see but other masks? Not men or women or children. Not the shadows of God.

There is a low sky and gentle mizzling rain but a promise in the light wind that the sun will shine before long. The red tricycle with green wheels has somehow or other found its way out to the yard. Lacking the sun the borders of oxalis are closed and colourless. Bertie is a poet and the trees have ears. And the lake. And eyes too. There it is, silent as if nothing had happened. But you can't fool me. The treacherous waves. You know what happened. You helped it to happen. The searchers in the black boats have not yet started work. Or do men search for murder weapons on the seventh day? Lough Muck, Loch na Muice, the lake of the pig, Pig's lake, what pig? *Me and Andy one evening was strolling, we were happy and gay you can bet, and when passing by Drumragh new graveyard, a young Loughmuck sailor we met.* She sleeps forever in new Drumragh on the wrong arm of the cross. *He brought us along to his liner that was breasting the lake like a duck. And that was the start of our ill-fated cruise on the treacherous waves of Loughmuck.* That now was the

first verse of the comic song: two drunks from the town astray
in these rural parts, falling footless in a dyke, suffering alco-
holic comas about an ocean cruise on the oval inland lake, a
comic laughing lake, sea-lions, sharks, alligators, whales, ship-
wreck, and a pity it was that the name of death, *oh the sights that
we saw as we waited for death,* had to be mentioned in the chorus
of the song: *There we lay on that beach quite exhausted till a man
with a big dog drew near. He shouted out, Hey, clear away out of this,
we want no drunk towney boys here.* Laughter and innocence were
gone. The shadow of the monstrous mythological pig brooded
over a landscape that could never free itself from vengeance
and old wrongs. A pig of an island, an island changed by the
magic of the Tuatha-de-Danaan into that mammoth of a black
pig crouching on the sea, so as to try to prevent the Milesian
wandering heroes from coming safely to haven on their isle of
destiny. What a destiny, to consort with murderers in the valley
of the black pig.

Corkman opens the boot of the car which has been reversed or
pushed back to the hayshed, in which there is another car, a
Ford Cortina. But it didn't come there during the night. No
noise. Must have been there before we drove from the happi-
ness of Donegal into the haunted farmyard.
　　—You're a learned man, Corkman says.
　　Bertie, like a statue of the Rifleman, stands in the shrubbery
away at the gable of the house.
　　—There she is. You'll like to know what's in her.
　　She is a stout squat creamery can, shining silver.
　　—One hundred pounds of ammonium nitrate mixed with
fuel oil and about three pounds of gelignite.
　　—A sweet cocktail.
　　—She'll do the job. Watch her. Technologically we've made
big advances.
　　Carefully he closes the boot: Don't bump her, old man.
　　—Advances? Towards what?
　　—That's the way we'll bugger the Brits. Technology.
　　The town hall, the post office, any innocent person who
might be in them or walking the street past them, Judge Flynn
doomed because of his virtue: a madman spoke behind the
mask, the man in the mask was mad.

—Some American says that shortly any fool will be able to make a hydrogen bomb in his own backyard.

—You read too much, old man.

Once upon a time a creamery can had been a harmless or lovely, even a musical object. Up and down the street in the town in which he was reared, the horses and carts from the farms would travel, bright with jingling cans, taking fresh milk to the creamery, taking away the skim milk for cattlefood. In Hamilton's smithy where three gigantic Presbyterian men, a father and two sons, swung their hammers and reddened the forge, the horses and the cartwheels were shod when the need arose: Presbyterian iron, and across the street his father and his helpers, all Catholics, including Bertie's poor fool of a father, provided the leather. Genuine co-operation: the horses had no sectarian prejudices. One large red-faced farmer-boy would sit sideways on his cart, outsized hobnailed feet trailing the ground and, fancying himself perhaps on the Oregon trail, would sing in the rural dialect: Rowl along, covered wagon, rowl along.

No shuddering shattering death in those bright cans.

Nowadays motor-trucks took the cans to a modern factory.

—Time's ticking away, Corkman says.

He agrees. What else is new? Corkman is a bore: and suddenly the brutal effrontery of the whole business freezes his blood and sets him shivering. What right have these brainless bastards with their half-baked ideas to crash in on the lives of better people, to bind and gag old women, set children whimpering, and himself bearing death and ruin to the town he loves. Ireland? What Ireland? Ulster? What Ulster? Multiplying like body-lice, the other crabs, in the hairy undergrowth, one madman produces another. He says to Corkman that, indeed, time is ticking away, that they're all closer to the grave than they were yesterday morning. He says: I heard of a man who defied a gang like you . . .

—Gang? Watch it, old man.

—And said: Murder me now. What would you do, Corkman?

—Try me and see. Nobody would miss your son, for starters. But listen to me now and listen good and no codacting. You can't take the short way into the town. They may be easy on a

Sunday morning at the roadblock but you might bump her on the ramps. She's as delicate as a virgin.

Then the backdoor of the house slams thunderously. Soldier's Cap has come backwards out through the doorway like a rocket and is flat on his ass and roaring. Bertie the imbecile, soldier of the legion of the rearguard like his father before him, is also flat but on his belly, shotgun aimed on the backdoor. Corkman says: Don't move, old man. Charlie Chaplin couldn't guard a henhouse. Has farmer boy a gun?

—He has the 'phone.

—It's small use to him. We fixed that. Be your age. Has he a gun?

—He has a shotgun somewhere.

—In the house?

Soldier's Cap rises, falls again over the green-wheeled red tricycle, comes crawling crabwise across the yard towards the hayshed and his master and the loaded car and the concealed can. Corkman calmly raises the pistol: Jesus, I could shoot him where he creeps. Only it wouldn't be worth the noise. The dung I have to work with. Where's the shotgun, old man?

Soldier's Cap crawls closer. Bertie leaps to his feet and, in a perfect imitation of a British paratrooper shooting down civilians in Derry on Bloody Sunday, races round the corner of the house, goes down, shotgun ready, on one knee, under a windowsill and close to the backdoor. Bertie has studied the art of war, or whatever it is, on the teevee.

—You may as well spill, old man. It's not in the house.

He may as well spill. His son hasn't a hope. He says: No shooting then. If so, no driving. The gun's up on hooks in the stable-loft.

—It's safe there. We'll get it later. And no conditions, old man. Who in hell do you think is boss around here?

Soldier's Cap has crawled into what he thinks is the shelter of the hayshed. He moans what seems to mean that his jaw is broken. He rises to his knees: and, fair enough, if his jaw isn't broken it, and his mask, are in some disarray: my son still has a good right, and it is mad Minahan. Then Corkman with care and deliberation kicks Soldier's Cap in the privates and the creature goes down again howling.

—A lesson in discipline, soldier. And now, old man. Into battle.

The pistol is pressed against the back of his head.

—Walk slowly across to within twenty paces of the door. Tell the idiot farmer boy to step out backwards, hands behind back. Women and children in kitchen and quiet. If not I'll shoot you in one kneecap. Also we'll run the milk delivery up the back-door and leave it there. Time's ticking away. The virgin's in the boot. Waiting to be bust. Fed-up fooling, old man. Soldier-boy on your feet. You stupid fucker. The Battle of Britain and Paddy Finnucane. And get the cuffs out of the Cortina.

He stirs mad Minahan more than briskly with his foot and the creature rises and hobbles, doubled-up and moaning, towards the hidden car. They pace across the yard. Quasimodo Minahan lurches behind. The borders of oxalis are stirring in expectation of the sun. The birds are busy. The birds sang around Dachau. The mouth of the pistol is not touching his head but he feels that it is. Cold shivering anger at outrage is not enough. You need guns and bombs and swinging ropes and the shooting of hostages. But here and now there's no help for it, no way out. If the milk has to be delivered any-where, better not at your own door. So his son steps out back-wards, hands behind his back, and Quasimodo, hobbling side-ways and groaning, snaps the cuffs on him in a flash and a click and, for better value, kicks him viciously on the shins. Corkman laughs again that astoundingly good-natured laugh and says: Chained in the market-place he stood, a man of giant frame.

Then: To the wheel, old man, to the wheel.

—Will my son be safe?

The humiliation, oh heart of Jesus, the humiliation, hoors, whores and worms.

—If he minds himself, and if you deliver the goods. He can't masturbate the way he is. He won't grow hair on the palms of his hands. To the wheel, old man.

—The women? My daughter-in-law? The children?

Bertie's father's awkward feet have walked into the house.

—No time, old man, for tearful farewells. Kiss them all you want when you come back. If you ever do. Time's ticking away.

The pistol, really touching his head, pushes him towards the car. His son stands silent, chained in the market-place amid the gathering multitude that shrank to hear his name, men without hands, girls without legs in restaurants in Belfast, images of Ireland Gaelic and free, never till the latest day shall the memory pass away of the gallant lives thus given for our land, images of Ulster or of a miserable withdrawn corner of O'Neill's Irish Ulster safe from popery and brass money and wooden shoes. These mad dogs have made outrage a way of life. To the wheel, to the wheel, to the wheel, time's ticking away, in the town the churchbells are ringing, Catholic, Church of Ireland, Presbyterian, Methodist, Baptist, all calling people away from each other to get them in the end by various routes, *variis itineribus* to the home in the heavens of the same omnipotent, omniscient, omnipresent Great Father with a long white beard, but why not unite here and now and not wait for then, come all to church good people good people come and pray, and the angel of death is at the wheel or on the wing, and ye know neither the day nor the hour.

Before him like a blood-red flag the bright flamingoes flew. The bright evil lake is behind him. The car runs well. To look at it, nobody would have a notion. This now is the crossroads and the longest way round is the shortest way home. And his still-silent, silvery passenger, glutted with fuel oil and gelignite and ammonium nitrate, might be discommoded into burping by the bumps of the ramps. Beloved, may your sleep be sound. She sleeps in New Drumragh. Death sleeps in the silver can. In Dublin long ago he had gone with her to see that movie about Venezuela and the wages of fear. A friend of his had even introduced them to the Frenchman who had written the novel: a tall man, visiting Dublin at the time, who wrote about dead-beats in a vile South American town, island of lost souls, taking perilous jobs, only the lost would take them, that was a pothole and a bad bump, driving nitro-glycerine or something to mines or quarries or was it oil-wells: the occupational hazard, a blinding flash over the ridge, scarcely an explosion, just a blinding flash and that was that

But at least those wrecks of men were paid to carry the stuff. More or less they went willingly. If they won through they had their ticket to somewhere out of hell. If they didn't, they felt no more pain. While I ferry murder to my town and its people so as to save my children, my children's children, an old deserted woman, a long white house. And on the cause must go, through joy or weal or woe, till we make Ireland a nation free and grand. Not even the Mafia thought of the proxy bomb, operation proxy, proxopera for gallant Irish patriots fighting imaginary empires by murdering the neighbours. Could Pearse in the post office have, by proxy, summoned Cuchulain to his side, could the wild geese have, by proxy, spread the grey wing on the bitter tide, could all that delirium of the brave not have died by proxy, Edward Fitzgerald, and Robert Emmet and Wolfe Tone? Corkman seemed semi-educated, and must know that poem, and also, let me carry your cross for Ireland, Lord, but let some other unfortunate fucker carry the bomb for me.

Proxopera, he says, and likes the sound of the word.

Proxopera Binchey, fit foe for the Red Baron, zooming in to attack, and dear God there was a bump that nearly stopped my faulty heart, my palms are sweating, my crotch is scourged and where in God's name is the brandy that was under the cushion in the back of the car? He finds it, and blessed be God, blessed be His holy name and blessed forever be the holy name of Hennessy, and stands on the roadway sipping, and breathing in the living morning. This is a quiet place, and a good place to drive the accursed thing into a field and be shut of it forever, except that he knows that some of them, not Corkman, not Bertie, not mad Minahan, but some fourth monster, and unmasked and like an ordinary human being, is watching him from somewhere, hedgerow, hilltop, to see does he truly deliver the goods.

Six weeks ago that man near Kesh, by the Erne in County Fermanagh, was ordered to take a loaded bomb into the town and simply drove it at sixty into a field and jumped out and scuttled for his life and the gunmen took off in panic, like shit off a shovel, in his car and didn't stop for twenty miles and abandoned his car beyond Ballyshannon: real true Irish heroes, they were, when their own yellow hides were in peril. Like the way they were all to stand and fight if the Brits went ahead with Operation Motorman and went into the Bogside in Derry, but on the day and night of Operation Motorman the heroes were safe across the Border getting heroically drunk in Bundoran on the ocean, a health resort of high renown. But at Kesh there were no hostages: and what would that Corkman and mad Minahan do to his son and his wife and children: soldiers of the Republic in their own eyes, kneecappers, murderers, arsonists, protection racketeers, decorators of young girls with tar and feathers, God, the oddities that in times like these crawled out from under the stones.

The green rolling landscape is happy all around him. Where are the watchers hiding?

Brandy breaks out in sweat on his brow. Time's ticking away. He's as lonely as Alexander Selkirk, lord of the fowl and the brute, lord of destruction and the day of doom. Into battle then. To the wheel. To the wheel. Get a good grip on myself. Another sip. More sweat, but the heart seems easy. A man of my age in Belfast was forced to drive a bomb to the Europa hotel, already bombed seventeen times, and had a heart attack and died, and the bomb didn't even go off: the cursed murderous cretins, and all the happy days I passed along this road on my way to the innocent lake and the vision of the white house of destiny: and now, out of humanity's reach, I Alexander Selkirk, on my own island and passing her holy grave without time for a prayer, must finish my journey alone.

Traffic is slight for a Sunday morning. Have the men of blood frightened the people from going to mass or meeting? Three cars overtake him and hoot at him in salute, and in the noise and reverberation of their passing he grips the wheel until his sweating palms hurt. He doesn't hoot back. They'll all be surprised to see me driving. God preserve any of them from stopping to make enquiries. An old woman – oddly enough he doesn't recognise her although he thought he knew everybody on this road – thumbs a lift and, out of habit, he is almost about to respond. She'll be amazed and annoyed that he hasn't. People in these parts were always generous about giving lifts. These morons have blighted the landscape, corrupted custom, blackened memory, drawn nothing from history but hatred and poison. Proxopera, proxopera lift up your voice and sing. So he sings, but softly: Going to mass last Sunday my true love passed me by. I knew her mind was altered by the rolling of her eye. And when I stood in God's dark light, my tongue could word no prayer, knowing my saint had fled and left her reliquary bare.

My true love passed me by. No, but I passed her by, in fear and without a prayer, when I passed the green spiked railings of new Drumragh. He sings again, this is as close to prayer as I can come: Ringleted youth of my love with your bright golden tresses behind thee, you passed on the road up above but you never came in to find me.

How dear to me now, doomed to solitude, a murderer by proxy, are my memories, how dear the ordinary details of life, a red tricycle with green wheels, a doll's pram, the rocks of Donegal, two crabs in a glass jar, the wrinkled face of an old woman, the winy body of a young woman, the bald head of my angry son, the voices of his children, the sound of the hooves of his horses, the oxalis opening to the sun now breaking out splendidly beyond my doomed town.

Spiked green railings surround the dead, the gravelled cross divides them.

Outside a Wesleyan hall in Belfast a woman has been found impaled on the railings. Foul play is not suspected. She fell from a window. Of a Wesleyan hall? Odd, very odd. And in Belfast, where for six years there has been nothing but foul play. Christ, there I went bump bump over a bridge over a small stream out of which, with the humble worm, I took my first ever brown trout. Has the creamery can moved? Rattled? How do you fall from the window of a Wesleyan hall and impale yourself on the railings? Shades of Shaka, the great Zulu, who amused himself by seating his enemies on pointed stakes and letting them sink to find their own level. A very painful happening, buggery by proxy, proxbuggery. But the

Turks had more finesse with a slender, pliable, tough rod tapped gently in at the anus and up and up, an expert job, and out at the back of the neck and one end of the rod lashed securely to the other and the victim raised on a pole to perish as soon or as slowly as he pleased. With their hammers and nails and carpentered crosses the ancient Romans were a crude bloody crowd. Proxopera in the highest, hosanna to the king.

Long ago she said in all innocence: Take my cherry.

They were sitting in an ice-cream parlour in O'Connell Street in Dublin.

He picked the cherry from the top of her phallic Bombe Cardinale, blunted multi-coloured obelisk of ice-cream, and told her what she had just said, and she blushed and laughed and laughed and blushed, and still I remember the first touch of the tip of my finger on the fragile membrane.

—She's as delicate, Corkman said, as a virgin.

Or was that what the bastard had said?

And that, God above, was another bad bump. St. Christopher, pray for me, who carried Christ on your back, I carry Lucifer, evil and a blinding light.

Once in an old churchyard that must have been in some eighteeth-century engraving, and beside a high Norman earth-work, a friend of mine and myself came on a Sunday on a newly-opened grave, opened to receive its guest on the Monday morning. Down, deep-down in the next door grave reposed a skeleton, not a bone out of place, but bed-clothes temporarily disturbed for the reception of the new guest. Inlaid to the brown clay, head tilted restfully back, hands joined together a little above where manhood or membrane might have been. She sleeps for the life of the world in new Drumragh where soon, perhaps, I may join her but, also perhaps, not with my bones in their proper positions. Before the city hall in Belfast people kneel around more than a thousand small white crosses, one cross for every person murdered in the name of Ireland or the name of Protestant Ulster. Bertie of the blundering hereditary feet talks of the Republic,

Corkman the crazy talks of technology, and I drive on, sick
with fear and an awful resignation, to bring death to my own,
to keep death from my own.

My father was a great man for bananas, treacle-bread and
oatmeal porridge. Three hundred and sixty-five days of the
year, three hundred and sixty-six in Leap Year, even on Christmas day and after the Christmas dinner, he would prepare and
sup his own oatmeal.

Once upon a time the country people held that human skulls
had healing properties, chiefly for the healing of epilepsy. You
broke off a little bit of the skull, ground it into powder and
drank it. That is, if you were an epileptic. Also, milk could be
boiled in the skull and given to the patient. Over there near
Keadue on the shores of Lough Key in the west of Ireland, the
skull of Turlough O'Carolan, the last of the bards, was so used
until somebody stole it from his tomb. To preserve the bard's
skull? Or to make a corner in the curing of epilepsy? In new
Drumragh she sleeps forever, her skull on a pillow and under
a canopy of Ulster clay. Goldsmith, Thackeray said, could have
heard O'Carolan and God of Almighty what am I thinking of,
broken-down pedant sitting on a volcano, Empedocles on
Aetna, and that was a bump and a bump and an 'alf and my
hands are so slippy they can hardly hold the wheel till the
vessel strikes with a shivering shock, even the roads have gone
to blazes since the troubles began, Good Heavens it is the
Inchcape Rock, as our ship glided over the water we all gazed
at the landscape we knew, we passed Clanabogan's big light-
house and the Pigeon Top faded from view: but, alas, as we
sped o'er the waters, we were all soon with horror dumbstruck,
for without any warning a big storm arose on the treacherous
waves of Lough Muck, and Sacred Heart of Jesus what now is
happening in my white house that I first saw and loved across
the waters of the lake that have been polluted forever: and
Bertie's father was a born fool for this night, when my father
was cooking the porridge, he steps into our kitchen with a
collection box, and all round his left bicep a tricoloured ribbon
oh, collecting cash for Caithlin Ni Houlihan, the Hag of Beare

and Caith Ni Dhuibhir, and Patrick Pearse and the sainted
dead who died for Ireland. Nowadays people die for Ireland
in the oddest ways.

—And what will you do with the money, says my father and
he carefully watching the bubbling oatmeal.

—Elect members to Stormont and Westminster, Mr.
Binchey.

—And what will you do then, Brian boy?

—The members will then abstain from attendance, Mr.
Binchey. They'll be abstentionist members.

—Bully for them. That'll save train and boatfare. And what
will you do then, Brian?

—Spread our propaganda among the Orangemen, Mr.
Binchey. Bring them round to our way of thinking.

—A laudable intention. And what then, Brian?

—Declare a republic, Mr. Binchey.

—Oh la dee da, says my father and goes on stirring the
porridge.

But how could Brian help it and the way he was reared, with
an uncle that was forever in and out of jail for Ireland and an
aunt that blew herself up making bombs for Ireland and a
mother that ran a restaurant and lodging-house always as
full of republicans as Rome before the Caesars, so that it was
regularly being raided by the Royal Ulster Constabulary, and
one night Brian's mother and Bertie's grandmother poured
from a second-floor window, and all for Ireland, the contents of a chamber-pot from under the bed of a drunken
journeyman-carpenter, over the shoulders of a police sergeant
who came knock knocking at the door: and the sergeant's
name was Poxy Thompson because of the pock marks on his
face and for no worse reason, and one of his shoulders was
lower or higher than the other. A family that was fierce Irish,
as they'd say in irony in Dublin; and now Bertie on his father's
feet and with a face like a faceless monster goes plodding
unbidden around the house of my boyhood dreams.

But Kyrie Eleison what is this on the road on a Sunday morning, smoke rising from the smouldering stump of what's left of
the Orange Hall where once that love-bewildered young Prot-

estant provoked a riot by footing the light fantastic with a papist girl. In this present Ulster world there's little place for the light fantastic: close to Newry town the U.V.F. or was it the U.D.A. murdered a showband.

My road drops down, doing a double bend, into a saucer of a valley. High, green, terraced banks, no turn left or right, no turning back, no way out except straight through: *There we were like two Robinson Crusoes far away from Fireagh Orange Hall. Though we starved on that rock for a fortnight, not a ship ever came within call.* Fireagh, here I come. And the Orange Hall has just gone. Up in smoke. Thirty or so people are in and around what's left of it. As close to the smouldering ruins as they dare to go. The flames have blackened the bushes on the high bank above. Sweet sight for a Sunday in a good autumn. No soldiers around. This is a fire. Not a fight. Thank God for that. But for what? One policeman raises his bluc-black arm. What can I do but stop? No use to say to him halt me at your peril. And the peril of everybody in this little valley. And of my son and his wife and Gary and Catherine and Minnie, Minnie Brown we're home again from Dungloe town.

—Good morning, Mr. Binchey. Bit of a surprise to see you at the wheel.

A decent fellow. I drank with his father. Also in the force. And a brother of his, a plain-clothes man, murdered in the town, twelve months ago. Sitting reading the paper at a bar-counter when two gunmen walked in. Into a pub in which he had had his first drink. And in which on my way from teaching I used to drink with his father, at the same counter at the same place. Tried to pull his gun. They shot him once. Crawled into the gents. They followed him and finished the job and shouted: We have you in the right place on the shithouse floor.

That pub would never be the same again.

—Good morning, constable. I wouldn't be at the wheel only necessity knows no law.

How true, how bloody true.

—We got back from Donegal last night. Margaret wasn't feeling too well. Robert's on the suspended list. As you know. So old grandad has to head off to the chemist. But I'm taking it easy.

—It's the best thing to do these days, Mr. Binchey. If you can. What do you think of that on a Sunday morning?

The engine purrs. He's afraid to cut it off. God only knows what restarting might do. The constable is a squat solid civil fellow with a squint, and his face smudged from the fire the way the soldiers, now and in this place, smudge their faces on night patrol, in my own town, dear God, battledress and camouflage in my own town. Could I tell him that time is ticking away? Could I tell him that someone in the crowd is watching?

—What happened, constable?

—I.R.A. I'd say, a reprisal for the Catholic Church at Altamuskin. The U.V.F. tossed a bomb into that.

—Oh, what a wonderful war.

—So now the U.V.F. will bomb another Catholic church. Or a Catholic pub. Then the I.R.A. will shoot a policeman or bomb a Protestant pub. And then the U.V.F. ...

—Was the brigade here?

—Couldn't make it. Fires everywhere this bloody morning. All a few miles outside town. Cornstacks. Barns. Anything.

Aha, the grand strategy, get the brigade away from the town, make straight the path for Binchey the Burner. Time's ticking away.

—They could be up to something else, Mr. Binchey. All this could be a diversion.

It sure as God could, except that diversion is not the word that Mr. Binchey, his ass squelching in a pool of sweat, his stomach frozen with fear, his mind running crazily on irrelevancies, would have chosen. What at the moment is relevant? Time's ticking away. Time's relevant. How long have I left? How long has anybody left? Half an hour after I place the bomb even at the remoter place, the Judge's house, say fifty minutes to an hour, constable, constable let me pass or I'll wet my pants or my heart will stop.

—These are queer times, Mr. Binchey, pubs and churches, women and children, my own brother, the Tower of London, and in London too the Ideal Homes Exhibition, a bomb by the escalator, sixty-five mutilated and eleven of them Irish, bad, mad times.

With utterly resigned terror Mr. Binchey recalls that the

constable's father was an amiable long-winded man. In the smouldering wreckage another constable has discovered something and the crowd has gathered around him. So if I go up I'll only bring this boy with me. The watcher, whoever he is, will be watching from a safe distance. That's the name of the game. Proxopera. Proxopera. He spells it to himself as a sort of charm to move the man to let him pass. But, hands on the door of the car, stooping down, square head half in the window, smudged face still smelling of good aftershave lotion, the young man in blue-black uniform one of the last surviving symbols of an empire gone forever into the shadows, is prepared to talk to Mr. Binchey, as venerable, as respectable, as comforting as the face of the town clock: this is an historic moment and I was a teacher of history and Latin and English literature, and time is ticking away.

—But one of the worst things of all, Mr. Binchey, was that business in the Catholic graveyard at Lisnagarda on the outskirts of Scarva in County Down. Even in the bloody graveyard nothing's sacred.

She sleeps, waiting for me, in new Drumragh, I come, I come, my heart's delight.

—I didn't hear about that.

—It happened, I'd say, when you were in Donegal. The caretaker of the graveyard, sixty-one years of age, a woman, walking in the graveyard in the morning, sees a wreath lying on the path. Purple plastic chrysanthemums and white roses. Thinks it was blown from a new grave. Picks it up. Boom. Boobytrapped. Sure as Jesus. Could you beat that, Mr. Binchey?

An awkward question, in the silvery can, constable my constable, time is ticking away, I'm boobytrapped like the white roses and purple plastic chrysanthemums, we may boom and go aloft together.

—Only a part of it went off or the poor woman was done for. As it was, hands, legs and body severely injured. An old lady. Sixty-one. In a consecrated graveyard. Blood running out of her, she staggered three hundred yards to the nearest cottage, rapped on the window and collapsed. Only one shoe and stocking on, blood everywhere. Something, she said, hit me on the foot when I lifted the wreath. God in heaven, wouldn't you think an old woman would be safe in a graveyard?

Every spring we lay on her grave a bunch of daffodils, a branch of green and golden whin.

—Nothing's sacred, Mr. Binchey. But I'd better not hold you up.

You'd better not indeed.

—And the odd thing, Mr. Binchey, is that a lot of these fellows, I.R.A. or U.V.F. or U.D.A., or ABCDEXYZ, if left alone wouldn't hurt a cat or a child. But get a few of them together and give them what they think is a leader or an ideal and they'd destroy Asia and themselves and their nearest and dearest.

A military truck comes from the direction of the town.

—Good luck, Mr. Binchey. And I hope young Mrs. Binchey will be well soon.

—Thank you, constable. And so do I.

Two soldiers walk towards them. They wave casually at Mr. Binchey as he goes on his way towards the town he was reared in.

Those two soldiers looked like lizards, protective colouring to be worn in the emerald isle, Ireland of the welcomes and the bomb in the pub and the bullet in the back. He remembers a time when the soldiers in the town dressed smartly, pipeclayed belts and shining brass badges, polished nailed boots, puttees rolled with precision, peaked caps at an exact angle, walking cane under the oxter the way you'd truss a chicken. They were part of the town then, too, even if they were also part of the far-flung empire: the Royal Irish, the Royal Inniskillings, the pipes playing Adieu to Bellashanny and the Inniskilling Dragoon as they marched from the barracks to the railway station and thence to Aldershot and India or Egypt or the West Indies or Hong Kong or the Burma Road itself. A soldier out for the evening could talk to friends on the street although regulations did not encourage them to loiter at street corners. They drank with the people in the pubs and no madman gloried in shooting them dead in the shithouse. They relaxed with the girls in and around a public park. Or, better still, in whatever private place a poor man could find. Nobody thought of them as an invading hostile army. No girl had her head shaved or was tarred and feathered.

But then we always had with us Bertie's father and the like of him.

Curious thing, but the only book I ever saw in the hands of Bertie's father was a copy of *Mein Kampf*. Not in his hands exactly, but under the oxter where the soldiers kept the canes. He had a stiff left leg and always wore a brown belted overcoat, and had no brains, and through 1939 and 1940 he was never without that book. Never did I see him open it to peek at the treasures within. Was he like the vagrant who was washed and treated at a delousing centre and was delighted to discover, buried under alluvial mud in his navel, a collar-stud he had lost six years before? Yet he carried, even if he didn't read, *Mein Kampf*, because since the Jerries were marching against and going to invade England, Hitler had to be a republican. Declare a republic, Mr. Binchey. Oh la dee da, says my father, and goes on stirring the porridge. And about the same time there was a crazy missionary father going around, a roaring beanpole of a man, preaching missions in rural and even urban churches, the purest Goebbels who had noebbels at all, and all about the Jews and the Freemasons, and the real names of the rulers of Russia, all ending in ski, until his religious superiors had to put a stop to his gallop and lock him up or something. Oh never fear for Ireland, boys, for she has soldiers still.

No pipeclayed belts, no shining brass badges, no girls in the park, no drinks with the people in the pubs. But soldier boys like lizards on a sunny Irish Sunday against a background of scorched hedgerows and a burned-out Orange Hall, black wicked guns carried at an angle, pointing upwards, Martian antennae. They hold on to their guns as if they might rocket into space. They whistle through their teeth so as to seem carefree. Young fellows from the other island who scarcely know where they are or what they're doing here or what in hell it's all about. Their boots are dull-black, rubber-soled. They can move as quietly as cats round corners or along alleys. In the old days you could hear the clatter of the nailed boots half a mile away: evil secrecies of the world we have lived into. Forty shades of green, ironically, the green above the red, over trousers and combat jacket. And over the bullet-proof vest, a life-jacket for very dry land, and tied down back and front. But only a black beret protects the head and where have all the tin hats and helmets gone?

Christ hear us, Christ graciously hear us, I'm gripping the wheel so hard that my left arm has gone completely numb, it's not there, it's amputated, I've only one arm remaining and the road is empty and the sun bright and high and I swelch in sweat but I'll make the bridge where the railway used to be before I rest long enough to shake and rub and exercise that arm back into existence. In Jefferson County jail in Alabama there's a prisoner who's in for using an artificial arm to kill a man – like the joker who killed Miss Kilmannsegg with and for her precious golden leg. He has two artificial arms and he complains that the people who run the prison won't let him wear them so that he can't eat, shave, brush his teeth, change his clothes or clean himself after crapping: but the prison people say that if he had his arms he'd hurt somebody, and there you are, like Ulster, an insoluble problem, and my left arm now hurts like hell so it must still be there but, *exaudi nos domine,* there's the bridge around a pastoral corner, lambs on the green hills gazing at me and many a strawberry grows by the salt sea and many a ship sails the ocean, and up a slight slope, and once up there I can survey the morning smoke of my own town.

There below me as I lean on the parapet and puff and sweat and sip the last of the brandy, the blood of Hennessy the God, is the Grand Canyon of my boyhood, now a choked-up formidable dyke where weeds and wild trailing brambles have smothered the magic well at the world's end. No train will ever again go through there bringing noisy happy summer crowds to the breakers at Bundoran. The world is in wreckage and these madmen would force me to extend that wreckage to my town below, half-asleep in the valley, my town, asleep like a loved woman on a morning pillow, my town, my town, my town. Declare a republic, Mr. Binchey, destroy the town, Mr.

Binchey. Who's watching me now? Where are they? And down in the Grand Canyon I ate sweet raw turnips and drank, from the rock, water as cool as Moselle. That spring will never be the same again, yet for what civilisation, my town, is now worth, we still have inherited something, we have many good memories. Now I see. Let them watch and damn them to the lowest pit.

Here where I lean, the parapet was once shattered by a runaway truck and during the repairs a boy wrote in the soft concrete the name he imagined himself by: Black Wolf. And I'm the man who was the boy who wrote Black Wolf, and the concrete hardened, as is its nature, and there the name still is, and would Black Wolf ever submit to what the madmen are now trying to force on me, and go on for the rest of his life remembering that to save his own family he had planted death in his own town which is also his family? And even if every blade of grass were an eye watching me, to hell with them, let the grass wither in the deepest Stygian pits of gloom, and blast and blind the bastards and Bertie Bigboots and Mad Minahan and that creepy half-literate Corkman. Now I see. Mud in the eyes is a help and, more than my son and his son, or the bees in the pink oxalis, I see there my town and all its people, Orange and Green, and the post office with all its clerks and postmen and red mail vans, and the town hall and its glass dome and everybody in it – from that fine man, my friend, town clerk, or mayor, for forty-odd years, down to the decent tobacco-chewing man who swabs out the public jakes in the basement, my people, my people. Under that glass dome I played as a young man in amateur theatricals, the Coming of the Magi, the Plough and the Stars, the Shadow, God help us, of a Gunman, and the return of Professor Tim and the Monkey's Paw and the shop at Sly Corner and Look at the Heffernans, and all the talk and all the harmless posturing and laughter, my people. Hissing into a sock or something Corkman couldn't know what a town is. Even by consenting for a moment to drive this load of death I've given these rotten bastards some sort of a devil's right over the lives of my people. What, after my death, will they say about me in the local papers, what would they remember: that I carried a bomb on a sunny Sunday to the town hall and the post office or to the

door of Judge Flynn who's one of the best men in the north
and who goes every day in danger: they've already murdered
a good Judge at his door in the morning and in the presence
of his seven-year-old daughter, and now I see and there she is,
the virgin, the sleeping beauty inaccessible in a sleeping wood,
and thorns and thorns around her and the cries of night? Did
she stir in her sleep? Did her guts rumble? My left arm stings
but it is alive again.

He places his left hand, palm flat, on the creamery can. He
strokes her as if she were a cat. He recalls harmless tricks of
boyhood, putting carbide in tins, boring holes in the tins,
clamping down the lids, dripping water through the holes,
listening for the hiss, putting matches to the holes, and delight-
ing in the bangs and the soaring tins: or tossing squibs over the
garden fences of crabbed old men. Down in the valley his town
is at peace and blue peace is on the hills beyond. This may be
farewell forever, the end of my ill-fated cruise on the treacherous waves of Lough Muck. He says to the can that, daughter of
Satan, you'll never get to where you were sent. The beleaguered white house is far away in another world, her
grave is very near. He closes the boot carelessly, turns the car
sharply on the road, and drives back towards the nameless lake
of the mad old women.

That pillar of smoke, of cloud, ahead of me cannot, surely to
God, be still coming from the corpse of the Orange Hall. The
smoke had died down before I left the place. Where does it
come from? Up the steep hill and into the tunnel of tall
beeches. Not yet russet enough to make the road seem warm.
Up and down this hill, through this tunnel, walked so often
that amazing family of strong, red-cheeked, flaxen-haired brothers and sisters, a dozen or more of them, clutching their
bibles and meditating, perhaps, on Lot's daughters and the
night before. All gone now. Where to? Somewhere in England? Lost in the last war? Did they separate or stay together?
House and place went to a stronger farmer who lives elsewhere. The house, a barn now like the barns behind it, and out
of the tunnel and close to the hilltop and the checkpoint Char-
ley and, under God, it's the barns are on fire, not smoke only

but fine dancing flames, another diversion, all the fun of the fair, to keep the army and police away from Binchey the Bomber! They'd burn all Ireland so as I could plant one bomb to burn what was left and get the Brits on the run. Who'd want to stay? The Irish have to. Some of them.

Only two soldiers, lizards, at the checkpoint. One looking one way, one another, for the enemy, for fire-bugs, for the brigade if it ever gets here.

Careful and slow, the ramp might bust the virgin.

So he says to one soldier, and is amazed at the cold steadiness of his own voice, many an old woman walked along this road to a lonely end: There's a bomb in this car, I want to dump it in the bog beyond, proxopera, a proxy bomb.

The first soldier says: Fuck.

Involuntarily goes back a step.

The second soldier says: Let me take the wheel, dad.

The first soldier says: I'll phone the squad.

Is gone.

—The wheel, dad.

—Why should you? It isn't your town.

—Hurry, dad.

—They have my house and family. The white house by the lake.

—Dad.

—Follow me. Keep far away.

He drives on. More rapidly. Fuck: to quote the first soldier.

Far behind he hears the siren of the brigade. Fuck, again. What does it matter? This road that I drive on is Suicide Road. Wages of fear. Many an old woman. Now an old, an aging, man. Dad, indeed. Grandad. A boy walked along this road to see a vision of his white house. Up and down on esker land, sandy humps, that the icebergs left behind. The lake is below, bog birch and sally bushes, nobody ever fished there, nothing there ever but death, the still water glistens, shimmers, dances, for a moment he sees two lakes, then one lake as large as the ocean, boundaries fading and undefined. Now here, where old withered women stumbled to meet the dark lover, should, surely to Satan, be the place for the virgin to awake, relax, open legs, abandon the membrane. A dry season, thank God, and wheels don't sink on the turf-cutter's path that goes through bog and birches, but bump, bump, bump, he goes, and branches crack against the windows and sides of the car and on and on, and why not now go on and on and the spirits of old dead women, with such hair too, shriek around him. The car stops. The front wheels sink. That's that. Out and away. Which way? To the lake? The road is back there, and the soldiers, some of them, he hears coming carefully after him. He, carefully also, goes towards them, not stumbling. It's not over. Every step is a step towards the white house. The harvest colours are splendid on the hills above and around the bog. Beech leaves will soon begin to redden. He walks between two soldiers. And the elder of Lot's daughters said to the younger: Come let us make him drunk with wine and let us lie with him that we may preserve the seed of our father, for our father is old, and there is no man left on the earth to come in unto us after the manner of the whole earth.

A voice, the second soldier, says: Dad, you're raving. Shock.

Somewhere behind there's a muffled boom. His feet are on the hard road. Strong arms are holding him.

—Let me see. Now I see.

They turn him round. The pillar of cloud rises out of the bog, birches and sally bushes. There's some flame and crackling. Judge Flynn is at home. The town goes about its Sunday business. He tells them about the old women who committed suicide in that nameless lake. The first soldier says effing lucky you weren't a suicide yourself.

—Careful, dad, says the second soldier. Here, lean on me.

There's a crowd on the road, around a Land Rover.

—All this, says the first soldier, is what my dad used to call a real Irish fuck-up. My dad, you see, was Irish, from Liverpool.

But the only thing he can see is a grainfield, red for the reaper. Beyond it somewhere is a white house.

—Home, he says.

—Careful, dad, says the second soldier. Some of us are on the way. You need a rest.

—Good news this morning, Mr. Binchey. Two of them blew themselves up in a car driving into the town of Keady. A loaded handgun was found in the wreckage of the car and police deduced that the men, one already dead in the garden of a roadside house...

You're nearer God's heart in a garden.

... and the second dying in the wreckage, had either been on their way to leave the bomb in Keady or to deliver it to someone else.

—The police could be correct in their deductions.

—When they go out to harm other people it's always to me a happy sight to see the harm come back to their own doors. God is just.

—Or to their own cars, Minnie. Or to other people's gardens. Once upon a time we used to talk of misguided youths.

—Who guided them or misguided them?

—Ireland. A long history. England. Empire. King William. The Pope. Ian Paisley. Myself. I was a teacher of history.

—With all due respect, Mr. Binchey, we all had the same history. How many people now in your time did you blow up and you as good an Irishman as the next?

—Two weeks ago I came close to it.

—But you didn't do it. You were a hero.

The treetops billow around his third-floor window, three shades of green, beeches turning russet. Through gaps made now and again by the billowing he glimpes a bright suburban road, a bend of a river, a bridge, his town, Venice, for the present preserved.

From the white house and the lakeshore Minnie Brown has come to him with fruit and flowers and the Sunday papers from Dublin and London: his son and daughter-in-law and grandchildren will follow later. The newspapers are filled with the most wonderful reading for an ageing man whose heart is not in the best condition. The crabs from Donegal are still alive and seemingly doing well. Minnie has survived the rascals and the blackguards and her long wrinkled face has the glow of a girl. A forty-eight-year-old father of six children, ranging in age from six to thirteen, has been killed instantly when gunmen burst into his brother's pub at Aughamullen on the shores of Lough Neagh and sprayed the public bar with bullets. The dead man is Patrick Falls, a chemist and a native of the area, but he has been residing in Birmingham for the past four years. He had previously a pharmacy business in Belfast, for sixteen years, but was forced to go to England when his shop was destroyed in an explosion. He had returned to his native Aughamullen a week previously to make arrangements for the building of a house for his wife and family and himself. On the night of his murder he had gone into the bar to allow his brother, Joseph, to have a tea-break. Only one customer was in the public bar when the gunmen entered. One of them killed Mr. Falls instantly. A second opened fire on the customer, seventy-year-old Alphonsus Quinn of Ardboe, wounding him in the arm. The gunmen fled to a waiting car and sped off in the direction of the Protestant area of Tamnamore...

Home is the sailor, home from the sea...

But on the other hand...

A sixteen-year-old boy who moved to Australia from Glasgow with his parents eight years ago has been murdered in rugged country near Adelaide. Police say the boy was clubbed to death. His body was found lying beside his new car. His father said the family had left Glasgow to escape violence in the streets.

And thus the whole round earth is every way bound by the gold chains about the feet of God.

—Now here's a hussy and a half, says Minnie.

She reads slowly, pointing, peering, asking for help with the more rugged words: Susan Shaw is the blonde who puts sheer enjoyment into Manikin cigars. Her abundant sex appeal has helped advertise everything from car-polish to riding saddles. She has nakedly graced the pages of the popular press...

—Look at her, Mr. Binchey, tearing her shirt off and her mouth open. No wonder the world is the way it is.

Mr. Binchey looks and is not displeased and makes no verbal comment. But to please Minnie he clucks a little.

—She gets twelve pounds a picture with her clothes on and two hundred and fifty in her pelt. Mr. Binchey, did you ever?

—Never, says Mr. Binchey.

Surprisingly Minnie, who hasn't much respect for sex, laughs until the tears flow down the gullies of her cheeks.

—Well now, says Mr. Binchey.

His father might have said: Boysaboys.

Or Ladeeda.

Or was Ladeeda only for politics and republics? He is tired, he cannot remember, the billowing movement of the treetops is lulling him asleep. But again to please Minnie he makes a heroic effort to keep awake and to listen to her and to go on reading the papers. He is after all a hero. Also: he feels she is hiding something. If he lets her talk she may betray herself.

—It says here, Mr. Binchey, that the I.R.A. blew up a young private soldier of the Ulster Defence Regiment as he was making a regular call on a sixty-eight-year-old house-bound widow. He was off duty and on a tractor and going to chop wood, a daily task to help the aged widow. All U.D.R. men have been warned (Mr. Binchey has had to help her with some of the words) to exercise caution in carrying out spare-time errands of mercy to help the aged and infirm.

—It's in an English newspaper, Minnie.

—Still.

The gullies of her cheeks are again wet but not, this time, with laughter.

—For all those blackguards care, Mr. Binchey, all of us old people could starve or freeze in our houses. If we had a house left to starve in.

She has betrayed herself. He is wide awake. The tree-tops are still, or seem to be. The town below is still unviolated. The gun attack which killed three men in the Belfast pub owned by former Stormont minister, Roy Bradford, is believed to have been the work of a Republican group seeking vengeance for the bombing of the White Fort Inn in Andersonstown in which two men died and six were seriously injured. Come landlord fill the flowing bowl, and an Irishman's pub is no longer his castle: it was all so unexpected, in seconds men who had been enjoying themselves and watching athletics on the teevee were slumped dead or wounded at the counter.

—What was that you said, Minnie?

He is still reading the paper.

—Sacred Heart of Jesus, they'll murder me, Mr. Binchey. You weren't supposed to know until you were up and about.

—Know what, Minnie?

—They burned the house, Mr. Binchey.

—They burned the house.

—Since then we've been living in Judge Flynn's.

—In Judge Flynn's.

—All except Mr. Binchey, Mr. Binchey. He's living in the barn to get the repairs going.

—Repairs. Judge Flynn is a good man.

—He is, Mr. Binchey. And his wife's a lovely woman, too.

—She is.

—It was the fellow with the gasmask. And the shotgun. He said they should burn the house to destroy fingerprints. And the Corkman laughed and said he thought that was the funniest thing he ever heard.

—Fingerprints.

—Mr. Binchey tried to get at them. It was then they shot him in the left knee.

—But Minnie, they can't destroy footprints.

—No, Mr. Binchey.

She doesn't know what he's talking about.

Convert the Orangemen, Mr. Binchey. Declare a Republic, Mr. Binchey. Burn the house, Mr. Binchey, to destroy fingerprints.

—They burned Portrush too, Mr. Binchey.

—They did indeed, Minnie. So why should we worry. I read in the papers about Portrush.

Eight buildings in the centre of Portrush, County Antrim, one of the major holiday resorts in Northern Ireland, were destroyed after a telephone warning that ten bombs had been placed in the town by the Provisional I.R.A.

You may talk of Bundoran, of Warrenpoint and Bangor, but come to Portrush if you want to be gay. Yes, Billy me boy, put your hand in your pocket, just spend a few ha'pence and come to the say.

That was in a comic song about the seaside resorts of Ulster.

Bracing breezes, silvery sands, booming breakers, lovely lands, come to...

No, that was about Bundoran where the Catholics go, not Portrush where the Protestants go.

But the Orangemen could now, couldn't they, burn Bundoran? Or pubs in Dublin? Or the Ark of the Covenant if they could find it, or the Pearly Gates or Uncle Tom's Cabin or the tumbledown shack in Athlone or the house that Jack built or the little old mud cabin on the hill? What anyway do people want with pubs, or all those houses, or hotels or churches or schools or libraries or happy holidays? Burn the bloody lot. Wipe out all the world's fingerprints.

The papers slither on to the floor and he falls half-asleep and Minnie sits there and cries silently.

There is a place in the lake called the Blue Stones. Twenty feet out from the shore and in shallow water two conical blue rocks stand up a few feet above the surface and look at each other as if they were in love, lovers turned to stone and unable for all eternity to touch or taste.

When he was twelve years old he owned a Brownie camera, a birthday present. His pal, Tony, and himself, both trouser-less, waded out to the Blue Stones. Tony balanced on one, he on the other. He peered and clicked and snapped Tony balancing, bare-legged, shirt-tail fluttering, and the snapshot was no sooner taken than Tony fell off into the water. Sitting on the shore in the July sunshine, Tony naked, his clothes spread out on a bush, they laughed and dried themselves and ate toffee and drank lemonade.

He can't now in his half-sleep remember when exactly it was that he had the terrible dream about Tony.

He, not Tony, is, in the dream, sitting alone by the great glowing range where his father used to stir the porridge. He is reading a book. Out in a scullery a voice keeps chanting, like the voice of a schoolboy learning something by rote. He listens more carefully. It is Tony's voice. He tiptoes to the door of the scullery. Tony is standing by a blackboard with chalk markings on it. He has in his hand a long, yellow, wooden pointer. He is spelling out something but it makes no sense. Then, as he watches, black hair grows on Tony's face and his upper teeth protrude like fangs: and he awakes screaming that Tony's going mad, Tony's going mad.

The odd thing is that at the age of eighteen Tony did go mad. A premonition? Or was the dream before or after the event? Either way, that was the end of the laughter of the water and the Blue Stones. A dream, like the dream of the white house. Somewhere, somewhere he still has that snapshot.

His eyes open again. Minnie has dried her tears. When I was a teacher, pin-stripe and pince-nez, my jokes in class were well-known, even became proverbial, so I may have given something to my town to be remembered as long as the last of my students live, then to be forgotten or attributed to someone else. Cathy comes in and runs to Minnie. At least my body will go intact to lie beside her, membrane by member, ghosts, to the final, far beyond this partial, day of doom. Gary comes in and runs to his grandfather's bedside. But by the living Jesus they should not have touched my house, my living dream seen across water and through tall reeds and beech trees, they should not, they should not have touched my living dream, mad Minahan, Bertie Bigfeet, Creepy Corkman whoever you are, I will see you all in hell. Her son comes in hobbling on a half-crutch. Followed by his wife, as rich a red wine as ever, carrying parcels and grandfather's clothes.

—Minnie, Minnie Brown, Cathy sings, we're home again from Dungloe town.

The crabs are dead within the last hour. The oxalis is past its best. The house is burned. There is no laughter around the Blue Stones. The lake will never be the same again. Tony the madman roars through his dreams. Oh, the sights that we see as we wait here for death on the treacherous waves.

—But not destroyed, his son says.

More than my town, more than my family, my dream of a white house.

—They did their worst, his son says. But they should have brought a professional pyromaniac with them. We kept it out of the papers.

—You could have told me.

By the living Jesus they should not have tampered with my dream.

—You had enough to recover from. We thought it better.

Minnie and his daughter-in-law and the children are by the window laughing at the antics of a crew of magpies in the swaying treetops. The town, still undisturbed, is far below. His son gathers the newspapers from the carpet, stooping and rising again with some difficulty. He says: You knew them.

—Two of them. That'll do to begin with.

—I felt you might know them.

—Oh, I've been watching people in this town for a long time. Their faces. Their families. The books they read. Even their feet. If you looked at little else but the way people walk you could write a history of a place. Boots, boots, boots marching up and down again. Kipling, you know.

Patiently his son says: I know.

And through a gap in the reeds he looks, as he waits for the perch, across the water at the white house. Reeds make one frame for the picture. Beech trees, set back from the avenue that leads up to the house, make another. He envies the people who own it, the lawn and flower-beds before it, the barns and varied outbuildings behind it. He has missed a strike. Tony is laughing. And the most beautiful thing of all, cutting across a corner of the lawn, a small brook tumbling down to join the lake. To have your own stream on your own lawn is the height of everything.

THE STATE OF IRELAND
has been set by Adams & Abbott in Mergenthaler VIP Baskerville, a fine transitional typeface designed about 1760 by the English printer John Baskerville. A controversial face which originally found more favor on the Continent than in England, Baskerville did not win popular acceptance until its recutting by the Monotype Corporation in 1923. Since then this widely used face has been adapted to use on the Linotype and for photocomposition. A round, open typeface, it is characterized by thin hairlines, slightly bracketed serifs, and generous proportions.

The book has been printed and bound by Halliday Lithograph Corporation. The photographs have been provided by the Irish Tourist Board and are reproduced by its kind permission.